…thor Brenda Novak is the au… …he has won many awards, in… …, the Bookseller's Best, the Book B… …oit Medallion. She also runs Brenda No… …se money …r diabetes research (her you… …ate, she's rai… …2.5 …llion. For more abo… …renda… …visit… …endanovak

Praise for Brenda Novak:

'Richly detailed with believable characters and gripping action . . . Brenda Novak just gets better and better' Carla Neggers

'Brenda Novak spins a taut, spine-tingling story with imagery so vivid it leaves you breathless' Christine Feehan

'Brenda Novak's seamless plotting, emotional intensity, and true-to-life characters who jump off the page make her books completely satisfying. Novak is simply a great storyteller' Allison Brennan

'Brenda Novak has carved out her spot among the masters of suspense and mystery' Sherrilyn Kenyon

'With great sensitivity and an exquisite flair for characterization, Novak explores the ideas of redemption, forgiveness, and the healing power of love' Booklist

'Novak never disappoints' *Romantic Times Book Review Magazine*

'Another engrossing addition to Novak's addictive series'
Library Journal

By Brenda Novak

The Evelyn Talbot Chronicles:
Hanover House (e-novella)
Her Darkest Nightmare
Hello Again

Bulletproof Trilogy:
Inside
In Seconds
In Close

Last Stand Series:
Trust Me
Stop Me
Watch Me
The Perfect Couple
The Perfect Liar
The Perfect Murder

Stillwater Trilogy:
Dead Silence
Dead Giveaway
Dead Right

Dundee, Idaho Series

Department 6 Trilogy

Fairham Island Books

Whiskey Creek Series

HELLO AGAIN

BRENDA NOVAK

First published in the United States in 2017 by
St Martin's Press, LLC

First published in Great Britain in 2017 by
HEADLINE PUBLISHING GROUP

1

Cataloguing in Publication Data is available from the British Library

ISBN 978 1 4722 4099 6

Typeset in Palatino LT Std 9.88/12.85 by Jouve (UK), Milton Keynes

Printed and bound in Great Britain by CPI Group (UK) Ltd, Croydon, CR0 4YY

Headline's policy is to use papers that are natural, renewable and recyclable products and made from wood grown in sustainable forests. The logging and manufacturing processes are expected to conform to the environmental regulations of the country of origin.

HEADLINE PUBLISHING GROUP
An Hachette UK Company
Carmelite House
50 Victoria Embankment
London EC4Y 0DZ

www.headline.co.uk
www.hachette.co.uk

HELLO AGAIN

One

We are all evil in some form or another.

The Night Stalker made that statement. Although Dr Evelyn Talbot had never interviewed Richard Ramirez personally, like she had so many other serial killers, and the opportunity was now lost to her since Ramirez died of cancer in 2013, she'd watched video footage of the interviews he'd done with others. In her opinion, he'd been pandering to the camera when he tossed out that little nugget, had been hoping to sound profound, far deeper than he actually was.

She ran into that a lot. So many of the psychopaths she studied pretended to be more than they were. Most weren't smart enough to pull off the charade. Even those who'd gone years before being caught and punished for their crimes hadn't done so because of any great intelligence. Often it was sheer luck, basic survival instinct or a lack of solid police work that got in the way. Or they looked completely benign – like Jeffrey Dahmer or Ted Bundy.

But the newly convicted Lyman Bishop, the inmate she'd just met with . . . She found him to be far more unnerving than any of her other patients. He was brilliant and *so* calculating – she grimaced at the pictures in his file, which lay open at her elbow – not to mention absolutely unflinching in his brutality. They called him the Zombie Maker, and for good reason.

Taking off her glasses, which she used now and then to avoid eyestrain, she leaned her head on the back of her chair and stared up at the ceiling of her office. It wasn't quite lunch and yet she felt like she'd put in a whole day. She'd been up late last night, preparing for her interview with Lyman Bishop. She had to stay one step ahead of him where and when she could, or she'd earn his contempt instead of his respect. If that happened, she might as well have him transferred somewhere else, because he'd do her no good at Hanover House. If she couldn't develop some type of rapport, she'd never learn who he really was.

He'd merely toy with her. He'd probably try to do that, anyway.

With a sigh, she put her glasses back on and continued typing up her thoughts and impressions. Although she typically welcomed every inmate who was transferred to Hanover House upon his arrival, yesterday she'd been in Anchorage with Amarok, her boyfriend and Hilltop's only police presence, visiting his father, who was ill. Lyman Bishop had spent his first night, Sunday night, at Hanover House before she could meet him. And whether this would be good or bad in the overall scheme of things she couldn't say, but he was everything she'd expected him to be.

When I tell a new acquaintance what I do for a living, I hear the name Hannibal Lecter far more than I do B.T.K. or John Wayne Gacy or that of any psychopath who ever really lived, she wrote. *Everyone seems to associate 'psychopath' with* Silence of the Lambs. *I've always eschewed that fictional representation. The men who commit murder for the sake of enjoyment are typically much more mundane. Even though I've met many dangerous men over the years, men who have committed stomach-turning atrocities, none has ever reminded me of Thomas Harris's character. Until Lyman. He's the only killer intelligent enough to elicit the association.*

She paused to remove her high school Homecoming picture from her top drawer. Jasper Moore, her first boyfriend, smiled back at her from twenty-one years ago. Young. Handsome. Seemingly guileless. So unlikely a killer. By looking at him, no one would believe that a short time later he'd murdered her three best friends and tortured her for days before slitting her throat and leaving her for dead. He'd been seventeen, she sixteen. That she'd survived was nothing short of a miracle. She'd been alive to name her attacker and to say what he'd done to her, and yet he'd slipped away, had never been apprehended in the two decades since, despite all her efforts with private detectives and the full focus of police.

She had her theories about how he'd managed such a feat; his wealthy parents must've gotten him out of the country right away. But with or without help, he was the only other psychopath she'd ever met whom she would categorize as being as smart as Lyman Bishop. Which was what made Lyman so intriguing and frightening to her. After hundreds of disappointments – like Anthony Garza, who'd exhibited similar behavior even if he wasn't quite as intelligent – having the opportunity to examine a mind so similar to Jasper's was thrilling.

At the same time, as Victor Hugo once said, *Nothing is so terrifying as this monologue of the storm.*

Was there a new storm on the horizon that had nothing to do with the massive cold fronts that routinely socked Alaska this time of year? When she'd met with Lyman, she'd gotten the bone-chilling sensation that he would change her life in some way . . .

He made me feel there is nothing I can do to stop him and others like him, which plays into my worst fear, she added to her notes. *That what I've been through will be for naught. That what I'm doing, sacrificing Boston and the association of the family and friends I have there to live in this frozen wilderness, will, in the end, mean nothing.*

The intercom on her desk buzzed, startling her, she was so deep in thought. With a glance at the clock, she pressed the button that would allow her to communicate with her receptionist, four-foot-nine Penny Singh. 'Yes?'

'Jennifer Hall is here.'

Right on time. 'Send her in.'

Sliding away from her computer, Evelyn stood in anticipation of greeting her guest. These days, she didn't visit with many victims or their families, not since she'd opened Hanover House a year ago. Working in the small, remote town of Hilltop, an hour outside of Anchorage, made her less accessible. And now that she'd accomplished her goal of establishing the institution, where she and a team of five forensic psychologists plus one neurologist could study the 'conscienceless' in great depth, she didn't have to appear on television quite so often, was no longer constantly in the public eye, lobbying for the necessary funding. She'd dedicated her life to unraveling the mysteries of the psychopathic mind. Now that she was free to pursue that goal as she had envisioned, she was consumed by her work and rarely let anything else interrupt. But when Jennifer Hall, the sister of Jan Hall, one of Lyman Bishop's victims, contacted her several weeks ago just before Christmas, Evelyn didn't have the heart to refuse to see her. Having been a victim herself, she couldn't help identifying with the suffering of others. She wanted to offer what peace and support she could, even if that didn't amount to as much as she wished.

'Dr Talbot, thank you for taking time out of your busy schedule to speak with me,' Jennifer said the moment she entered the room.

Only twenty-five, with long dark hair and wide brown eyes, Jennifer was attractive, but Evelyn barely glanced at her face. Almost instantly her gaze fell to the other woman's swollen belly as if dragged there by magnetic pull. That Jennifer was expecting had nothing to do with their meeting, which was, no doubt, why she hadn't mentioned it, but Evelyn was transfixed. She'd been thinking about babies a lot lately. Amarok had mentioned marriage for the first time a month ago. She'd pretended not to hear him when he made the comment – something about getting her a ring if she'd ever agree to marry him – and he hadn't brought it up since, but she'd been contemplating whether she could make that commitment. To him. To anyone. She was thirty-seven. If she was going to have a family, she needed to do so fairly soon. She'd just never imagined such a traditional future for herself. Not with Jasper still on the loose. The most heartbreaking thing she could imagine would be for him to come after one of her children . . .

'No problem,' she said. 'I can't believe you were willing to make the trip.'

'Jan was more than my sister. She was my identical twin.'

Fortunately, Lyman's file contained no postmortem photographs of this particular victim so Evelyn didn't have a terrible image of a murdered Jan Hall pop into her head. He'd been convicted on circumstantial evidence alone. He'd been in the area and didn't have an alibi. He'd kidnapped and murdered other girls who looked similar. And Jan's underwear had been found in his house with his other 'trophies'.

'I understand,' Evelyn said. 'And I'm sorry. I can only guess at how painful it must be for you to . . . to carry on without her.'

Jennifer blinked rapidly. 'Sometimes I wake up at night and I'm positive she's alive, you know? It's like I can feel her, feel that tight connection. Then morning comes and . . .'

With it, reality. Evelyn knew all too well how *that* went. Despite the passage of so many years, she still had dreams of talking and laughing with her best friends from high school, all three of whom were gone, thanks to Jasper. 'And you lose her all over again.'

'Yes,' Jennifer said quietly.

Evelyn gestured toward the proof of her pregnancy. 'When are you due?'

'I have only a month left.'

'And your doctor let you travel so far from Minneapolis?'

'I didn't consult him. I had to meet you, and I knew it would be easier before the baby than after.' Her attention briefly shifted to the window, which showed another cold and dreary day. 'I couldn't imagine bringing something as pure and innocent as a newborn into this place, where there're so many evil men, even if they are behind bars.'

Evil. Once again, Evelyn was reminded of Richard Ramirez's words and the question that drove her: what made some people more evil than others? And why did those people *enjoy* inflicting pain on the innocent? 'I hope I can help in some way. Please, sit down.'

As Jennifer levered herself into the chair across the desk, Evelyn perched on the edge of her own seat and smiled to ease the younger woman's anxiety. 'What can I do for you?'

Propping her purse on what little remained of her lap, Jennifer leaned forward. 'I need to know where my sister's body is. I need to reclaim it, to give Jan a proper burial. Then maybe I'll get to feel she's in a good place, at peace. And I'll have somewhere I can go to grieve and say good-bye. I need to create an ending for this terrible chapter in my life.'

Evelyn clasped her hands in front of her. She hated to disappoint her earnest visitor, but if Lyman Bishop hadn't provided this information to date, chances were good he had a reason – if only to continue to torment those he could. The police would've asked him, would've made every effort, including offering to let him serve his time somewhere other than Hanover House. Most inmates weren't excited to be sent to such a cold and foreign place, so far from friends and loved ones. 'Dr Lyman is . . . difficult to deal with.'

'Difficult?' Her bitter laugh sounded slightly hysterical.

'An understatement, for sure,' Evelyn agreed, but she hadn't been referring to his behavior as she knew it. So far, he hadn't acted badly in front of her. She'd been referring to his complexity and how hard he was to read.

'He wouldn't tell the police anything. The day they captured him, he asked for a lawyer and said nothing more. Wouldn't speak to the media. Wouldn't testify in his own defense.' Jennifer grew earnest again – or maybe 'determined' would be a better word. 'But there must be something that can be used to . . . to entice him. Something he wants.'

'Like?'

'From what I've heard, having money can make an inmate's stay much more pleasant, and he's used to the finer things of life. He's some kind of foodie, from what I've heard. I don't have a lot, but I'm willing to give anything I've got.'

'He just arrived here at Hanover House. Those luxuries will become more important as he grows weary of doing without them. Until then, I doubt he'll be sufficiently motivated.'

'You're saying . . . we should wait?'

'I think that would be smart. Give me time to get to know him, to figure out what makes him tick – as much as that might be possible. Once he and I fall into a routine, maybe I'll be able to determine what, if anything, will give us the best chance.' If she could find a chink in his armor, she'd exploit it. But she wasn't confident she'd be able to get additional information out of him. Gaining any leverage on someone who was incarcerated for life and had nothing to lose wasn't easy.

With a wince, Jennifer closed her eyes. 'It's been two years since she went missing,' she said when she opened them again. 'I'm glad her murderer has been caught and that he's in prison. I know I'm luckier than most, that there are those who never get justice. You – you're one of them, and I'm sorry for that. But I have to . . . I have to be able to put her to rest. For my own peace of mind.'

Evelyn closed Lyman's file, in case Jennifer happened to realize whose it was. This distraught young woman didn't need to see the photographs it contained – although she'd probably seen some of them at his trial. 'Trust me. I'd love to be able to help. But dealing with a man like Lyman Bishop is a bit of a chess game. If he figures out how badly we crave the information, he'll be sure to withhold it. He might even taunt us with the fact that he has something we want but can't get.'

'*Why?*' Jennifer cried. 'What pleasure could he possibly get from keeping the location of Jan's remains a secret?'

'It's not pleasure so much as power,' Evelyn explained.

'So you can't reason with him? Can't bargain with him?'

Evelyn scrambled to come up with something that might ease Jennifer's mind without promising more than she could deliver. 'I can try, but it would be a mistake to offer him incentives or concessions right off the bat. He'll surmise the level of our desperation, and then we may *never* get what we want.'

Dropping her head, Jennifer pinched the bridge of her nose.

'Jennifer, what is it?' Evelyn asked, trying to catch her eye.

She looked up. 'What do you mean? I just told you.'

'We could've discussed this over the phone. What made you come all the way to Alaska at eight months pregnant?'

Tears welled up, but she set her chin and wiped them away. 'My mother's been diagnosed with pancreatic cancer.'

More tragedy . . . 'I'm sorry to hear that.'

'So am I. My father died of a heart attack when I was fifteen. Then Jan fell into the hands of that . . . that monster you have here. And now this. My entire family will soon be gone.'

'You'll have your baby,' Evelyn said, hoping to encourage her.

Her hand covered her extended abdomen. 'I may not keep her. I haven't decided. She'd probably be better off with someone else. I don't have a lot to offer.'

'It's a girl?'

'According to the ultrasound.'

'And the father? He isn't in the picture?'

'No. He got his ex pregnant about the same time I found out I was expecting and went back to her.' Fresh tears caught in her eyelashes, a few even slid down her cheeks, but she stubbornly dashed them away.

'That must be heartbreaking.'

'I'll deal with it. Somehow. I just . . . I can't stand the thought of my mother dying before we can get Jan home and buried. We should be able to share that moment, to have the chance for all three of us to be together one last time. It's her dying wish.'

Evelyn would love to help fulfill that wish. But they were talking about Lyman Bishop, someone she already knew she'd have to handle very carefully. 'How much time does your mother have left?'

'The doctors have given her three months.'

Which was an estimate, of course. She could die sooner as easily as later. 'I'll do the best I can, look for any angle, every opportunity. I promise. Just . . . give me a couple of weeks.'

'A couple of *weeks*? With only a sentence or two from him this could all be over. In *seconds*!'

'And yet most of these guys carry that sort of information to their graves.' Evelyn stood so that she could hold out the box of tissues she kept on her desk.

'What if *I* were to talk to him?' Jennifer asked. 'What if . . . what if I were to make a personal appeal? Would that make *any* difference?'

'I doubt it. You have to understand what most psychopaths are like. They do what they do because they are the only ones who matter to them. If they want something, they take it, even if it means lying, stealing or manipulating anyone and everyone around them. If inflicting pain gives them pleasure, they see no reason they shouldn't have the gratification. Unless they choose to, they feel no empathy.'

Jennifer dabbed at her eyes, smearing her mascara in the process. 'What about his sister?'

When Lyman was sixteen, Marianna, his mother, left the family for another man. Shortly after that, Lyman's father committed suicide, so Marianna took the kids. But after only a year, her new love interest made it plain that he wasn't willing to maintain a relationship with her if that relationship included the children. So she delivered Lyman and ten-year-old Beth to the closest mall to shop for the day and never went back. When Lyman and his sister finally made it home by riding the city bus, the house was empty, completely cleaned out. Marianna and her boyfriend had moved without a forwarding address. From that point on, Lyman lived on his own and finished raising his little sister – all while getting a doctorate using government grants and loans and working two jobs. Beth seemed to be the only person he cared about. He'd had a few romantic relationships, but none that had lasted more than four or five months.

'What about her?' Evelyn asked.

'She sobbed throughout the trial. She seemed to care about him. Maybe there's some way to get in touch with her. Maybe he'd do it for her.'

Evelyn couldn't believe that would work. First, Beth would have to agree to try to get the information out of him, and it was possible she felt too much loyalty. Despite what he'd done to other women, he'd taken care of her when she had no one else. Second, unlike the intelligent Lyman, she'd had developmental issues growing up. By all indications, her IQ was well below average, so she might not understand much more than the sudden loss of her brother. Third, she would have to come to Alaska in order for an appeal to have the kind of effectiveness they were hoping to achieve. A letter or a phone call wouldn't be the same. Evelyn wasn't even sure Beth was capable of traveling on her own.

For all of those reasons, enlisting Beth wouldn't be easy. But Evelyn was willing to talk to her, to determine if there wasn't *something* that could be done. 'I'll make a few calls, see what I can find out.'

'Okay.' Clasping her tissue in one hand and her purse in the other, Jennifer stood. 'Thank you. I'll be at the motel in town – The Shady Lady. You'll have to call there to talk to me, since there's no cell service in this godforsaken place.'

Ironically, since she'd once thought of Hilltop in the same way, Evelyn couldn't help being offended. She knew how much Amarok loved this place, had become converted to its incredible beauty, freedom and fresh, if cold, air. But she didn't react. She was more concerned about the fact that Jennifer still sounded as though she expected quick results. 'Okay, but please be aware that my efforts might not culminate in the information you want, especially before you leave.'

'I'm not going anywhere,' she said. 'Not until that bastard reveals where he put Jan's body.'

Evelyn heard the steel in her voice. *'What about the baby?'*

'There are doctors here, aren't there?'

'In Anchorage, I'm sure. But—'

'Hopefully, we'll be able to find out where he put Jan's body in the next few days or weeks, so I can go home.'

Evelyn didn't welcome the pressure of having a pregnant Jennifer Hall in town. She'd barely met Lyman, had no idea what to expect from him. He could easily refuse to speak on the subject.

But she had a sister of her own, knew she'd feel the same if she were in Jennifer's shoes. 'I'll do what I can.'

'Thanks,' she said, and Evelyn walked over to hold the door while she left.

Evelyn had returned to her desk and opened Lyman's file again, was just flipping to the beginning, looking for the name of the Minneapolis detective who'd handled his case, when Jim Ricardo, the neurologist she'd hired to replace Dr Fitzpatrick, who'd quit before he could be fired last year, poked his head into her office.

'You got a minute?'

She almost said she didn't. She had a busy day ahead and her mind was on other things. But she figured she might as well hear him out, address whatever he needed and get it over with. It was a relief that she no longer had to tiptoe around Dr Fitzpatrick, who'd made her life so unpleasant. At forty-one, Dr Ricardo didn't have the experience of Fitzpatrick, who'd been older, but he also wasn't trying to wrest control of the institution away from her. If she had to pick one over the other, she'd take Dr Ricardo all day, every day. 'Sure. What's up?'

'I was hoping to use our new inmate in a study.'

'Lyman Bishop?'

'Yes.'

'The empathy study?'

'We could use him for that, too. But I was thinking of another I'd like to start, one designed to determine if those diagnosed with anti-social personality disorder can more readily suppress the autonomic nervous system's response to deception.'

'And thus pass a lie detector test.'

'Yes.'

Early studies, studies by David Raskin and Robert Hare back in the late seventies, suggested psychopaths could not beat a polygraph any more easily than regular people, but those findings had since come under dispute. Some claimed that psychopaths' lack of fear of punishment or reprisal should make them less susceptible to the stress registered by others. She could see why Ricardo would be eager to answer the question one way or another – or at least provide further insight. But she wasn't ready to let anyone else interact with Lyman. 'Sounds interesting, but I'd rather you not use Bishop.'

'Why not?'

'He's so new. Give me a chance to work with him for a few weeks, to determine how cooperative he's willing to be and where he might be able to offer the most to our efforts.'

Ricardo peered more closely at her. 'You've never barred me from using someone before. Why is he different?'

'As you know, most people with anti-social personality disorder don't have good impulse control, which means they lack the self-discipline to get through extensive schooling—'

'Unless you believe that some of the world's greatest business leaders are psychopaths,' he broke in. 'The case has been made for that, remember.'

He had a point. Psychopaths were more attracted to business than any other profession. Many were also policemen, lawyers and surgeons. But she wasn't talking about law-abiding psychopaths, and Ricardo knew it. 'They might be psychopaths, but they don't kill people. Of the subjects *we* get, few are as educated as Dr Lyman. He was a biomedical researcher at the University of Minnesota – a fruit fly geneticist, to be exact – who has contributed a great deal to cancer research.'

'Are you sure?'

His sarcasm took her off guard. 'I don't follow you.'

'Maybe, like that researcher from the University of Iowa who altered some of his samples to boost HIV vaccine test results in order to achieve more grant money, he cheated somehow.'

She could see why someone might suspect that. Psychopaths weren't often the sort of people who put in a lot of hard work. If it was possible to bend the rules or get around some prerequisite to what they wanted, they often did. 'From all I've heard so far, his work seems to be unimpeachable. He did whole genome DNA sequencing with another geneticist, making it possible to determine what types of cell mutations are causing cancer.'

'In flies.'

'Human cells likely undergo the same process.'

'Sounds noble, but I doubt he restricted his bad behavior to murder. You know how criminally versatile most psychopaths are.'

That was true, too, but Evelyn got the impression Lyman Bishop had a code of ethics he lived by even if it wasn't the same as a 'normal' person's. What he'd done for his sister was admirable. 'Regardless, I don't want him purposely throwing off our findings for his own amusement. Please, leave him to me.'

Although he obviously wasn't happy with her response, Ricardo nodded. 'All right. Let me know when he's cleared.'

'You're anxious to work with a smart psychopath?' she asked.

'They're all smart.'

'Cunning, manipulative and deceptive, perhaps. But not as smart as Dr Bishop.'

'Now you've piqued my interest.'

'I'll turn you loose on him soon.'

'Okay.' He picked up the calendar on her desk and flipped it to the current day, which she hadn't yet bothered to do. 'By the way, Annie's planning a dinner for Friday after next. She's lonely, living so far from family. She was hoping that you and Amarok would be interested in coming.'

If Ricardo's wife couldn't take the isolation or the darkness and the cold, which were so prevalent this time of year, he'd eventually have to pack his bags and return to San Francisco, where he was from. Evelyn didn't want to lose him. She'd just replaced the two members of the team she'd lost last year. She figured she needed to support this dinner and any other social event Annie devised, but she wasn't always comfortable around the other woman. Annie was odd and a tad overbearing. After working with difficult personalities all day, Evelyn preferred to socialize with less complicated people. 'Of course. We'd be happy to join you. What would she like me to bring?'

'I have no idea. She's driving to Anchorage today to pick out the centerpiece and china and such. I'm not sure why what we've got won't do. That woman has dishes coming out of her ears. But if shopping gives her a goal and keeps her happy, I'm all for it.'

Like Evelyn, Ricardo had a true fascination for their work. While so much of deviant behavior appeared to be self-serving, it rarely produced the desired results – not in the long run. Psychopaths destroyed their own lives in the process of destroying others. Why they couldn't see that, or didn't seem to care, was another mystery, one Evelyn hoped to explore in more detail with Dr Bishop, who'd destroyed his ability to care for his sister, his ability to further his work and his freedom. 'She can let me know. I'm sure we'll have a wonderful time.'

'Thanks.' He started for the door, then paused. 'She's also going to see an obstetrician while she's there.'

'She might be pregnant?' Evelyn hadn't seen one pregnant woman since coming to Hilltop, not until this morning. Now she'd seen one and was hearing about another?

'I'm hoping. I'm afraid she'll insist we start fertility treatments if we don't conceive soon, and . . .'

He seemed to be searching for the right words.

'And that would add more stress to an already-challenging transition,' Evelyn supplied.

His lips curved into a ghost of the smile he'd given her the day she hired him, letting her know his situation at home was already far from ideal. 'Yes,' he said, and walked out.

Evelyn stared after him. Maybe if Annie could conceive, she'd be more fulfilled, more content, in Alaska – and Evelyn would be able to hang on to Jim.

Returning to Bishop's file on her desk, she finally located the detective's name and picked up the phone to call him. She was still thinking about Annie and Jennifer, and whether a baby might be the right thing for her own life, when Penny knocked and poked her head into the room.

'What is it?' Evelyn asked, phone in hand.

'Lyman Bishop would like to speak to you.'

'Again?' She hung up before the phone could ring. 'Why?'

'He won't say.'

She thought of Jennifer Hall. Maybe this was a good thing, the opportunity she needed. 'Have two correctional officers bring him to any interview room that's open.'

Two

'You have beautiful eyes, but I'm sure you already know that.'

Evelyn stared placidly through the plexiglass that separated her from Lyman Bishop. 'Thank you.'

'What color are they?'

Determined to play along rather than have him perceive her as critical or sensitive, she allowed him to say what he wanted to see where it might go. 'Hazel.'

He squinted as he leaned forward. 'I thought they were green. It's difficult to tell from here.'

For good reason . . . The separation accomplished by the plexiglass kept her safe. 'They look lighter some days than others,' she told him.

'With those thick eyelashes and long, dark hair . . . What a nice combination.'

'Is that why you wanted to meet with me? To compliment me on my appearance?' she asked.

He chuckled, then sobered so quickly she almost thought she'd imagined his levity, which didn't fit the situation in the first place. 'Does it surprise you that I can't stop thinking about you?'

The psychopaths she dealt with often tried to be evocative – by pledging their love or admiration or, more often, by making sexual innuendos. They wanted to matter, and nothing made them feel more like they mattered than eliciting a strong response. Apparently, Bishop, a soft, middle-aged white man with glasses, nondescript brown eyes and pattern baldness, was no different in that regard, despite his intelligence. But if he was angry at being sent to Hilltop, so far from his sister in Minnesota, he didn't show it. Like all Hanover House inmates, he wore an orange jumpsuit. He also wore handcuffs and a belly chain, since he was out of his cell, although he could just as easily be sitting there in a lab coat for the calmness with which he moved and spoke.

Evelyn considered his manner to be a welcome change from the more aggressive behavior of some of the other men. Many acted out, especially when they first arrived. Anthony Garza, who'd given her so much trouble just after Hanover House opened, was a glaring example. And yet, although she was relieved in a way, she found Bishop more discomfiting. Deception, after all, was the tool that had worked so well for Jasper all those years ago. He'd blindsided her – at sixteen, before she could fully grasp how terrible some people could be.

'Not at all.' She tried to imagine why Lyman Bishop had called this meeting. What was he trying to accomplish or put in play? She got the feeling he was methodical to a fault, did nothing without a reason. 'Since we met only a few hours ago, and I explained that I'll be visiting with you regularly from now on, I suppose it's only natural for you to be curious about me.'

He sat on a stool, which was bolted to the floor – the only furniture afforded to him – and folded his hands in his lap. 'I doubt it has anything to do with curiosity, but . . . yes, I'm going to enjoy our sessions. We should have a lot to talk about.'

'I can see where *I* might think so,' she responded. 'I'm intrigued by the way psychopaths view the world. But what could you find so interesting about me?'

She half-expected him to go back to admiring her features, was glad when he proved he could be deeper than that, more in keeping with her expectations of his intelligence and education.

'You're a survivor,' he said. 'You're fighting back. That's something I can admire.'

Once he'd learned where he'd be incarcerated, he'd probably read everything he could get hold of on her and her work. He could've heard about Hanover House even *before* he was apprehended. She'd conceived of creating an institution dedicated to such work in graduate school and had started lobbying vociferously for it as soon as she completed her residency. Her crusade for a place where she and others could develop the tools necessary to combat the psychopathy problem had played out in the media, which was partially how Jasper had been able to find her – although he'd disappeared again – just before she moved to Alaska. 'So you know about Jasper.'

'Yes. What he did must've come as a terrible shock.'

One Lyman probably vicariously enjoyed. 'Yes. But it's not a subject I'm willing to talk about.' So many of the inmates tried to probe her anguish, she'd made it her policy not to speak of her past. She was here to learn about them, not the other way around.

'We all have our . . . sensitive issues.'

'Are you referring to what your mother did?' Since he'd been callous enough to bring up Jasper, when they were barely acquainted, she felt it important to let him know she could play the same game.

There was a slight tightening to his jaw, but his expression didn't change otherwise. 'Yes. I'll never forget that day.' He bit off each word as if it tasted bitter in his mouth but a moment later smoothed out his hands, which he'd balled into fists. 'It also came as a terrible shock, of course.'

'You can't feel good toward her.'

'I hated my mother. Although my experience wasn't nearly as *violent* as yours, it was still . . . painful.'

In ways, it might've been *more* painful. So did he eventually track her down and kill her?

Someone had. When Lyman would've been thirty, she'd been shot at point-blank range as she got out of her car late one night and left where she fell on the drive. But no one had ever been charged for her murder. There'd been no witnesses and, other than the bullet that'd stopped her heart, the police could find no forensic evidence at the scene. Lyman was the primary suspect. He didn't have an alibi. But the MO had been so different from his later killings there wasn't anything to tie him to her death – other than motive.

'I'm sorry for what you went through,' she said, and meant it. No child should ever have to endure such heart-wrenching abandonment. Who could say how different Lyman might've turned out if he'd had a better mother? Not all psychopaths had terrible childhoods. Surprisingly, some had good parents and very little early trauma. But the most violent ones had almost always been abused or neglected in some way.

'Thank you. I think we'll get along nicely, even if I don't believe you know what you're doing.'

She blinked at the unexpected barb. 'That's blunt, wouldn't you say?'

'I've often been accused of being too blunt. But I admit, I don't see the purpose of pretense. If I'm a skeptic, I believe it only fair that I make my position clear up front.'

She could see why he'd never been able to maintain a steady relationship. He might be intellectually smart, but he wasn't nearly as adept at mimicking normal social interactions as most psychopaths. 'I'm not sure I understand. Are you skeptical of *me* or my profession?'

'The jury is out on you – a bad pun under the circumstances.' He chuckled but stopped when he realized she wasn't laughing with him. 'But your profession? That's a different story. I'm sorry if I've offended you,' he added.

'Are you really?' she asked.

He seemed confused. 'What?'

'Sorry for offending me?'

After thinking for a moment, he shook his head. 'No, I guess I'm not. I find it illogical and even ridiculous that I must apologize for the truth when there is no ill will intended.'

So he'd attempted to use a social device even though he didn't understand it. She found that interesting. It showed effort. 'Psychology has always had its critics, Dr Bishop. You're hardly the first.'

'Perhaps that's true. But even you must admit we critics have a solid argument.'

'Except that I could come up with an equally compelling argument with which to take the opposite side.'

'Compelling argument – or justifications? Certainly you've heard of the reproducibility crisis and the University of Virginia psychology professor who couldn't replicate so many important psychological studies.'

Of course she'd heard of Brian Nosek. Only thirty-five of the one hundred replications he and his colleagues performed fully supported the original studies – creating a black eye on her industry. But humankind couldn't give up on trying to understand their own mental processes. They had to forge ahead, perform more and more studies, as she was attempting to do, in all areas but specifically psychopathy, or there'd never be any real help for the innocent victims who so often suffered when they came up against someone like Bishop.

'I'm familiar, yes.'

'That doesn't make you doubt – even a little?'

'No.'

'Once someone is damaged, they're just damaged. There's no help for them.'

Was he talking about himself? 'That's a pessimistic view, wouldn't you say?'

'Again, what's the point of hiding from the truth?'

'I've seen a lot of growth and change in damaged individuals. I believe I'm one of them.'

'You're *completely* recovered? Self-actualized as B. F. Skinner or another humanist might put it?'

She wasn't sure she could state *that*. She still struggled at times. Healing was one thing. Forgetting and refusing to let what happened change certain things about her – like her ability to trust – was something else. 'We all have a choice. I'm turning what happened to me into positive energy.'

'As opposed to me, for instance.'

'If you killed your mother and those young women, yes.'

'Apparently, you can be blunt, too.'

'You said you preferred the truth.'

'Fair enough. If I killed my mother and the others, you'd be right.'

'But you didn't.'

'I've already told you that.'

She glanced at her watch. They could go back and forth on this later. There'd be plenty of time. 'Listen, I'm afraid we'll have to continue our discussion later. I have other appointments. So if that's all . . .'

'Not quite.' He stopped her before she could reach the door.

She turned in expectation.

'I hear you had a visitor today.'

Evelyn felt the hair rise on the back of her neck. She'd been thinking of Jennifer all along but hadn't planned on mentioning her until the last possible second, as if the matter were merely an afterthought. How had he beaten her to it? 'You heard about that?'

She knew how the COs talked. Rumors swept quickly through the prison side of the facility. Hilltop was such a small town – only five hundred people – that there wasn't a lot to offset the boredom other than the small aberrations in each day. But this was ridiculous. Jennifer had only been gone fifteen minutes when Lyman sent word that he'd like an audience.

'Apparently, the woman who came wasn't from around here,' he said. 'And she was quite attractive. Almost as attractive as you.'

She ignored the compliment. 'I can't imagine why information of a visitor would be of any interest to you.'

His chains, looking sorely out of place on such a seemingly harmless and docile man, rattled as he stood and approached the glass. 'Was it Jennifer Hall, by any chance?'

For a split second Evelyn considered lying but thought twice. If he ever caught her being dishonest with him, she'd lose his trust, and that trust could prove valuable in the future. No matter how badly she wanted him to cooperate for Jennifer's sake, she had to look at the big picture. 'Yes, it was. How'd you know?'

'Her description, of course. And Jennifer was expecting during the trial. I could hardly take my eyes off her. I'm fascinated by childbirth and motherhood.'

Evelyn suppressed a shiver at the thought of this psychopath staring down the twin of the woman he'd murdered so cruelly – or having any interest in her baby. 'Because . . .'

'It was like seeing a ghost.'

'As if Jan was there, watching.'

'Yes. I had Jan in one of my graduate classes. She was a bright student, somehow more attractive than her identical twin. That sounds odd, I know. But she had a certain . . . zest for life. An intangible trait, if you will, that I admired.'

He'd admired her so much that she became an obsession. He went to her apartment and kidnapped her, probably at knifepoint. Then, if he followed the same pattern used for other victims, he gave her a frontal lobotomy to make her more compliant and, if she survived that, used her for whatever purpose he wanted. Until he killed her, of course. 'And now she's gone.'

'Yes, it's tragic.'

Oddly enough, he sounded sincere, as if he mourned her loss as much as anyone. 'So why did you kill her?'

At this point, many of the psychopaths Evelyn interviewed would say, *I had no choice . . . She made me . . . She wouldn't shut up . . . She was going to leave me . . .* Something that placed the blame squarely on the victim for provoking the behavior.

Evelyn arched her eyebrows as she awaited Bishop's response.

He shook his head. 'I *didn't* kill her.'

'You might as well be honest with me, Dr Bishop. You've been convicted.'

'Despite the lack of evidence.'

'Still. There's little hope of getting out. You wouldn't have been sent *here* if you had any chance with an appeal.'

'Regardless, the truth remains.'

He could be *so* convincing. But those inmates who didn't blame the victim often pleaded their innocence, despite overwhelming proof to the contrary. Psychopaths could lie about something they'd admitted only two minutes earlier – and never bother to account for the discrepancy. 'I suppose that means you won't reveal the location of her sister's remains.'

He bowed his head. 'I would if I could.'

'Excuse me?' He'd spoken so low she could barely hear him.

He jerked his head up, but he didn't repeat himself. 'That's why Jennifer came all the way to Alaska?'

'Yes.'

'And you weren't even going to ask me?'

'I was still thinking about the best way to approach you.'

He rubbed his lower lip, mumbling words she couldn't hear.

'Would you please speak up?'

'Has she left? Is she heading back to the Lower 48?'

'Not quite yet. I told her I didn't hold out much hope, but she doesn't want to take no for an answer. So . . . is there any way to convince you to change your mind?'

He didn't answer; he stared off into space.

'Dr Bishop?'

'I wish I could help her,' he said, coming back to himself. 'I'd do so in a heartbeat.'

'You *can*,' Evelyn insisted.

'I told you. I don't know where the body is.'

'From what I've read in your file, you have a fondness for fine wine and good food. With the right excuse, I could make your stay here much more comfortable . . .'

Once again, his gaze dropped to some point on the floor and stayed as if anchored there. He seemed to be drifting inside of his own mind, watching a scenario of some sort play out.

She gave him a few seconds. Then she said, 'Dr Bishop?'

He looked up.

'Are you ready to tell me where you disposed of Jan Hall's remains?'

He frowned. 'I liked Jan. I liked her a great deal.'

'That doesn't answer my question.'

'The answer is no.'

Evelyn curled her nails into her palms. 'Will you *ever* be willing to divulge that information?'

Lines of consternation appeared on his forehead as he gazed back at her.

'Well?'

'You should have Jennifer go home. We wouldn't want her having that baby alone in Alaska.'

For a few seconds Evelyn had been hopeful. Despite her pessimistic predictions when she'd been speaking to Jennifer, she'd felt like she was reaching Lyman Bishop, that he was about to give up the location of Jan Hall's body. And then . . . nothing. He'd retreated inside himself, closed up – leaving her all the more frustrated for that brief moment of hope. The crazy thing was that he'd seemed so sincere, as if he really wanted to help. So why hadn't he? What stood in his way? Was the promise of a few worldly pleasures not enough? Did he believe he might receive a better offer later?

Her heels clacked against the cement floor as she marched back to her office. The inmates were being served lunch. If she skipped eating herself, which she did quite often, she could garner a few minutes to prepare for her afternoon. Thanks to a rather large grant from a victims advocacy group, Hanover House had recently been afforded the same high-field magnetic resonance imaging technology as some brain research centers. With such equipment, she could replicate a study performed by scientists in the Netherlands, where eighteen psychopaths were shown short movie clips of two people interacting with each other. The psychopaths' ability to empathize with depicted emotions was measured against that of a control group who watched the same clips. The findings of that study indicated that psychopaths showed less activity in the region of the brain associated with empathy, which didn't come as a surprise. But the study also showed that, when they were asked to try to identify with what the people in those films were feeling, the activity in the brains of those with psychopathy was not dissimilar to that of the control group, suggesting that psychopaths *can* feel empathy when they choose to. That was revolutionary! She and Dr Ricardo planned to use a much larger sampling of psychopaths to determine whether psychopaths autonomously switch between empathy and non-empathy depending on their personal goals, desires and/or certain social situations. Her findings, if conclusive, could lead to the possibility of therapy helping to heighten a psychopath's ability to keep that 'empathy switch' on, providing the first effective treatment for those with the disorder.

The idea of accomplishing that, something that might make a real difference in criminology, was her dream.

Maybe she was close. Maybe she'd be able to take the Netherlands study one or two steps further . . .

She'd just returned to her desk when Amarok called. Since she was already using her lunch hour to keep up with the demands of her day, she didn't really have time to talk, but neither would she miss the opportunity. Although Amarok was seven years younger – no one she should take seriously since she didn't plan on living in Alaska forever and she couldn't see him being happy anywhere else – it was easy to lose sight of those practicalities. He was the first man she'd been able to sleep with since Jasper. She'd grown to trust Amarok in a way she trusted no one else, which was more important in her life than love.

Although . . . she loved him, too. There was no getting around that. She'd fallen hard for the handsome trooper – and seemed to be falling harder with each passing day.

'Hey, babe. How was your morning?'

She couldn't help smiling at the deep rumble of his voice. The memory of the way he'd made love to her last night, so tenderly, evoked a warm, tingly sensation. In many ways, she was like a teenage girl who was just beginning to explore her sexuality. Jasper had caused her to shut down that whole area of her life, but Amarok had rekindled her desire to be with a man, reintroduced her to physical pleasure. He was giving back everything Jasper had taken. No matter how things ultimately turned out between them, she'd always be grateful. 'Eventful.'

'That sounds ominous. I hope nothing too terrible is happening.'

When they'd first started seeing each other, all hell was breaking loose at Hanover House. She assured him that it was nothing like before. Then she explained about Jennifer Hall's visit and her meetings with Dr Lyman Bishop.

'What's Bishop like?' he asked.

'Calm. Low-key. Thoughtful. Rational. Intelligent.'

'That doesn't sound like the kind of man who could – what did you call the procedure he performed on his victims?'

'Ice-pick lobotomies. Like what Dr Walter Freeman did back in the fifties and sixties.'

'Right. Freeman jammed an ice pick through his patients' eye sockets to scramble their brains. I remember now. Fucking gruesome.'

He didn't understand why she insisted on working with the type of men she did. But after they'd survived last year, when Dr Fitzpatrick was undermining her authority and Anthony Garza was becoming a real threat, Amarok had stopped complaining about her job. He understood that she couldn't quit. She felt destined to do this, *had* to do it – not only for herself but also for all the other victims who'd suffered at the hands of a human predator.

'He was trying to render them docile. Manageable. *Controllable.*'

'So he could use them as sex slaves.'

'So he could have ultimate power, ultimate control – for whatever he wished to do.'

'And then he killed them.'

'Maybe he only killed the ones in which the lobotomy didn't exactly work. If I had to guess, I'd say he had varying results. He probably turned some victims into vegetables he couldn't care for. Some probably died of infection or other complications. And maybe others were rendered docile, as he wished. Two years passed from the time one victim went missing to the time her body was found – and it was just going into rigor, so it was a fresh kill. He must've kept her that long.'

Silence.

'Let's talk about something else,' she said. 'I can tell this is upsetting you.'

'It would upset anybody!' he snapped. 'Which is why I worry about you, being constantly immersed in details of the worst of human behavior.'

'I'm fine. I have a certain . . . clinical separation.' That wasn't always true, but it was better if he believed it. 'Anyway, I'm starting the brain imaging I was telling you about later today. I'm so excited.'

His response was slow in coming, but he let her change the subject. 'I wish you luck with that.'

'A lot of good could come of it.'

'But it's going to take many hours of work.'

'Yes.'

'So let me guess – you'll be home late again?'

'I'm afraid so.'

'There's a storm coming in, Evelyn.'

'I'll try to beat it.'

'Call me before you leave. I'd rather pick you up than have you fight your way home alone.'

'Won't you be out helping Phil clear the roads?'

'I might be, depending on when you finish up. But leave me a message, just in case. I'll come if I can.'

After what'd happened last year, he was extra vigilant about her safety. And with Jasper still out there, somewhere, she appreciated even the small sense of security that evoked. 'Okay.'

'I'll talk to you later.'

She caught him before he could hang up. 'Amarok?'

'Yes?'

'Did I tell you Jennifer Hall is eight months pregnant?'

'No.'

'Well, she is.'

He hesitated. 'Why's that significant, babe?'

She propped her head up with one hand. She shouldn't have mentioned it. 'It's not. Never mind.'

She disconnected, but he called her right back.

'You're not getting my hopes up, are you?' he asked.

She sighed. 'Can you see me pregnant, doing this job, Amarok?'

'No. Each day would be agony for me, worrying that one of those assholes might get hold of you. It's hard enough as it is.'

What was she thinking? He was right. She couldn't create the possibility, couldn't put either one of them through that. 'I have to go. We'll talk about it later, okay?'

He ignored her attempt to get off the phone. 'Couldn't you set up a private practice? I mean, if you were to get pregnant? We could compromise, couldn't we? You got Hanover House up and running, which was your dream. Now let other scientists do the actual research. You could keep an eye on your brainchild from outside the walls, become a consultant.'

'What would I have to gain from leaving Hanover House – as long as Jasper's out there, Amarok? He could kill me far easier than anyone in here.'

'We always circle back to that bastard, don't we?'

'Yes. And that might never change. He's had a lifetime to perfect the act of killing. I have no doubt that's what he's done. Which means he'll be even harder to catch than before.'

'We have to stop him, or you'll never be able to live in peace.'

Sadly, that was pretty much what it came down to. But the reason Jasper had never been caught wasn't lack of good police work. Seasoned detectives had done all they could; there just weren't any leads. Amarok himself had scoured the case files, searching for any small detail that might've been missed. Some clue that'd been overlooked. Some possible way to track Jasper.

There wasn't one. So far, Jasper had managed to outsmart them all.

'I've made a good life, in spite of him,' she said.

'It won't ever be complete, not when you're constantly looking over your shoulder.'

'He hasn't gotten me yet,' she said. But they both knew he was out there. Waiting. Planning. That he'd made a second attempt on her life after twenty years left little doubt. 'Be careful in the storm.'

Three

As far as Jasper Moore, aka Andy Smith, was concerned, a prison wasn't an entirely bad place to work. He needed experience as a CO if he hoped to get close to Evelyn Talbot again.

Tilting back his chair, he leaned against the wall of the warden's outer office and imagined leaving his wife and her two irritating daughters once and for all and heading for the final frontier. He'd been to Hilltop before – once – and knew exactly what it looked like.

He closed his eyes as he conjured up the tiny town and the feel and smell of Evelyn. Then he had to lower his chair and shift, because he didn't want the warden's assistant, when she came to get him, to notice that he had a major woody. Dreaming about getting a job at Hanover House and working with the only woman who'd ever gotten away, without her even realizing he was there, always gave him an erection. She'd be ripe for the taking. Since she hadn't seen his face when he'd made his last attempt, she didn't know about the cosmetic surgery his parents had paid for years ago, when he was in Europe.

'Officer Smith?'

He came to his feet as soon as Devon Shirley called his name.

'The warden is ready to see you,' she said.

After looking her up and down, he grinned to suggest he liked what he saw, and she flushed. She was married and hadn't yet lost all the baby weight from her last pregnancy, but she was mildly attractive. He could have an affair with her . . .

No, he refused to threaten what he had going. All he needed or wanted from Florence Prison was a sterling recommendation; he could get laid anywhere.

'He in a good mood?' he whispered to Devon, still flirting with her.

'He's not happy about the stabbing this afternoon.'

'That was unfortunate.' But entertaining . . .

The way she flipped her hair and looked up at him from under her eyelashes indicated she found him attractive. But that came as no surprise. He made sure to stay fit, stay appealing. His innocent-looking face was probably his best lure.

'Having an inmate die in such a violent way doesn't make the institution look good,' she said.

It did, however, save the taxpayers a shitload of money. As far as Jasper was concerned, that wasn't a bad thing.

'*What the hell are you smiling at?*' the warden bellowed.

Jasper hadn't realized his boss had come to stand in the doorway.

'Nothing.' He adopted a much more solemn expression as he crossed over to the inner office.

The warden looked like George S. Patton – and came off just as tough and determined. His scowl didn't disappear, but he backed away so that Jasper could get past him and gestured toward the chair positioned in front of his desk. 'Sit your ass down.'

'Yes, sir.'

With a sigh that suggested he was nearly at his wits' end, he took his own seat and glared at Jasper. 'What the hell happened today?'

'One inmate shanked another. There was nothing I could do to stop it.'

The warden studied him closely. 'This is the third time someone has been stabbed while you were in the vicinity.'

So what if Jasper overlooked a weapon here and there or occasionally passed a shank to an inmate? As far as he was concerned, they could all kill one another. 'Bad luck on my part.'

'Are you telling me there isn't more to the story?'

Jasper didn't like the tone of his voice. 'I'm not sure what you're asking me,' he said. 'You've seen the security tape. I had nothing to do with it.'

The warden stretched his neck as if he was trying to offset a headache. 'Yeah, I've seen the tape. I'm not accusing you. It's just damn coincidental that you've been at Florence for only fifteen months and yet you've been on the scene of three of these publicity nightmares.'

'Only two inmates have died. I managed to save the other one.' He hadn't had any choice. The security cameras would've revealed his lack of action had he not broken up the fight.

'We still lost two men,' the warden said.

'That's better than losing all three.'

The warden sat in silence for several seconds, but he seemed more frustrated than truly suspicious. He merely wanted someone to rail against. 'I have to retain control of this prison,' he said.

'I understand that, sir. I just happened to be at the wrong place at the wrong time on three separate occasions.'

'Damn violent inmates,' he muttered.

Jasper leaned forward. 'Are you okay, sir? You're a little pale.' Word had it he'd had a heart attack in the months before Jasper started at the prison. From what Jasper could see, it looked as if he was ready to have another one.

The grizzled old warden glanced up. 'I should be asking *you* that. You should see a psychologist to help you deal with what you've witnessed.'

He reached for the phone on his desk, obviously intending to see to that right away, but Jasper came to his feet. 'That won't be necessary, sir. I don't believe a psychologist can do anything for me, so I'd rather not waste my time and the state's money.'

He lowered his hand, leaving the phone alone. 'You're okay without any help? *Really?*'

'I feel fine. Going through something like a stabbing . . . it's upsetting, of course, but I knew when I started at the prison that I might see some harrowing things.' Although he drew his eyebrows together so he'd look pained as well as sincere, he didn't feel remotely bad. Why would he? At least the stabbings were interesting to watch.

'I'm glad you can be so objective,' the warden said. 'But I hear you're thinking about leaving us. That you'd like to work for that psychopath prison in Alaska – what's it called? Hanover House?'

'Yes. I've applied online.'

'Why leave here just to do the same thing somewhere else?'

'The beauty and freedom of Alaska appeals to me. I think I'd love it up there. Why?' His heart beat faster. 'Have you heard from them?'

'Not yet.'

Jasper tried not to get discouraged. It'd only been a week or so. 'If you do, I hope you'll give me a good recommendation. I can cope with this kind of work. I think I've proven that.'

'Considering the inmates they have up there, they need officers with nerves of steel. Anyway, what do I do with you now? Do you want to go back to work or head home for the day?'

'I was actually hoping to take a couple of days off to . . . to come to terms with the stabbing. You know, go on a short vacation, get a change of scenery. Then I'll be good as new.'

'Of course. A vacation sounds ideal. Take the rest of the week – with pay.'

'Are you sure? I'd hate to cause a scheduling problem.' It was only Monday. That gave him four weekdays and the weekend.

The warden made a shooing motion with his hands. 'I'm positive. I wish every correctional officer was as diligent as you are,' he added.

Jasper bit the inside of his cheek so he wouldn't smile again. He'd turned this around so handily he couldn't help being proud of himself. And now he had six whole days to spend exactly how he wanted – doing what he loved best. 'Thank you, sir. You don't know how much your good opinion means to me.'

Jasper waited until he was out of the prison and to his car before releasing the mirth bubbling up inside him. But then he put the top down on his wife's Mustang despite the cold – even Arizona could chill off in January – and laughed all the way home. He was brilliant. If only he could tell his wife about *this.* She wouldn't be happy he was going out of town, but she had to work, so she'd live with it.

Amarok rubbed his eyes. He'd been sitting at his desk, reading crime reports, for so many hours the words were beginning to run together.

'Hey, Sarge.'

He glanced up as Phil Robbins opened the door and stomped the snow off his boots. Phil was one of the Public Village Safety Officers who helped Amarok keep the peace in spring and summer, when Hilltop received its usual influx of hunters and fishermen. He also manned a truck like Amarok's that had a shovel on the front and helped clear the roads in the winter. 'What's going on?'

'Storm's gettin' bad.' Phil peeled off his gloves and made a bee-line for the coffeemaker. 'Shit, it's cold out there.'

'You able to keep up?'

'So far I'm managing okay. After I defrost a little, I'll make another pass.'

'You need any help?'

'Will later. Someone needs to plow out by the prison to make sure those folks can get home. Unless you'd rather I go out there so you can handle the roads here in town.'

'No, I'll take the prison.' He wanted to pick up Evelyn anyway.

'Okay.' Phil's spoon clinked against his cup as he stirred in cream and sugar. 'What're you working on?'

'Nothing,' he muttered, but he was working on the same thing he'd been working on since he'd fallen in love with Evelyn Talbot. And Phil wasn't fooled. Evelyn didn't know how much time he spent trying to track Jasper down, but Phil did. Phil was in the trooper station too often; there was no hiding it from him.

'Jasper Moore again, huh?' he said.

Amarok sifted through several crime scene photos. They turned his stomach. As a police officer, he was willing to do what he had to do, but he wouldn't have asked to be included in this dark shit. He hated seeing what one person could do to another. The callous disregard for human life made him angry, which was probably why he preferred to remain in Hilltop, where he'd been born, rather than move to a more urban area. The wide-open Alaskan countryside still seemed safe and innocent by comparison.

But he wasn't going to allow Jasper to continue to terrorize the woman he loved. That dragged him into Jasper's fucked-up world, even if he didn't care to be there. 'Yeah.'

A skeptical expression settled on Phil's ruddy face. 'Do you think you'll ever really find the bastard? You've been searching for months – an entire *year* – and it doesn't seem as if you've made much progress.'

'When you're looking for a needle in a haystack, you have to sift through a hell of a lot of hay,' Amarok said.

'You're devoted. I'll give you that.'

'Process of elimination. I'll find him eventually.'

Phil came to stand over Amarok's shoulder while sipping his coffee. 'By contacting every police department in America and asking about any unsolved murders?'

'That's right.' Evelyn herself said that Jasper wouldn't stop killing on his own. He had to *be* stopped or he'd go on and on. That meant if they were hoping to find him they had to look for the carnage he left behind. Given all the unsolved murders out there, identifying which ones could be attributed to Jasper wasn't easy. Even Amarok had to admit that. He was using his intuition, which meant he could be wrong – about so many things. But he had to do *something.*

Fortunately, he felt fairly safe making *some* assumptions. If Jasper was obsessed with Evelyn, it fell to reason he'd target women who looked like her. Also, because he fancied himself to be something special, Amarok doubted he'd bother with the unattractive or the old. That left Amarok searching for pretty female victims, age twenty-five to forty, with dark hair and hazel eyes who'd been tortured extensively before death. The real problem came in when the victim's remains were found in such a state that no one knew what the woman had looked like. Amarok had to pass over those even if they could be what he was searching for. 'Determination can make a big difference.'

'I agree. But if the experienced detectives who investigated Dr Talbot's case couldn't come up with anything . . .'

At only thirty years old, Amarok didn't have a lot of homicide experience. Until Hanover House was built, Hilltop hadn't had a murder for over a decade, and that'd been a domestic dispute that his predecessor hadn't had to do a whole lot to solve. 'Most of those detectives have a lot of other cases to work at the same time. They don't know Evelyn, don't care about her personally. And, since it's winter, I've got time. As long as everyone around here behaves themselves, I may break up a drunken brawl at the Moosehead once in a while and help you clear the streets.'

'You do a lot more than that. There's always someone who's after you for help with one thing or another.'

Amarok didn't answer. He didn't want to think about the devotion he felt to Evelyn because he wasn't sure he could rely on her in the end. She made no secret of the fact that she planned to move back to the Lower 48 eventually.

'In any case, I've learned not to bet against you once you set your sights on something,' Phil added.

'I'll find him,' Amarok confirmed. 'It's just a matter of time.'

'It's too late for me to call Bishop's sister, don't you think?' Evelyn held a glass of Salmonberry Wine – her and Amarok's favorite – loosely in one hand as she sat with him on the couch of his cabin-like bungalow, high heels off, feet up, in front of a roaring fire. They'd just returned from the prison and yet Sigmund, her cat, had already managed to find her lap. Amarok's Alaskan malamute, Makita, had been with Amarok all day as he was most every day. But now Makita slept at the periphery of the room, well away from the heat of the flames. He much preferred the cold.

'Didn't you say she lives in Minnesota?' Amarok asked.

'Yeah.'

He had one arm around her. The fingers of that hand toyed with pieces of hair that'd fallen from her ponytail. 'What's the time difference?'

'Three hours.'

He checked his watch. 'Yeah. Definitely too late.'

'Darn,' she said, although she couldn't help feeling a bit of relief that she was really off work for the night. 'It took the detective on Bishop's case several hours to get back to me, and then I was so busy that I couldn't call, and yet I've got a twenty-five-year-old Jennifer Hall, who's eight months pregnant and weathering her first Alaskan storm, waiting for word from me at The Shady Lady.'

'Ms Hall should be safe enough. Margaret Seaver at the front desk will take care of her if she gets nervous. Just call Bishop's sister first thing in the morning. That should be good enough.'

She finished her wine and set her glass on the coffee table before snuggling closer to Amarok. Living with him was so nice. She'd never forget the fear that used to cause her stomach to cramp every time she entered her empty house or condo. With Jasper on the loose, she never knew when he might strike, had to check every closet, every nook and cranny, before she could relax. Of course, she'd gotten a lot more take-home work done when she lived alone. But that was because she didn't have a life. 'I'll *have* to wait. It's nearly midnight there.'

He took a sip of his own wine. 'How'd the brain imaging go?'

They hadn't been able to talk much on the drive home. The wind had been howling, the snow falling, and Amarok had mostly been on his radio, checking in to see that Phil had finished the final plow for the night. 'We ran into some complications and had to start over a couple of times, so we managed to get only a few scans done,' she told him.

'You can handle the rest tomorrow, can't you?'

He spoke with a wry smile, and she understood why. He always teased her about how driven she was, told her she needed to relax and pace herself. 'I've got my regular appointments with various inmates in the morning, but I've blocked off most of the afternoon to be able to continue the experiment.'

'You'll get it done.'

'Eventually,' she agreed. 'How was *your* day?'

'Better than most.'

'In what way?'

He stared thoughtfully into the fire as he took another sip of his wine.

'Amarok?'

'I found something that feels . . . right. The type of thing I've been looking for all along.'

She leaned away from him so that she could look into his face. She loved the contrast of his blue eyes with his black hair and dark beard growth, the strength of his jaw, the fullness of his lips. But right now she was more interested in what he was saying than his good looks. 'What do you mean?'

'Three weeks ago, the bodies of five women, aged twenty-eight to forty-three, were found not far from a burned-out barn on an abandoned farm a few miles into the desert outside of Phoenix, Arizona.'

The image of the shack where Jasper had tortured her immediately was conjured in her mind. 'Why would you be interested in these particular murders?'

'I wasn't interested at first. I considered this case one of several other possibilities. But I followed up with the detective who's investigating it this afternoon. And now that the victims have been identified, I'm almost certain the person who killed them was Jasper.'

'Why?'

'All five women have the same physical characteristics you do.'

Chills rolled down Evelyn's spine. Amarok wanted to catch Jasper as much as she did. She was fairly certain he spent quite a bit of time searching, but he didn't typically mention what he found. She understood that he didn't want to drag her through the hills of hope and valleys of disappointment. Finding anything of value was such a long shot. But *this* . . . this sounded promising.

'Did you bring home the photos?'

'I brought home all the information I've been able to glean so far.'

'Then why are we sitting here drinking wine? Why didn't you say something sooner?'

'Because it can't be healthy to keep forcing you to relive the past. I was thinking I'd see what more I could find out before bringing it to you. Determine if there's any way to eliminate these murders from my list of possibilities. But that would be much harder to do without your unique perspective.'

'I relive the past every day, Amarok. I can't escape it. That's why we need to catch him. And that's why you need to quit trying to preserve my peace of mind. *Five* victims who resemble me? That's got to be more than a coincidence.' She nudged Sigmund off her lap and stood. 'Where're the pictures?'

'In my satchel.'

She retrieved his satchel – and spread out the photographs on the table.

'What do you think?' He carried his glass over and poured himself more.

Evelyn could hardly breathe. The corpses were in varying stages of decomposition. The one that had been dead the longest had been reduced to bones. The most recent victim, however, wasn't. The ligature marks on her wrists and ankles, and the fact that her hair and eyebrows were burned off, even some of her fingers, made Evelyn ill. Jasper hadn't done those same things to her, but they were things he would've done had he thought of them – things she wouldn't put past him.

Amarok touched her arm. 'You okay?'

She nodded.

He drew her attention to the pictures of the victims as they'd been in life, photographs the police had added to the file after the bodies had been identified. 'To a greater or lesser degree, they all look like you, right?'

He hadn't mentioned the other similarities – with the structure and the fire. Jasper loved finding an old building he could use to torture his victims. When he was done with it, he burned it down. He'd tried to burn down the shack in which he'd tortured Evelyn all those years ago – while she was still in it. To this day, she didn't know why the fire went out instead of killing her and destroying all the evidence.

'Evelyn?'

She felt a tear roll down her cheek. She wasn't crying for herself and what'd happened to her in the past but for these women and what they'd suffered more recently. 'God, I hate him,' she whispered, covering her mouth.

He put a comforting hand at the small of her back. 'Can you see the resemblance?'

She nodded. 'Yes. This one . . .' She pointed to the third picture from the left. 'It's almost like looking in a mirror.'

Four

Amarok had found Jasper's 'signature'. Evelyn was sure of it. Over the past year he'd mentioned several unsolved murders where the victims looked like her, but with only one body here and one body there, sometimes states apart, it was difficult to determine if the physical similarities were merely a coincidence. Having five women discovered at a single kill site made it obvious they were all murdered by the same perpetrator. And learning that every one of them had the same hair and eye color Evelyn did made her confident Amarok had, at the very least, pinpointed a specific time and place where Jasper had lived for several years – long enough for one body to have turned to bones. This might be what the detective in Boston, who'd inherited her case since the original detective retired, needed in order to find Jasper.

Evelyn was so excited she couldn't sleep that night, and she knew Amarok could tell. He pulled her to him to get her to stop tossing and turning, but that did little good. After only a few hours, she slipped out of bed and went to the kitchen to work.

When he got up at six and found her at the table on her computer, he frowned as if to say he'd known better than to share the news about those victims in Arizona.

Averting her gaze, she pretended she'd only crawled out of bed a few minutes earlier. 'Morning.'

'Morning,' he grumbled.

Silence fell as he poured himself a cup of the coffee she'd prepared a few minutes earlier. Then he said, 'How are you going to get through such a busy day on no sleep?'

She couldn't say for sure, but she wasn't about to add any support to *his* side of the argument. 'I'll manage. I've done it before.'

He leaned one hip against the counter. 'Evelyn, you're running yourself ragged.'

She pulled closed the sweater that she'd donned to help ward off the morning chill and walked over to him.

'What?' he said when she offered him a grin.

'I'm glad you told me about Arizona. I'm excited, not upset.'

With a sigh, he set his coffee aside, drew her to him and rested his chin on her head. 'I understand that, but we're a long way from catching him. You can't be up walking the floor every night until then.'

She slid her arms around his lean waist as she settled into his embrace. 'But this is it, Amarok. I feel it like I've never felt it before.'

'It's got to be Jasper,' he agreed. 'But just because he was in Arizona two years ago doesn't mean he's there now.'

'There's a chance. People get comfortable. They like familiar territory, especially killers. That's why so many take victims from the same area over and over.'

She could feel his chest rumble as he chuckled, so she pulled away. 'What are you laughing at?'

'You,' he replied. 'I guess there's no protecting you against disappointment.'

'I can be pessimistic about Jasper, too. No one knows that better than you. But it's the hope that we'll win in the end that keeps me going.'

He sobered. 'Still, you can't keep driving yourself like you do.'

When she pressed her lips to his, he hesitated as if he wouldn't let her cajole him out of his concern. But then his lips parted and he met her tongue in that familiar give and take she loved, and his hands slid up her back to hold her closer.

'God, you can kiss,' she murmured against his warm, soft mouth. 'You're pretty good at a few other things, too.'

He leaned his forehead against hers. 'Are you ever going to marry me, Evelyn?'

Her heart nearly stopped. She wouldn't be able to ignore this comment like she had the other one. He was waiting for a response. 'I love you,' she replied. 'There's no question about that.'

He scowled at her. 'That's not what I asked.'

'I can't promise anything long-term, Amarok. Committing to you means committing to Alaska, too. You'd never want to leave this place.'

'This is where I belong.'

'Exactly my point.' He wouldn't be quite so at home anywhere else.

'So where does that leave *us*?'

'For right now, I'd rather not live without you. If you feel the same about me, I guess we just . . . go on as we are.'

'You're saying we wait and see.'

'Yes.'

He shoved a hand through his hair. 'I hope this goes my way.'

'Or . . .'

'I'll find out what it feels like to have my heart broken, something I've managed to avoid for thirty years.'

Once again, she felt torn. Was she doing the right thing allowing herself to get so close to him? 'I don't want to hurt you, Amarok.'

'It's too late; I already care.' With that, he set her aside to get a bowl of cereal. 'Have you called Lyman Bishop's sister?'

'Not yet.' She returned to where she'd been sitting at the kitchen table. 'I was waiting for you to get up, didn't want to wake you by blabbing on the phone.'

'Go ahead. You've got to be itching to cross that off your "to do" list.'

Evelyn didn't pick up her phone right away. She preferred to spend a few minutes with him, since he was available. They chatted while he ate, but when he went to get a shower she called the number the Minneapolis detective had provided to her yesterday.

The phone rang several times and never did forward to any type of voice mail. Evelyn hung up and called again, to no avail. She even tried to reach Beth periodically throughout the day. No one ever answered. It was Friday, just after breakfast, when Amarok was once again in the shower, that Evelyn finally heard a slurred, 'Hello?'

Evelyn hesitated. Had Lyman's sister been drinking? Even three hours later, on Minnesota time, it was early for that. 'Is this . . . Beth Bishop?'

'Yes. Who's this?'

Again, Beth's voice sounded . . . strange. Maybe she hadn't been drinking. Maybe she'd been taking meds. Evelyn had no idea what illnesses she might have. 'This is Dr Evelyn Talbot calling from Hilltop, Alaska.'

'Did you say you're my doctor?'

Evelyn heard relief in those words. 'No,' she clarified. 'Not *your* doctor. I'm a psychiatrist at the facility where your brother has been incarcerated.'

'What?'

Speaking much slower, Evelyn chose simpler words. 'I'm at the prison where they put your brother.'

'Lyman's there? Can I talk to him?'

'Not right now.'

'Why not?' she demanded, her voice rising as if she was about to cry. 'I'm cold. He has to come turn on the heater. It won't work for me.'

Evelyn curled her fingernails into her palm. Was there no one looking after this unfortunate soul? 'Could a neighbor come over and check the heater?'

'I can't let anyone in.' She lowered her voice, mimicking someone. '"Never, *never* answer the door, Beth. Do you hear me?"'

'That's what Lyman told you?'

'He said I won't ever get another white powdered donut if I do.'

Had Lyman taught her to refuse visitors because he had secrets he hoped to keep hidden? Or was he trying to protect his sister? And is that why Evelyn had had such difficulty reaching her? Maybe she'd been there all the time but just wouldn't pick up. 'You like white powdered donuts?'

'They're my favorite. Lyman says they make a mess. But I always clean up. I sure wish I had a donut now. I like Oreos, too. We need to get more Oreos. Lyman won't be happy when he gets home. He'll say I ate the whole package—'

'Beth?' Evelyn had to raise her voice in order to be heard.

'Can I talk to Lyman?' she said instead of answering.

'He's not here right now. Listen to me. Have you had breakfast?'

'There're no more cookies. No more donuts, either.'

'That's not breakfast. What do you have?'

'Oatmeal. But I hate oatmeal.'

'That's what you had this morning?'

'Yes. Tell Lyman I ate it like a good girl. Maybe then he'll come home. And buy more donuts.'

'I'll let him know if you'll tell me what you had for dinner last night. Can you remember?'

'Oatmeal.'

Evelyn rose to her feet. 'Again?'

'That's all that's left.'

'You don't have any milk or bread or meat?'

'I should hang up. Lyman wouldn't want me talking to you. I don't even know you.'

Evelyn spoke quickly in an effort to stop her. 'I'm your brother's doctor, remember? He asked me to call. He's checking to see what food you have.'

'Can I talk to him?'

'I might be able to have him call you later. For now, just look through the cupboards.'

After several minutes of hearing Beth mumble and then sing to herself somewhere away from the phone, Evelyn almost hung up. She didn't think Lyman's sister was coming back. But then Beth picked up the phone. 'Oil.'

Evelyn was mildly surprised she'd remembered her task. 'You have some oil in the cupboard?'

'Yes.'

'Anything else?'

'That's all.'

'What about the fridge?'

'Nothing.'

'No eggs? No milk? No bread?'

'I love bread,' she said. 'I like it when Lyman makes toast. With strawberry jelly. When he comes home he's going to bring some bread and make toast with strawberry jelly. All I can eat of it. And he'll turn on the heat.'

'What is it?' Amarok asked.

Evelyn jumped at the sound of his voice. She hadn't heard him come into the room. She held up a finger to let him know she'd answer in a moment. 'Beth, stay by the phone, okay? Your brother will call you in an hour or so. Do you know what an hour is?'

She didn't answer the question. 'Lyman's going to call me?'

At least she understood that part. 'Yes.'

'Now?'

'In a little bit.'

'Can he hurry?' she pleaded. 'Will you tell him to hurry?'

What was going on here? Had this woman been left to her own devices? Because it didn't sound as if she was capable of taking care of herself. 'Yes. I'll tell him to hurry,' she promised, and disconnected.

Amarok was waiting for an explanation. 'What'd she say?'

'We never got around to talking about Jan Hall. Beth's more disabled than I thought. I'm fairly certain she's sitting in Minneapolis with hardly any food in a freezing house.'

'Why didn't Bishop tell anyone that she might be in dire straits?'

'I have no idea,' she said. 'But as soon as I can get to Hanover House, I'm going to find out.'

'You've spoken to my sister?'

Evelyn was so concerned about Beth Bishop she was pacing on her side of the interview room. 'Yes. And she didn't sound good.'

He lowered his head but said nothing.

'When's the last time you talked to her?'

No response.

'Dr Bishop?'

'I quit calling.'

'When?'

'After the trial.'

'Because . . .'

'Because it was too upsetting,' he replied. 'She'd cry for me to come home, and there was nothing I could do. I couldn't even make her understand why I couldn't.'

Resting her hands on her hips, Evelyn paused in front of the plexiglass. 'How disabled is she?'

'Her mind is like that of a fifth-grader.'

'A ten-year-old.'

'Yes.'

'Who's taking care of her?'

His narrow shoulders lifted in a shrug.

'What does that mean?' Evelyn demanded.

'Now that I'm locked up, there's no one to take care of her!' he snapped in a sudden flare of temper. 'Do you think there's a line of people waiting and hoping for the chance?'

Evelyn studied him, tried to imagine what was going on behind those innocent-looking brown eyes and couldn't. 'It sounds as if the heater's broken. Or the utilities have been turned off.'

'I wouldn't be surprised.'

'Aren't you concerned, Dr Bishop?'

'I should've killed her,' he mumbled. 'It would've been a mercy to both of us.'

'What'd you say?'

'Of course I'm concerned!' He lifted his gaze from the floor. 'She's my *sister.*'

'So why haven't you made it clear to anyone that she needs to be institutionalized? How is it that she's living on her own?'

'I tried institutionalizing her – once.' He spoke as if it was difficult for him to retain his patience, but he didn't allow his voice to rise a second time.

'When?' Evelyn demanded.

'A decade ago.'

'And?'

'It was a mistake. When I went to visit, she had a black eye and scratch marks on her arm. The attendant told me she stumbled into the door.'

Evelyn hated these types of stories, but, unfortunately, she heard far too many of them. 'She couldn't tell you what happened?'

'She said the man who put her to bed "hurt" her.'

'Did you lodge a complaint?'

'Of course. But it was her word against his, so ultimately it went nowhere. According to them, her injuries didn't prove anything.'

Given the amount of rage Bishop had had to cope with in his lifetime, Evelyn almost felt sorry for him.

Actually, she *did* feel sorry for him. That was the problem. She hadn't lost her empathy, even for people who typically felt none, which meant she could still get drawn into their lies and their lives – and be victimized again, even if it wasn't in a physical sense. 'So you . . . what? Took her home?'

'Yes. That was when I accepted that I would likely be caring for her the rest of my life.'

Evelyn drew in a deep breath. She'd dealt with heartbroken parents, shocked wives and children who'd suddenly been cast adrift, extended family who'd had to step up and take care of a convicted loved one's responsibilities. But she'd never confronted a situation like this and was at a loss on the best way to handle it. 'Certainly your arrest made it clear that you would no longer be able to look after her.'

'I wasn't willing to see her go back to such a place, not with the memories she has. I told the police I needed some time to teach her how to care for herself, but they wouldn't listen. They thought they'd caught a serial killer, that I might escape if they didn't lock me up without a second's delay and throw away the key.'

'You expected special treatment? That they'd shuttle you back and forth to your house to take care of Beth?' If he thought she'd criticize the police, he was wrong.

'A little human kindness could've made all the difference,' he mumbled, now sullen.

'You could've shown some human kindness yourself – to all the women you murdered.'

'I haven't killed anyone,' he said, but with enough defeat to tell her he didn't expect her to take him seriously or even respond. 'I thought I'd be found innocent and set free, that I'd be able to go about my business. So I hired a colleague from the college to look after my sister in the meantime – Teralynn Clark, the janitor who cleans the lab every night. Given the astronomical amount of my legal fees, I could only afford an hour or so of her time each day, but an hour was all Beth needed. Someone to make sure she had groceries, that she was taking her bath and was able to get her favorite TV programs and games on her iPad.'

'You told me she has the mind of a ten-year-old.'

'But she *isn't* a ten-year-old. She's only six years younger than me. And she was used to being alone while I worked. I convinced myself we'd be able to muddle through until I was released.'

Evelyn tucked a stray wisp of hair behind her ear. 'But they convicted you instead.'

'Yes.'

'Is Teralynn Clark the one who brought Beth to your trial each day?'

He winced. 'You know about that?'

'Jennifer Hall told me Beth was there most days, crying in the gallery.'

'Teralynn thought it was funny to torment me by hurting someone I care about – saw it as vengeance for my "victims".'

'Is Teralynn still taking care of her?'

'No. There's no money left. Once I realized I wouldn't be going home, I started writing to various institutions, asking for help. But they all cost money, and I haven't got any. So far, I haven't received a response, but you understand what prison mail is like. It's monitored. For all I know, some correctional officer threw away those letters rather than allow me to obtain the reprieve I seek.'

Evelyn hated to think that might be the case, but she had to admit it was possible. Not all of those in corrections were above reprisal. 'If someone went out to check on her, would she even open the door?'

'Probably not.'

'Are you the one who taught her to be so cautious?'

'Of course. Would you want a ten-year-old opening the door if you weren't home? There are some sick people out there.'

Was he trying to be funny? Or did he really not see himself as one of those 'sick' people?

Either way, Evelyn didn't comment. She was more concerned with the possible emergency at hand. 'You're saying that this Teralynn Clark has done nothing to alert the authorities to Beth's situation.'

'I can't say for sure. I've written Teralynn, as well, asking her to check in, but haven't received a letter from her, either.'

'Can you give me Teralynn's number?'

He rattled it off from heart.

'Not many people bother to memorize phone numbers these days,' she said.

'I don't memorize them,' he told her. 'I have a photographic memory.'

'Somehow that doesn't surprise me.'

He came to his feet. 'Does this mean you're going to make sure Beth is taken care of?'

His relief seemed sincere. 'It does. It also means I'm going to ask her where we might find the body of Jennifer Hall's dead sister.'

She watched for any alarm on Lyman's part, but he merely shrugged. 'Good luck with that,' he said.

Because she'd already signaled into the camera for the COs to remove Bishop from the room, the door behind him opened right when she wished she had another few seconds with him. So far, Bishop had been careful to say and do all the right things. He'd managed to plant a tiny seed of doubt in her brain that a man who'd taken such loving care of his mentally handicapped younger sister could also kidnap, rape and maim innocent young women at random. But there'd been something in his 'good luck' that set off alarm bells in her head – a cavalier attitude that indicated he was unconcerned with the threat of punishment. Maybe he was even eager for the challenge that trying to manipulate her presented.

'You did it,' she said. 'I know you did it.'

He didn't get the chance to respond. She wasn't even sure he understood what she meant, and she didn't explain. It was enough that *she* knew he'd killed those women, that he wasn't an innocent party unjustly locked up.

But it wasn't ten minutes later that her faith was shaken – thanks to a call from her mother.

'Have you heard the news?' Lara asked.

It'd been a long week. Evelyn wanted to sink into her seat and kick off her heels. Instead, she remained standing; she could tell that her mother was upset. 'No. What are you talking about?'

'Mandy Walker.'

'What about her?'

'She's been kidnapped and murdered.'

Limp and suddenly cold despite the fact that she'd been plenty warm a moment earlier, Evelyn supported herself by using the desk until she could ease into her chair. 'You're talking about the Mandy I knew in high school, aren't you?'

'Yes. She was in your class, remember?'

How could Evelyn forget? Although she and Mandy had lost touch soon after graduation, they'd hung out a great deal during senior year. Mandy and four or five others had been part of the group of friends that had once included the three girls murdered by Jasper. After Marissa, Jessie and Agatha were gone, Evelyn had grown closer to Mandy than any other friend, as close as she could tolerate in the immediate aftermath of her attack. Fear of loss had hampered her relationships ever since, was a problem she encountered even with Amarok. Sometimes she'd wake up in a cold sweat, thinking Jasper had killed Amarok just because she loved him.

'I can't . . . I can't believe it.'

'Her ex-husband found her when he went to drop off their kids. Can you imagine?'

No, Evelyn *couldn't* imagine. What were the chances that *four* of her high school girlfriends would die by the hand of someone else? 'What was the manner of death? Was she beaten or—'

'They don't know yet,' her mother broke in. 'The poor thing had been tortured so badly they couldn't immediately tell what killed her. The autopsy should reveal more.'

'She'd been tortured? Like me?' Evelyn's words came out a mere whisper, but her mother must've heard, because she responded correctly.

'Maybe worse. Even if he'd let her live, she would've been impaired for life. I read in the paper that whoever killed her gave her a frontal lobotomy.'

Evelyn bolted upright. *'What'd you say?'*

'You heard me. He purposely damaged her brain!'

'With an ice pick,' she muttered.

There was a moment of stunned silence. Then her mother said, 'How'd you know?'

Five

Evelyn was still staring at her computer, reading and rereading the article she'd pulled up on Mandy Walker's slaying, when Penny knocked and stepped into the room. 'Dr Talbot?'

With a steadying breath, Evelyn pulled her gaze from the screen. 'Yes?'

Penny looked confused. 'I've been buzzing you. Why haven't you answered?'

Evelyn had been so caught up that she hadn't heard the noise. She'd blocked out everything else, couldn't quit thinking about the bodies of the three friends she'd discovered in the shack where she'd been tortured herself twenty-one years ago. Their images would be forever etched in her mind. 'I was concentrating on something. What is it, Penny?'

'Dr Fitzpatrick is on the line.'

'Fitzpatrick?' Evelyn hadn't heard from him since he quit Hanover House and left Alaska a year ago – and she'd been glad for that. As far as she was concerned, he'd gotten off easy after what he'd done, even if his career was all but over. 'I have nothing to say to him. He knows that, and so do you.'

'I told him you wouldn't accept his call, but he insists he has something to say that you should hear. It involves an old friend of yours – a Mandy Walker?'

How did he know she was friends with Mandy? Regardless, she'd heard the news and wasn't about to give him the opportunity to get involved in her life again. Sure, she would never have been able to establish Hanover House without his support. She'd been relatively new to the industry when she started lobbying for a place to study psychopaths in depth. It was his sterling reputation that had helped solidify the necessary backing. But during the years they'd been associated, he'd become infatuated with her. There at the end, he'd even *stalked* her.

She grimaced as she remembered how he'd tried to kiss her when they were working late one night and how he'd turned on her after, when she refused him.

These days, she didn't even like the sound of his name.

'I've heard the news,' she said.

Although she expected Penny to leave right away, her assistant lingered in the doorway.

'What is it?' Evelyn asked.

'I feel kind of sorry for him. I know he caused a lot of problems last year, problems that could've led to the closure of Hanover House, which would've ruined everything you've worked so hard to achieve. I don't blame you for being angry. But he's apologized several times. He feels bad; he just told me so again. And I think he's sincere.'

Penny could afford to be sympathetic. She didn't know about the stalking behavior, only that he'd performed some 'inappropriate' studies with the men and sabotaged Evelyn's ability to run the institution. That was what Evelyn had told the press, too. She'd had to smooth everything over to some degree, couldn't give the impression that she didn't have control of the facility and its staff. Her detractors would pounce on that immediately. There were too many dangerous men inside of Hanover House to allow for any internal strife.

'I'm not holding a grudge,' Evelyn said. 'We simply have no reason to remain in contact with each other.'

'Okay. I'll tell him,' Penny responded, but she was so reluctant that Evelyn changed her mind.

'Fine. I'll tell him myself,' she said. 'Put him through.'

The door closed. Then Evelyn's phone began to ring.

A bone-deep reluctance almost caused her to go back on what she'd said. Amarok wouldn't like her engaging Tim Fitzpatrick, and, psychologically speaking, Amarok had the right of it. But, telling herself she'd make it quick and get it over with, she picked up the phone. Maybe if she finally allowed her former colleague to say what he wanted to say, 'the end' would really be 'the end'.

'What can I do for you, Tim?'

'I'm not looking for any favors,' he said.

'Then what?'

'I'd like to apologize.'

'You've already apologized. Several times.'

'To everyone around you, to anyone who would give you a message and tell you how terrible I feel, but not directly to you.'

'Because it's not necessary. An apology won't change anything.'

'I hate that I've lost your respect, Evelyn. All I ask is that you give me a chance to redeem myself.'

Redeem himself? In what way? If he thought she'd ever work with him again, he couldn't be more mistaken.

'Tim, we started the first research center of its kind. That put us under a lot of pressure. Moving to a place so foreign to both of us added even more stress. It's understandable that there would be some hiccups in the beginning. Let's be grateful we were able to accomplish what we did and agree to go our separate ways.'

If it helped him to believe she could dismiss what he'd done that easily, fine – as long as he stayed out of her life.

'I was going through a difficult time,' he said. 'I'd lost sight of who I am and what I want to be. Please don't define me by my worst deeds. Now that I'm not actively engaged in . . . in anything productive, I'm lost, Evelyn.'

She closed her eyes. She wouldn't – *couldn't* – allow him to prey on her humanity. He was suffering the consequences of his actions. He needed to go about rebuilding his career without her. 'That isn't my problem, Tim.'

'But don't you see? When you become unsympathetic, you're no better than they are.'

A shot of indignation stiffened her spine. '"They"? Please don't tell me you're comparing me to the psychopaths we study!'

'No, of course not,' he said. 'I'm just saying that you've never been a hard-hearted person. Surely you can understand how ... how I got caught up and ... and made a mistake.'

'Tim, I wish you well. But I'd rather not have any contact.' She wasn't about to let him cajole her into accepting him back into her circle of associates. It was bad enough that his protégé, Russell Jones, still worked at Hanover House. After what happened with Fitzpatrick, she'd thought Russell would give up and quit. He hated Alaska. But he hadn't turned in his resignation and didn't act as if he was going to. Was Russell's continued presence the reason Fitzpatrick thought he could weasel his way back in?

'Even on a professional basis?' he asked, as if he was shocked.

'You said you weren't calling for a favor.'

'But we have so much in common. We both live to work. We both enjoy the same kind of work. We've both made groundbreaking strides in psychology. And we could do so much more in the future if we collaborate. Certainly, affording me a few crumbs of professional help, now that I need you instead of you needing me, can't be asking for too much.'

'We tried working together, Tim. You couldn't maintain the professionalism required to be successful as a team.'

'But I was never any real threat. Look at you. You have everything. You've got Amarok' – whom he'd treated as a romantic rival; he'd even suggested that she was overreaching by dating such a younger man and Amarok wouldn't stand by her in the end –'and a successful career,' he continued. 'The sky's the limit for you.'

'Where are you going with this, Tim?'

'Isn't it obvious? I'd like to work again, to be useful in some way.'

Her boss at the Bureau of Prisons wouldn't allow it even if she relented. 'Janice would never agree.'

'Now that the emotions of the last year have calmed down and

Hanover House is on a strong footing, you could put in a good word for me. Maybe she can use me at a different prison, if not Hanover House.'

'There's no chance of that.'

'Then include me informally – on a consultation basis. I'm not asking to be paid. Not at first. If I prove myself, perhaps our association could evolve into a paid position. I have to be part of something that matters or my life has no meaning.'

He had no right to ask her for *anything*. 'Penny said you were calling about Mandy Walker,' she said.

'I was. In case you haven't heard, she's been murdered.'

The way he blurted that out told her he didn't care how it might affect her. He was contacting her for his own sake. But she wasn't going to accuse him. 'I know. My mother just called with the news.'

'I thought Mandy's death might have something to do with Jasper. It'd be like him to try to hurt you by killing more of your friends, wouldn't it? As some sort of message?'

An uneasy prickle rolled down Evelyn's spine. The thought had crossed her mind, which was why she'd immediately searched for whatever she could find on the murder. But hearing someone else say those words made what had been a sneaking suspicion that much more viable.

She prayed whoever killed Mandy wasn't Jasper. If it was, there was a strong possibility he might target more of Evelyn's friends. She was the one he wanted, but since she was out of reach, this was a perfect way to land a blow from thirty-five hundred miles away.

'The perpetrator performed a lobotomy,' she said. 'That doesn't sound like Jasper.'

'No, that sounds like Lyman Bishop.'

She gripped the phone tighter. 'I see you've been keeping up on what's happening here at Hanover House.'

'Of course. Hanover House was my baby, too. I can't help being interested. The whole country is interested in what's going on up there. The fact that Bishop was sentenced to Hanover House brought up the old arguments about whether such a place is worth the investment, whether it's safe, whether it's even possible to treat such men. You're familiar with the litany of our opponents.'

Our opponents. He still included himself.

'They're painting it as a showdown – you against the latest and greatest in twisted psychopaths,' he said.

'I wish the press would stay out of it and let me do my job.'

'You have to be careful where they're concerned. Public opinion is important – and you could easily lose it.'

How ironic that *he'd* point out the danger! He'd done as much as anyone to besmirch the institution's reputation.

Or was that some kind of veiled threat? Would he try to sabotage her again?

'I understand what's important here,' she said.

'What's Bishop like?'

The change in subject led her to believe he was trying to keep her on the line as long as possible, to reestablish their old camaraderie. 'He doesn't come off like a killer. But you, of all people, know that most of these men don't.'

'He's been in the news a great deal. So have the gruesome details of his crimes. Jasper could have read about his methods. Maybe he decided to emulate them.'

'Someone else could've read about his methods as easily as Jasper. It's even possible that we've incarcerated the wrong man.'

'Do you honestly believe that?'

She recalled the moment when she thought she'd noticed a telltale sign that Bishop was guilty. Could she trust what she'd learned from dealing with so many psychopaths over the years? Or was she merely prejudiced by how many times she'd interviewed guilty men who tried to paint themselves as innocent? Psychopaths were *such* convincing liars, and Bishop could be better than most. According to various studies on the brain, lying required more intelligence than telling the truth. 'No. How did you hear about Mandy, Tim?'

'I live here, remember? It was on the news.'

'I'm terribly sorry about what's happened – more than I could ever say. But . . . I'm wondering how you knew she was a friend of mine. I'm sure I've never mentioned Mandy to you before. I would have had no reason to. Don't tell me *that* was on the news.'

'It was! Your association with the victim is not something the press is going to miss, Evelyn. You've been in the public eye too much yourself for that detail to go unremarked.'

'They connected it that soon? Her body was found yesterday!'

'Some journalist is doing his job. He's familiar with your story, where you're from, and with the fact that Jasper already murdered three of your other friends – and was never caught. That's a sensational piece, wouldn't you say?'

'I'll be honest, Tim. I'm not comfortable with having you get involved.'

'Seriously? You're still holding a grudge?'

'You act like what you did wasn't any big deal!'

'It wasn't!'

'*What?* You *spied* on me! Took photographs of me changing clothes. Superimposed my face over pornographic images you used in various studies with the dangerous men I interview on a weekly basis.' And, although she didn't mention it because she knew he'd only try to justify his actions, in the end, before he was exposed, he'd undermined her authority and tried to usurp her position at Hanover House.

'But I never touched you, never actually hurt you.'

'So? You could've cost me this institution!'

'You would never have gotten that place off the ground if it wasn't for me. I've been going stir-crazy – for a whole *year* – with nothing of any import to do. Have some pity, for God's sake. Isn't leaving Hilltop in shame and being exiled for twelve months punishment enough?'

She recognized several things that were oddly familiar in his response. A lack of true remorse. Mitigating excuses. An unwillingness to accept the consequences of his own actions. The way he minimized what he'd done in order to make her feel as if she were overreacting. It scared her. Once again, he was behaving more like the men she studied than the renowned psychiatrist she'd once believed him to be.

'I'm hanging up now, Tim. I'm sorry that you're not actively engaged in a project you enjoy, but with your background and your talents, there are plenty of opportunities out there. You need to find one and forget about Hanover House.'

'Wow,' he said. 'How ungrateful can you be?'

'You're the one who destroyed my trust.' She hung up, but before she could even catch her breath Penny knocked and came in to drop off a file she'd requested.

'How'd it go with Dr Fitzpatrick?' she asked.

Evelyn rubbed the goose bumps from her arms. 'I shouldn't have taken that call.'

It wasn't easy to get hold of Teralynn Clark. Evelyn got her voice mail three times before Teralynn called back, and by then Evelyn was well into brain imaging and couldn't pull away. The clock indicated five twenty when she finally connected with Lyman Bishop's lab janitor.

'Teralynn, this is Dr Evelyn Talbot at Hanover House in Alaska.'

'I've heard of you.' She sounded excited, as if Evelyn was some kind of celebrity. 'I'm sorry I missed your earlier calls. I work nights, so I shut off my phone when I sleep during the day.'

'That's perfectly understandable. I'm glad I didn't manage to disturb your rest.'

'I've seen you on TV,' she announced.

'I've been in the news quite a bit over the past four or five years.'

'I'd say. People *love* to talk about you and what you're doing – a young, beautiful female doctor studying all those serial killers in such a remote place. It's . . . creepy.'

'I'm hoping a lot of good will come from it.'

'Me, too. But doesn't it frighten you? If just one of those killers gets loose, you're in trouble. Even if he doesn't kill you, the government will probably shut you down.'

Evelyn stretched her neck. 'I understand the threat.'

'How's Lyman behaving?'

'He's been rather . . . subdued, but we haven't had him here long.'

'You'll have to watch him closely. That one can fool you. I *completely* believed he was innocent, that he would never hurt a soul. I mean, I've been in his house. I've had dinner with him and his retarded sister.'

Evelyn stiffened. 'I don't believe that's a term we use anymore.'

There was a slight pause, then a degree of bewilderment. 'What are you talking about?'

'"Retarded". "Intellectually disabled" might be a gentler way to put it.'

Another pause. Then Teralynn said, 'Is she on the phone with us? Can she hear me?'

'No, but *I* can.'

'You're *that* concerned about his retarded sister? I mean . . . *intellectually disabled* sister?'

Evelyn waved as Penny stuck her head in to say good-bye. 'Why wouldn't I be? To my knowledge, she hasn't killed anyone, has she?' she said to Teralynn.

'No, but she didn't do anything to stop him.'

Evelyn rose to her feet and began to pace the short distance across her office. 'Was she capable of stopping him? Did she even know what he was doing?'

'I bet she did. She didn't challenge him in *anything.* Far as she's concerned, he can do no wrong even still. I tried to tell her what a sicko he is, but she just covered her ears and shook her head. The sun rises and sets on her dear brother.'

'He *has* been the one to take care of her,' Evelyn pointed out. 'She's indebted to him in that regard.'

'I guess.'

'Have you seen any evidence to suggest he *hasn't* taken good care of her?'

'No, but who can say what they've been doing in that house? For all we know, he's been crawling into her bed at night, using her at will. A man who could rape and murder innocent strangers would probably have no problem sleeping with his own sister.'

Evelyn wasn't sure why, but she was tempted to refute that. Teralynn was right; there was no telling what Lyman might've done to such a defenseless person. But there'd been no allegations of incest or that kind of abuse in his file. And ironically, considering the crimes he'd been convicted of, Evelyn preferred to give him the benefit of the doubt. Maybe it was because she hated his selflessness when it came to Beth to be tainted in such a terrible way.

Or maybe it was because she disliked Teralynn *immediately*. 'Is that why you brought her to his trial?'

'No, I-I did that just to be nice,' she stuttered, taken off guard.

Evelyn pivoted at the wall. *'Nice?'*

'Yes, she wanted to go. She begged me to take her.'

To the trial? Or to her brother? After talking with Beth, Evelyn believed Lyman on this one. Teralynn had enjoyed the drama, liked feeling as if she had some role in it and didn't mind that her actions weren't in his sister's best interest – or his, for that matter.

'You mentioned that you've been in the Bishops' house, when Lyman was there.'

'Yes. Several times. Scares the hell out of me to think of it now.'

Evelyn found her chair again. 'He never did anything . . . threatening? Never drugged you or tried to get you to stay over?'

'No. He was the perfect gentleman, acted grateful I'd be willing to come. But I bet he would've tried something if he thought he could get away with it. I bet that was coming.'

Evelyn began to doodle on the pad next to her phone. 'He told me you looked after Beth once he was arrested.'

'I did. I took excellent care of her, too.'

'You must be a very kindhearted person.'

'I do what I can.'

Evelyn rolled her eyes. Given the fact that she was paid and Beth was likely without food and heat since the money ran out, Teralynn's high opinion of herself hardly seemed warranted. 'Who's looking after her now?'

'I have no idea. I suppose family of some sort.'

She'd mumbled the last part, making it difficult to decipher. *'Family?'* Evelyn repeated. 'I wasn't aware that Lyman had any close family.'

'He doesn't. Not *close* family. But surely there's someone . . . somewhere.'

Evelyn couldn't detect a hint of conviction in those words. Teralynn knew otherwise. 'When was the last time you saw Beth?'

'Just after Lyman was convicted.'

Since he hadn't been transferred right away, due to some red tape regarding the cost, and then the weather in Anchorage, which had turned ugly, forcing them to postpone his flight, that was three weeks ago.

'I stopped over, made sure she had supper after the sentencing,' Teralynn added, as if she'd been more than thorough.

Evelyn glanced at her calendar, even though she didn't need to. 'That was at Christmastime.'

'Yes. Two days after Christmas, to be exact.'

'Was someone else there at that time?'

She paused; then she said, 'No.'

'Then how did you know it was safe to leave Beth on her own?'

'I assumed someone would be coming to take over for me. Lyman only hired me for a short time. It wasn't as if I agreed to take the job indefinitely. He doesn't have the money to pay me even if I was willing to pop over there every day. Matter of fact, he still owes me two hundred dollars.'

'Have you written to him about that?'

'Of course.'

'And what did he say?'

'He doesn't have it. Where's he going to get it now?'

'He said so?'

'No. He didn't answer. That's how grateful he is for my help.'

Her response didn't ring true here, either. Lyman had mentioned writing Teralynn several times out of concern for his sister. Evelyn got the feeling the janitor was simply covering for her own selfishness and insensitivity. 'I see. Okay. Thank you for your time.'

'That's it?' she said. 'Beth – that's all you wanted to talk about?'

'Did you expect something else?'

'I thought you might ask me about *Lyman*. Don't you study serial killers?'

'I do. How well did you know him?'

'I cleaned his lab for more than five years. We struck up a friendship of sorts, before I realized what kind of person he is and all that. I'm about the only friend he's ever had.'

Even she hadn't been much of a friend, Evelyn thought.

'Several reporters have called already, wanting to talk to me,' Teralynn added proudly.

'It sounds as though you've enjoyed the attention.'

'What?'

Evelyn had muttered those words beneath her breath. 'I said, "What's your opinion of him?" '

'He's smart, but he doesn't know the first thing about how to get along with people.'

'He was a troublemaker?'

'Not at all. He was just . . .'

'Easily overlooked?'

'Yeah. Mostly kept to himself. I'm not even sure how he got those women he murdered to go home with him.'

'But you believe he figured out a way.'

'They found all those panties in his house, didn't they? Seven – or was it eight? – pairs of them.'

Evelyn felt a headache coming on, and talking to Teralynn wasn't helping. Something needed to be done about Beth, and Evelyn could already tell that Teralynn wasn't going to be part of the solution. Evelyn wasn't sure she wanted someone like Teralynn taking care of Beth, anyway – wasn't convinced she'd be humane enough. 'It was eight. I'll let you go. Thanks again.' She was about to hang up when she pulled the receiver back to her ear. 'Ms Clark?'

'Yes?'

'Did you ever see him with any of the victims?'

'Jan Hall. She came to the lab to help out whenever she could. She was fascinated by his work, wanted to do the same thing. I believe she was hoping to intern for him.'

'You clean the lab each night. Do you clean the rest of the building?'

'Yes.'

'Do you have an idea where he might've disposed of Jan's body? Could there be any place at the college? Maybe a furnace room or a-a place where the trash goes?'

'There's no body in the science building – at least none that shouldn't be there,' she joked. 'I would've found it by now – God forbid. Anyway, the police have already checked the entire campus.'

Evelyn tossed her pen aside. 'I'm sure they did. Before you go, can I ask you one more question?'

'Of course.'

'Did you get the impression that Lyman cares about his sister?'

'I guess so,' she replied. 'As much as he's capable of caring. Psychopaths don't really care about anyone, right? Isn't that what I heard you say on TV?'

'They don't care about others nearly as much as they care about themselves,' she confirmed.

'Even their families? That's hard to imagine.'

'For those of us who have empathy and easily connect with others, yes, it is.'

'So . . . they fake it?'

'Sometimes they model the behavior they see around them, to fit in, to go unnoticed. You saw how he treated Beth. Did he seem kind?'

'Very. That's what's so surprising. I guess you never know some people, huh?'

That was true. Evelyn had had the same thoughts about Jasper. He'd turned out to be completely different from the perfect athlete, student and boyfriend he'd seemed to be, had shocked her and everyone else who knew him. And yet . . . there *were* signs, if she'd been aware or mature enough to spot them. For one thing, he'd loved being the center of attention and grew bored the instant the focus of any group he belonged to shifted elsewhere. And he'd never been the type to put himself out for the sake of someone else, not like Lyman Bishop had done for his sister. None of the men she'd studied were willing to care for another person as dutifully as Lyman seemed to have cared for Beth. Not beyond putting on a show for praise or to prove how great they were. Not when it was real work on a consistent day-to-day basis and there was nothing in it for them.

If Lyman enjoyed murder, why hadn't he made his life easier and killed his sister? He could've gotten away with it. From what Evelyn could tell so far, no one had been keeping track of him or Beth. No one cared about them. Beth had been living on her own without anyone noticing for weeks, and Evelyn had no idea how much longer that would've gone on if she hadn't had reason to call Beth.

But Lyman didn't kill her. He didn't even institutionalize her. He bought her the powdered donuts and Oreos she loved.

As far as psychopaths went, Bishop seemed to be unique.

Six

Evelyn met with her new inmate several times the following week but didn't feel any more settled about his culpability. Bishop's many contradictions troubled her. Not only had he stood by his mentally handicapped sister, he'd gone to college and earned his degrees – she'd checked with his alma mater to be sure they were real – and he'd maintained a demanding job over a number of years with no problem. He even had an electric car, for crying out loud, and a solar system on his house – both of which indicated he was socially conscious. According to his rap sheet, he'd never even had a speeding ticket!

She hated the thought of an innocent man getting caught in a net cast for an evil soul who was preying on women, especially a man like Bishop, who could contribute so much to society otherwise. But then she reminded herself of the evidence police had recovered from his house. If he was innocent, where would he have gotten the victims' underwear? And was it a mere coincidence that his mother had also been murdered?

Of course not. So it didn't matter that he didn't seem to fit the stereotype of a psychopath. Stereotypes were dangerous to begin with, something she couldn't afford to be influenced by. No self-respecting psychiatrist or psychologist could. So while the much-used PCL-R, the guide designed by Canadian psychologist

Robert D. Hare to assess the presence of psychopathy in individuals, focused on twenty personality traits that could, on the surface, appear to support a basic narcissistic stereotype, she had to take into account how diverse and unique human beings could be. Just because Bishop seemed functional in most areas of his life didn't mean he wasn't dangerous or violent. He was smart enough to know what signaled trouble to those who'd be looking for it – and how to avoid exhibiting those traits and behaviors. That was all.

As she pulled into the only motel in town, a collection of lodge-like single-story cabins made of wood and strung together like the beads of a necklace, she looked for a parking space less encumbered by snowdrifts and found one close to the office. They'd just had another storm, one that'd come and gone without wreaking a great deal of havoc, which was nice. But they had a lot of winter yet to survive. She wasn't overly optimistic that future storms would be so gentle. Not if last year served as any indication.

She couldn't help recalling where she'd been twelve months ago on the morning after one of their worst snowfalls. She'd been with Amarok, identifying Lorraine Drummond's severed head. Lorraine used to run the food service program at HH and had been such a nice person—

Blocking that memory almost as soon as it broke upon her mind, Evelyn got out of her SUV and waded through the snow in the rubber boots she wore over her shoes. Nothing as bad as what'd happened to Lorraine – and then Danielle – could happen again because Evelyn had weeded out the bad employees and gotten Hanover House running on a nice even keel. She missed Lorraine, would never forget her, but she couldn't dwell on that loss, or the loss of Danielle, whom she hadn't known nearly as well. She was waging a war against the conscienceless, could never weaken, give up or retreat. *Someone* had to do *something*, for the benefit of every person who'd ever been victimized.

Evelyn had been here before, twice earlier in the week, to check in on Jennifer. She knew where to go – to Room #8, in the corner. She waved at middle-aged Margaret Seaver, the diminutive manager who'd watched her pull in, as she made her way carefully over the icy sidewalk.

'Hey, Doc, how're things going over there at Hanover House?'

Margaret had come out to greet her, so Evelyn paused to chat for a moment despite the biting wind. She liked Margaret, so she would've taken the time anyway, but she also made an effort to build relationships in Hilltop in order to tear down the 'us' versus 'them' mentality she'd had to contend with when she and the rest of her team of doctors first arrived in town. Not everyone had accepted her – or them. Her Boston accent, her socioeconomic status and her Ivy League education made her too different. And many locals weren't happy about the kind of facility she was bringing to town. Who'd want a bunch of serial killers living only a few miles away?

No one, which was why the federal government had chosen Alaska. The forty-ninth state in the union hadn't had the population to put up much of a fight. So Evelyn couldn't blame Hilltop's residents for being a bit resentful, especially toward her. She was the face of the institution.

Fortunately, she'd made some friends here in spite of that rocky beginning. Of course, it helped that she was in a relationship with Amarok. Everyone loved Amarok, so if *he* thought she was okay, they were more tolerant . . .

'All's well at Hanover House,' she told Margaret. 'How are things here?'

The streaks of silver in Margaret's coarse black hair almost glittered in the floodlights bearing down on the parking area. It was always so dark in winter. 'The same. Nothing ever changes. But I'm satisfied with my predictable life.'

She lived a *simple* life. That was what Evelyn thought most often – that life up here was simple.

'I hear you have a new inmate, a cancer doctor or something,' Margaret said before Evelyn could utter a quick good-bye and get on with her errand.

Margaret must've been talking to Jennifer or someone else in town. Nothing happened at Hanover House that wasn't discussed, in great detail, in Hilltop. Evelyn often wondered what the locals had done for entertainment before she'd established the facility. 'A geneticist, yes.'

'Who used an ice pick to cut into his victims' brains?' She wrinkled her nose. 'That's sick! Who would even think of such a thing?'

'He probably learned of it in college. I did.' She'd also reacquainted herself with the information once she learned of Bishop, so what she'd read was fresh in her mind. 'Believe it or not, there were people who once paid doctors to perform ice-pick lobotomies – back in the fifties and sixties.'

Margaret's breath misted on the cold air, softening the many lines in her brown, leathery face. 'Why would anyone pay to become a vegetable?'

Evelyn hugged herself for warmth. 'Not everyone became a vegetable. Some lobotomies seemed to be successful. Anyway, there wasn't a lot of help for the mentally ill at that time, none of the medications we have today, so—'

'So they thought cutting into someone's brain might be a good idea?'

'Sounds far-fetched, I know. They believed "craziness" came from an excess of emotion and cutting certain nerve connections would relieve that emotion.' She raised a hand to block the wind from her face. 'In their defense, they were sort of desperate for *some* answer. The asylums of the day were overcrowded and people were desperate for ways to help their loved ones. That's how we got the lobotomy. The neurologist who invented it in 1930-something was awarded the Nobel Prize.'

Margaret's jaw sagged, revealing the gold caps on her teeth. 'You don't say!'

'It's true. But it was another guy, an American neurologist, who performed the first transorbital lobotomy.'

'I don't even know what that is,' she said with a self-deprecating chuckle.

'It's just another name for the ice-pick lobotomy, one that sounds a bit more sophisticated. Drilling through the skull was a long and laborious process, so they decided to go in through the eye socket where the bone is so thin you can see light through it. A Dr Freeman could do the procedure in ten minutes, and he did thousands over the course of his career. He even performed them in front of crowds.'

Margaret rubbed her arms. She was wearing a sweater, but she'd come out without a coat or other outer layer. 'So Bishop was copying him? Could he have been experimenting to see if there was a better way to do it than before?'

'I'm guessing he was curious what various jabs and cuts would do. But I doubt he had any illusions that he was helping anyone, not like Dr Freeman and those who performed lobotomies back in the day.'

Margaret blew on her hands. 'Wow. As if it's not cold enough out here. That just gave me chills. Good luck with that one, Doc. He sounds like a doozy.'

'He's not the only doozy.' Not all of her subjects were known serial killers. Only 46 out of 320 inmates, since they'd added another wing last summer, had been classified that way. The rest were repeat offenders who exhibited strong psychopathic traits and were in for lesser crimes. Those men would one day be released, which was almost *more* frightening, since statistics indicated that psychopaths were highly likely to reoffend.

'I guess not,' Margaret said. 'I don't know how you stand being around them, to be honest.'

Sometimes even Evelyn didn't know how she stood it. What compelled her to do battle with what so many people preferred to ignore?

She'd been attacked and tortured herself, for one. She'd felt the terrible helplessness, which was worse than the pain. And Jasper had gotten away, escaped justice. Such gross unfairness was too galling for anyone to suffer. But still. Why couldn't she put the past behind her and try to forget, like her parents hoped and prayed she would? Forge ahead without the daily reminders she faced in her current life?

She couldn't say for sure. She just felt . . . compelled. Compelled beyond her ability to resist. Maybe it was her residual anger against Jasper. Maybe rage created her relentless drive. But she was going to do all she could to protect the unsuspecting.

'I'm hoping to make a difference,' she said simply.

Margaret smiled at her. 'You're one brave lady.'

Evelyn chuckled. 'Amarok would probably call me foolish, if he came right out and said what he thinks.'

'No. Not Amarok. Anyone can see how much he admires you. And it takes someone special to impress him.'

Evelyn reached out to squeeze her arm. 'Thank you. Now go inside. You're freezing.'

'You're here to talk to Jennifer again?'

'Yes.'

'Have you found out where Bishop put her sister's body?'

'Not yet, but I'm still trying.' Evelyn slid her keys, which she'd been holding, into her purse before waving good-bye and approaching Jennifer's room.

Jennifer answered almost immediately. 'I thought I heard voices. Come in.'

Evelyn stepped into an overheated room with the television playing. She set her purse on a small corner table and sat in the only chair while Jennifer perched on the edge of the closest bed.

'So? What do you think?' she asked. 'Have you made any progress since we talked last? Is there any chance of finding out where my sister is?'

Evelyn clung to that moment in the very beginning when Bishop had seemed a trifle glib – when she'd decided, for herself, that he *was* a psychopath regardless of any indication to the contrary. It'd seemed so clear to her then, as if he'd been exposed. There was also how he'd behaved when they first met, how he'd talked about her appearance. That could've been as innocent as he'd pretended, a few simple compliments from someone who wasn't remotely savvy in a social sense, but she'd run into that heightened awareness before with the men she studied.

Bishop had seemed to get more 'in character' and do better with his 'persecuted innocent charade' from there, however. 'I've made it clear that his life will be much easier if he provides the information we want.'

'And?'

'So far, he hasn't taken the bait. I'd like to say something encouraging to you here, but I'm all out of hope. I'm afraid he's too smart to ever reveal that information.'

'What does "smart" have to do with anything?' she demanded.

'If he tells you where he . . . where he put Jan, he'll be admitting to her murder. We've talked about that.'

'He's been convicted! He's in prison for life without the possibility of parole.'

'That's true. But he's appealing. And I suspect he's playing a game. That he's trying to make me believe he didn't do it. He's hoping to enlist my sympathy so that I'll put in a good word for him if it ever comes to that, so he can eventually get out.'

'You won't fall for that, will you?' Jennifer gasped.

Evelyn could feel her own pulse at her temples. 'No, I won't fall for that – not without significant proof that he's innocent.'

'There will be no proof.' Her lip curled in disgust. 'They found Jan's panties at his house.'

'I know.' Evelyn was glad for that, glad the evidence made it so obvious, because everything else seemed sort of murky. That was the nature of studying human behavior – what seemed clear one minute could be hopelessly clouded the next.

'So what do we do now?' Jennifer asked.

Evelyn hauled in a deep breath. This was her opportunity to get Jennifer to do the right thing for her baby. They'd been going back and forth for seven days, but Evelyn needed to draw a line. 'You should go home. Why have your child in this cold, foreign place where you have no family to support you? Won't your mother want to be there for the birth?'

Jennifer glanced away. 'She and I don't talk about the baby. She didn't like that I ever took up with Kevin. He wasn't a good person, and she knew it. But I wouldn't listen to her. Being with him, living that kind of fast and easy lifestyle, somehow made it possible for me to cope with losing Jan. He was like a . . . a drug that deadened the pain. Watching me ruin my life was hard on my mother, who was already grieving over Jan. Now I feel guilty about making things worse for her. But I couldn't face reality at the time. You can understand that, can't you?'

The pain and regret in Jennifer's voice hung heavy in the air. Leaving her purse on the table, Evelyn stood and wrapped her arms around the younger woman. She was crossing boundaries she probably had no business crossing. It was possible Jennifer wouldn't welcome the comfort she was trying to offer. But she couldn't resist trying to share the younger woman's pain.

At first, Jennifer froze as if she didn't know how to react – or whether she should react – to this unaccustomed familiarity with someone she'd known such a short time. Evelyn told herself to let go and move away before the situation could become any more awkward. But just before she could, Jennifer melted into her and clung tightly as she began to sob.

The television droned in the background while Evelyn stroked Jennifer's back and murmured, 'I'm sorry – I'm so sorry.'

After several minutes, Jennifer straightened and Evelyn backed up. 'You have every right to be hurt and angry,' she said. 'I wish I could change what happened, make it better. But there's no going back. You have to make the future better. Do you understand?'

'How?'

'Go home. Spend what time you can with your mother. I promise I'll continue to do everything possible to help on this end.'

Jennifer sniffed but said nothing.

'Will you go? So I don't have to worry about something happening here and you not being able to make it to the hospital? With the storms we get this time of year, the roads can become impassable. You've seen the weather this week. You could wind up having that baby alone. Right in this motel room. You don't want that, do you?'

A tear dripped off her chin before she could catch it. 'No.'

'So you'll listen to me? Go before we get another storm?'

'I will, but first . . . I want to talk to Bishop myself. I can't leave without doing everything in *my* power to find Jan.'

Evelyn shook her head. 'I'm not sure that's a good idea.' What if he surprised them both and began to regale Jennifer with the blood-curdling details of her sister's last minutes on earth? That could throw her into labor. Many of the psychopaths Evelyn worked with would jump at the chance to toy with her in that way.

Question was . . . would Bishop?

'I have no idea what he might say,' Evelyn warned.

'I don't care what he says. I want the chance to confront him. To plead for my sister.'

Evelyn considered the possible ramifications.

'Please?' Jennifer begged. 'Then I'll go home and make a better future. I promise.'

'Regardless of the outcome?'

'Regardless of the outcome.'

If Bishop had any way of harming her physically, Evelyn would've said no. But she trusted the security of the facility, trusted her staff after a year of getting to know them. She also felt reasonably assured Bishop wouldn't do anything to destroy the meek image he'd been trying to create. 'Okay. As long as I can be present.'

'That's fine.'

'Then we have a deal. Arrange for a flight out late tomorrow evening, if possible. And come to the prison first thing in the morning.'

Jennifer nodded solemnly. 'Thank you.'

Seven

When Evelyn stopped at the Moosehead after leaving the motel, she was looking forward to an hour or two when she could talk and laugh, maybe have a drink or play a game of darts. She didn't want to think about Bishop or her work anymore tonight. As determined as she was to continue pushing forward with her research, the responsibility, the pressure and the frustration she dealt with on a daily basis could, at times, become too much.

She parked in one of the only spaces available, at the far edge of the lot, and trudged through the snow to the entrance. The second she could hear the beat of the music permeating the walls, she knew she'd come to the right place. A year ago, a visit to the Moosehead wouldn't have been such a positive experience. She'd been too much of a 'cheechako' then, would've felt out of place. But the local pub was slowly becoming as much a part of her life as it was everyone else's. She often joined Amarok there at the end of a long day. That little bit of socializing, more than anything else, had helped mitigate the animosity she'd sensed when she first arrived in town.

Amarok smiled the moment he spotted her weaving through the crowd. 'There you are,' he said when she reached him after responding to the greetings of several others.

He'd left her a message at the prison to stop by if she got off work in time. But she would've looked for him there, regardless. He had to spend a fair portion of his time at the pub if he hoped to maintain law and order. Drunken fights broke out there all the time. Brawling seemed to be a favorite local pastime, even when no one was angry. Shorty, the owner of the Moosehead, occasionally arranged boxing matches on weekends, which, of course, invited some gambling, too. There'd been one yesterday. As long as it didn't get out of hand, Amarok turned a blind eye. It was all harmless fun, for the most part. As the extent of the area's police force, he stopped by the tavern for networking purposes as much as anything. Doing so helped him bond with the community.

'How'd it go with Jennifer?' he asked as he helped remove Evelyn's coat.

She climbed onto the stool next to him. 'Good. I think. She's going home tomorrow.'

'You got her to agree to that? Don't tell me Bishop coughed up the location of her sister's body.'

'No. And I doubt he ever will. I've met with him several times. He's too determined to convince me that he's not the killer everyone thinks he is.'

'So you talked some sense into her – for the sake of the baby.'

'We made a deal, yes.' She didn't have time to explain the deal before Shorty, who tended his own bar most nights, came to get her order.

'I'll have a glass of chardonnay.'

'Course you will, Doc. I know what you like,' he said with a wink, and went to make the pour.

As soon as she removed her gloves, Amarok took her hands and rubbed the cold from them. 'You look tired. Maybe we should head home early tonight.'

'I'm okay,' she insisted. 'I'm just . . . facing something I haven't seen before, something that reminds me a lot of Jasper.'

'With Bishop?'

'Yeah.'

'I thought Jasper was handsome, popular, charming. I don't get the impression Bishop fits that description.'

'He doesn't. He's the opposite. Plain. Average. Nondescript. But he also comes off as smarter, more capable – essentially more "normal" – than most psychopaths.'

'Harder to detect.'

'Exactly. Like Jasper.'

He took a swig of the beer sitting in front of him. 'You know how I feel about statements like that. There is no one-size-fits-all diagnosis. People are too different.'

'I agree. But I've seen certain similarities among the men I've studied, and they've remained consistent throughout my work. So there are some commonalities.'

'There'll always be exceptions, Evelyn.'

Was that what Bishop was? An exception? If so, how would she ever be able to point to one personality type and say, *Stay away from this kind of person*? And, short of accomplishing that, would she ever be able to save anyone?

Molly Granger, Shorty's stout older sister, who helped out at the bar, delivered Evelyn's wine because Shorty had become engaged in an animated conversation down the bar.

'I'm going to image his brain. Put him in the empathy study. I can't wait to see how he compares, not only to the control group, but to the other psychopaths.'

'It'll be interesting to learn the results.'

Phil Robbins, who'd been dancing with a single mother named Heidi Perth when Evelyn came in, grabbed Amarok's shoulder, interrupting their conversation. 'Hey, man. I'm heading home. If you need to be at the airport by seven, we'd better leave first thing in the morning. The weather's so changeable. You never know what we might encounter on the road.'

'Sounds good to me.'

'Should I pick you up at home then?'

'Might as well. Then I won't have to leave my truck at the trooper post.'

'Okay. I'll be at your place at five.'

'I'll be ready,' Amarok said.

'Doc.' Phil acknowledged Evelyn with a nod before heading for the door, where Heidi was not so discreetly waiting for him.

'What was *that* all about?' Evelyn asked when Phil and Heidi were gone.

Amarok wiped the condensation from his mug. 'I'm flying to California tomorrow.'

Evelyn blinked in surprise. This was the first she'd heard of any trip. 'Since when?'

'Today.'

'But . . . you've never been outside of Alaska. Never been on a commercial airliner. Why are you going now?'

'Jasper's parents live in San Diego.'

Evelyn was fully aware of that – she just hadn't made the connection. She still had a private detective on retainer. He checked in with the Moores every couple of years on the off chance they'd decide to cooperate and reveal some snippet of information that might lead to Jasper's arrest. But they'd stonewalled for so long, Evelyn had given up any hope of enlisting their help. 'You're not going to see *them*!'

He clinked his beer against her glass. 'I am.'

'*Why?* If they won't talk to my PI – any of the PIs I've sent over the years – they won't talk to you.'

'Never know. It's worth a shot. Maybe I'll make a better case, prove more persuasive.'

'You'd have to hold a gun to their heads,' she grumbled. 'They're *so* delusional where their son is concerned. I can't imagine what excuse he conjured for three murders and a fourth attack, but they seem to believe what happened wasn't entirely his fault. That it was a onetime "mistake".'

'The blind love of a parent . . .'

'Not many parents could be *that* blind.'

Amarok stared into his beer. 'If he's still in contact with them, they could be the key to unraveling the whole thing.'

'They're the ones who helped him escape when it happened.'

'Sometimes people change their minds. Time can be a cop's best friend. I wish the police were watching their house.'

'So do I, but it's Boston's case, and they don't have jurisdiction.'

'San Diego should be helping.'

'I'm sure if we had some specific request, they'd help if they could. But they're not willing to spend the kind of money twenty-four-hour surveillance would require, not when catching Jasper that way is such a long shot. No one knows for sure that he's retained contact. Even if he has, he could go years without seeing his folks. The police can't spare the manpower to watch the Moores day in and day out, year in and year out.'

Amarok tipped his beer at someone who brushed past and said hello. 'You were going to ask San Diego PD to check the Moores' phone records again. Have you heard back on that?'

She took a sip of her wine. 'I have. I just haven't mentioned it because it's so discouraging. The judge refused to grant us another warrant. He said we can't continue to invade their privacy.'

A muscle moved in Amarok's cheek. 'Jasper's smart. But he's no smarter than we are.'

Jasper had outwitted her so far – her and the army of detectives and private eyes she'd worked with over the years. He'd escaped capture as recently as a year ago last summer. Before she left Boston to open Hanover House, he'd rammed into her car in the middle of the night while she was on her way home and dragged her from behind the wheel to his own car.

If only he hadn't been wearing a mask when he did that. If only she'd gotten a glimpse of his face before she escaped. A fresh composite would've given police something new they could publicize, since the photographs they had now were so outdated.

'Maybe I should go with you,' she said.

'No. You're busy here, and I'd like a shot at this myself.'

She turned her glass on the varnished wood. 'I'm not sure I want you getting that involved.'

His eyebrows shot up. 'You're kidding, right?'

'There's no telling what he might do if we draw his attention your way.'

'Stop it, Evelyn. We've gone over this before. I can take care of myself.'

It would only take a moment of surprise. One moment when Amarok was caught off guard –

'Hey.' He lifted her chin and looked into her eyes. 'Quit worrying. Battles require some risk, right? Isn't that what you always tell me?'

'Yes, but I'm not willing to risk *you*.'

'This is *my* decision.'

She sighed. She'd already lost Marissa, Jessie and Agatha to Jasper. He might've killed Mandy, too.

'I'm not one of your girlfriends. I'm a cop,' he said, as if he could read her mind.

Forcing a smile, she nodded. 'So are you going to see your father before you go?'

'If I can.'

'How's he doing?'

'Last I heard he'd stopped throwing up. They think it's a bad case of food poisoning, but he should be fine.'

With Bishop arriving in Alaska at virtually the same time, it'd been a relief that they could trust Amarok's stepmother to look after Hank this past week. 'I'm glad to hear that.'

Evelyn nibbled at her bottom lip.

'What is it?' he asked.

'How long will you be gone?'

'Only as long as I have to be. I'll keep in touch.'

'Why don't *I* take you to the airport?'

'There's no need. You have to work.'

She did have that appointment in the morning. 'I guess you're right. I have to let Jennifer speak to Bishop before she'll leave.'

'What does she have to say to him?'

'I have no idea. Maybe she merely needs to vent her rage. Their meeting should prove interesting. I only hope she doesn't get too riled up. That wouldn't be good for a woman in her condition.'

'You're willing to take that chance?'

'I'm tired of everyone deciding what's best for victims except the victims themselves. She's come all the way to Alaska. As long as Bishop will agree to see her, I'm going to give her the audience she's requested – and hope I don't live to regret it.'

Shorty came by to ask Amarok if he'd like a refill on his beer, but he didn't answer. Something else had caught his attention. He lifted his hand in a 'hold on' gesture as he stared up at the television affixed to the wall over the bar.

'What is it?' Evelyn murmured. Then she saw for herself. A banner crossing the screen read: *Tainted evidence throws conviction of 'Zombie Maker' into question.*

Her eyes riveted on the screen and her ears strained to pick up the anchorman's voice, but they'd caught only the tail end of the story. The image and topic changed before she could hear any of the details.

'Isn't that what they called Bishop?' Amarok asked. 'The Zombie Maker?'

Evelyn felt slightly nauseous. 'Yes.'

'What are you learning?'

Evelyn glanced up to find Amarok standing behind her. As soon as they'd walked in, he'd greeted his dog while she made a beeline for the desk, where she could open her laptop. 'That news report we saw *was* about Bishop.'

Nudging Makita aside, Amarok dragged over another chair and sat next to her. 'What'd the detectives do wrong?'

'The story's just breaking, so there's not a lot of information out there. From what I can tell, the lead detective, a Detective Gustavson, fabricated the most damning evidence.'

'Which was . . .'

'The panties. In court, he testified that the search of Bishop's house produced the panties of various victims. Eight in all. Apparently, that's been called into question.'

'By whom?' He scratched Makita's head. 'Who or what brought this to light?'

'The detective's ex-girlfriend started it. I guess they've broken up since the trial. She called the press to say he placed that evidence in Bishop's attic so it would be found by the search team.'

Forgetting about his dog, who was resting his muzzle adoringly on Amarok's thigh, he gripped his own forehead. 'Holy shit!'

'No kidding.'

'I bet he regrets the breakup now, even if he didn't before.'

The wry note in Amarok's voice indicated he was teasing, but he had a point. 'The timing is certainly suspect,' she said. 'Maybe it's not true. Maybe it's just sour grapes and she's after revenge.'

'Does she say why she came forward?'

'Claims it's because of Mandy Walker's murder.' She scrolled through the article until she found the section where that was addressed. 'See? Right here.' She pointed at the screen as she read aloud, ' "I couldn't live with myself, knowing what I knew. I was afraid Detective Gustavson was wrong about Bishop, and I didn't want to see an innocent man spend the rest of his life behind bars." '

'Whether the evidence is good or not doesn't necessarily have any bearing on his guilt,' Amarok said.

'True, but it will have significant bearing on his conviction.'

'Surely Gustavson can prove these allegations false. Has there been any rebuttal from him?'

'Not yet. This will launch an internal investigation if it hasn't already. He'll probably have to keep mum until it's over, and that could take some time.'

'If she's telling the truth, he'll lose his job.'

'Without question,' she agreed.

'That's a lot to put on the line. So, if he did cheat, why'd he do it?' Makita whined and then barked, and Amarok started petting him again.

'She says he was determined to impress his superiors and the community by solving "the big case". That he was hoping to be promoted, had his sights set on becoming chief of police someday.'

Amarok leaned forward to read over her shoulder. 'That isn't good.'

'No. If Gustavson planted the evidence, they'll release Bishop. They'll have to.'

'Maybe they *should* release Bishop,' Amarok said. 'Maybe he didn't do it. Then he can go home and continue his cancer research and take care of his sister.'

Evelyn had turned what she'd learned about Beth over to the Minnesota Department of Human Services, which had brought in the correct county's Adult Protective Services to investigate. She'd been playing phone tag with Louise Belgrath, the person who'd been assigned the case, had been assured they were doing everything possible, but she hadn't heard exactly what that entailed. 'I wouldn't be happy to see him released.'

Amarok adjusted Makita's collar. 'Why not?'

Evelyn closed her eyes and pinched the bridge of her nose.

'Evelyn?' he prompted.

Dropping her hand, she lifted her head to look at him. 'I think he's guilty, Amarok. I think he's one of the craftiest killers I've ever met, one that will continue to take lives as long as he can.'

'What makes you believe that? You've only been meeting with him for a week. And you told me yourself he doesn't fit the mold.'

'I can't explain it,' she said. 'It's just . . . gut instinct. Whenever I meet with him, my "bullshit" meter goes crazy.'

He got down on his knees and slipped his arms around her waist. 'Are you sure it's not that you've become jaded? That you're now seeing every inmate as a conscienceless monster? Once they go into that orange jumpsuit, it'd be easy to lump them all together – especially after working with such people as intently and as long as you have.'

She stared down at him. 'It's possible.'

'So let the system do whatever it's going to do.'

'Meaning . . .'

'Keep your mouth shut,' he said with a grin.

'You're suggesting I don't state my opinion?'

'For a change. Yes.' He was chuckling when he said that, but he sobered quickly. 'If you publicly oppose his release and he's innocent – or everyone else grows convinced he's innocent, thanks to the way the investigation was handled – you could lose a lot of credibility.'

'That's true. But what happens if I say nothing, Amarok?' She combed her fingers through his thick dark hair. 'What if he goes free, and another unsuspecting woman loses her life? I'm afraid I'll feel responsible.'

'Why? You're not the one making the decision.'

'I'll be a party to it if I don't fight his release.'

'So that's what you're going to do?'

She backed off. She didn't want to upset him and couldn't say yet, anyway. 'I'll do some testing and hope I know what to say if it ever comes to that.'

Eight

As Evelyn drove through the foggy darkness to Hanover House early the following morning, she felt a little sad. The weather here could cause some depression. A lot of people complained of the 'winter blues'. But that wasn't her problem. She was so caught up in her work the world could come tumbling down around her and she wouldn't notice, unless someone pointed it out to her. That news piece about the tainted evidence in Bishop's investigation had her on edge. Mandy Walker's death made that uneasy feeling worse, and so did hearing from Fitzpatrick again.

'"Nothing is so terrifying as this monologue of the storm,"' she mumbled. That sense of impending doom was back. It didn't feel like a good time to have Amarok gone. She'd grown accustomed to riding home with him if it was storming, having dinner with him if they both got off early enough and snuggling up to him in bed. Sleeping in an empty house would feel strange – lonely. She was afraid the next few days might teach her just how much she'd come to rely on having him in her life, and she wasn't sure she cared to know. The more he meant, the more she stood to lose – and, after losing her best friends in such a horrible way in high school, she never wanted to feel such pain again.

But she couldn't dwell on what-ifs, not where Bishop, Jasper, Fitzpatrick or even Amarok was concerned. She had to get over to the prison and determine whether Bishop was willing to meet with Jennifer. Jennifer was scheduled to arrive almost immediately.

Evelyn greeted the COs handling security at the entrance and, once they'd checked her in, took the elevator to the second floor of the mental health wing.

Penny wasn't at her desk when Evelyn walked through the double glass doors that separated the offices from the labs used for brain imaging and other studies, but she knew her assistant would arrive soon. Penny wasn't late; Evelyn was early. Before she'd moved in with Amarok, she'd often beat everyone else to work. After she'd moved in with the handsome trooper, she typically came in at eight, like the others. Some mornings she was tempted to sleep even later, if he also had the time.

She wished they'd had a quiet half hour together this morning, but they'd both been rushed . . .

She buzzed the prison side of the facility as soon as she sat down and asked for two officers to bring Bishop to Interview #1. Then, because that always took some time, she picked up the phone to listen to her voice mail.

She'd received a message from her sister, Brianne, her only sibling, expressing sympathy over Mandy's death.

Sorry it's taken me so long to call. I was away for the weekend and Mom didn't want to ruin my trip, so she just told me what happened to Mandy Walker Thursday night. I'm terribly sorry. Are you handling it okay? Must bring up horrible memories. It's brought up horrible memories for me, too. Those days while you were missing . . . well, I try not to think about them, but I'll never forget. Call me if you'd like to talk. You know where to find me.

Evelyn hadn't allowed herself to grieve over Mandy's death. She and Mandy hadn't spoken in a number of years. As long as Evelyn was in Alaska, she felt so removed she could almost pretend that Mandy was alive and well – except for what her death might say about Bishop, of course. What was going on? Was there a copycat killer on the loose? And was that copycat killer Jasper, playing games with her as Fitzpatrick had suggested?

Her next message was from Preston Schmidt, another member of the team. He had a terrible cold, said he wouldn't be in today. Then she received a message from Fitzpatrick. She almost deleted it as soon as she heard his voice. Hadn't she made herself clear? She didn't want any contact! But curiosity got the best of her.

Have you seen the news, Evelyn? They're going to vacate Bishop's conviction. They can't continue to keep him behind bars, not if the detective tampered with the evidence. I hope he isn't a serious threat to society. You and I should both test him, independently. Try to determine if this guy is really a psychopath. Call me if you'd like me to come up there.

Evelyn couldn't believe her ears. He refused to take no for an answer! 'I'm beginning to think *you're* the psychopath,' she muttered, and deleted his message as she should have in the first place.

The intercom buzzed almost the second she hung up the phone.

She pressed the button. 'Yes?'

'Bishop's waiting for you in one.'

She glanced at her watch. Seven fifty. She had ten minutes before Jennifer was due to arrive. 'Thank you,' she said. 'I'm coming.'

Bishop looked like he hadn't slept since he arrived at Hanover House. He stared at her from a pale face with dark rings below his eyes.

'Morning,' she said.

He didn't answer.

'Now that you've had a chance to settle in a bit, how are you adjusting?'

Lowering his head, he mumbled a response she couldn't quite make out.

'Excuse me?'

'I'm *not* adjusting,' he stated more clearly. 'The food here is deplorable. I can't eat it.'

'Most days I eat here myself. Saves me from having to bring a lunch. What's wrong with it?'

'It's homogenous, salt- and butter-laden garbage – an insult to the palate.'

'Trust me, it's superior to what you'll find in other prisons.'

Except for those in solitary confinement, most of the inmates had televisions in their cells. Many had radios, too. And they talked among themselves when they could. She wondered if he'd heard the news about the panties. Of course, if *he* hadn't put them in the attic, he had to know someone else did. But, judging from his slumped shoulders and sagging jowls, he didn't seem to be aware that the detective on his case had been called out for it. He'd be more encouraged if he were.

Evelyn hoped his ignorance would play in her favor. Maybe it was fortuitous that Jennifer had come to Alaska and Evelyn had set up this meeting, because even if Bishop hadn't heard about the spoiled evidence, it wouldn't be long before he did. His attorney would be calling to suggest they file one motion or another to start the process of having his case reviewed. Then the opportunity Evelyn had at this moment would be lost. If Bishop gained *any* hope of getting out, he'd be much less likely to meet with Jennifer – or tell them anything of value.

'Do you sleep here, too? Because the mattresses are hard as concrete.'

'I'm afraid my hands are tied there—'

'Another bad pun,' he broke in.

She didn't remember the first one, but that wasn't important. Sometimes he focused on the most insignificant details. 'It's true. Thick mattresses make good hiding places. And anything with springs, well . . . we have to be careful what we allow the inmates to have. Some can and do make weapons out of almost anything.'

'That's right – you had a stabbing here a year ago.'

'Yes. One that was nearly fatal. We'd like to avoid that in the future, so certain things have to be the way they are.'

He gazed dismally at the painted cinder-block walls. 'The injustice of what's happened to me is almost insufferable.'

If he was innocent, what the detective had done *was* unconscionable. 'Fortunately, the human spirit is quite resilient.'

'I believe I've proven that.'

'What you've accomplished, if serial killer is *not* part of your résumé, is admirable.'

'I'm no killer, Dr Talbot. What killer would take care of his own mentally handicapped sister?'

None that she knew of. But she'd dealt with enough psychopaths to understand that the smartest ones created a compelling cover. 'Most claim to be innocent regardless of what they do or don't do that's commendable. Anyway, I was wondering if you might be interested in participating in some of our studies.'

'Today?'

'Why wait any longer? It's been more than a week since you arrived.'

'No. Thank you,' he added, as if he was determined to be polite under any circumstances.

She lifted her eyebrows. 'You're not eager to get out of your cell?'

'I'm not feeling up to it.'

'It would put you back in a clinical setting,' she said, tempting him.

'I prefer to be the scientist, not the subject.'

'Scientist or subject, the studies should be intellectually stimulating. Why not relieve the boredom? You might be able to offer a perspective different from our own.' She held her breath, hoping her appeal to his vanity might prove successful.

Forgetting that his chair was bolted to the floor, he tried to scoot it forward only to mutter a curse when he realized he couldn't change anything. 'What kind of studies?'

'We have one going on right now that's designed to determine whether those who exhibit psychopathic traits can more easily beat a polygraph than a control group can. We also have one that measures empathy via magnetic resonance imaging. I'd like to include you in both.'

He folded his arms as well as he could while wearing handcuffs. 'I don't know. You have no idea how upsetting what I've been through is. I'm not sure I'll ever recover. The police were out to get me. That's all I can figure.'

She was far more prone to believe that now. But she was also reluctant to give away what she'd learned about the evidence used to convict him. 'You'd like being part of the studies. And we could celebrate with a glass of wine at the end of the day. Have you ever tried Salmonberry?'

'No.'

She never provided any of the inmates with alcohol, but Jennifer had mentioned that Bishop considered himself a bit of a foodie, and he probably hadn't had a glass of wine since he was arrested. Given the length of his trial, that was months and months ago. 'It's a dry Alaskan wilderness wine made from wild salmonberries hand-picked on Kodiak Island. I predict you'll love it.'

'That's my best offer?' he said glumly. 'A single glass of wine?'

'I'm afraid so. It's more than the others get.'

A thought seemed to strike him, causing him to perk up. 'You're not afraid that I might skew your findings?'

'Why would I be afraid of that?'

'Because I'm not a psychopath. Give me the PCL-R. You'll see.'

He sounded *so* confident, confident enough to make her question her own intuition. Maybe she was wrong about him. 'Okay, I'll do that as soon as we have the chance, in the next couple of days.' She'd been planning to, anyway. She thought it might be the only thing that could help shore up what she felt in her gut or throw her to the other side. 'Right now I have something else I'd like you to do.'

'You want *more* from me?'

'Yes, and this favor might not be as easy as the others to grant. Jan's sister is still in town. She's asked to speak to you.'

He got up. 'What's the point of that? I've told you. I don't know where her sister's body is. How could I know? I didn't kill her. I didn't kill anyone!'

'I've conveyed your response to Jennifer. She'd like to meet with you anyway, if you're willing.'

'I'm *not* willing! She'll just accuse me.'

'You told me you cared about Jan.'

His eyes narrowed as if she'd caught him on something. 'I did care. A great deal.'

'Then prove it. Meet with Jennifer for the sake of Jan's memory. Have some compassion for her suffering sister.'

The way he looked at her made her wonder what he was thinking. He was so careful not to let his thoughts register on his face. She'd never met anyone so guarded, so disconnected from his or her own body language.

Maybe that was what frightened her about Bishop. If they let him go, she doubted they'd ever catch him again, even if he was guilty.

'Fine,' he said, and took his seat.

Jennifer was shaking when Evelyn showed her in.

'Don't worry,' she murmured, giving the younger woman's back a reassuring rub. 'There's no way he can hurt you.'

Resting her hands on her rounded belly, she sat slowly behind Evelyn's small utility table.

Evelyn hadn't known what to expect from this encounter – some level of emotionality, she supposed. But there were no tears or recriminations. Just silence. The two stared at each other, almost without blinking, for at least three minutes. Evelyn was about to ask Jennifer what she had to say when Bishop finally spoke.

'I'm sorry about your sister.'

'No, you're not,' Jennifer responded.

He shrugged. 'If you won't believe me, there's nothing I can do. I didn't hurt her.'

'That's a lie,' Jennifer insisted. 'I don't care what you or anyone else says, I *know* you did it. I was there at the trial. I saw the way you looked at me. You'd almost begin to salivate when I walked into the room because you were reliving what you'd done to her, imagining the way you'd touched her or hurt her, maybe even the way you killed her.'

Evelyn saw a leap of emotion in Bishop's eyes, but, masking it almost immediately, he shifted his gaze to her. 'I don't see how this will get us anywhere.'

It already had. It'd given Evelyn a glimpse of what Jennifer had seen in court. But it had also made Evelyn more afraid than ever that Bishop would be released. There was a level of excitement inside him when Jennifer talked about Jan that was so palpable even Evelyn could feel it. 'Compassion, remember?' she said, hoping to keep him engaged so she could witness more of his reaction to Jan's identical twin.

'Where's your compassion for *me*?' he demanded. 'For a man whose whole life has been ruined? An innocent man unjustly accused and imprisoned?'

Evelyn returned his level stare. 'Stop playing games, Dr Bishop. You're not innocent; you're just clever. But you can't fool me.'

His pouting demeanor twisted into an evil, sort of gleeful expression. 'I'll *never* give you what you want!' he snapped.

The change that came over him was so sudden and so opposite to anything he'd shown her before, Evelyn felt stunned. The whole episode reminded her of something from a horror movie where the main character was possessed and his head had just started spinning.

She and Jennifer had caught sight of the demon hiding inside . . .

'Get me out of here!' he yelled.

Evelyn was shaking as badly as Jennifer by the time the guards removed him from the far side of the room. By 'what you want' he'd meant the location of Jan's body. That was an admission; Evelyn was convinced of it. He'd just been careful to couch what he'd said, to say the words in such a way that he could claim he meant otherwise if she ever repeated them – or played the video of this meeting in court. All of her interactions with the prisoners were recorded.

That he felt confident enough to do what he'd just done was absolutely chilling. He believed he was so convincing, so good at acting the innocent, he could take on even her – and win.

Maybe he *was* aware of the evidence scandal. Maybe he knew he had a good chance of getting out – and she wouldn't be able to stop it.

'We got nothing from that,' Jennifer said. 'That was a big waste of time. I'm sorry for the trouble I've put you to. But at least I had my say.'

Evelyn drew a steadying breath. 'Don't be sorry. It wasn't a waste of time. As a matter of fact, I'm *glad* you came up here.'

Jennifer seemed surprised. 'You are?'

'Yes. I needed to see exactly what I just saw.'

The question was . . . would it make any difference?

Nine

Evelyn left four messages for the detective on Bishop's case before he finally called her back, and by that time it was her lunch hour.

'This is Detective Gustavson.'

The voice on the other end of the line sounded beleaguered. She waved for Penny, who was in her office going over some paperwork with her, to step out and give her some privacy. 'Thanks for returning my calls,' she said.

'Figured you'd just keep after me if I didn't.'

The door clicked as her assistant shut it on the way out. 'That's true. I'm nothing if not persistent.'

'What can I do for you?'

'As I told you in my messages, I run Hanover House – or at least the mental health unit—'

'I'm aware of you and your work, Dr Talbot,' he broke in, his voice brusque.

She felt awkward, hated to intrude at what had to be a bad time, but this was important. 'I'm sorry to bother you, but I . . . I have to know. *Did* you plant that evidence? Will Bishop be getting out?'

There was a long pause.

'Detective Gustavson, please. Be honest with me.'

After another extended silence, she got her answer: 'Yes.'

That word sounded wrenched from him, but there it was. He'd

cheated. He'd plucked the 'fruit of the poisonous tree', as such illegally obtained evidence was sometimes referred to in criminal justice circles.

Shit. Evelyn covered her face. *'Why?'*

'Because I had no choice. He's guilty. Guilty as sin, Dr Talbot. He may not have been up there with you long enough for you to recognize that, but *I* know it. And I knew it then. You should've seen how he challenged me when I first called him in for questioning, how he smiled at me. I had no doubt he'd go on killing until I stopped him. Problem was . . . he's too smart, too good at making sure he lures his victims in without alarming anyone. I couldn't get anything solid on him. So I . . . I figured out a way to get the job done.'

'The end justified the means, in other words.'

'Do you think *he* plays fair? Do you think the women whose brains he cut into before raping, torturing and murdering them thought that was fair?'

'I'm not judging you,' she said, hoping to diffuse the surfeit of emotion that came bursting through the line. Obviously, Gustavson was defensive. No doubt he'd already been criticized from all sides – his superiors, the press, the community, perhaps even his own family. 'Maybe . . . maybe under the circumstances, I would've been tempted to do the same,' she told him. *If* she was certain, how could she not be tempted? She couldn't be hypocritical enough to pretend otherwise, given her determination to stop such predators. She wished someone would see to it that Jasper was put behind bars whether it was through legally obtained evidence or not.

And yet . . . due process of law was there for a reason.

'The mistake I made wasn't *planting* the evidence.' Although Gustavson was calmer now, it sounded as if he was almost in tears. 'It was wrestling with my conscience over it and sharing that struggle with someone I loved and trusted, someone who turned on me in the end. My ex may be trying to make it sound as if I did what I did to enhance my career. But that's not true. What kind of man would do something like that for the sake of ambition? I did it for the community. To get him off the streets. To stop him before he could hurt anyone else. I swear it. He was too smart, and I was desperate. That's all.'

Whether that was true or not, Gustavson seemed earnest enough that she believed him. Probably because she also felt Bishop was guilty. That he would continue to kill. 'Then I'm sorry for what you're going through. It'll be a long, rough ride. And now . . . now Bishop will get out. You realize that.'

'Yes.'

'Have you admitted the truth to anyone else?' If he hadn't, maybe the investigation would peter out and nothing would change, but Gustavson dashed all hope of that.

'Of course. I had no choice. Lindsey set me up, turned over a conversation she recorded on her cell phone.'

'No!' Evelyn gasped.

'Yes. Can you believe that? No good deed goes unpunished, as they say. I tell you I was doing the world a favor. I put my reputation and my career on the line to stop a killer. Now *I'm* the one who'll be hurt by it, and he'll walk free – after murdering eight women, probably more. I just turned in my resignation and am cleaning out my desk, so the investigation won't take long. Be prepared to send him home.'

'Do you know Beth?' she asked before he could hang up.

'His sister? I've met the poor thing. She was there when we were doing the search, huddling in the corner, frightened half to death. And she came to the trial.'

'What do you make of a serial killer taking care of someone like that? It's a bit of a contradiction, wouldn't you say?'

'It's no contradiction,' he scoffed. 'If I had my guess, he's the one who turned her into the imbecile she is.'

Evelyn felt her jaw drop. 'Are you *serious*?'

'We're talking about a man who performed lobotomies on his victims. I'm guessing he started on her. Used her to practice, for God's sake!'

The thought of someone's *brother* doing such a terrible thing made Evelyn sick. And yet . . . what Gustavson said resonated with what she'd seen of Bishop so far – made sense of a piece of the puzzle that hadn't fit before.

'I wouldn't put it past a psychopath of Bishop's caliber,' she admitted.

'Then you're one of the few who truly understand what he is.'

'Is there anything I can do to help?' she asked.

'Just stay out of the way. You're doing good work, but all the bleeding hearts out there who care more about the rights of criminals than victims would love to take you down with me. The last thing you need is to get mixed up in this mess.'

What he said was true. She'd been lucky to escape last year's media scandal. But he wasn't the only one who believed Bishop would go out and reoffend.

That meant she was already mixed up in it.

Amarok had no trouble finding the exclusive development where Jasper's parents lived, but he wasn't sure how to get through the iron gates of the tall fence that enclosed it. After coming so far, he was reluctant to use the intercom on the small brick edifice between the exit and entrance. If the Moores could turn him away that easily, he was fairly certain they would.

He parked and waited, hoping someone else would approach and punch in the correct code so he could pull in behind him or her. But it was a quiet afternoon with little activity in the neighborhood. He sat there for fifteen minutes before he spotted another vehicle. And that vehicle wasn't going in the entrance; it was coming out the exit.

In case this would be his best chance, he waited just long enough for that car to get out of the way. Then he punched the gas pedal of his cheap rental and rocketed through the exit, barely making it before the gate closed.

When brake lights flashed on the Mercedes that'd inadvertently let him through, he imagined a moment of panic on the driver's part. '"Dear me,"' Amarok mocked. '"I fear I've let a piece of common trash through the gate!"'

He didn't wait to see what that driver would do; he sped past a series of fountains and man-made lakes into the sprawling neighborhood. He was determined to reach the Moores' doorstep before anyone could stop him, wanted to confront Jasper's parents face-to-face rather than let them hide behind some intercom or fence.

The homes in this small but elite neighborhood were spread out for privacy and sat on large lots. The lots had to be large because the houses themselves were enormous. Had he come earlier, he was certain he would've had no trouble following a lawn service, housekeeper or handyman through the gate. These weren't the type of people who mowed their own lawns, cleaned their own houses or mended their own fences.

Amarok found Stanley and Maureen Moore's sprawling stucco mansion at the end of a cul-de-sac on grounds worthy of a museum. Of course, growing things in San Diego was a lot easier than in Alaska this time of year. This mild-weathered, completely domesticated area was the exact opposite of the wild, rugged place where he lived.

Some people – *most* people – loved San Diego. But he wasn't overly impressed. He preferred Alaska.

After parking across the street, where he could drive away without having to back down some windy drive lined with pagoda lights, he left his jacket in the car – it was too warm to wear it – and grabbed the file he'd brought with him.

The entrance to the Moores' house was more elaborate than any Amarok had ever seen – except, perhaps, on television. The overhang had to be thirty feet high. The light that extended down from it looked like a giant piece of contemporary art.

He couldn't admire Jasper's parents' wealth, however, not when they'd used it to rob Evelyn and Jasper's other victims of the justice they deserved.

With a glance over his shoulder to be sure that the Mercedes hadn't found him, if the driver had even tried, he rang the doorbell and heard a long melodic chime. 'What the hell's wrong with a simple ding-dong?' he muttered. Then he held his breath, hoping he'd find someone at home.

After thirty seconds or so, footsteps approached from the other side. The heavy wooden door swung open and a petite, attractive woman wearing a turtleneck with a fitted tweed jacket and tan slacks peered out at him. 'Yes?'

Elaborate diamond rings adorned her fingers. A strand of pearls hung from her neck and matching pearl earrings dangled from her ears. 'My name is Sergeant Benjamin Murphy.' He flashed his badge. 'Are you Maureen Moore?'

'I am . . .'

He could've guessed from her resemblance to the picture he had of Jasper – Jasper's senior portrait that had run in the high school yearbook even though Jasper had already been on the lam at that point. Amarok had studied that photograph often over the past year, wondering how Jasper might've changed in the years since, what he must look like today. Since his last attack, Evelyn's private investigator had had the same photo 'aged' using a new computer program that helped with police work, but Amarok was afraid to rely *too* heavily on the result, simply because there was a chance it wasn't correct. 'I flew here all the way from Alaska to speak with you.'

'Alaska?' Her carefully manicured eyebrows drew together. 'Oh God. Don't tell me you have any connection to Evelyn Talbot or that ghastly prison she's created.'

'Actually, I do.'

Subtle lines at the corners of Maureen's eyes and above her top lip revealed her age. She had to be sixty. But, from a distance, he would've guessed she was much younger. He figured that was what having a good physical trainer, dye job and Botox could do for a person.

'Hanover House is located on the outskirts of Hilltop, where I live,' he explained. 'But I don't work there. I happen to be the local law enforcement.' He left out the fact that he was personally involved with Evelyn. He didn't see where that was pertinent to the conversation.

'Don't tell me something's happened to Evelyn—'

'You mean like what happened to her twenty-one years ago, when your son tried to murder her? Or what happened to her eighteen months ago, when he made a second attempt on her life?'

Her cheeks flushed. 'Jasper didn't kidnap her again. She made that up as a-a publicity stunt to get the police and the media once again interested in her case. She was about to move to Alaska, so that was her last chance to launch another search before she left the area. Or it was one of the psychopaths she's worked with. She's studied so many, who can really say?'

'You honestly believe it wasn't Jasper.'

'How did you get in here?' She glanced around him, but he knew she couldn't see his vehicle.

'I came in the exit,' he replied.

'You *what*?'

'I didn't have the code. But I felt it was important to show you what I've found.' He lifted the manila envelope he'd brought with him.

Instead of showing interest, she blanched. 'I don't want to see it.'

'Hiding from the truth won't change it, Mrs Moore.'

'My husband's not here. He – he won't like that I'm talking to you. You'll have to come back later.'

She started to close the door, but he stopped it with one hand. '*Please,*' he said. 'Try to look past your love for your son and imagine the grief your son's victims and their families must feel.'

'It's not like I don't have sympathy for them,' she said. 'What Jasper did before, it . . . it breaks my heart. But he was high on acid when he killed those girls. He didn't know what he was doing. He thought they were zombies!'

That was what he'd told his parents? How he'd convinced them to help him and stand by him all these years? 'What about Evelyn? He imprisoned her for three days while he was attending school – and baseball practice. *Tortured* her whenever he could slip away. Slit her throat!'

'She got those injuries trying to escape. He only acted as he did because she threatened to tell and he panicked. He was afraid – afraid of going to prison for life for something he didn't even mean to do. Surely you can understand the terror of a seventeen-year-old boy who was smart enough to know he'd be tried as an adult.'

'I understand how much *you* want to believe what he told you,' Amarok said softly. 'And I understand how tightly you've had to cling to the excuses he provided – to justify your own actions. You seem like a decent, caring individual.'

'I am!'

'Then why are you helping him? That makes you partly responsible! And more women are dying, Mrs Moore – at the hand of your son.'

'No!'

'Yes. Surely you must wonder, in some small part of your mind, what if? Maybe it's time you looked at the evidence with an open mind. That's all I'm asking. Then I'll go.'

Her chest lifted as she drew a deep breath. 'Stan won't be happy,' she muttered, obviously torn.

'Then we'll speak quickly and privately, before he gets home.'

At that moment the Mercedes that'd inadvertently let him through the gate pulled up to the curb and the driver yelled out across the broad expanse of lawn and shrubs. 'Maureen, this man isn't bothering you, is he?'

Amarok thought that would bring an abrupt end to the conversation, that Maureen would lean on the driver's support. But she didn't. 'I'm fine, Scott. Thank you. This man is . . . he's a friend of the family,' she said, and opened the door to admit him.

'Okay,' Scott responded. 'Just wanted to be sure. Have a nice evening.'

As he drove off, Amarok stepped into the cathedral-like entrance with its black-and-white-checked flooring, crystal chandelier and elegant grandfather clock, which ticked softly in the hushed silence. 'Thank you. What I have to say will only take a moment.'

Maureen didn't seem pleased by her own decision, but she didn't change her mind and throw him out. She beckoned him into a sitting room off to one side that was stuffed with antiques. 'There hasn't been any new evidence in years,' she said. 'Evelyn didn't even get a look at her attacker's face eighteen months ago. So . . . what is it you have in that envelope?'

He opened the flap and withdrew a sheet that contained a collection of color pictures.

'Who are these women?' she asked when he showed it to her.

'Their names are written on the back.'

'I don't recognize them, don't know them.'

He handed her Evelyn's picture. 'Do you see the similarity? How much they look like her?'

'There's more of a resemblance to some than others,' she hedged. 'But so what? What are you getting at?'

He pulled another sheet from the folder. 'This is what those women look like after being tortured and murdered.'

With a yelp-like sound, she dropped that sheet as soon as she realized it contained crime scene photos. 'Who the hell do you think you are? Get out!' she yelled.

'Give me one more second,' he said as he retrieved what she'd dropped. 'These women? They were murdered just outside of Phoenix over the past five years, near a burned-out barn very similar to the shack in which your son killed Evelyn's friends. So if Jasper's been living anywhere near the northwest side of Phoenix, you need to speak up.'

She was blinking rapidly, trying to avoid tears. 'I-I don't know where he is. It's not Arizona.'

If she didn't know where he was, then how did she know it wasn't Arizona? 'Could it be Boston? Where he was eighteen months ago? Because another of Evelyn's friends has been killed there, a woman both Jasper and Evelyn knew in school. You might've heard about it. Her name was Mandy Walker.'

'Yes, I've heard, and I remember Mandy. We had her over to the house a time or two. But Jasper had nothing to do with her death. That was some other . . . some other person – the Zombie Maker or a-a copycat. Surely you've read about the Zombie Maker. Maybe you've even met him. He was sentenced to Hanover House.'

'You think Mandy's killer was someone from Minnesota? That's where all the Zombie Maker's crimes have been committed.'

She looked shaken, unsure. 'It could be.'

'Don't you find it a bit of a coincidence that the victim was another close friend of Evelyn's?'

'It *must* be a coincidence,' she insisted. 'Jasper's a good family man these days – a husband and father. He would never hurt anyone like he did before.'

So she did have contact with him . . . 'But he *does* live in Arizona. In Peoria, right?'

When she didn't contradict him, he thought he was getting somewhere. He hoped she might reveal more. But a booming voice came from elsewhere in the house. 'Maureen? Where are you? Are you ready to go to dinner or what?'

Stan was home. The house was so large they hadn't heard him come in.

The rest of the color drained from Maureen's face. 'He can't find you here!'

'I'll hide, do whatever you want,' he whispered. 'I'm not out to cause problems for you. I realize you're a victim in all of this, too. So take my card and think about what I've told you. Think about the fact that no parent of a psychopath wants to acknowledge that their child could cause so much harm. It's gut-wrenching. But you can't let the pain stop you from doing what's right. You have to be brave, even if it means turning in someone you love.'

'Stan'll never forgive me if I do.'

'I believe your son murdered these women, Mrs Moore. He chooses victims that look like Evelyn, as these do, because she is the person he's fixated on, the person he really wants. And he will continue to kill – again and again – if you don't stop him.'

She didn't respond. There was no time. She went to the door and called out, 'I spilled a little wine on the carpet and am cleaning it up! Will you grab my purse from our bedroom?'

After her husband answered that he would, she peered out until she felt assured that he'd gone upstairs. Then she showed Amarok out the back.

Ten

Finished with brain imaging for the day, Evelyn returned to her desk to find she'd received several messages from various reporters. Most were from the Minneapolis area, but there were a few who represented national papers and news programs. They all wanted to speak to her about Lyman Bishop.

She knew, as Detective Gustavson had advised, she'd be better off staying out of the firestorm. Hanover House would most likely be better off, too. That was the only thing that gave her pause. She hesitated to let what Detective Gustavson had done get in the way of what she might be able to accomplish with the resources at her disposal. But the only weapon she had to fight back against Bishop was her professional opinion on his culpability, and because of the danger she believed he posed she had to alert the community as to where she stood on the issue.

After wiping her palms on her wool slacks, she picked up one of the message slips and dialed someone named Sebring Schultz – a man, judging by the voice on the recording.

'*Star Tribune.*'

'Mr Schultz?'

'Yes?'

'This is Evelyn Talbot in Alaska, returning your call.'

'Thanks for getting back to me, Dr Talbot.'

She drew a deep breath. 'No problem.'

'Do I need to explain what I'm calling about?'

'No, you're not the only person to have contacted me.'

'So? What do you think of what you're hearing?'

'Frankly, it frightens me.'

'That this case includes such police corruption? That Bishop could be an innocent man unjustly stripped of his liberty?'

'No, that news of what Detective Gustavson did will lead to the release of a very dangerous man.'

'You believe Bishop is guilty.'

'I haven't had much time to work with him. I've tried to analyze him to a degree, to create some official notes, but he's been very careful to only show me a certain façade, which makes that hard. At this point, with what's happened, what small chance I did have has disappeared. I doubt he'll cooperate, am guessing his lawyer would advise him not to, since that could be perceived as an unnecessary risk. But, yes, even though he's only been here a short time, I believe he's guilty.'

'How can you say that, Doctor? He was convicted on evidence that was planted in his house!'

She frowned at the clock, hated the way the seconds and minutes ticked away toward Bishop's release. 'That has no bearing on his guilt, Mr Schultz, only on *proving* his guilt. That's the sad thing here. What Gustavson did was wrong. But those panties weren't the only evidence. Just the most damning.'

'I've interviewed several of the jurors. The conviction turned on those panties.'

'I understand that.'

'Are you also aware that another woman was murdered by "The Zombie Maker's" MO *after* he was imprisoned?'

'Of course. The victim was a personal friend of mine. I'd be unlikely to miss that. But I believe someone else committed that murder.'

'Let me guess . . . the man who attacked you and was never caught?'

'Given Mandy's connection to me, it's a possibility. As for the murders Bishop has been convicted for, he knew each of the victims. He had no alibi for the nights they went missing. And let's not forget the murder of his mother some years ago. The perpetrator was never caught.'

'Maybe he had nothing to do with that. Maybe that was just bad luck all the way around and it wasn't him.'

Evelyn rolled her shoulders, trying to ease some of the stress knotting her muscles. 'After meeting him, I don't think so.'

'But if you haven't tested him, what are you basing your opinion on?'

'I've spoken to him, Mr Schultz, on more than one occasion.'

'You couldn't have spent much time with him. That can't be all of it.'

'I assure you, it isn't.'

'So it's the circumstantial evidence you rattled off to me.'

Evelyn cleared her throat. She'd known she'd meet with a certain amount of skepticism, that it wouldn't be easy to take the stand she was taking. Bishop hadn't been with her long enough. She wished news of the tainted evidence could've broken six months from now. Maybe by then she would've had more credibility when sharing her opinion of Lyman Bishop. 'No. I'm merely pointing out that even if the panty evidence is thrown out, nothing has come to light to show he *didn't* kill those women. The police can't rule him out; they just can't keep him behind bars.'

'Where *you* think he belongs.'

'Judging by what I've seen of him so far, yes.'

'What have you seen that leads you to such a conclusion, Dr Talbot? Could you be more specific?'

'I'm sure you won't be satisfied with my answers, Mr Schultz. If I were you, I'd be equally skeptical. But every once in a while I come across someone who causes the hair on the back of my neck to stand on end.'

'You can tell psychopaths from regular people just by meeting them.'

When she heard the derisive tone of his voice, she considered trying to explain what she'd glimpsed, briefly, in that meeting with Jennifer Hall but decided against it. He'd only pick that apart. Truth was – she had nothing substantial with which to defend her position. But she still wasn't willing to relinquish it. 'No. Occasionally my intuition warns me about some people, that's all. I'm sure yours does, too. How else would you know who to trust when doing interviews or writing a story?'

'I try to rely on *facts*, especially when it might ruin someone's life.'

'We don't always have the luxury of having all the information so perfectly laid out and clear. As a matter of fact, we rarely have that luxury. A large proportion of the men I work with claim they're innocent. Perhaps, if they'd had a different jury looking at what the prosecution presented, they'd be free today. In other words, it almost always comes down to opinion, and in my *professional* opinion, letting Bishop go means more women will die.'

'So where do we draw the line?'

'That's the debate, isn't it? I wish I had the answer, but I don't. I can only tell you that if I'm going to err, it's on the side of protecting the victim, not the perpetrator.'

'Will you stand by what you've said? Can I quote you?'

He'd taken such an adversarial stance, Evelyn guessed she wouldn't be represented well in whatever he chose to print and wished she'd let his call go unreturned.

But she hadn't. She needed to give him an answer.

She thought of Jennifer Hall, sitting in that interview room with tears streaming down her face, and hoped she wasn't letting her empathy speak for her intuition. 'Yes.'

'*Who* came by?' Jasper turned on the single lightbulb dangling over his workbench in the garage, where he'd gone so that his wife wouldn't hear him. He didn't speak to his parents often. He was fairly certain that only by assuming they were always being monitored – if not by police, then by one of the private investigators

Evelyn had hired – had he managed to escape being caught. Whenever his parents wanted to get in touch, they'd text him from a borrowed or disposable phone the name of his favorite baseball team as a boy – Red Sox. He'd then call the number that text originated from, if he could get safely away from his family long enough to do it. His wife, Hillary, believed his parents died in a car accident when he was eighteen. He'd had to tell her that so she wouldn't expect to meet them or associate with them. She had no idea he'd ever been Jasper Moore, and it was imperative she never find out.

'A Sergeant Benjamin Murphy from Hilltop, Alaska,' his father replied. 'That place where Evelyn lives these days.'

Jasper felt his muscles bunch, but he kept his voice as calm and even as possible. 'I didn't even know she was in Alaska.'

There was a slight pause. Then his father said, 'But we've talked about it. And it's been all over the news.'

He'd gone a bit too far in his feigned indifference, so he attempted to prop up the lie with more convincing statements. 'To be honest, I try to shut it out, if I can. Why would I ever think of Evelyn? Her name alone reminds me of what I'd rather forget.'

'I wish what happened twenty-one years ago would go away, too,' his father said. 'It *was* dying down, until someone kidnapped her eighteen months ago. That's what has started it up again.'

'You know I wasn't anywhere near Boston when that happened.' Although he had, briefly, moved his family there, he'd known better than to tell his parents. They'd guess immediately that Evelyn was the draw. Why else would he go back to where he'd committed his original crimes? The Boston police were still looking for him. 'I think she made it up, like I told you before, to whip everyone into another frenzy. She won't move on. She's still out there, even after all these years, demanding an eye for an eye.'

'I understand why she'd crave justice,' his father said. 'I really do. But putting you away isn't going to change the past, and it certainly won't change her life as it is today. She's recovered and gained a lot of fame and opportunity from that terrible incident. It's given her a solid career. So what's the point?'

'There *is* no point,' Jasper replied. 'I mean . . . maybe if I was really a danger to others, as she claims. But I'm not.'

'She *has* to say you're a danger. Then tracking you down is about protecting the innocent, which is far nobler than sheer revenge.'

Hearing his father talk like that made Jasper a lot more comfortable. He hadn't lost his parents' support. 'What did Sergeant Murphy say?'

'I wasn't the one who talked to him. He left before I got home. But I'm looking at the business card he gave your mother right now.'

'He left her a card?'

'Yes.'

'As if he expects to hear from her?'

'I guess.'

'Is Mom with you? Can you put her on the phone?'

'She's inside the restaurant. We're in the middle of having dinner with some friends.'

Jasper began to pace in the dim, enclosed space. His van was parked outside at the curb, so his wife's Mustang was the only vehicle in the garage, but that still didn't leave a lot of room. 'What phone are you using?'

'My friend's. I told him mine was out of battery and I needed to step out to make a quick business call.'

'Mom didn't mention the sergeant's visit in front of your dinner companions—'

'Of course not. I could tell something was wrong with her on the way over, before we met up with them. So I kept asking, and she finally told me about Sergeant Murphy.'

Finally? 'Why would she hold back?'

'I guess she didn't want to upset me, didn't want to ruin the evening. I would've let you know instantly, but since I couldn't use one of our phones, I had to wait until it would seem natural to ask for someone else's. Fortunately, when I said mine had died Mom piped up that she hadn't brought hers and Jared, my partner on some oil deals, offered his.'

'So you're talking on Jared Somebody's phone?'

'Yes.'

'Thanks for being cautious, Dad.'

'No problem. We're in this, too, you know. If they catch us communicating with you, they'll charge us with obstruction of justice. They've told us that.'

'They won't catch you. They haven't yet, have they? We just can't get sloppy. That's why I asked.' Jasper couldn't afford to let any problems crop up now. He was just about to move in for the coup de grâce. The funny thing was, Evelyn had worked with so many psychopaths over the years that even his parents wouldn't know it was him when he finally killed her.

'I can't erase this call from his call history,' Stan was saying, 'so if Jared happens to reach out because he doesn't recognize this number and he's curious or something, say you're Chase Johnson and that you and I are involved in a housing development project together.'

'Will do. Anyway, I don't have much time, either. So why don't you tell me what Mom had to say about Sergeant Murphy.'

'She just said he tried to upset her. To spook her by telling her that you're out there, killing more women.'

Jasper had bumped into Sergeant Murphy – or Amarok, as the locals called him – when he visited Hilltop back before Hanover House ever opened. He hadn't liked the trooper from the beginning, but he'd liked him even less once he'd realized that Amarok and Evelyn were together. What the hell did the trooper think he was doing, traveling all the way to San Diego to bother Stanley and Maureen? 'That's crazy,' he said. 'No way could I be hurting anyone. Hillary would know if I was going out at night. She wouldn't put up with that for a minute. And I work during the day.'

'That's what I told your mother, but he had some pictures with him,' he said.

Jasper felt a muscle begin to twitch in his eye. This wasn't what he wanted to hear after his first day back at work. Having to return to that damn prison was hard enough after being off for six days – and making the most of those days. 'What kind of pictures?'

'Photographs of several women who've been murdered.'

Curling his free hand into a fist, Jasper pivoted to head back across the cement floor. 'Where did he get those?'

'I guess he got them from the police or something. Your mom said the victims looked like Evelyn – same color hair and body type. And Sergeant Murphy claimed the bodies were found just outside of Phoenix.'

Although his father didn't add *not far from where you used to live,* Jasper knew that was the reason behind this call. Amarok had managed to shake their faith. Now they were looking for reassurance, and Jasper didn't have a lot of time in which to soothe their fears. Hillary could come looking for him any second. He'd promised to help the girls with homework while she took a bath. She said he owed it to her after being gone all week.

'That has nothing to do with me, Dad,' he said. 'I have a family now, a family I adore. I would never do anything to threaten their peace and happiness.'

Jasper guessed his father would respond to that argument because he would never allow anything to threaten his own family. Stan felt what most men felt – and what Jasper couldn't.

'I know,' his father responded. 'It's a beautiful family, too.'

Jasper had provided them with pictures. His folks were so excited about being grandparents, even though they couldn't see Miranda and Chelsea in person due to the risk and the fact that Hillary didn't even know they existed. The photographs Jasper showed them on the rare occasions they met also made Hillary, Miranda and Chelsea seem real, helped his parents to believe he was the normal husband and father he purported to be.

'Because of the second chance *you* gave me, I've made good,' Jasper insisted. 'I could never tell you how grateful I am for how you've stood by me all these years, Dad. I don't take that lightly, would never make a mockery of your love by hurting someone else. I don't have any desire to act out because I don't do drugs anymore – not even experimentally, like I did back when . . . when everything went so wrong.'

'That's what I told your mother.'

'It's true. Thank God I can't remember what happened. I was so high . . . it's all a blur to me.'

Fortunately, he didn't bring up the fact that he couldn't have been high the entire time – for days in a row – or someone would've noticed. His parents seemed content to overlook what they could. 'That was a tragedy for everyone – including us,' his father said. 'People don't think we've suffered, but we've lost regular association with you, our only son. We can't even get to know our daughter-in-law or our grandchildren.'

'I feel terrible about that. But it could've ended much worse, if not for you.'

'We believe in you, Son. We always have.'

Stan sounded convinced and satisfied. Jasper had managed to pacify him. But that didn't mean Evelyn's cop lover would leave them alone. 'You don't think Amarok will come back, do you? Mom told him to stay the hell away, didn't she?'

'Amarok? Who's Amarok?' his father asked.

Jasper's breath lodged in his throat as if it had suddenly congealed there. He'd been so stressed about Hillary coming out to find him in the garage and jumping to the conclusion that he was calling another woman – or whatever else her jealousy inspired – that he hadn't been monitoring his words carefully enough, and now he'd screwed up.

Shit! What was he going to say? He hoped the sergeant's nickname had been given in the press or on the Internet somewhere – possibly attached to a quote regarding Hanover House coming to town. If it wasn't and his father decided to check, it'd look awfully strange that Jasper had somehow known Sergeant Murphy's nickname.

His saving grace was that his father wasn't likely to check, he told himself. Even if he did, Jasper would cover for it somehow. He'd gotten away with lying to his parents for most of his life, hadn't he?

'Isn't that what you said his name was?' he asked, hoping to make up for the slip.

'I said it was *Benjamin Murphy,*' his father clarified.

'Sorry. We don't have that great of a connection. I must've misheard you. Or I picked that up in some news report or something.' He could hear his wife calling his name from the back door of the house, checking to see if he was in the yard. She was coming; he had to go. 'Listen, thanks for letting me know what's going on. But I have to get off the phone. I promised Hillary I'd help the kids with homework tonight.'

There was a pause that seemed to be filled with renewed uncertainty.

'Dad?'

'Right. No problem. Of course. And don't worry. Everything's fine here.'

Jasper let his breath seep out in relief. 'Thanks. Tell Mom not to talk to anyone connected to Evelyn or the police. Why put herself through the grief?'

'I've told her that a million times.'

'So why'd she let this guy in?'

'She said he was . . . different, more convincing somehow.'

'He's after the same thing all the other cops are. Stay away from him.'

'I doubt he'll be back. He lives in Alaska, so it's quite a trip.'

The distance didn't matter. Amarok seemed determined. He'd made a bold move, flying all the way to San Diego to approach Stanley and Maureen.

One that required nerve.

And one for which Jasper was determined to make him pay dearly.

Eleven

When Amarok's call came in, Evelyn was in the conference room analyzing the brain scans with Dr Ricardo. Her colleague walked out to get a cup of coffee so she could have a few minutes to talk. She turned away from the laptops they'd set up and stood and stretched her back as she did so. 'How'd it go?' she asked Amarok.

'Better than I expected,' he replied.

She walked over to the large expanse of windows and gazed out at the tall chain-link fence, topped with razor wire, illuminated by the perimeter lights. 'That's encouraging.'

'I believe Maureen feels bad about what her son has done and wonders if she should've acted differently. It's Stanley who's standing in the way.'

'*He's* the one protecting Jasper?'

'Well, they both are. She's sticking with her husband, for the time being. But the good news is that she seems to be struggling with her conscience.'

Could that be the case? Would the Moores ever be willing to face the truth about their son? *'Really?'*

'That's how it felt to me.'

Evelyn was almost afraid to get her hopes up. She'd waited so long for any kind of justice. 'What'd she say to give you that impression?'

'She said Stan wouldn't like that she was talking to me. Yet she *did* talk to me. And I learned that they do have contact with Jasper.'

'She *told* you that?'

'In so many words. She said he couldn't be out murdering people because he's now "happily married".'

'Oh God. As if the two are mutually exclusive. I guess she's never heard of Linda Yates, Darcie Brudos or Judith Mawson'.

'I'm sure she hasn't. *I* don't know who they are.'

'Well, I'm sure you'd recognize who their husbands once were. And so would Maureen Moore.' Evelyn pitied the poor unsuspecting soul who was now living with the man who'd not only slit Evelyn's throat but also started the fire meant to consume her body. After all these years, she could smell the smoke as if it were sweeping through the room where she stood at this moment. 'I'm sorry for whoever he's drawn into his web.'

'I'm more worried about the kids.'

'*He has kids?* That's even worse news.'

'According to his mother, he's a real family man these days.'

'Makes me sick.'

'Do you think they're in danger – or are they too important as a cover?'

'Using them as a way to hide might be enough to keep them safe. But . . . I can't even begin to guess. With someone like Jasper, anyone he associates with – or bumps into – could be in danger. He's a cold-blooded killer. Someone who enjoys inflicting pain on others. Someone who actively looks for opportunities to indulge his sick fetishes. So it all depends on what strikes his fancy in any given moment, and what he thinks he can get away with.'

'If I get the chance to talk to her again, I'll let his mother know the children he's raising could be in trouble. Maybe then she'll open her mouth.'

'Jasper's wife and kids are probably dying of emotional starvation, even if he isn't hurting them physically,' Evelyn mused.

'I'm surprised such a cold, selfish guy can keep a wife.'

'If I know him, he's making sure she thinks the failings in their marriage are her fault. He blamed me the entire time he was torturing me. If I hadn't been so nosey. If I hadn't shown up when I did. If I hadn't shoved my way in and spotted Marissa, Jessie and Agatha dead. On and on. *You asked for this, Evelyn.*'

'His days are numbered, babe,' Amarok said, pulling her back from the precipice of those memories. 'We're getting closer. His mother also gave away the fact that he's living in Arizona, and I got the impression that it's not far from where those five bodies were found.'

'Just like you suspected.'

'Just like I suspected. I might've gotten more out of her, but Stan came home. That spooked her so much she rushed me out the back door so he wouldn't see me.'

'Wow. She really *is* concerned about how he might react.'

'No doubt Jasper has caused a fair amount of turmoil in their marriage.'

'I'm glad you went down there, Amarok. For the first time, we have somewhere to start looking.'

'When I called the detectives in Peoria to tell them there may be a connection, they mentioned that there was an attempted abduction in Casa Grande two days ago.'

'Casa Grande?'

'It's south of Phoenix, not quite part of the metropolitan area but close. Some woman escaped a man who threw her in his van – a man who was wearing a mask.'

That sounded familiar, but a lot of rapists and murderers wore masks. 'How'd she get away?'

'The details are still murky, but I've been told she jumped out while her abductor was merging onto the freeway. And she has the same hair and eye color you do, like the others.'

'How far is Casa Grande from Peoria?'

'About an hour and twenty minutes.'

'That's not very close. It may not be related.'

'It's within the realm of possibility. You know how people move around metropolitan areas. Anyway, the detectives are willing to have her look at the age-enhanced photo of Jasper, so I figure it's worth a shot.'

'How will that help? Didn't you say her abductor was wearing a mask?'

'Maybe she won't be able to identify him as the man who threw her into the van, but she should be able to tell us if she's ever seen him before. If he's been following her, or he works at the same place she does or lives nearby, that'd be a notable coincidence.'

'True.'

'Maybe Jasper has moved. Or he works in Casa Grande. To get to Casa Grande, you just take Ten South.'

'So you e-mailed the detectives that photo?'

'No. I told them I'd bring it with me.'

'Now you're going to Phoenix?' she asked in surprise.

'It's not too far out of the way.'

'I already have to sleep by myself tonight.' She was partially teasing and knew he'd get that, but she did want him home.

'I'll be back before you know it.'

She could hear the smile in his voice. 'Have you had a chance to call and check on your dad?'

'I have. He's fine.'

'Good.' She ducked her head and lowered her voice because Dr Ricardo had come back into the room. 'I love you,' she murmured.

'Then marry me,' he said, but he didn't wait for her to respond. He disconnected.

Dr Ricardo indicated the computers. 'You ready to get back to work?'

She returned the cordless phone to its base and sat down, but Russell Jones poked his head into the room, interrupting before they could make any progress.

'There you are,' he said when he saw her.

She studied him. 'You've been looking for me?'

'When I was coming back from my last interview, Dr Wilheim said you were downstairs, so I thought you were still busy with the brain scans.'

'We're taking a look at some of the results.'

'And?'

'We can't draw any conclusions yet. We haven't even created our baseline.'

'Everything takes time.'

'Exactly.'

He didn't leave, but neither did he indicate why he'd been searching for her. He shoved his hands in his pockets and stood there, leaning against the doorjamb.

'Did you want to speak to me?' she asked.

His gaze shifted to Dr Ricardo and back to her before he responded, which meant he was hoping to have a word in private. 'If you have a minute.'

Rather than make Dr Ricardo feel he had to leave the room again, Evelyn got up. 'Sure. Let's go to my office.'

Russ had gained at least fifty pounds since she and Fitzpatrick first hired him. He wheezed as he followed in her wake, as if crossing the reception area had become almost too arduous for him.

She stood back in order to give him sufficient room as she showed him in. Then she closed the door. 'How've you been, Russ?'

'I'm holding my own.'

'I mean on a personal level. I know it was hard on you when . . . when Sally decided she wasn't coming to Hilltop.'

'Yeah, well, I've since figured out why. She's met someone else. We don't really talk anymore.'

'I'm sorry.'

'It's okay. I've met a couple of other women online. One gal is a social worker in Canada. Canada's cold, too, so she seems like a good possibility.'

'I hope that works out for you.'

'So do I.' He wiped the sweat on his upper lip; it seemed like he was always sweating, even in the winter. 'It's getting damn lonely up here.'

Part of the reason she'd expected him to head back to the Lower 48. She still wasn't sure what was keeping him at Hanover

House – unless it was uncertainty that he'd be able to find a job with the same pay and benefits. Because he was so sloppy in his personal hygiene and attire, he didn't interview well. She wouldn't have hired him herself if Fitzpatrick hadn't insisted he come along. 'Especially during the dark months,' she agreed.

'How would *you* know?' he teased. 'This is the second winter you've been with your handsome state trooper.'

'I admit it's nice to have someone to go home to.'

'Yeah. I'd like that,' he said wistfully.

Reluctant to get too caught up in his maudlin approach to life, Evelyn brightened her smile. 'You'll meet the right one eventually.' *If* he didn't run her off with his general pessimism. He was a nice guy in other ways. And he was only twenty-nine. It wasn't as if he'd been searching his whole life. Evelyn didn't feel there was any reason to panic. 'So . . . what did you want to talk about?'

'Tim called. He's been trying to reach you.'

'I'm aware of that.' She'd been ignoring Fitzpatrick's calls and e-mails, hoping he'd eventually give up and go away. 'I'm not interested in having another conversation with him.'

'But what he has to say could be important.'

'In what way?' she asked. 'He doesn't even work here anymore.'

'He has a feeling that whoever killed Mandy Walker is going to strike again – and that the victim will be another one of your high school girlfriends.'

The heater hummed in the background and yet she felt as if a cold breeze had just swept through her office. 'How would he have any idea what's about to happen?'

'He didn't care to go into it with me. Said I needed to get you to call him. That's all.'

'Does he know something that hasn't been reported in the media?'

Russell lifted his sloped shoulders. 'I have no idea, but he feels strongly that certain potential victims should be warned.'

'The press is taking care of letting everyone know that there's a killer on the loose, Russ.'

'People spread out after high school, Evelyn. Some leave the area. I agree with Tim. Anyone who associated with you back in the day should be contacted.'

She hadn't wanted to face that Mandy's killer might go to the trouble of looking up other friends. 'I doubt those who have left the area are in any danger.' Unless it *was* Jasper. She could see *him* going to the extra trouble of tracking down mutual acquaintances and traveling to wherever they lived. For him, that would only add more intrigue to the game. She could recall interviewing at least one serial killer who'd made it his practice to travel to a different state to find each new victim. Such a completely random method had made him extremely difficult to catch, and he couldn't be the only one smart enough to think of that.

So was Jasper doing the same thing? Amarok said he had a wife and children. How easily could he get away from them?

She hoped his family hindered his mobility, at least to some degree – not that Linda Yates, Darcie Brudos or Judith Mawson had proven to be much of an impediment to their serial killer husbands.

'Fitzpatrick just wants to talk to you. Will you call him? Please?'

Evelyn was tempted to smash something against the wall. She didn't want Fitzpatrick in her life – for any reason. 'No.'

'That's ridiculous. Maybe he can help save a life.'

'He shouldn't even be involved in this! What could he know that the police don't?'

'He's in Boston, Evelyn. He's been studying what happened to Mandy. Maybe he's noticed some small detail about the killer that the cops haven't.'

'Then he should make what he's found plain to the detectives, not me. Now, if you've said what you needed to say, I have work to do.'

His heavy jowls swung as he shook his head. 'I told him you'd refuse.'

'Good.' If she didn't relent, maybe Fitzpatrick would start to believe she really meant to keep him out of her business.

Squeezing past her portly colleague, she headed back to the conference room.

That night it was cold and musty in Amarok's garage, which was so small he could really only use it for storage. Evelyn was wearing a heavy coat and a hat but no gloves. She needed to be able to feel as she searched for her 'Jasper' collection. When she'd sold her condo in Boston and moved to Alaska, she'd stored most of her memorabilia in her parents' attic – all the pictures and keepsakes from when she was a little girl. But she'd brought everything that could be related to Jasper and his attack, including the police files, the media clippings, the reports she'd received from the various private detectives she'd worked with over the years, even the love notes Jasper had written way back when. Her high school yearbooks were with that stuff. She was hoping to find them.

Although she'd left Sigmund in the house, she'd brought Makita out. With the wind whistling through the eaves, the trees scraping against the house and Amarok over a thousand miles away, she couldn't help feeling isolated and alone in the vast wilderness that made up most of Alaska. But she had plenty of other things to think about.

Makita sniffed around the garage as she clamped a flashlight under one arm and climbed a ladder to reach the trapdoor that led to where Amarok had put her boxes when she sold the house she'd been living in before moving in with him.

Her stuff appeared to have been shoved to the back already. As she rearranged everything so that she could reach it, she discovered a box of Amarok's that contained some pictures of him with his ex-girlfriend. She'd heard that Samantha Boyce was returning to Hilltop. She didn't know when, but she wasn't looking forward to it. Apparently, Samantha was as good a hunter as any man and planned to open her own guns and ammo shop. Amarok rarely spoke of her. He claimed he'd never truly been in love before Evelyn. But if Samantha hadn't meant that much to him, why did he still have their pictures?

Evelyn held the flashlight closer. Not only was Samantha attractive; she also had more in common with Amarok. His life would be so much simpler if he got back together with her or someone else who'd been raised here. Someone who had a love of the area and would never want to leave. Someone who wasn't putting herself at risk by associating with psychopaths on a daily basis.

Amarok hated that Evelyn was so immersed in 'that dark shit', as he put it.

Sam was also closer to his own age . . .

As she continued to dig around, something scurried toward her, causing Evelyn to scream and jerk back so fast she nearly fell from the ladder. Makita barked and darted over, as if he might be called on to defend her, but she was laughing by the time he pranced at the base of the ladder in eager anticipation. She'd just startled a mouse or a rat, probably harmless, but she didn't care to come in contact with it.

Heart pounding, she shoved the box with those pictures of Amarok and Sam out of the way and began rifling through her own stuff. She had no business getting distracted like that. If Fitzpatrick was right, time could be of the essence.

As soon as she located the right box, she found the yearbook from her junior year and carried it into the house. She planned to go through it page by page and make a list of the people she felt Jasper might target, if he was the one who'd killed Mandy. Once she had some idea who might be in danger, she could warn those on Facebook via a personal message tonight and figure out how to contact the others tomorrow.

The phone rang before she could get too far.

'You home safe?'

It was Amarok. Since it was getting late, she'd expected as much. He sounded tired, yet he'd made the effort to check in with her one last time before going to sleep.

He'd always been protective, thoughtful . . .

'Yeah.'

'What are you doing?'

'Looking through my old yearbook.'

'Why? I thought you preferred to forget high school – at least when you're not at work.'

'I do. But with Mandy Walker murdered, I thought I'd try to figure out if someone else might be targeted – and, if so, who.'

'How will you do that?'

'By looking through the pictures, trying to anticipate who Jasper might assume I care about most. Who might be an easy target. Who he didn't like. Basically, I'm hoping something jumps out at me.'

'How's it going?'

'It's not going yet. I barely started.'

'You managed to get your yearbook out of the garage by yourself? Didn't I put that box up above the ceiling?'

'You did, but I can use a ladder. I may not be able to hunt like Samantha Boyce, but I can retrieve my own storage.'

He went silent. Then he said, 'Samantha Boyce? What made you mention her?'

Resting her head on the back of the couch, Evelyn stared up at the ceiling. 'Maybe it's the pictures I found.'

'What pictures?'

'The ones in a box next to my stuff.'

'I don't remember putting them there, so they can't be too significant.'

'If they aren't significant, why are you keeping them?'

'I guess I don't see any reason to throw them away. She was an important part of my life for two years. It's not like I hate her. If anyone has hard feelings, it would be her. I'm the one who broke off the relationship.'

Sigmund, who'd curled up on the couch next to Evelyn, purred as she stroked his thick, soft fur. 'Why'd you do that?' she asked.

'Why'd I do what?'

'Why'd you break up with her?'

'I've told you. She wanted to get married. I wasn't ready.'

'You're ready now.'

'Evelyn, I'm older. And I want to marry *you*, not her. What's going on? Are you jealous or . . .'

'I'm not jealous,' she said, but she realized instantly that was a lie and she was pretty certain he could guess the truth. 'I mean, okay, I'm jealous. When we were at the diner not long ago, Sandy Ledstetter told you that Sam's coming back to town, remember?'

'I remember.'

'You didn't act like it was any big deal.'

'Because it *isn't* a big deal.'

'Even though you'd probably be better off with . . . with someone like her?'

He sighed through the phone.

'I'm just keeping it real,' she said.

'I appreciate that. But if I wanted someone like her, I'd be with someone like her. You know that. So where is this coming from?'

When she didn't answer, he said, 'Oh wait. I get it. I've started pushing for more of a commitment and that's spooked you.'

She couldn't argue; it was true.

'Listen, you can relax. There's no pressure.'

But there *was* pressure. She understood why he'd want to make their relationship more permanent. It felt natural, like the next step. She just wasn't sure she could make him happy at that level – that they could make each other happy. They came from two completely different worlds, which would never be more apparent than once they started having children. And Evelyn couldn't help thinking about what'd happened with his mother. Would she be just as unhappy here in Alaska? Would they eventually split? 'Samantha's more like you. More like what you might need.'

'Quit dangling Samantha in front of me!' he said. 'Why are we even talking about her? I love *you*. I'm the one who wants to get married, remember?'

'I want to marry you, too. I'm just afraid to do it.'

'You need to stop being afraid. Everything's fine.'

She rubbed her forehead. 'Okay.'

'How's Makita?'

Whenever she got too uptight, he directed the conversation to something mundane, as if to remind her that she was freaking out for no reason, that nothing had changed. 'I think he's wondering where you are. And he's avoiding the heat of the fire, as usual.'

'And Sigmund?'

She turned through her yearbook as they spoke. 'He's here on the couch with me.'

'Good. Okay, as long as all is well on the home front, I'll let you go. I'm exhausted. And it's two hours later here, so it's going to be hard to catch up on my sleep.'

She wasn't ready to say good-bye, though. She was imagining the feel of his muscular chest, bare, against her skin, the sight of the Inuit word for 'life', which was tattooed on his biceps and in full view whenever he held himself above her, and the heavy-lidded expression that claimed his face in the second before he reached climax.

'Evelyn?'

She drew a deep, calming breath. 'I'm here.' She wanted to tell him what was going through her mind, how the thought of his mouth on her breast as his hands moved over her body made her crave him inside her. She'd made a lot of progress since she met Amarok, but she still struggled with sexual intimacy. That was another reason she felt as if someone else, someone without the hang-ups she had – like Samantha – might make him happier. She was hoping to have phone sex with the man she loved, and yet she didn't know how to initiate it.

'What's going through that head of yours?' He sounded slightly confused and a little curious.

Embarrassed by the carnal images she'd conjured, she squeezed her eyes closed. 'Nothing. I'll talk to you in the morning.'

'Are you sure?'

'Yeah. There's nothing to worry about.'

'Okay. Good night.'

When he hung up, she sagged against the couch. She should've *told* him what she wanted, should've acted on the desire he inspired.

She had no doubt he'd like it. But she couldn't. Where would she start? How would she bring it up?

'I can't wait to fuck you again,' she whispered.

Hearing her use that kind of language would've shocked him. She was rarely aggressive in the bedroom. Even when she did initiate sex, she didn't approach him nearly so boldly. But at least she had the desire to take charge, for once. That proved she was finally overcoming what Jasper had done, despite the setback of that close call eighteen months ago, didn't it?

Yes! Amarok would be proud of her. He was always careful not to be too forceful when he touched her, not to arouse bad memories. She'd once asked him if holding back bothered him and he'd said it didn't, but she had a hard time believing that. Before they made love for the first time, he'd essentially told her he didn't want to feel like he couldn't let go and be himself, didn't want to feel as if he had to treat her like a china doll that might shatter at any moment.

'I can't wait until you fuck me again,' she said, testing the words on her tongue for a second time. They certainly weren't subtle.

'That's progress,' she muttered. 'Maybe someday I'll tell *him*.'

Sigmund had crawled into her lap. She slid him to one side and fanned herself, trying to overcome the deluge of hormones her brain had just dumped into her bloodstream. Then she reopened her yearbook.

The pictures brought the past back so vividly. Any sexual awareness or desire that remained was crushed beneath the heavy boot of those memories. Jasper . . . There he was swinging a baseball bat during a game. There he was in the team photo. And there he was with his arm slung around her at his locker. He'd been so popular that the yearbook team had taken a lot of photographs. They would've been removed once he killed three fellow students and almost killed her, but the yearbook had already gone to press.

She'd been so innocent when she loved him. She wondered what he was like now – and yet she felt like she knew, like he'd been with her ever since, casting a shadow over everything she did.

They had to catch him . . .

'Who else might you attack?' she asked while turning the pages. She flinched when she saw Marissa seated with Agatha out on the quad where they ate lunch. Her friends had been beautiful girls, and so fun.

Jessie had been the number one seed on their female tennis team. On another page, she smiled for the camera while wielding her racquet.

'Jasper, you are such a bastard.' Although it grew increasingly more difficult, Evelyn continued to study each page, to reacquaint herself with the people she'd known back then. But when the trip down memory lane didn't seem to serve any greater purpose, she began to wonder why she was putting herself through the agony.

She was about to give up and set that book aside when she ran across a picture that made her blood run cold. It'd been so long since it was taken she'd completely forgotten about it, but there she was, sitting around a big sign she was helping to paint for the Homecoming pep rally with Agatha, Marissa, Jessie, Mandy – and Charlotte Zimmerman.

This was what Fitzpatrick had found. He must've requested a copy of the yearbook from the school or something, because Evelyn knew the second she stumbled across that particular page it had to be what he'd been calling about.

Every girl in the picture had been murdered – or, in her case, almost murdered – except Charlotte.

Was she next?

Twelve

Jasper startled when his wife came up behind him. 'There you are!' she whispered. 'What are you doing in here?'

'Just watching her sleep.' He'd been imagining what it would be like to put a pillow over Miranda's face, was trying to figure out some way he could fulfill that desire without screwing up his plans for Evelyn. The fantasy gave him an outlet, something fun to think about when the pressure he felt living with Hillary and her girls grew to be too much for him. 'She's such a sweet thing.'

Hillary slipped her hand in his. 'Sometimes I get the impression that she drives you crazy. It's comforting to know you care about her.'

He'd learned that staying as close to the truth as possible worked better than too bold of a lie. 'She does drive me crazy sometimes. But kids are kids. Of course I care. I'm her father.'

His wife rested her head on his shoulder as she gazed lovingly at her sleeping daughter. He could tell she was assuming he felt the same emotions she did. It was a proud-parent moment, even though he didn't feel a thing, except a mild repugnance for the very gullibility that enabled him to function as he did.

'She's got a big, warm heart, doesn't she?' Hillary said. 'And she's such a good sister to Chelsea.'

Miranda was trusting, too. He had that going for him. If he could only figure out the right kind of accident – one that had no connection to him – he'd be golden. But he wasn't sure if or when he'd be able to come up with a viable plan. He had other, more important things to deal with and figured that was just as well. If he harmed Miranda, he'd be breaking his own rule, the one most tantamount to his success.

'Do you have to work in the morning?' Hillary asked.

'No.'

'They gave you *more* time off?'

He could hear the surprise in her voice. 'I requested it.'

She pulled back to look in his face. 'Why?'

He shook his head. 'I can't return to the prison. Not yet. I need more time.'

'To . . .'

'To recover!' he snapped in full voice. 'What do you think?'

When Miranda stirred, Hillary lifted her hand to get him to be quiet and pulled him from the room. 'I'm not saying what you went through was easy, honey,' she said in a placating way. 'I'm just . . . wondering what's going on. We haven't discussed any of this.'

'I'm sorry I couldn't give you any advance notice. I thought I'd be okay, but . . . that stabbing. It's still screwing with my head. I need to go away again, take some more time.'

The concern on her face made her look old in the dim light filtering into the hall from the kitchen. 'Wouldn't it be smarter to see someone who could help you through it?'

'You mean a shrink? Hell no! I've explained how I feel about all that psychology mumbo jumbo.'

She spread out her hands. 'So what do you plan to do instead?'

'What I always do when I need to come to terms with something. I'm taking off for a few days.'

'To think.'

'Yes!'

'But you just got back! You've only worked one shift.'

'I told you, I wasn't off long enough.'

She rubbed her forehead. 'Where will you go this time?'

'The Grand Canyon.'

'It's winter.'

'It's not that cold there. And even if it is, I've got a coat.' He'd billed himself as someone who loved nature, who used it to 'find' himself, so he thought she'd buy the destination. In reality, he wasn't going anywhere close to the Grand Canyon.

'What if I hired someone to watch the girls, took a few days off and went with you?' Hillary asked.

'There's no time for that.'

'Why not? I could make the arrangements first thing in the morning.'

'Because I'm leaving *now*.' He pivoted and headed to their bedroom so he could pack his duffel bag.

Hillary came after him. 'But wouldn't it be more fun to have a companion? Someone to travel with? I could help with the long drive, give you someone to talk to.'

Except that he was only driving to the airport. 'No. I'd rather not leave the girls with someone else. Who could say how they'd be treated? I've told you what my babysitter did to me.'

'That was terrible – unthinkable.'

It was also untrue, but the lie served his purpose. Whenever she asked to come with him, that 'incident' gave him an excuse to fall back on, one that made her believe he loved the girls as much as she did and didn't want to see them come to any harm.

'I'll be careful, get someone trustworthy,' she added.

'You never know who you can trust. My parents thought the bastard who raped me was "a nice young man", didn't they? But look what he did, and how badly it screwed me up.' The same lie excused so much – why he often grew aloof, angry, distant, or was unable to sustain an erection during regular sex. Even why he liked the violent type of pornography she'd discovered on his computer. That 'rape' when he was only seven covered it all – and made her empathetic at the same time. 'I'll feel better if you're taking care of Miranda and Chelsea and the house. That's what I need right now,

Hillary. To feel confident that you and the girls are fine while I pull myself together.'

She fell silent as she watched him pack. When he finished and closed the zipper, she said, 'Do you have any idea how long you'll be gone this time?'

'A few days.'

'I really wish you'd try seeing a psychologist instead.'

He lifted a hand. 'Don't start. Don't make this any harder on me than it is already.'

She fell silent. When he glanced up, he found her staring dejectedly at the floor, but he didn't have it in him to mollify her. The revulsion he felt when he touched her was growing worse by the day.

'I'm sorry. I agree that this isn't fair to you,' he said. 'But I'll make it up to you when I get back, okay?'

She didn't answer, and he didn't bother trying to convince her. He couldn't even bring himself to kiss her good-bye. 'See you soon,' he said as he threw his duffel bag over his shoulder and brushed past. His flight didn't leave until morning, but he had somewhere he had to go before he left – or Christina would be dead in that RV when he returned. As weak as he'd left her, she couldn't last much longer. If he waited until after he got home, he'd have to deal with the stench of her decomposing body. It was hard enough to keep that RV smelling decent, what with all the body fluids he dealt with.

Besides, he didn't see any reason to miss the grand finale.

Don't worry, Christina. It's all going to be over with soon . . .

According to what Evelyn found on Facebook, Charlotte Zimmerman worked as a paralegal for one of the bigger law firms in Boston. Although she now went by her married name of Pine, Evelyn had been able to confirm that she was the right Charlotte from her picture and because she was connected to so many other people who'd gone to their high school. Evelyn left a message before going to bed and checked first thing in the morning, as soon as she arrived at work. But she didn't receive a response until mid-morning.

Thanks for reaching out. How are you, Evelyn? It's been so long since we've talked. I'm sad that we didn't stay in touch, but I've seen you on the news and read various articles in the paper about what you're doing. You're an inspiration to victims everywhere. It's nuts to think I know someone who's been through what you went through – and that I know others who've been killed. But the craziest thing of all, at least to me, is that I know the person who's responsible for those crimes. I guess I can admit to you now that I had a crush on Jasper, for years. I was so jealous of you – that you were the one he wanted. I'm ashamed of it now. But he was so handsome, so smart and popular. It's hard to believe someone like that could be any different from what he appears to be on the outside. I wondered when Mandy died if there could be any connection. I've had a few people from high school contact me about it. Anyway, I appreciate the warning, even though it terrifies me. Should I contact the police or what do I do next?

Evelyn wasn't sure what advice to offer. She wanted to tell Charlotte to leave town and tell no one where she was going until the person who killed Mandy was caught, but what if that never happened? Charlotte had a family. She couldn't disrupt her life, and her husband's and children's lives, forever.

It's great to connect with you, too, she wrote back. *I've been so obsessed with my work finding out why people like Jasper do what they do I haven't stayed in touch with anyone, and that's a sad thing.* She'd actually withdrawn from those she'd known in high school to avoid the memories, and the sense of loss she felt that none of them could replace her best friends, but she didn't go into that. *As far as what you should do, I wish I had a great answer for you, a way that you could stay safe without leaving Boston. But I don't. Moving would be your safest bet, because I doubt the police can or will be able to help you. They have no idea whether you will really be targeted, or if Mandy's death was merely a terrible coincidence. This is all me. I just saw that picture of us making the Homecoming sign last night and felt a chill go through me. It's possible I'm being paranoid and there's no danger. Just keep an eye out. Don't go anywhere alone. Don't leave your kids alone. Put an alarm system on your house today, if possible. Carry pepper spray and know how to use it. Make sure your number is unlisted. Get rid of any and all personal information on your Facebook page and alert everyone you know not to tell anyone anything about you.*

The door opened as Russell Jones poked his head into her office. 'What are you doing?'

She looked up. 'I'm working. What are you doing?'

'I was just on the prison side, meeting with the warden about one of my patients who's been acting up. While I was there, Bishop's attorney called and told him he'll be released soon.'

She grimaced as she scratched her arm. 'I was fairly certain it would come to that.'

'I heard him asking the guards if he could speak with you.'

Why did he want to talk to her? So he could rub it in her face that he was going to walk free despite the fact that she believed he was guilty? 'What could that be about?'

'I have no idea. I asked, but he clammed up when I came onto the scene.'

'I have no incentive for getting him to participate in any of the studies while he's here, so at this point we'll just let him sit in his cell until the order arrives to release him.'

'The order will take a few days, at least. Maybe you could continue to evaluate him. Give him a rating on the PCL-R.'

'What good would that do?'

'It would be something you could put in his file, in case it comes out in the future that he is dangerous. You believe he killed those women, don't you? That's what I read in an article I found online this morning.'

Sebring Schultz's article was out? She wondered how he'd portrayed her – and planned to look it up as soon as she could get rid of Russ. 'How'd you find that?'

'I have a Google alert on our names, the name of the institution and several other key words, like "serial killer". It came up.'

She'd had that service once, too, but turned it off when things got ugly last winter and there was bad press popping up all over the place. 'I'd love to evaluate Bishop, but I don't see why he'd agree.'

'He's feeling pretty smug at the moment. Thinks he beat the

system. I bet if you play him right his arrogance will tempt him to try to prove that he can outsmart you and any test you give him. That could be valuable for our research, if nothing else.'

For once, Evelyn agreed with Russ. 'Okay. I'll send for him. See what I might be able to glean from his brief stay.'

'There you go.'

She smiled at him. 'Thanks, Russ.'

'You bet.' He went out but came right back in. 'Even though I know I shouldn't bring this up, I got another call from Fitzpatrick last night. He's certain that whoever killed Mandy Walker will strike again, and soon. Are you sure you won't call him?'

She sent the message she'd typed for Charlotte Zimmerman Pine. 'I'm sure. Tell him he doesn't have anything to worry about. It's all handled.'

Whether Vanessa Lopez, the woman lying in the hospital bed in Casa Grande, Arizona, looked like Evelyn was hard to tell. Her eyes were so swollen she could barely open them, and she was bruised and scraped all over. According to Mike Sims, the detective from Peoria who'd brought Amarok down to interview her, she had a broken collarbone, her leg was fractured in three places and she'd all but pulverized her wrist reaching out to brace her fall when she jumped from the vehicle of the man who tried to abduct her four days ago.

'I'm sorry to bother you.' Catching her eye, Amarok left Sims at the entrance of the room, speaking to her doctor, and walked over to the bedside. 'This can't be an easy time,' he said, and handed her his card. 'I'm Sergeant Murphy.'

She gave him what was obviously the best smile she could muster. 'Detective Sims told me you were coming, but I never dreamed you'd be so handsome. I doubt *I* could look any worse.'

He chuckled. 'You're a brave woman to have done what you did.'

'Not brave at all. I knew it would only get worse if I let him take me wherever he was taking me. He was so . . . angry and violent. Have you ever seen *I Survived*?'

'I've seen an episode here and there.'

'Then you understand what I'm talking about. I kept remembering what some of those women have been through and decided that wouldn't be me. If I was going to be hurt or killed, it was going to happen while I was trying to escape.'

Finished with the doctor, Detective Sims came to stand on the opposite side of the bed. 'Vanessa, I'm Detective Sims from Peoria, the one who spoke with you on the phone two days ago and again this morning.'

'You're investigating those murders outside of Phoenix.'

'Yes. How are you feeling?'

'Better now. All the broken bones have been set, and the doctors have disinfected my wounds. I'm hoping the worst is over.'

'Can you tell us what happened?' Amarok asked.

'You mean, from the beginning?' She looked to Sims.

'Please,' Sims confirmed. 'Pretend you haven't told me anything.'

'Okay, well, I work at a tattoo parlor.'

That surprised Amarok. She didn't have a single tattoo that he could see. 'You do?'

'My brother owns it. He's the one who's tatted up. I've never been interested in jabbing needles into my skin, but I can run a business, so we make a good team.'

'I see.'

'I might get a tattoo eventually,' she mused. 'After working with him for the past six months, I'm starting to appreciate his work.'

'Maybe he could tattoo the word "survivor" on your lower back or ankle or somewhere,' Sims suggested.

'He'd be happy to do that.'

'So the man who tried to abduct you, was he a customer?' Amarok asked.

'Not that I know of. I'm not sure where he came from.'

Amarok would've been disappointed, but she'd already told enough to Detective Sims that he was expecting that. 'Do you have any idea how or why he picked you?'

'None. I've never had any trouble – not until Saturday night.'

'What happened then?'

'Everyone at the shop had gone home. We close at midnight, so I turned the sign around like I usually do and started to clean up. I'd just finished vacuuming and went to take the trash to the bin behind the building. That's when he grabbed me. I didn't hear or see anything, didn't know I was in danger, until he came up from behind.'

Amarok was jotting the details on his notepad so he'd have them in writing. 'He had to be hiding back there, waiting for you.'

'I guess. Once he grabbed me, he dragged me around to the side of the building, where he had a vehicle.'

'But he was wearing a mask.'

'Yes. It was dark anyway. I'm not sure I could've gotten a good look at his face even if he hadn't been wearing a mask. It all happened too fast.'

'What else did he have on?'

'Nothing unusual. A sweatshirt and jeans, tennis shoes. But he's a white man. I can tell you that much. I could see the skin on his hands in the cabin light of the van when he stuffed me into the back and tied me to a ring on the floor. And he might be married.'

'He was wearing a wedding ring?'

'A plain band.'

Too bad the ring wasn't more distinctive. 'Any tattoos, moles or birthmarks on those hands?'

'No. But they were clean, if that tells you anything. There was no motor oil or dirt under his nails. His van was spotless, too. I pegged him as a clean freak.'

That wasn't good news, either. Sloppy perpetrators were so much easier to catch.

'He actually . . .' Her words fell off.

'He actually . . . what?' Amarok prompted.

'Well, this is going to sound weird, but it felt like he had a nice build. And he smelled good – clean with a hint of expensive cologne. No cigar or cigarette smoke. No body odor or bad breath.'

'How tall would you guess he was?'

'He wasn't short. I'd say he was about the height of my brother.'

'And how tall is that?' Sims asked.

'Six two. Somewhere in there.'

Sims spoke again. 'Any idea on weight?'

'He's thinner than my brother, so . . . one ninety-five? Two hundred? He was strong, I can tell you that. He threw me around like it was nothing.'

'What about his voice?' Amarok asked, jumping back in. 'Did he say much?'

'Not a lot. He cursed when he couldn't get the knot tied as quickly as he wanted. Hit me, too. I remember him laughing when I lifted my arms in an attempt to defend myself.'

'Can you tell me anything about the vehicle?'

'It was a dark-colored minivan. Clean on the inside, like I said. The seats had been removed in back. That's all I can tell you. I wasn't thinking straight. My mind was racing.'

Could this be Jasper? Amarok wondered. Or was he grasping at straws? 'Where's your brother's shop?'

'In a little strip mall here in Casa Grande. I can give you the address.'

Amarok wrote it down. He planned to drive by. He had the time. His plane didn't leave until early tomorrow morning. 'Did you get the impression this was something he'd done before?'

'If I had to guess, I'd say yes. He acted very confident. He said, *Wait until you see what I have in store for you.*'

'And what did you say?'

'Nothing. I'd loosened the ropes he'd used to tie me, so I yanked open the door and flung myself out.'

'He didn't stop? Come back for you?'

'There was another car coming. Fortunately, the driver pulled over when she saw me fall. I'm guessing he spotted her headlights and panicked, because he sped away.'

Sims had told Amarok that the driver of the car who'd helped Vanessa had gotten the license plate number of the van as well as the make and model. She'd said it was a Mazda van. But when they traced the information, they learned the plates had been stolen from another vehicle in a nearby apartment complex.

'I bet if he'd known it was an elderly lady, he would've stopped,' she said. 'At eighty-one years old and barely five feet tall, Mrs Paxton wouldn't have been hard for someone like him to overpower. I'm fortunate he didn't know.'

'You're lucky she was in the area,' Amarok said.

'She was coming home from the birth of her great-grandson, or she wouldn't have been. Maybe no one would've been there, and I wouldn't be sitting here with you today.'

Amarok pulled out the pictures he'd brought with him. 'Can you tell me if you've ever seen anyone who looks like this man? This was him twenty-one years ago, and this is what he might look like today.' He tapped the age-enhanced photo to get her to focus on it.

She bit her lip as she studied both pictures. 'Hard to say. He looks sort of like a guy who stops in at the 7-Eleven where I get gas. I'm pretty sure I've seen him there a time or two.'

'Which 7-Eleven is that?'

'It's in the same strip mall as the tattoo parlor.'

'That helps. Thank you for being willing to meet with me.'

She returned the photographs of Jasper. 'If I think of anything else, I'll let you know.'

'Please do.'

Sims thanked her, too, and they started for the door. But she called to them before they could reach the hall. 'After I heal, will it be safe for me to go back to work? I mean . . . you don't think he'll come after me again, do you?'

Amarok exchanged a glance with Sims, who dipped his head to indicate he'd let Amarok field this one. 'He could.' If it was Jasper, Amarok wouldn't put it past him. The fact that Vanessa had escaped, thereby denying him his fun and putting him at risk, could make him angry at her personally – meaning he could turn her escape into his justification for a vendetta similar to what he had going with Evelyn. 'If you return, I wouldn't close up alone anymore.'

'I won't.' She lifted his card to take a closer look. 'Wait a second.

You're from Alaska? Why did you come all the way from Alaska to ask me about an abduction attempt in Arizona?'

He didn't want to tell her he thought she might've been abducted by the same man who nearly murdered Evelyn Talbot, the famous psychiatrist. If Jasper was in this area and he read that in the paper, he might move somewhere else. 'We believe this guy has been preying on women for a while, in many different states.'

'Even Alaska?'

Fortunately, Detective Sims jumped in. 'Sergeant Murphy is especially good at these kinds of cases. He's just helping out.'

'So you think the guy who attacked me is the one who killed those women in Peoria?'

'I can't say for sure, but it's a possibility,' Sims said. 'I plan to stay in close touch with Casa Grande PD, just in case.'

'I see. Well, I hope you catch him,' she said.

Amarok gave her a parting smile. 'So do we.'

Thirteen

'I bet you're sorry now.'

The petulance in Lyman Bishop's voice made him sound childish, definitely at odds with his IQ. But sometimes the men Evelyn dealt with acted no more than ten or twelve. In most cases, their emotional development had been arrested by some childhood trauma, which trauma, of course, contributed to their criminality. Considering what Bishop had suffered, Evelyn could easily understand if he'd been psychosexually stunted. She felt bad about the pain he'd suffered and any damage that resulted, felt bad for anyone who'd been hurt as a child. But she didn't like him. She didn't trust him, either. Although many psychopaths could be charming, a craft they honed in order to draw in people they could then manipulate, he wasn't capable of that approach. He reminded her more of a recluse spider – the type of hunter that built an innocent-looking web, then sat back out of sight, waiting for prey to get caught in it. 'For?'

He regarded her from his stool on the other side of the interview room. 'For saying all those things you did. For assuming I'm guilty in spite of my many protestations. Surely by now you've heard that the panty evidence used to convict me was planted in my attic. *I* didn't put those panties there. Even if I was guilty, I wouldn't be stupid enough to do that,' he added under his breath.

'Where would *you* put them?' she asked.

'Nowhere that could be tied to me,' he replied. 'But, like I said, I'm innocent.'

She adjusted the scarf she'd draped around her shoulders to help keep her warm in the drafty prison. 'Detective Gustavson was wrong to resort to the measures he took. We can agree there.'

He studied her carefully. 'That hardly sounds as condemning of Gustavson as I would expect.'

'I feel sorry for him,' she explained.

'For *him*?'

'I spoke to him. This has ruined his career.'

'As well it should!'

'Not if you're guilty and he was being honest when he said he only did it to get you off the street. If that's true, I almost see it as . . . noble.'

'You can't listen to him, can't *admire* him. Of course he'd say that. He's got to cover for what he did somehow. But I'm innocent, like I've told you from the beginning, and before I go I'd like to hear you acknowledge that.'

She didn't have to acknowledge anything. He acted as if she'd slighted him personally, but she'd had nothing to do with stashing the panty evidence or locking him up.

She was, however, loath to let him go. Maybe he wasn't a psychopath, but she thought he was, and one of his caliber rarely fell into the net of the criminal justice system. 'Just because Gustavson acted wrongfully in order to get a conviction doesn't mean you're innocent, Dr Bishop.'

His mouth formed an affronted O. *'You still don't believe me?'*

'It doesn't matter what I believe. As you say, they're going to vacate your conviction. You're going home – for now.' From there, the district attorney would have to decide whether to retry him, this time without the panty evidence, but Evelyn highly doubted that would happen. That evidence was too integral to the case. They'd have to wait and hope they could find other forensic proof of his culpability.

'For now?' he repeated.

'Unless a witness steps forward. Or something else comes to light.'

'You'd like it if something else came to light.'

'I assure you, it isn't personal. I merely want to keep the community safe.' She stood as if that were all there was to it, and he came to his feet at the same time.

'So you're fighting my release?'

'There's not much I can do to "fight" it. I *am* telling anyone who will listen that I think you'll kill again.'

'How dare you!'

'It's my job. And I try to be as honest as possible.'

'*Honest?* You can't see past your own prejudice. What kind of a scientist are you? You don't deal with the facts. You let emotion, and the past, control you.'

'If you've let *your* past turn you into a serial killer, then you do, too.' She couldn't help pressing, hoping his temper would erupt and he'd reveal his true self again, like he had when meeting with Jennifer.

'I'm *not* a serial killer! You can't lump me in with all the other psychopaths in here, can't discount me as if . . . as if I'm no better than the dirt beneath your feet!'

'It hasn't been my intention to mistreat you. But I've seen nothing to convince me that you're innocent, and I won't say you're innocent until I'm sure.'

He approached the plexiglass, put his palms on it. 'I would've told you where to find Jan Hall's body, if I could,' he said, now almost boy-like.

'No, you wouldn't,' she insisted.

Without warning, the 'sweet supplicant' smacked the glass, causing an odd *wah-wah-wah* to reverberate around her. 'Oh my God!' he railed. 'What will it take to convince you? Give me the damn PCL-R! You'll see!'

'I can't.'

'Why not? It only takes three to four hours, and that's if you're being especially diligent – but I would expect nothing less of you.'

'You're obviously familiar with it.'

'So?'

'You know what traits I'd be looking for and how to avoid exhibiting those traits so that you score well below "severely psychopathic". That means an interview will do me no good. And I can't base my evaluations on your institutional records, since this is the first time you've ever been arrested.'

He dropped his hands. 'You could use other collateral information, but you know that, too, will indicate I'm as normal as anyone else.'

'Not necessarily. Only failed psychopaths wind up in prison.'

'Not only do you think I'm a psychopath; you think I'm a failed psychopath. What can I do to prove otherwise?'

She tossed her pen onto the table. 'Take a polygraph if you'd really like to convince me you had nothing to do with those murders.'

He waved her words away. 'I'm not stupid enough to do that.'

'Why not? Do you have something to hide?'

'My lawyer would never agree.'

'It's not up to your lawyer, Dr Bishop. It's up to you. And if you're innocent, you have nothing to fear.'

He began to pace in short, agitated strides. 'Who would administer it?'

'We have two professional polygraph examiners who drive over from Anchorage each day. You can take your pick between them.'

'I don't know that one is any better than the other. Why would *I* pick?'

'I'm offering you that as a courtesy, I guess – to show I'm not trying to railroad you.'

'A meaningless gesture, maybe even a ruse, given they both would probably do anything they could for you. If I decide to take the test, you can pick yourself.'

'Fine.'

He smoothed the few hairs he'd combed over his bald pate again and again as he thought it over. Then he said, 'They're helping with the study you told me about?'

'Yes.'

'Even if the results prove me truthful, you'll say I "beat" it. Isn't that what one of your studies is about?'

'All data so far indicates that psychopaths can't beat a polygraph any easier than anyone else, so there will be no reason for me to disbelieve the results.'

He said nothing, just continued to run his fingers over those meager strands of hair.

'What do you have to lose?' she added. 'This is only between you and me. Even if you fail, polygraphs aren't admissible in court.'

A stubborn, almost arrogant expression settled on his face as he stopped messing with his hair, quit pacing and lifted his chin. 'I'm not going to fail.'

Evelyn tried not to show her surprise. Russ had been right. Bishop had something to prove. 'Is that a yes?' *Do it. Take the bait . . .*

'Why not? I don't have anything to fear from you.'

He'd accepted her challenge. He couldn't resist it. He had to win, *had* to show her. But that propensity only added to the conviction she felt that he was, indeed, a killer. She'd seen that 'no one gets the better of me' trait in many of the psychopaths she'd studied.

Jasper possessed it, too. That was what made her so sure he was still out there, hoping for another chance.

'What are you doing?'

Evelyn turned to see Dr Ricardo standing in the doorway of Lab #4, where she was working with Lido Thomas, the polygraph examiner she'd chosen.

'We're preparing to give Lyman Bishop a lie detector test,' Evelyn told him. 'Since this is probably a one-shot deal, we have to be ready before he gets in here, have to decide what to ask and how to ask it.' She tapped the file she'd been using to brief Lido. 'Even the order of the questions is important – all part of matching wits with him.'

'So we won't be continuing to evaluate the brain scans this afternoon?'

She could tell he was put out. 'Not today. Didn't you get my message?'

'I got it. I was just surprised. I asked to include Bishop in the polygraph study when he first arrived, and you put me off.'

'Things have changed.'

'Yes, they have. And not for the better. You put me off, and now I've been looking forward to making some progress on the empathy study. I consider it some of the most promising research we have going, but almost every day something comes up.'

'I hate to let these other things interrupt. I agree that we're garnering some great information with the scans. But the polygraph study is still as important as it ever was.'

'Not when it comes to Bishop. We're no longer sure he *is* a psychopath, which would throw him out of it right there. From what I hear, he's about to be released, anyway.' He gestured at the blood pressure cuff that would soon be centered over Bishop's brachial artery, the rubber tubes, called pneumographs, that would be fastened around his chest and abdomen, and the electrodes, or galvanometers, that would be attached to two of his fingers. 'Whatever results you get with this won't stop that.'

When Lido hesitated in making sure the equipment was properly attached to her computer, which would register Bishop's blood pressure, breathing rate, pulse and perspiration so that the information could be evaluated using a mathematical algorithm-based program called PolyScore, Evelyn nodded to indicate she should proceed. 'That may be true. But it can help me determine where I stand on the issue.'

'Judging from the article Tim Fitzpatrick sent me this morning, you've already taken a stand. Which, I admit, seems a bit reckless. What you do and say reflects on Hanover House, Evelyn. You get this wrong and it could make you, and me and the rest of the team by association, seem like a bunch of quacks.'

'You shouldn't be communicating with Fitzpatrick,' she said. 'You're beginning to sound like him.'

'He has a point! We could lose the public support we currently have and our funding would likely go with it. Then Hanover House would become a regular prison, and we'd be sent home. Is that what you want?'

Evelyn touched the examiner's sleeve. 'Lido, would you mind giving us a few minutes?'

'Not at all.' She scurried from the room, obviously eager to avoid the awkwardness of this confrontation.

'Jim, I hope I don't have to remind you that Fitzpatrick would've been fired had he not resigned.'

He sniffed as he crossed his arms in a show of stubborn determination. 'I'm aware of that, yes.'

'Are you also aware of the reasons?'

'He admits he made some mistakes,' he said, gesturing with one hand, 'but he cares a great deal about our success and—'

'Did he tell you he kept a file on me that included the floor plans of my house?' she interrupted. 'That he collected so much information on me that he had contact info for my parents and sister – even a copy of my college transcripts?'

'No . . .'

'He used to follow me home at night and take pictures of me changing from outside my bedroom window, Jim.'

He looked suitably shocked.

'And, worst of all, he used Photoshop to put my face on naked female bodies engaged in various sexual activities – pornographic pictures – which he then showed to the inmates.'

His jaw dropped. 'That's the most unprofessional thing I've ever heard!'

'Well, you might consider his lack of professionalism the next time you receive a call or an e-mail from him. He talks a good talk – can be quite convincing. But his side is never a side you want to be on.'

'You're right,' he mumbled. 'I'm sorry I ever listened to him. But this has nothing to do with Fitzpatrick, Evelyn. What he did a year ago doesn't change what you're doing now. Did you *have* to take a stand on Bishop? Couldn't you have said that he hasn't been here long enough to make a determination and leave it at that?'

'You wish I would've remained neutral.'

'Seems to me that would have been the most prudent course, yes – considering what's at stake if you get it wrong.'

'I gave my honest opinion, Jim.' She hoped. Those second thoughts hadn't gone away. 'I can't always be so interested in saving my ass that I forget the reason I'm in this business to begin with.' She pointed at the computer and polygraph equipment. 'Maybe this will give us some indication of whether I'm right or wrong.'

He didn't seem convinced. 'Polygraphs can be beaten.'

'Yes. I'm not unrealistic enough to think this is some kind of magic bullet. Polygraphs are subjective. They depend a great deal on the examiner's experience and ability to detect what a "normal" response looks like for each individual subject.'

'Not to mention there is no standard of behavior for when someone is telling a lie!'

'Lido is good, though. I trust her. And I won't waste the opportunity to get inside Bishop's head. If this could tell me something I didn't know before, something that might help someone later on, I'm going to do it.'

'You mean when he kills again.'

'Possibly. Or new evidence comes to light. Police rely on polygraphs all the time, so they have *some* value, even if they can't be used in court.'

'Most people in the criminal justice field believe they're eighty to ninety-nine percent effective, but I've seen considerable research that refutes that. I'd guess seventy percent would be high.'

'Still, this gives us more information instead of less,' Evelyn said. 'And more information is always better.'

'I can't argue with that.' With a sigh, he walked over and flipped through the file she'd been using to brief Lido. 'Will you use the control question technique or the concealed-information technique?'

'Control question. I tried to call Detective Gustavson to get his opinion on the best strategy. But he's not picking up, and without his help we're better off avoiding the concealed-information technique.

We don't know enough about Bishop's crimes to be effective with that.'

'Makes sense. Have you developed your control questions, then?'

Bishop's physiological reactions to the control questions would be compared to those of the relevant questions, making them the most important part of the test. 'We've developed a few.'

'Like . . .'

Lido knocked as she came down the hall, drawing their attention to her approach. 'Sorry to interrupt, but I was afraid to be gone too long. The subject should be here any minute.'

Evelyn checked her watch. Lido was right. They were almost out of time. 'I'm glad you're so conscientious. Why don't we take the last few seconds to go over the control questions with Dr Ricardo?' She figured he might catch something she'd missed or have some advice to offer, but they didn't get the chance to collaborate. The guards were bringing Bishop to the lab. Evelyn could hear the clink of his ankle chains as he made his way toward them.

Fourteen

Jasper had the code to the gate of his parents' housing enclave. Usually he approached their place under cover of darkness, but today he didn't feel like waiting. He had to get back to Arizona and his work at the prison sooner rather than later – before he stretched the warden's patience too thin and got himself fired. That meant he couldn't dawdle on this trip, couldn't waste five or six hours twiddling his thumbs.

Coming in the daytime would be okay, he told himself. He didn't have anything to worry about. What were the odds that Evelyn was still paying for a private investigator to watch his parents' house?

Slim to none. It'd been too long. His parents hadn't noticed anyone for quite some time.

Even if she *was* paying someone, Jasper was betting he or she had grown lax. Eighteen months ago, Jasper's encounter with her had been brief. It'd been a full twenty-one years since he'd caused any real damage. That lessened the immediacy of the situation. And no one else in his parents' neighborhood would have reason to pay him any mind. Even if someone saw him and made note of it, he looked nothing like he used to. The surgery had seen to that. He just couldn't let anyone get the license plate number of his rental, because if the police ever had reason to they could trace it back to 'Andy Smith' and he had to keep that alias clean if he planned to work at Hanover House.

Leaving the car at a strip mall, where seeing a white Volkswagen sedan wouldn't seem unusual to anyone, he walked the three miles to his parents' housing development, slipped through the main gate and made his way to their cul-de-sac.

He went around the house, out of sight, to knock, but his mother took her sweet time answering, as if she couldn't imagine who'd be banging on her back door in broad daylight. When she finally came into the kitchen, peered out and saw him, she smiled, but he felt like that smile was lacking some of its usual excitement and warmth.

That concerned him; it also made him angrier with Amarok . . .

'Jasper! What are you doing here?' she asked when she'd unlocked and opened the door. 'Get inside before someone sees you.'

'No one will see me back here. Your yard is almost as big as a city park,' he said, but he stepped into the kitchen so she could close the door before pulling her in for a hug. The easiest way to reach her heart was to allow her to hold him for a few moments. He was still her 'baby', she'd tell him whenever they embraced. She felt all kinds of protective motherly emotions he didn't understand, but he was glad for them. Her attachment to him, although surprising after so many years, often worked in his favor.

'I've missed you so much,' he said.

Normally, she would've squeezed him tighter. Like Hillary, she loved hearing the mushy stuff. But today she didn't beam with happiness and pride.

Something had changed, all right.

'I've missed you, too,' she responded, but let go almost immediately.

'Aren't you glad to see me?'

'Of course! But . . . what are you doing here? Especially during the day?'

'Don't worry. I was careful. I had to pay you a visit. It's been too long. Where's Dad?'

'He's at his office. Did he know you were coming? Because he didn't say anything to me.'

She didn't seem entirely comfortable being alone with him. The color in her cheeks told him she was flustered.

'No, I thought it would be fun to surprise you. I brought some more pictures of the girls. Hundreds of them,' he said, and pulled his digital camera from his jacket pocket.

She seemed to relax as she began to scroll through the pictures of Chelsea's birthday party, which they'd held at a pizza parlor. Typically, he only brought a few pictures that he printed out on Hillary's home printer so his parents could keep them, but he hadn't had time to prepare for this trip as well as previous visits. He'd only thought to grab the camera from the back of the minivan as he was rushing off to catch his plane.

'What beautiful children, honey. I wish I could know them.'

'They have their other grandparents,' he said.

The sudden crease in her forehead showed that she was taken aback; he'd spoken too carelessly, had somehow hurt her. 'Not that it's the same as having you,' he corrected. 'I'm just saying . . . at least they're not without support.'

'Right. I'm glad for that, too,' she mumbled.

He hurried to change the subject. 'You got a new painting, huh?'

She glanced over her shoulder to see what he was looking at. She didn't even remember, he realized. That was how much money his parents had. They bought expensive art, jewelry, antiques, fine rugs, boats and luxury cars without blinking an eye, while he and Hillary had to scrape to put food on the table and pay the rent. As much as his parents had helped him financially through the years, sometimes he resented the disparity between them, resented that he had to ask for their help and wouldn't be able to inherit when they passed.

Everything they had should belong to him someday and would have if only Evelyn had died in that shack like she was supposed to.

She'd ruined his life – and deserved what she was going to get.

'I guess we did get that painting since you were here last.' His mother spoke rather indifferently, so used to getting whatever she wanted she didn't even appreciate it anymore.

'It's been ten months.'

'Right. Since March,' she said. 'Are you hungry?'

'I could use a quick bite. What do you have?'

'Should I make you an omelet?'

'Perfect.'

'I'll get that going and finish looking through these while you eat.' She set the camera on the breakfast bar as he followed her around to the kitchen proper.

If Hillary only knew what kind of people he came from, he thought as he looked around. She'd be so impressed if she ever saw his parents' house . . .

'Dad said someone named Sergeant Murphy stopped by to see you,' he said, slouching into a seat at the kitchen table.

She'd just opened the giant built-in refrigerator, but at the mention of Amarok she looked back at him. 'Yes, from Alaska. I guess he knows Evelyn.'

'Of course he knows Evelyn. There're only a few hundred people in Hilltop – not including all the psychopaths, of course. Hanover House almost doubles the population. Great place to live, huh?'

She didn't answer. She put a carton of eggs, a block of cheese, an onion and some previously cooked bacon on the counter. 'He – he showed me some pictures—'

'Of five woman who've been murdered. Dad told me that, too,' he said with a grimace. 'Various details of that case have been on TV. It's terrible, gruesome. Last I heard they hadn't caught the guy who's responsible, either. But Sergeant Murphy's wrong. It wasn't me.'

'Their bodies were found in Peoria.'

Jasper schooled his features so he wouldn't give anything away, but he was seething inside to think that Amarok would make so much trouble for him. He was also surprised, couldn't figure out how Amarok knew he was behind those killings. How had Evelyn's boyfriend picked up on them, out of all the killings in America? And from where he lived in *Alaska*?

Regardless, this could ruin everything. Jasper had to convince his mother that he was innocent so she wouldn't give Amarok any information, and the best way to do that was to bristle at the accusation her simple statement encompassed. 'I don't live there anymore, Mom.' He leaned forward as if he had nothing to hide and was angered by the mere suggestion. 'As you know, these days I'm over an hour away – two if there's traffic – in Florence, where I'm working hard and taking care of my family.'

'But you *did* live there. And these women – Sergeant Murphy said they were murdered over the past five years.'

She was pressing the issue? She'd never done that before, either. She was usually so eager to believe him, she'd accept almost anything he said, whether it made complete sense or not. 'So maybe I was there when *some* of them were killed,' he said. 'That doesn't mean *I'm* to blame. Lots of people live in Peoria.'

Tears filled her eyes as she studied him. 'Jasper, I-I couldn't take it if you . . . if you were the one who killed those poor women. What you did when you were younger . . . I've tried to be as understanding as possible, what with the drugs and . . . and all that. But I'll be honest. It's been hard. Sometimes I wake up in a cold sweat, having dreamed the worst things a mother could ever dream. So I hope you're being truthful with me.' She lowered her voice. 'Please tell me you're being truthful.'

He hated that stupid, imploring look on her face, wished he could wipe it off. 'Of course I'm being truthful!' he snapped. 'I can't believe you'd even ask me that!'

When her gaze softened, he knew the outrage he'd added to his response had been convincing. That or a similar response worked whenever he was accused of anything. He just had to get angrier than the person questioning him and whoever it was backed down.

'Mom, would I come back here, stay in touch, if I was some . . . serial killer?'

Her shoulders slumped as she sagged against the counter. 'I don't know.' She rubbed her forehead. 'I don't want to think so, but . . . sometimes I get confused. Sergeant Murphy was so certain.'

'Sergeant Murphy's an asshole.'

She lifted her head. 'You know him?'

'Of course I don't *know* him. But he must be an asshole if he's trying to pin those murders on me. It's more of Evelyn's bullshit, like claiming I attacked her last summer – in Boston of all places! As if I'd be stupid enough to go back to Boston!'

'You *would* know better than that,' she agreed, as if it brought her some relief.

'I've screwed up in the past, but I'm not an idiot,' he said. 'Jesus, am I going to be accused of every murder that happens – by my own mother?'

At last, she smiled again, and this time it seemed to come more naturally. 'I'm sorry, Son.' She walked over to touch his cheek with a hint of the old tenderness. 'Of course you can't be to blame for everything. Let's call your father and have him come home. He'll be so upset if he misses you.'

'I'll call him. Where's your cell?'

As she grabbed her purse and began rummaging around inside it, he couldn't help noticing the flashy diamond rings on her fingers. Her jewelry alone was worth thousands. He wished he could get hold of just one of those rings, knew a gift like that would go far toward placating Hillary when he got home . . .

But then he saw something that interested him even more. His mother had a stack of money in her purse, secured by a rubber band, that was at least an inch thick.

'Whoa! Why are you carrying so much cash?' he asked.

'Your father and I are going to Vegas tomorrow for the weekend,' she replied, as if it were nothing.

She had to have three or four thousand dollars in there! She and Stanley were just going to blow through that money?

Jasper felt he could put it to better use. A few thousand would go far toward getting him set up in Anchorage.

It was possible his mother would give it to him. His parents had helped him quite often over the years; he just had to think of the right approach.

Maybe he could say that Miranda had cancer – tell them that was the real reason he'd come to see them.

He imagined tearing up as he claimed he couldn't cope with the possibility of losing his stepdaughter and didn't know how he was going to pay for her treatment.

But he wasn't convinced he could make himself cry. He'd long since lost the ability to do that.

'Here you go,' his mother said when she found her iPhone amidst her keys and sunglasses and that fat stack of cash.

She handed it to him and he turned away from all that money, but he couldn't quit thinking about it as he dialed his father's office.

Stan answered right away. 'Maureen, what is it? I told you, I have appointments this afternoon.'

'It's me,' Jasper said.

All the pique left his father's voice. 'Where are you?'

'At home. With Mom.'

'What are you doing there?'

'I was missing you guys, so I decided to come for a visit.'

'You were able to leave Hillary and the kids?'

'I witnessed a stabbing at the prison where I work, so they gave me some time off. I told Hillary I needed to get away on my own.'

'She doesn't know you're in San Diego, though—'

'Of course not. I told her I was driving to the Grand Canyon.'

'Does that mean you'll be staying with us for a few days?'

'No, I'll only be here for a couple of hours, as usual.'

'I wish it could be longer.'

Jasper could think of a lot of things he enjoyed more than pretending to be a loving son. The minute he convinced his folks that Amarok was merely trying to stir up trouble, he'd be done here – although he was now also hoping to walk away with at least some of the bills in his mother's purse. 'Me, too. But we can't risk it. You know Evelyn. She's determined to find me, will never give up.'

'Yes, I'm aware of that,' he said dryly.

'So can you see me?'

'Of course. Give me a few minutes to rearrange my schedule and I'll be there.'

'I'll be waiting,' he said, and hung up.

His mother had finished cooking his omelet. She put it on a plate and set it in front of him before bringing the camera over. She chuckled when she started looking through the photographs again and saw one of Miranda giving Chelsea a piggyback ride. She watched a short video he had of the girls swimming in their pool, too, and marveled at how attractive their mother was.

Hillary was no Evelyn, Jasper thought, but, as a nurse, she made more money than the other women he'd been dating at the time, so he'd considered her to be his best option.

'You're still happy in your marriage?' his mother asked.

'Of course. We've been together seven years now,' he said, as if those years had been the best of his life.

'That's nice.' She didn't mention his first wife, and he was glad of it. He'd told them Selma was too materialistic and needy, that *he'd* broken off the relationship. But she'd been so desperate to move on she'd slipped away while he was at work and left him her entire net worth, just so that he wouldn't fight the divorce.

He'd liked her more than he did Hillary. Or maybe it was that he respected her. On some level, she seemed to know what he was, to understand that she needed to get clear of him as soon as possible, while Hillary kept begging and cajoling and believing the most stupid lies.

He was thinking about the fact that he'd soon be rid of Hillary, too, when his mother gasped and dropped his camera.

It hit the floor with a solid thud, and he stopped chewing. 'What's wrong?' he asked, confused by the horror on her face. He'd never felt the emotion behind that expression himself, but he'd grown quite familiar with that look. It was the one he most liked to create on the faces of his victims – what appeared right before they wet themselves.

'What's wrong?' he said again.

She knocked over her chair in her hurry to get out of it, and that caused her to fall herself.

Shocked, since he hadn't done anything wrong, he grabbed her wrist so that she couldn't go any farther and retrieved the camera.

Then he saw what she'd seen – a picture of one of his victims, naked with her legs tied apart, a gag in her mouth and a pipe shoved into her vagina. That picture reminded him of one of his most enjoyable days last summer, was some of his best work, but he could understand why Maureen wouldn't appreciate it.

'Oh shit. I left *this* on there?' Somehow he'd forgotten to delete that batch when he'd downloaded to his laptop, which was password protected, and he hadn't noticed because he'd taken so many shots of the kids since. It was a miracle Hillary hadn't stumbled across it. He would've checked before handing off his camera, but he'd been rushing around too much, hadn't put the same amount of thought and preparation into this trip as he had the others.

He blamed Amarok for that, damn it. Evelyn's boyfriend had screwed up everything.

'You did it! You k-killed those women! You're *still* killing,' his mother screamed. 'And we *believed* you. We helped you evade the police!'

'Don't feel bad. The ones I killed . . . they deserved to die. There are so many stupid women out there, *too* many,' he said, but she could hardly breathe, wasn't calming down.

He could tell there would be no convincing her.

'My God! It's *our* fault. Evelyn tried to tell us, to warn us. Now there's no way to make what we've done right. That blood is on *our* hands, too. What am I going to do?' She was straining to get away from him, to reach her cell phone. But he couldn't have that.

'You're not going to do *anything*,' he said, and calmly dragged her over to the counter, where there was a nice selection of kitchen knives.

As soon as Stan got home, he pulled into the garage and lowered the door. He didn't want the sight of his car to act as an invitation to visit for any of the neighbors who might be out walking a dog or pushing a stroller. He so rarely got to see his son that he was loath to let anything interrupt. He and Maureen couldn't afford for anyone to know they had a special visitor in the first place. Jasper had already taken a risk in coming here.

He wondered how Maureen felt about seeing their son. Stan had told her that he could not be the kind of lifelong murderer Evelyn insisted he was. What'd happened in high school was a freak thing, a terrible tragedy caused by the influence of mood-altering drugs. Jasper had outgrown that experimental teenage phase; they had no reason to worry about him continuing the behavior.

After today's visit, maybe she'd believe him. She'd been so despondent lately, so unsure that they'd been right to help Jasper stay out of prison. Stan had watched her take Sergeant Murphy's card from her purse, had seen the way she stared at it when she thought he wasn't paying any attention. So he'd stolen it when she wasn't looking and thrown it away. He wouldn't allow her to call the cops. He'd never loved anything so much as the blond-haired, brown-eyed boy they'd created together, would do anything to protect him. Like he told her, being a parent was never easy, but loyalty – that was what mattered in a family.

After grabbing his briefcase, since he wasn't expecting to return to work until after the weekend in Vegas, he pocketed the keys to his Lexus and went in through the mudroom, past the laundry room and his wife's craft room, to the large family room and kitchen that looked out on the backyard.

No one was there.

Where could they be? He hesitated, listening, but he couldn't hear voices. Of course, the house was seventy-five hundred square feet, big enough that he wouldn't be able to hear his wife and son, or anyone else for that matter, if they were in the far reaches. Although he couldn't see Maureen taking Jasper on in a game of billiards, he figured they could be upstairs in the rec room. Or they could be in the library with the door shut. Maybe Jasper felt less exposed there.

'Maureen?'

He received no answer, but he didn't dare call his son's name instead. The silence was so complete that he was beginning to fear the cops had figured out Jasper was in town and had busted in to arrest him *and* Maureen.

Depositing his briefcase on the floor near the couch, Stan pulled his cell phone from his pocket. He was about to call his wife when he noticed some red drops that weren't normally on the wall in the kitchen.

What was *that*?

His heart began to chug with the rhythm of a steam engine as he stared. The same red drops were everywhere – on the refrigerator, the wall, even the ceiling . . .

A moment later he realized they weren't merely 'red drops' – they were blood.

'What the hell?' Something terrible had happened. But what?

As he rounded the bar, an ominous, terrible feeling swept through him, smashing the eagerness and confidence with which he'd walked into the house.

'Maureen?' he called again, this time in panic, but he found her only two steps later. She was on the floor near the kitchen table, lying in a pool of her own blood.

'No!' With her head cocked at such an odd angle and her eyes open but seeing nothing, he could tell it was too late. She was dead.

He dropped to his knees so he could scoop her into his arms and scream out the pain he felt at her loss. But as he gathered her to him, he saw the knife protruding from her chest. Jasper had to have done this. He was the only one here with her. But *why*? Why would their son turn on *them*?

And where was he now?

Fifteen

Evelyn stood on the other side of the two-way mirror, watching as Lido Thomas finished up the pretest interview, which was intended to acquaint the subject with the procedure, and began hooking Lyman Bishop to the polygraph equipment attached to her computer. Evelyn hoped they hadn't rushed this too much, that they'd prepared adequately for such a smart subject. Strategy was everything when using a lie detector test, but she'd been so afraid that Bishop's lawyer would intervene or Bishop would change his mind, she'd had to move fast.

Jim Ricardo stood beside her in the secret observatory. Since he'd made it clear that he didn't agree with what she was doing, she wasn't pleased to have him there. But she decided not to ask him to leave. She knew that wouldn't come across well, and she hated to get into another adversarial relationship, like she'd had with Fitzpatrick. Finding good psychologists and neurologists, ones who were willing to leave their friends and family in the Lower 48 and come to Hilltop, was too hard.

'Please state your full name.' Now that Lido had Bishop attached, she was beginning the in-test phase.

'Lyman Roosevelt Bishop.'

Bishop seemed perfectly relaxed, despite all the cords and sensors.

'Can you tell me where you were born, Mr Bishop?'

'That's *Dr* Bishop,' he replied. 'I have my doctorate, just like your esteemed lead psychiatrist. I'd appreciate you affording me the same respect you give her.'

Taken aback, Lido cleared her throat. Fortunately, she resisted the temptation she must've felt to look toward the two-way mirror. 'Okay. No problem. *Dr* Bishop it is. Can you please tell me where you were born?' she asked again.

'Minneapolis.'

Lido gave him a few more irrelevant questions to make sure they were both comfortable before diving in. Then she threw in a control question. 'Have you ever told a lie to get yourself out of trouble, Dr Bishop?'

'Yes.'

Ricardo nudged Evelyn. 'Honest so far.'

He was joking, but Evelyn didn't think it was funny. So much depended on the control questions. They could've used a no there, needed Bishop to tell a white lie so that they could get some standard by which they could measure his other responses.

'Have you ever hurt anyone?' Lido asked.

'Yes.'

He didn't elaborate, didn't attempt to excuse himself by clarifying that he hadn't caused any *physical* damage or that the pain had been incidental, like accidentally hitting someone with a door. Evelyn got the impression that he understood not to embellish his answers, that he'd prepared for this. What with all the information on the Internet, it wouldn't be hard to learn the techniques that worked best. He could've done some research after he was first arrested, in case he had to face a polygraph somewhere down the line. Maybe that was why he'd agreed to take the examination – he was curious to see if he could beat it, wanted to test his prowess and gain some experience.

To Lido's credit, she moved on as if she wasn't disappointed by that admission. 'Have you ever harmed an animal?'

'No.'

Evelyn wished she could see the graph that was appearing on Lido's computer. Many psychopaths first acted out by torturing animals.

'Have you ever tortured a human being?'

His gaze shifted to the wall behind which Evelyn stood, as if he could see her watching him. He was looking right at her. Did he know she was there? Many tests were performed in places where subjects could secretly be observed, but neither she nor Lido had said anything to give that away. 'No.'

'Have you ever committed any other kind of crime?' Lido asked.

'No.'

This time Evelyn nudged Ricardo. 'We got one there. He's done something at some point – lied on his taxes, jaywalked, thrown garbage out the car window, used a park for which he skipped the fee.'

'We'll see if it makes a difference,' Ricardo responded.

'Are you hoping against me?' Evelyn asked.

'Of course not. I'm just not certain this is worth our time, like I told you before.'

It didn't have to take *his* time. Evelyn almost mentioned that he was free to go on about his business but, once again, chose to keep her mouth shut.

'Did you know Jan Hall?' Lido asked.

Bishop scratched the side of his face. 'Yes.'

'Did you kill Jan Hall?'

'No.'

'Do you know where her body is?'

'I don't even know that she's dead.'

'You know she's been missing for two years.'

'Yes.'

'You also know that she went missing a year before you were brought up on murder charges.'

'Yes.'

'Did you know Patricia Vanderbilt?'

'Yes.'

'Did you kill Patricia Vanderbilt?'

'No.'

Lido didn't need to ask about Patricia's body. That had been found. It was her autopsy that proved she'd had a lobotomy, that whoever had killed her had first cut into her frontal lobes.

Lido went through the rest of the 'ice-pick' victims, and he answered the same for all – confidently, without any hesitation.

'Did you collect any trophies from your victims?'

'I didn't have any victims,' he replied.

Smooth . . .

'So you didn't put those panties in your attic?'

'No, ma'am. I think it's become clear that Detective Gustavson, who investigated the case, planted that evidence. Obviously, he had an agenda, needed to put *someone* away.'

'Wait a sec,' Evelyn murmured to Ricardo. 'Why is he starting to open up and talk when he's been so careful not to?'

'I'd say he's gaining confidence,' Ricardo responded. 'That or he's trying to prove he's not afraid of this, of you.'

Evelyn was willing to bet it was the latter. He thought he could outsmart her.

'Is it true your mother was shot at point-blank range in her own driveway?' Evelyn heard Lido ask in the lab.

'I wouldn't know,' Bishop replied.

'Is there something about the question that's unclear?'

'I wasn't there. But, according to what I've heard, she was shot at point-blank range in her own driveway.'

Lido took a moment to study what his physiological responses indicated on her computer screen. Then she said, 'Did you ever go visit your mother at the house where she was killed?'

'No.'

'Did you love your mother, Dr Bishop?'

He set his jaw, but his voice didn't change. 'No.'

'Were you sad when she was killed?'

He paused; then he said, 'Yes.'

'If you didn't love her, why were you sad?'

'Because she was supposed to love me.'

'Do you believe she did love you?'

'Her actions proved she didn't.'

'So you had no contact with her before she died.'

'Not for a number of years.'

'That means you were never at her house, that there would be no reason for your DNA to be there. Is that correct?'

A smile curved his lips as he once again turned his gaze toward the two-way mirror. 'As I've learned the hard way, sometimes the police plant evidence in order to win a conviction. Now that the authorities have my DNA, I can't be sure where it might turn up.'

'Is that a yes or a no?' Lido pressed.

'That's a no. My DNA would have no reason to be there, not without some sort of intervention on the part of someone else.'

The questions continued for twenty minutes. Lido asked all the things Evelyn had spoken to her about. She even rephrased questions she'd already asked, hoping to get a better reading. Evelyn had to hand it to her – she was good. But a signal she gave with her right hand, one they'd agreed to use before, indicated that the test wasn't working out the way they'd hoped.

'It's inconclusive,' Ricardo guessed, catching that sign, too.

Lido was winding down. The examiner didn't have anything else to ask. But Evelyn wasn't ready to let Bishop escape the machine, wasn't about to let the results be 'inconclusive' – not if she could help it. She had one more question, one she hadn't discussed with Lido. Just in case Bishop was innocent, she'd thought it would be going too far.

'Desperate times demand desperate measures,' she muttered, and, ignoring Ricardo's surprise, she hurried out of the room and into the lab, where she whispered in Lido's ear. After that, instead of leaving, since Bishop obviously understood she'd been observing him anyway, she stood behind the examiner.

'How old was Beth when you gave her the lobotomy?' Lido asked, repeating what Evelyn had told her to say.

His eyes flared wide, then narrowed as they focused on Evelyn. She'd managed to surprise him, to throw him off balance. But he didn't answer the question. He started to take off the sensors and other equipment. 'I'm done,' he said. 'You're not interested in the truth. You're only trying to trap me.'

'Why would a question about your sister be a trap, Dr Bishop?' Evelyn asked.

He didn't answer that, either. 'I've tried to be your friend, Evelyn. I've tried to give you what you want. And this is what you do?'

'You didn't indicate the test would be restricted to certain questions,' she said.

That evil, frightening look she'd witnessed once before, when Jennifer Hall was visiting, stole over his face again. 'You're no better than my mother,' he whispered. 'And you deserve the same thing – a bullet right to the face.'

That blast of hate felt like a gale-force wind. Evelyn steadied herself with one hand against the wall. 'You did it,' she said. 'You killed your mother and all those other women, too.'

'You're crazy,' Bishop said.

'Am I?' she challenged. 'Then how did you know where your mother was shot? The police have never revealed that to the public.'

He jumped up so fast that the few cords still attached to him jerked Lido's laptop off the table. It went crashing to the floor as he shouted, '*You're* the monster! Here's hoping Jasper Moore finally gets it right.'

Stunned by the vehemence of those words, Evelyn blinked in surprise. 'You're being recorded. You realize that.'

'Not by this,' he said, and stomped on the computer until he'd mashed it.

Evelyn called for COs. They poured into the lab within seconds, but by then she feared it was too late to save the data from the polygraph.

'You have *nothing* on me!' Bishop called as they dragged him out. 'In another week or two I'll walk free, and you won't be able to do anything to stop that!'

A pair of bloody footprints led out of the kitchen.

Had Jasper left?

Stan could only hope he'd been spooked by his own horrific act and run. But that didn't make much sense. Jasper had killed before. And Maureen had been stabbed over and over, well beyond what was necessary to take her life. Obviously, Jasper wasn't bothered by his own actions. He had to be the psychopath Evelyn had long accused him of being. He knew that Stan was on his way – that Stan would find Maureen dead and finally understand how badly he'd been played. In spite of all the help they, as parents, had given him, Jasper had killed his own mother. He'd destroyed any chance he had of getting future help, which was what made this situation so dangerous.

Careful not to make any more noise, Stan scooted away from his dead wife. He couldn't bear to look at her any longer. He was as much to blame for her death as Jasper was. He'd refused to see their son as he truly was, even when she'd tried to get him to look at the situation more objectively.

His own culpability made him cringe. He'd left his wife of forty years vulnerable, and she'd suffered a tragic end – one that he would now likely suffer himself.

If he didn't want that to happen, he had to call for help, get the police to come as soon as possible, he told himself. He needed to think beyond the betrayal, the confusion and the pain. But he no longer had his phone in his hand. He couldn't even remember what he'd done with it. It was almost as if he was in shock.

Maybe he was in shock. He felt nauseous, cold, clammy.

His phone, he reminded himself. He must've dropped it. The darn thing couldn't be far . . .

As he wiped his hands on his suit coat to rid them of Maureen's blood, his eyes darted around the kitchen. No cell. But he didn't hear any noise, either. Did he have a chance to get out of the house, to run to a neighbor's – or hide? He doubted Jasper had left, at least for any length of time, but he could be upstairs, ransacking the house, looking for valuables. Maureen's purse had been dumped out not far from her body. That told Stan her murder had been as callous as a murder could be, that Jasper had stabbed his mother thirty or forty times and then gone through her purse as if it were nothing.

So had he killed her for the money?

No, that couldn't be it. They'd given him money many times and would've given him more if only he'd asked.

Stan winced as he glanced back at his wife, but he couldn't allow what he saw – the terror and heartbreak it brought – to incapacitate him. Already he felt like he was about to throw up, and he was shaking so badly he wasn't sure he had the strength or coordination to move.

Don't think. Don't feel. That's not Maureen lying there. This is a nightmare. The only way to make it stop is to get out.

Afraid that Jasper would come into the family room as he was getting to his feet, he crawled around the bar. Then he leaned to the left, so he could see around the couch to where he'd left his briefcase. His phone should be somewhere in between him and that case. He'd had it when he walked in. But he saw no sign of it, and he wasn't going to take any more time to look.

His pulse raced as he considered his options. Although the back door was closest, the yard was fenced. If Jasper came after him, he'd be trapped before he could get through the gate. The garage would be no better. His car was there, which seemed to offer some safety, but Stan doubted he'd have the chance to get inside it. The garage entrance was the farthest away.

He'd go for the front door and run across the street, he decided. The people who lived there were retired and more likely to be home than the neighbors to the left or right, but before he could make a move his phone went off.

From the sound, it was close. Terrified that the noise would bring Jasper from upstairs or wherever he was, Stan longed to find it and silence it, but the moment he got to his feet he froze.

Jasper was sitting in the recliner. 'Looking for this?'

He held up Stan's cell, but it was the cast-off blood on his face and hands that caught Stan's attention. He'd never seen anything so revolting, even in the movies. 'She was your *mother,*' he said, gaping at him.

'And, for the most part, I liked her,' Jasper responded, as if what he'd done didn't mean anything at all. 'She just saw something she shouldn't have. I couldn't trust her after that.'

'What'd she see?' Stan asked. 'The *truth*?'

'A version of it, I guess,' he replied with a shrug. 'Regardless, it's a moot point now.'

Stan felt his jaw sag. 'You feel *no* remorse, *no* sadness? Your own mother meant *nothing* to you?'

'I told you I liked her.'

'Liked her,' he echoed in disbelief. 'She loved you so much she would've given her life for you!'

He sighed audibly as he rose. 'Then you have nothing to feel bad about, because that's essentially what she did. It was her or me.'

Stan stepped back, hoping he'd be able to get to the front door, in spite of the furniture that blocked his path. 'You killed those women, didn't you?'

'What women?'

'Have there been that many?'

'At least thirty or forty. I haven't counted in a while. But I've been killing a long time. The numbers start to add up.'

Stan took another step back. 'They're going to catch you someday.'

'I doubt it. They never catch the really good ones. I move around, know what kinds of victims to target, how to cover my tracks. There are too many people in the world. I actually perform a vital function. As far as I'm concerned, there needs to be more killers like me.'

Stan tried to gauge whether or not he could reach the door if he turned and ran. He doubted it. He wondered if he could talk Jasper down, get him to change his mind. But how? He couldn't appeal to Jasper's emotions. Jasper didn't seem to have any. He was so casual about murder, so confident. That scared Stan worse than anything. Jasper didn't think Stan had a chance, and that made Stan fear it was true. 'What about the women that sergeant from Alaska asked about? Did you kill them?'

'I did. I'm still surprised he made the connection, though. I can't wait to ask him how he figured it out.'

'You're going to *ask* him?'

'Yes. And then I'm going to kill him. He deserves it. He's been fucking Evelyn. Thinks he can protect her. If you ask me, he's asking for it.'

'So you *have* kept track of her.'

'Of course. Don't play stupid. You know that from when I called him by his nickname on the phone. You just chose to overlook that along with all the rest.'

'Because I wanted to believe you were normal! That you weren't some kind of creature I can't even begin to understand!'

'Now you're being unkind,' he said. 'I don't think that will help the situation; do you?'

Stan felt for the vase on the table behind him. 'What made you into such a cold bastard?'

'I've often wondered myself, but I don't have the answer. Maybe you should ask Evelyn. She's the one doing all the research.'

The smooth glaze of the vase against his palm gave Stan hope, but it wasn't as if Jasper didn't notice what he was doing.

'I wouldn't touch that, if I were you,' he said, lifting the knife. 'You don't want to piss me off.'

'*Piss you off?* You're going to murder me! How much worse can it get?'

'If any of my victims were still around to talk, they'd tell you it can get *a lot* worse,' Jasper said. 'Well, Evelyn *is* still around, and she's tried to tell you, to tell everyone. The questions are: would you rather die a quick death that allows you to retain some dignity? Or a slow, painful death, where I force you to suck my dick?'

'How could you be my son?' Stan cried. 'You're a *monster*!'

Jasper rolled his eyes. 'Are you really any better? The police could've put me behind bars when I was seventeen if you hadn't intervened. Then all of the women I've killed would be alive. Mom would be alive, too. Your name was the last thing she muttered before she collapsed, by the way. You have to at least take responsibility for your own gullibility.'

'You lied! And you manipulated me!'

'I only told you what you wanted to hear. Anyway, everyone manipulates everyone else. That's how the world works. I just happen to be better at it than most. You expect me to apologize for that?'

Stan had never felt like a greater fool. For so many years, he'd loved and protected an illusion. 'I hope you rot in hell.' He threw the vase, but he was so rattled he didn't have his usual strength.

Jasper laughed as it crashed and broke at his feet. 'At least you decided to make this fun,' he said, and leapt over the couch separating them.

Stan ran for the door, but he was more than two decades older and fifty pounds heavier. Jasper was on him within seconds. Still, Stan wanted to fight, to unleash the rage that suddenly boiled up to replace the fear. But an excruciating pain seized his chest, radiating so strongly down his left arm that he couldn't use it.

'My heart!' he gasped, struggling for breath before Jasper could even stab him.

Jasper frowned in disappointment. 'Damn. That's going to ruin what I was hoping to be an enjoyable afternoon,' he said, and stood and watched as the pain grew worse and worse, studying Stan as if he was fascinated by the spectacle of watching someone die.

Sixteen

Evelyn stopped by the Moosehead on her way home. It'd been such an exhausting day she'd left a little early, but she wasn't ready to spend the evening alone in Amarok's bungalow.

'Hey, Doc!' Shorty called as she approached the bar.

The place wasn't crowded yet, but she knew it'd fill up as the night wore on. Even Wednesdays could get busy.

'Hi, Shorty. Can I get a bowl of your sister's homemade chili and a piece of corn bread?'

'You bet,' he replied. 'Won't take but a minute.'

She sat at the bar, picking at a bowl of nuts and watching a basketball game on TV while she waited.

'When's Amarok due back?' Shorty placed her food, along with some silverware and a napkin, in front of her.

'Tomorrow. Why?'

He began wiping down the counter. 'Just wonderin',' he said as he moved away.

It didn't take much food to fill Evelyn up. After a few minutes she pushed her bowl to one side and put some money out to take care of the bill. She was about to leave when Russell Jones came in and claimed the stool next to her. 'Thought I might find you here.'

'Do I hang out here that often?' she asked.

'Since you've gotten with Amarok, you come in several nights a week.'

'I guess I do,' she admitted. 'And you know that because you come in even more.'

He shrugged. 'I like this place. Beats heading home to an empty house.'

'I'm discovering that for myself.'

After pulling the bowl of nuts closer to him, he tossed a few in his mouth. 'I hear the polygraph didn't go so well.'

'Actually, it went far better than I expected.'

'Really? Lido said Bishop broke her computer.'

'He did, but we'll replace it. And since she kept it backed up, we'll only lose Bishop's data.'

'Isn't that bad enough? You wanted him to take that lie detector test for a reason.'

She decided to linger awhile and have a glass of wine, so she asked Shorty to bring one when he returned to collect her leftovers and dishes. 'I got what I needed out of it,' she said to Russ as Shorty walked away.

'Meaning . . .'

'He knows something about his mother's death, something that the police never revealed to the public.'

'Is it significant enough to indicate he killed her?'

'I'd say so.'

'Nice. So what are you going to do about it?'

Shorty returned with her wine and put a beer in front of Russ at the same time. They both thanked him before continuing their conversation.

'I'll share the information with whatever detective takes over the Zombie Maker cases, of course,' she said. 'Maybe it'll convince them to keep an eye on Bishop once he's back in circulation.'

Russ sucked the foam off his beer. 'Doesn't what we're doing ever seem like a losing battle to you?'

'I try not to think of it that way. Who knows what we might find and how that might change the world? We only lose if we give up.'

'Whoa!'

Evelyn could tell by the sudden excitement in his voice – and the fact that he'd turned to stare at a tall blonde – that he was no longer talking about work.

'Who's *that*?' he whispered.

Although Evelyn didn't recognize her, it seemed as if everyone else at the Moosehead did. Several people went over to hug her and welcome her back, but it wasn't until she came closer that Evelyn realized who she was. She'd never met her, but she'd seen pictures.

Amarok's ex-girlfriend was here already? 'You've got to be kidding me,' Evelyn muttered.

Russ was still staring. 'About what?'

'It's Samantha Boyce,' she explained. 'Amarok used to date her.' *That* was the reason Shorty had asked when Amarok would be back. It wasn't the casual question he'd pretended. He'd learned Samantha was in town and was curious how Amarok would respond to her presence. All of Hilltop would be curious, which meant that she and Amarok would receive more than their fair share of attention over the next few weeks.

'And he let her go?' Russ said, with exaggerated shock.

Evelyn arched her eyebrows at him, but he failed to notice until she didn't answer. 'What?' he said, glancing back to see why. 'Did I say something wrong?'

'No.' Evelyn finished her wine and got up. She didn't care to sit through the welcome home party. The others might be excited to have Samantha back in town, but Evelyn was not.

Evelyn couldn't wait to see Amarok, especially because he ended up spending a couple of days helping the detective in Peoria and didn't get home until Saturday morning. Fortunately, it was the weekend, so she didn't have to work and could meet his flight. But she wasn't sure what she'd say to him if he brought up marriage again. She hadn't been able to quit thinking about Samantha since seeing her at the Moosehead. Samantha had been ready to settle down when she was with Amarok before. He'd admitted as much. So she'd probably be even more ready to settle down now. She'd probably want to have kids right away, too, which was something he'd been talking about. And she came with none of the emotional baggage Evelyn did, had never been attacked. Their sex life – and the other aspects of their life together – could be easy and uncomplicated.

Even Samantha's job would make Amarok happier. Running a guns and ammo store could be dangerous. Samantha could get robbed. But that held true for anyone who dealt with a retail store. Samantha wasn't delving into the minds of psychopaths every day, wasn't likely to become the object of their murderous fantasies. Neither did she have to constantly check over her shoulder in case the man who'd tried to kill her twice in the past would make a third attempt.

Why would Amarok ever choose to be with someone like her over someone like Samantha Boyce?

He claimed it was because of love. Love seemed important right now. But would it be enough to carry them through years, possibly decades?

Evelyn feared it wouldn't, that he'd only regret marrying her someday. On a purely practical level, she was damaged goods.

'Why couldn't Samantha have come back next year?' Evelyn grumbled as she circled around the airport for the fourth time, waiting for Amarok to appear on the curb outside of Baggage Claim. Maybe by then Evelyn would have decided whether or not she could make the kind of commitment marrying Amarok would require and wouldn't feel threatened by having someone who seemed far more perfect for him waiting in the wings.

As she returned to Arrivals, she slowed once again. His plane was supposed to have landed twenty minutes ago. Was it even in yet?

This was where a cell phone would come in handy, she thought. But then she saw him, standing on the sidewalk in his jeans, boots and big coat, his bag in one hand. She loved the way he looked, all rough-hewn Alaskan male. She loved the confidence with which he moved, too. And she loved the way he talked. He didn't use a lot of superfluous words. He kept life simple, but he always meant what he said and did what he promised.

His lips curved and his expression softened the moment he saw her, suggesting he'd missed her as much as she'd missed him.

In that instant Evelyn feared she didn't have a good choice when it came to their relationship. Either she broke up with him now, which would be almost impossible while she was still living in Hilltop, or she allowed all that other stuff she was worried about to destroy their relationship in bits and pieces over the years.

'How was your flight?' she asked as he tossed his bag in the back.

'Long.' He climbed into the passenger seat and leaned over to kiss her, but as far as she was concerned that kiss was far too brief. He was focused on the traffic around them and getting away from the airport, but she was thinking of the other night, when she'd wanted to have phone sex with him and couldn't tell him. She craved the feel of his hands on her right now, wanted to drown in the desire he evoked rather than continue to entertain all of the things that'd been going through her mind.

'Everything go okay while I was gone?' he asked.

She merged into traffic. 'We muddled through, but Hilltop definitely isn't the same without you.'

His mouth quirked up on one side. 'Good thing I'm back.'

When she shot him a smile of her own, he ran a finger over her cheek. 'How are things at work?'

'Let's not talk about work,' she replied.

'Because . . .'

'We'll deal with that later.'

He hesitated. 'Then . . . should I tell you about my trip?'

'No.'

'You're not interested to hear what happened?'

She could easily discern the surprise in his voice. 'We've got the whole weekend. There's no rush.'

'What's going on with you?'

She didn't answer. She just turned into the first motel she could find and cut the engine.

'What are we doing *here*?' he asked.

'Getting a room.'

He seemed as surprised as she'd expected him to be. 'I could hear *me* saying that, but *you*?'

'I'm serious.'

'We'll be home in a few hours.'

'We have to stop by and see your dad while we're here, don't we?'

'That'd be nice, but it shouldn't take long.'

Grabbing him by the lapels of his coat, she pulled him over to kiss him, long and hard. 'I can't wait.'

His eyes darkened with desire. 'Whoa! No problem. I'll go register.'

He went inside and came back a few minutes later.

'What's gotten into you?' he asked, teasing her as he led her to their room and unlocked the door. 'I've only been gone four nights. With the hours we've both been working, we've gone longer than that before. You're acting as though it's been months.'

He obviously liked that she'd initiated this; he was just taken aback. 'I missed you,' she admitted. 'I missed you a lot.'

She barely let him get inside the room before she started stripping off his clothes. He kicked the door shut, but then he pulled her to him, kissing her again – deeper and wetter and with more promise.

'I'm going to leave more often if this is what I get when I return,' he murmured against her lips.

'All I've been able to think about is your mouth on my neck, my breasts—'

'This calls for putting my mouth in a few other places, too,' he said, and swept her into his arms to carry her to the bed.

Evelyn stared up at him as he removed her clothes. Although she'd managed to get his coat and shirt off, he was still in his jeans. He had his shoes on, too. But neither one of them seemed to care about shoes. They were in too big of a hurry, and he didn't need to use his feet. She was much more interested in the rest of him.

'You taste like honey,' he told her as he kissed her. 'No one has ever tasted so good, not to me.'

Fisting her hands in his hair, she kissed him back, using the thrust of her tongue to mimic what she craved.

He groaned as his mouth left hers. 'Holy shit, Evelyn. You make me crazy. All I have to do is think of you to want you.'

He licked her collarbone, her breasts, her stomach. 'Is this okay?' he asked, sounding breathless when he held her knees apart so that she couldn't shield herself from his view.

Normally, she couldn't allow him to pin her down in any way. She didn't like feeling exposed, didn't like being so vulnerable, which was why she only let him make love to her in the dark and, even then, in a gentle, somewhat repressed manner.

It was time to push beyond that, however, to escape the shadow of her past and make love freely, expressing what she felt without letting what Jasper did hold her back.

This is Amarok. He'll never hurt me. 'I like it,' she said, even though she was slightly worried she might not be able to follow through with what she'd started.

His teeth flashed as he gave her one of his sexy grins. Then he used his shoulders to keep her knees apart and slid his hands up under her, pulling her toward his mouth. 'Wait until you feel this.'

When his tongue touched her, Evelyn gasped and closed her eyes. She was determined not to focus on the fact that she felt small and easily overpowered in comparison to his big, muscular body. He'd stop the second she asked him to. That was what she had to remember.

But why would she ever ask him to stop? The way he used his lips and teeth caused her to gasp and squirm in a good way. She could feel the tension building, could feel the kind of climax that so often eluded her – when she let all of that other stuff get inside her head – drawing close, like a swell rising out to sea that was quickly turning into a giant wave thundering toward the shore.

'Yes!' she whispered. 'That's good!'

Amarok tightened his grip on her, holding her in place so that her movements couldn't interrupt his ministrations. He was determined to make her come; she could tell he wanted that as much as she did. 'It's just me, Evelyn,' he said, surprising her by rocking back on his haunches for a moment. 'I've never hurt you, and I never would. So let go, okay? Let go and *trust me*.'

She did trust him. And she proved it. Not long after his mouth returned to her and his tongue continued its erotic work, her body jerked with the first wave of a powerful climax.

When it was over, he smiled proudly as he leaned over her. 'You did it. And you screamed so loud I thought the neighbors might start banging on the walls.'

He was joking about the screams, but she had been more vocal than usual. 'You haven't seen anything yet,' she told him, and reached down to undo his pants. 'I believe you have something else for me, and it's in here.'

Finally, he kicked off his boots so that he could remove his pants and boxers, and she felt a strange sort of female pride when she wrapped her hand around his erection. 'This is pretty impressive,' she teased.

'Maybe you can help me figure out how to make the most of it,' he said, and spread her knees again. He was so much more aggressive than usual. Evelyn got the impression he was too caught up in what he was feeling to remember to take the usual precautions – to move slowly, to follow the 'rules' they'd established over the past year so that she could be comfortable making love. Usually he let her be on top, so she'd never feel threatened. But she could tell that he was enjoying taking charge, and she wanted to let him express his sexuality without feeling as though he had to rein it in. She wasn't the only one who mattered. There had to be freedom, for both of them.

'I'm sure I can,' she said.

He started to settle himself between her thighs. 'What about a condom?' she asked. 'Don't you have one?'

'I do. It's in my wallet.'

She reached for his cast-off jeans, but he caught her hand. 'I don't want to wear it,' he said as he stared down at her. 'You're the woman I plan to marry, Evelyn. Let me come inside you.'

That frightened her. She wasn't sure she was ready for a baby. But the doctors weren't sure she'd be able to have one, anyway. They'd done all they could to repair the physical damage caused by Jasper, but her periods hadn't been regular since then. If she refused, maybe they'd be arguing about a moot point. Besides, Amarok's lips had returned to her neck and then her ears, making it almost impossible to remember why it would be such a terrible thing to cast aside their only form of birth control.

'Can I?' he breathed, his voice raspy as he held himself ready to push inside her. 'Will you let me make love to you the way I want to?'

She caught his face in her hands. 'Are you testing my level of commitment, Amarok?'

'Maybe,' he admitted.

He waited. When she didn't speak, he reached for his jeans. 'If you're not ready, it's fine.'

She stopped him. 'I'm ready,' she said, and pulled him inside her.

As Amarok began to move, Evelyn let her mind and body go. The more she concentrated on the rhythm, the easier it was to get caught up in it, to simply enjoy herself. Even her subconscious was starting to trust Amarok, to recognize the difference between him and Jasper, she realized. She wasn't tempted to freeze up or panic. This was another victory.

'Are you close?' Amarok asked.

The pleasure was intense, too intense for speech, so she nodded.

'Then look at me. Let me watch you.'

Her eyes met and locked with his as her second climax hit – this one was even better than the last. She cried out as her muscles contracted, gripping him that much tighter.

A satisfied expression claimed his face, which disappeared as, with a final thrust, his eyes closed and he let himself go.

Afterwards, Amarok seemed as reluctant to pull away from her as she was from him. They remained tangled up together, listening to each other breathe, for several long minutes as they recovered.

'That was perfect,' he said at length, breaking the incredible calm.

'Well, you really know what you're doing,' she responded with a throaty laugh.

He leaned up on one elbow. 'No, this one was all you, babe. You're always doubting yourself, wondering if you're not measuring up somehow, not able to meet my sexual fantasies or desires.'

She ran her thumb over the rough beard growth on his jaw. 'And . . .'

'Just for the record, that was the best sex I ever had.'

'Because I didn't make you wear a condom?' she teased.

He sobered and pressed his lips softly to hers. 'Because I love you.'

'What if we just created a baby, Amarok?'

'I'm okay with that. I'll be even happier.'

She rubbed her flat stomach, trying to imagine what it would feel like with a baby inside it. 'I hope you know what you're doing, Sergeant.'

He put his hand over hers. 'I know what I want.'

'And that is . . .'

'You and as many babies as you'll give me.'

'Now you're talking about having a big family? What am I getting into?'

He nipped playfully at her neck. 'We can start with one.'

The thought of carrying Amarok's child, of being a mother, sort of excited her – until she realized that they hadn't solved their problems. They were just ignoring them.

Seventeen

Evelyn had been dozing off in the motel with Amarok. They'd enjoyed a relaxing and fulfilling two hours. An interlude that left her languid. But Amarok was beginning to stir. He wasn't one who could lie around for long periods; he had too much energy. That was usually the case for her, too. She almost always had something to do or somewhere to be, which was probably why the past two hours were so remarkable. These moments in time, when the demons of her past finally disappeared from her consciousness, were rare, memorable.

'Do you really think the police will keep a close eye on that convenience store by the tattoo parlor?' she asked as he, noticing that she was coming around, got up to dress.

'You mean where Vanessa Lopez thinks she might've seen someone who looks like that age-enhanced photo of Jasper?'

She hadn't prefaced her remarks. They were simply an outcropping of what she'd been thinking since she started returning to full wakefulness. 'Yeah. The 7-Eleven you told me about on the phone.'

'They'll visit there periodically, have the clerks keep an eye out and report back if they see someone matching his description.'

She got up to recover her clothes, which were on the floor where Amarok had thrown them. 'Which the clerks may or may not remember to do.'

Having donned his boxers, he pulled on his jeans. 'I stopped by there myself. The guy I talked to knows Vanessa. He's eager to help catch her attacker. I'm guessing the others will feel the same, so they'll do what they can.'

She had to extract her panties from her jeans, since he'd peeled them both off at once. 'I guess I'm just so used to dead ends that I'm growing pessimistic.'

He retrieved her bra for her. 'It's been twenty-one years,' he said, handing it to her. 'Your hope is bound to flag now and then. You're only protecting yourself against more disappointment, anyway.'

'But you think the long wait might soon be over?' She tried to hide the desperation in her voice. She'd wanted to see Jasper caught for so long she couldn't even imagine what that day would be like. 'That we're getting closer than we've ever been?'

'If we can get through to Jasper's mom, gain her support, we've got a great chance. And I got the feeling that's a distinct possibility. She's torn.'

'Does she know about the attempted abduction in Casa Grande?'

'She might've seen it on the news, but *I* didn't mention it to her. I didn't find out about it until after I'd left her place, and I haven't called her back. Not yet. I want to give her plenty of time to think about the Peoria killings, to wonder if her son could be involved, before I speak to her again. Vanessa Lopez gives me something to go back to her with.'

Evelyn smiled as she ogled his bare chest.

'What?' he said. 'You keep looking at me like that and we'll never leave this motel.'

'I'm not sure I want to.'

He walked over and lifted her chin with one finger. 'We can stay longer.'

He made her feel safe, whole. 'No. Let's go see your father.' She finished dressing by yanking on her sweater. 'When will you call Maureen?'

'Monday.' He sat on the bed to lace up his boots. 'I'd rather not take the risk that Stan will be home, which is more likely on the weekend.'

'Makes sense,' she said as she watched him. 'Dare we reveal that Vanessa believes she's seen someone resembling Jasper's age-enhanced photo at the 7-Eleven near where she works?'

'Definitely not.'

'That might help convince her that he's still active, still killing.'

He switched to the other foot. 'But she could mention it to Jasper, and then he'll never go there again. We can't *count* on her help; we can only hope for it.'

Evelyn bent to pull on her sheepskin-lined boots. 'If he's living in that area, or she knows he works in that area, it might be enough to build her doubt.'

'It'll be especially damaging if he lives in Peoria and works in Casa Grande or has some other connection to both cities,' he mused.

She combed her fingers through the tangles in her hair. 'I don't have a comb in my purse. Do I look okay?'

He chuckled as he walked over to smooth a lock of hair out of her face. 'You look fine.'

'If that's true, why are you laughing?'

'Because you also look thoroughly . . .'

'Ravished?'

'That would be the less vulgar way to put it. Looking at you, it's obvious what we've been doing.'

'Then we can't go see your father!'

'I'm sure my father knows we're sleeping together. You live with me, remember?' He winked at her. 'But just to be nice, I'll get a brush out of my luggage.'

'You're *so* generous.'

'Don't say I never did anything for you.'

She picked up the phone.

'Who're you calling?'

'I'm checking my voice mail. Do you need to do it, too?'

'No, I'll check from my dad's.'

'This is so archaic,' she grumbled.

'What? No cell coverage? They have cell service here in Anchorage.'

'Little good it does me since I no longer have a phone.' And why would she buy one? She rarely came to Anchorage.

'I think your iPhone has been harder for you to give up than association with your family,' he said wryly.

'You sound surprised, but I can't argue with that. Other than Brianne, who's awesome, my family makes my life more difficult. A smart phone would make it a lot easier, if only there was service in Hilltop.'

'Might be a hassle to be tied to landlines at home, but at least we aren't walking around staring at electronic devices instead of each other.'

'True,' she allowed. 'Anyway, you don't have to worry. After the past two hours, I don't feel like complaining about anything.'

He came up behind her and hauled her against him. 'Good. We'll have to take the time to make love like this more often.'

She didn't have the chance to respond. Her voice mail had picked up. She had to listen if she didn't want to miss her messages.

Evelyn, this is Charlotte. I appreciate you offering me your number. That was – that was nice. Still, I hate to bother you. You must be busy. And I'm probably just being paranoid. But it feels as if someone's been watching my house, watching me. *Whenever I go anywhere, I keep glancing into the rearview mirror. To be honest, I haven't spotted anyone or anything I could call the police about. It's that this terrible feeling won't go away. I was hoping you might . . . I don't know, give me someone to talk to about my fear. Anyway, it's the weekend, so maybe you're not available. Just call me when you get in, if you don't mind. I was able to download that file you sent – the age-enhanced photo of Jasper? If he really looks like that, he's still handsome as the devil. And that makes him even more dangerous, doesn't it? What woman* wouldn't *go home with him?*

She left her number, which Evelyn jotted on the hotel pad near the phone before moving on to her next message.

Evelyn, I don't understand why you won't call me back.

Fitzpatrick. Making a sound of irritation, she reached for the delete button, but the message was short enough to play out before she could push it. *Jasper's back in Boston. We could catch him, if only you'd work with me.*

'What's wrong?' Amarok asked, concerned by her reaction.

'Fitzpatrick keeps calling me on the Boston murder. Wants to be involved.'

'In what way?'

'He mentioned coming to Alaska to evaluate Bishop. I'm assuming he'd also like to develop a psychological profile of the killer so we can prove that it matches Jasper's profile, and try to guess who his next victim will be.'

'Can't he call Boston PD and offer his services?'

'I doubt they'd talk to him without me paving the way. They know me, not him.'

Amarok asked another question, but the next message stole her attention. Although the voice was somewhat familiar, it was also childlike, which baffled her. *Who is this?* Telling Amarok to hang on for a second, she hit the replay button.

Hello? . . . Is my brother there?

There was a long pause, as if the caller expected an answer, didn't understand how voice mail worked.

I have this number. Who is it? . . . Lyman? Who's going to take care of me?

She hung up before giving her name, but Evelyn knew it was Beth Bishop. She must've figured out how to call the numbers in her phone history. Was she going through them, searching for her brother? Maybe Louise Belgrath, the social worker Evelyn had been in contact with, had helped Beth call in hopes that she could talk to Lyman . . .

The rest of Evelyn's messages were from the other psych team members. Preston Schmidt told her he couldn't make the staff meeting Monday morning. Jim asked if she'd be willing to come in today or tomorrow to finally get to those brain-imaging comparisons.

Normally, she would've been there working overtime whether he joined her or not. But now . . . she wasn't willing to give up her weekend with Amarok.

'What's Fitzpatrick's number?' Amarok asked when she put down the phone.

'Don't call him,' she said. 'Ignoring him should work – eventually.'

'Doesn't sound like it's worked so far. I'm all for making his boundaries a bit clearer.'

'Don't say anything inflammatory, Amarok. I don't want him coming after *you*.'

'Coming after me?'

'I know. Not everyone's a killer.'

'Just most of the people *you* work with.'

They were already back to the subject of her work, which he didn't like. But perhaps he had a point: her view could get skewed. Why not let Amarok speak to Fitzpatrick? Maybe he could get him to leave her alone.

After giving Amarok the number, she sat on the bed while he dialed.

'Dr Fitzpatrick?' she heard him say. 'This is Sergeant Murphy from Hilltop . . . Calm down; she's fine . . . No, nothing's happened to her . . . Yes, we're aware of the possibility . . . I'm working on it . . . We'll catch him . . . I appreciate the fact that you'd like to help, but Evelyn doesn't want anything to do with you . . . It's not about holding a grudge; it's about moving on. I'm sure you can understand that . . . This isn't one of those instances . . . I'll take care of her. Just proceed with your life and let her proceed with hers, okay?'

When he hung up, Evelyn let her breath seep out in a long sigh. 'What'd he say?'

'That this is no time to let your feelings over last year get in the way. That he has a great deal more experience than you do. That you should take advantage of his knowledge and expertise – and other such bullshit.'

'He agreed to let it go, though?'

'I didn't give him a choice. You ready?'

She stood up, but the memory of Beth's bewildered voice made her stop. 'I have to make one call.'

'To who?'

'Someone who's a bit lost.'

Amarok leaned against the wall to wait as the phone began to ring. Evelyn was willing to bet Beth was right there, listening to it, but was too scared to pick up. She was scared of everything now that she didn't have her brother in her life. Louise Belgrath, from the Minnesota Department of Human Services, had had great difficulty getting Beth to open the door.

'No one home?' Amarok asked.

Evelyn had opened her mouth to reply to him when she heard a soft, 'Hello?'

Yes! Bishop's sister had found the courage! 'Beth? This is Dr Talbot. Do you remember me?'

'No.'

'We spoke a few days ago. I'm in Alaska, with your brother.'

'You are?' Relief. Desperation. 'Can I talk to Lyman?'

'He's not with me right this second. I just wanted to let you know that he'll be coming home. You have nothing to worry about.'

'Tonight?' She sounded desperate.

'Not tonight, but it could be as soon as a week or two. Can you make it that long?'

'Will he bring donuts?'

'I hope so.'

'Tell him I'll take off my clothes. I'm taking them off right now.'

Evelyn stiffened. 'Why are you doing that?'

'So I'm ready.'

'For what?'

'To suck on his tummy banana. And I won't cry this time. Tell him I won't cry even if it chokes me.'

Tummy banana? Evelyn had never heard a penis described in that way, but what else could Beth be talking about?

'Hello?' Beth said when Evelyn didn't, couldn't, respond. 'Did you hear me? Tell him I'll swallow it all, and I won't cry.'

Nauseated, Evelyn put a hand to her stomach. 'You don't have to take off your clothes.'

'But he'll be mad if I don't!'

Evelyn squeezed her eyes closed. 'He puts his . . . tummy banana in your mouth?'

Silence.

'Does he put it anywhere else, Beth?'

Spooked – probably because of the somber tone of Evelyn's voice – Lyman's sister began to backpedal. 'No. N-never mind. I can't . . . I can't say that. I'm not supposed to say that. Please don't tell him. He'll be so mad!'

'And what does he do when he's mad?'

She began to cry.

'It's okay, Beth. You can tell me. He's told me a few things already,' Evelyn lied.

With a loud sniff, she stopped crying. 'He has?'

'Yes. He told me he hurts you with his tummy banana. And you don't like it.'

'Because it chokes me,' she said, almost with a whimper. 'And if I cry, he pulls my hair and hits my head. *Bam, bam. Deeper, Beth. Suck it, damn it. Suck it like it's the best damn lollipop you ever had.*'

Bile rose in the back of Evelyn's throat. What had Lyman Bishop done to his poor sister? He'd had her with him – without anyone following up – for so long. Detective Gustavson had crossed a line he should never have crossed, but if he hadn't fabricated that evidence Beth would've remained in Lyman's control, possibly indefinitely.

'What is it?' Amarok murmured.

She waved him off. 'What if Lyman never comes home, Beth?'

'He *has* to come home. Who's gonna take care of me?'

The devil she knew was better than the devil she didn't. Evelyn had seen that idiom in action so many times. She could've spent an entire career studying Stockholm syndrome alone. Beth had formed an attachment to her abuser, beyond the familial one, regardless of the pain he caused her. She probably believed she *deserved* the pain or provoked him with bad behavior. 'Someone from the state brought you groceries, didn't they?'

'Someone from *where*?'

'A lady – a lady came to your house with some food.'

'I remember.' She sounded guilty as she continued, 'Don't tell her, but I ate all the Oreos.'

'I won't say a word. And do you know why?'

'No . . .'

'Because you can trust me.'

'I can?'

'Yes. I was just thinking that maybe she and I could find somewhere else for you to live. Would you like that, Beth? Would you like to live with someone who is kind and would never choke you or hit you or do anything else that hurts?'

Amarok sat down next to her and took her hand.

'Will I get Oreos?' Beth asked. 'And can I watch TV?'

'Of course.'

Evelyn still expected her to refuse. People who'd been abused for so long, especially by a family member, had a difficult time believing life could be any better. They were too dependent on their abuser. So it surprised Evelyn when Beth said, 'Okay. Just don't tell Lyman what I said.'

'Or . . .'

'I don't want to say. *That's what you get if you can't quit crying!*'

Evelyn squeezed Amarok's hand for strength and reassurance. 'I won't tell Lyman. I promise.'

'Do I get my Oreos now?' Beth asked.

'No, but you will get them soon,' Evelyn promised. 'Very soon.'

When Evelyn hung up, Amarok brought her hand to his lips. 'You okay?'

'I have to get Beth away from her brother. She can't be living with him in that house after he gets out.'

'I heard enough to understand why. That's twisted beyond belief.'

She thought of Lyman's reaction to her question about Beth's being his first lobotomy and felt vindicated. He'd taken his sister's mind and, with it, her ability to resist or escape. It was little wonder that he'd use the same technique on other victims. Why not, if it had worked so well with his sister?

'I'm sure we don't know the half of it.'

She allowed Amarok to pull her head to his shoulder and breathed deeply, filling her nostrils with the unique scent of the man she loved. Life was so much easier with him standing beside her. But she couldn't be sure he'd always be there. Part of her insisted she'd be a fool to allow herself to depend on him – to depend on anyone.

Although Evelyn called Louise Belgrath, Beth Bishop's social worker, as soon as she and Amarok returned home from Amarok's father's house, Louise didn't pick up and she didn't return the call. It wasn't until Monday, when Evelyn was waiting for the lunch she'd asked one of the kitchen workers to deliver to her desk, that she finally got the chance to speak to Louise. Then she was glad to have had the conversation, but she knew it, in and of itself, was merely a starting point. Louise did agree to go out and interview Beth using more pointed questions than those she'd raised in their initial meeting – which, like Evelyn's first call with Beth, hadn't turned up anything. Louise also agreed to make sure Beth saw a doctor to check for evidence of physical abuse. If Bishop *was* mistreating his sister, as Evelyn now firmly believed, they needed to put together a case to prove it.

Problem was Bishop hadn't had access to his sister in some time. If there were scars or other signs of trauma, he could say they came from when she'd been in that institution. Unless it was obvious the wounds were recent or rather shocking, chances were the state wouldn't spend the kind of money required to perform an MRI, which was the only way to prove that he'd performed a lobotomy. Other than two black eyes, which healed quickly, the transorbital lobotomy left no scars, and it would be almost impossible to remove Beth from Lyman's control without proof that she was in danger. It wasn't as if they could rely on Beth's testimony. She could recant the whole 'tummy banana' story as soon as she realized that she'd gotten him in 'trouble'.

Still, Evelyn was determined that Beth would not be living with Lyman Bishop after he was released. If they could prove he'd caused her harm or injury, he could be prosecuted criminally, could even be locked up again, if only for a few years. Getting more than five to ten would be difficult, but at least they now had a loose thread they could tug and hope for the best.

In another week or two I'll walk free, and you won't be able to do anything to stop that! he'd shouted at the end of the polygraph.

'We'll see,' she muttered, and dialed Charlotte Zimmerman, whom she'd also had difficulty reaching over the weekend.

'Charlotte?' Evelyn spoke as soon as she heard someone say hello.

'Yes?'

'It's Evelyn Talbot.'

'I saw your name come up on caller ID. How nice to hear from you. I got your message. I would've called you back, but I haven't been home. I had my mother-in-law watch the kids so that my husband and I could get away for a couple of days. I couldn't stay in Boston. Couldn't go on with life as usual.'

'I understand. Fear can be debilitating.'

'And yet you've lived with it for twenty years.'

'I'll be glad when Jasper's caught.'

'Will that ever happen?'

'I have to maintain some hope.' As she'd proven to Amarok on various occasions, some times that was easier than others.

'Of course.'

They chitchatted about old times and caught up a little. Then Evelyn launched into what she'd really called to say. 'In the message you left on my voice mail, you mentioned feeling uncomfortable, as if you were being watched.'

'Maybe it's just my imagination. That's what my husband believes.'

'Have you ever felt this way before?'

'No. I've always felt safe and secure. But someone's been calling the house – and hanging up the second I answer. That's never happened before, either, not so consistently.'

'Have you told the police? Maybe they can check your phone records, see where that call has been coming from.'

'I've called them. The person I spoke to said someone will get back to me. But I haven't heard from anyone since. I got the impression my complaint wasn't much of a priority. They're too busy investigating violent gangs, kidnapping and murder to mess with the small stuff.'

Although Evelyn was hesitant to say it, murder often started with stalking, and calls like the ones Charlotte had described could certainly be evidence of unwanted and undue attention. That sixth sense that made her uncomfortable could be telling her something. 'Make them take you seriously. Demand they do something. Tell them you were a classmate of the girls who were murdered twenty-one years ago – and Mandy, who was murdered more recently. That you're afraid you might be targeted next.'

'I *tried* to explain that, but the person I was speaking to seemed to feel as if I was being paranoid. Maybe the detective who calls me back will be more concerned.'

'I hope so.'

'Me, too. I sure wish it was summer. I'd take the family and go to California, somewhere far away from here.'

'I'd do it anyway, if it's at all possible.'

'I can't. The kids are in school. They have sports besides. And even if I could get off work, my husband couldn't, not for more than a few days. I'd have to leave him behind if I planned to stay longer than a regular vacation.'

'Then find out who's making those calls, okay? I'll feel better once we know.'

'Can *you* contact the Boston PD?' she asked. 'Maybe they'll listen to you.'

'I've already left a message for Miles Dressler, the detective on my case, to give him a heads-up. Hopefully it'll help.'

'Thank you. I can't tell you how grateful I am.'

'It's the least I can do. We have to band together to stop someone like Jasper.'

'I agree.'

Penny came to the door as Evelyn was hanging up. 'Sergeant Amarok's on line two.'

'Thank you.' She pressed the blinking light. 'Hi there. How's your day going?' she asked.

'I just tried to call Maureen Moore,' he replied.

Evelyn tensed at the edge in his voice. He was upset; she could tell. 'She wouldn't speak to you?'

'She *couldn't* speak to me.'

'Why?'

'An officer from San Diego PD called me back.'

Evelyn gripped the edge of the desk with her free hand. 'Because . . .'

'They're monitoring all the calls coming in on that number.'

'They got the warrant, after all? They're trying to catch Jasper?'

'They may not realize that's who they're looking for, but he's got to be responsible.'

'For . . .'

'Stan and Maureen have been murdered, Evelyn – and the house was torched afterwards.'

Eighteen

When the phone went silent, Amarok could sense Evelyn's reaction and cursed under his breath. No matter what they did, Jasper was always one step ahead of them. Every time he and Evelyn, or the police for that matter, had any kind of lead, Jasper did something to throw them off his trail, to send them back to square one.

This setback, in particular, hurt. Amarok had been so hopeful. For the first time since he'd met Evelyn, he'd believed the end of that era of her life might be in sight, that soon Jasper would no longer hover over every decision she made. They'd had sex without a condom yesterday, for crying out loud. They wanted a *baby.*

Then this . . .

Now he understood why Evelyn was so wary of letting the hope that'd taken such deep root in him carry her too high. What if Jasper showed up in Hilltop? What if he came when Amarok was out dealing with something else – a hunting accident miles from town? If that happened, he could come home to discover the kind of scene the police officer from San Diego had just described to him.

He closed his eyes against the image *that* conjured in his head – of finding his bungalow nearly burned to the ground with Evelyn's body, Makita's and Sigmund's, maybe even his own child's, inside. 'Bastard,' he muttered.

'He murdered his own parents?' she said, as if she still had the power to be surprised. 'Turned on the very hands that had and probably were still feeding him – money and whatever documents he needed to move around and gain a new identity? If that doesn't show you the extreme narcissism we're dealing with, nothing will.'

Amarok carefully arranged the stapler, in-box, penholder and letter opener on his desk. 'I feel responsible,' he said, sharing the chest-crushing guilt that had descended on him almost instantly. 'If I'd never gone there, never spoken to Maureen, I have no doubt she and her husband would be alive.'

'You don't know that, Amarok,' Evelyn argued. 'Anyone close to a psychopath, especially one as wily and ruthless as Jasper, has reason to fear. It's entirely possible you had nothing to do with it.'

He wanted to believe her, so he said, 'He emptied his mother's purse.'

'There you go. Maybe he went there and they refused to give him any more money, because I'm sure they've given him plenty in the past. There's no way he could've gotten by, not in the beginning, without their help.'

But the timing indicated it wasn't about the money. Maureen had been about to do the right thing, to finally open up about her son. Amarok could feel it. And he'd been the impetus to that. Jasper must've figured out what was at stake, must've felt the same conflict inside his mother Amarok had sensed. So Jasper took steps to eliminate the threat she and her husband posed. And, just like that, two more people were dead.

'He wouldn't even have been out and capable of murdering them – or anyone else – if they hadn't helped him get away in the first place,' Evelyn said. '*They* are to blame, not you. But I'm sorry, Amarok. Your life was so much simpler before I came into it.'

'Don't start with that.' He wondered if she was thinking about yesterday, too – if she was regretting letting him come inside her. 'I'm not giving up. I'll get him.'

'I know you will, but you must be sickened and . . . and

disappointed. It might even be tempting to blame me for all the . . . "dark shit" that's come into your life. I'll take responsibility for that. I worry about how it will affect you all the time, feel bad that loving me involves you in something that never would've touched your life otherwise. I've often told you you'd be better off without me—'

'Stop.'

'Okay, but let me say I didn't ask for this fight. He brought it to me, when I was only sixteen. I had no defenses, nothing with which to protect my heart or my body. This situation is sort of like . . . I don't know . . . Hitler, I guess. The world didn't ask for Hitler to do what he did, either. But he had to be stopped, even though it required so many lives, so much loss and sacrifice. So you see? I have no choice. I *have* to fight back. What Jasper has done and is doing has consumed most of my life. I've sustained wounds that may never heal and scars that will never go away. And yet I won't back down. I won't cower in the corner and hope someone else steps in to do the dirty work, won't give way beneath the evil onslaught of what he and others like him do. Nothing will ever convince me to do that. I'd rather face him again and die than let him go on unopposed.'

Amarok swallowed a sigh as he scratched his head. She was an extraordinary woman. Maybe that was why he loved her so much, why he couldn't seem to love anyone else. But he understood what she was telling him. Caring for her would always be a risk. They'd probably never be able to establish the kind of life he dreamed about. 'I know. And I'm standing right beside you.'

'That's the thing. You don't have to stand there. *I* have no choice. But *you* do. It's not too late. I suggest you think about . . . us. Think about how long Jasper, and my work, might impact our lives and our relationship – what it could mean if . . . if we ever have a family together.'

Resting his head on the back of his chair, he stared up at the ceiling. She was so sure he couldn't hack it in the end, she kept warning him off.

'You have so much to offer,' she said. 'You could have anyone.'

'I'd rather not hear that right now,' he said, and hung up. Then he yelled, 'Damn it!' and swiped all the things he'd just arranged off his desk.

'Why are you wasting your time with me?'

Meeting with Lyman Bishop on the heels of learning about the murders of Maureen and Stan Moore required fortitude. Given the fact that she was already upset, Evelyn wasn't eager to confront the extreme emotions he evoked. But what she'd learned from Beth gave her no choice. She had to do something – everything she could to help that woman – while she had the chance. Once Bishop was released, she would have no more access to him, no more opportunity to get him on tape. While he was here, however, if she could push him in the right way he might provide her with something revealing, a comment or an expression that could one day be played before the jury at his trial.

'I just spoke with your sister.'

He said nothing, but he no longer bothered to pretend he was the cowed, soft-spoken, innocent scientist, no longer bothered to put up the façade behind which he hid from others. That polygraph test had crushed any hope he had of fooling her, and he knew it. But the people he encountered in his regular life had no reason to look close. She had no doubt he'd go back to what had worked for him before.

'She had some interesting things to say,' Evelyn continued.

'She doesn't make sense half the time,' he responded. 'Nothing she tells you can be taken seriously.'

'Even if it involves your "tummy banana"?'

A muscle ticked in his cheek, but, other than that, Evelyn could see no sign of distress. He was hanging on to the news that he'd soon be released, believed he had everything under control despite what *she* thought of him. 'What's a tummy banana?'

'Even if you didn't already know, you should be able to figure that out.'

He gestured dismissively. 'Not necessarily. Beth's full of inane chatter. That's all she's capable of.'

'Since the lobotomy, you mean.'

That tic in his cheek grew more pronounced. His pupils narrowed, too – filled with hate. 'I have nothing to say to you. I want to go back to my cell.'

'You'll go back when I say,' she responded. '*I'm* in charge here. Not you.'

'And you claim psychopaths like control . . .' he muttered under his breath.

'Are you contradicting me?'

'*You're* the psychiatrist. *You're* the one who's done the studies,' he replied with a shrug.

'Isn't that what the lobotomies were about, Dr Bishop? Power and control? Creating the perfect victim? Someone who could never leave you? More women, like Beth, who have no ability to argue or fight – or even tell on you?'

He gazed at her from beneath half-lowered eyelids. 'I wouldn't know. I've never performed a lobotomy.'

'And, despite what your sister told me on Saturday, you've never forced her to perform fellatio on you?'

'Of course not. That's disgusting,' he replied, but she could tell he didn't find it disgusting at all. What he found disgusting was the fact that she'd dare question him on it. That she'd dare interfere in his relationship with his sister, whom he felt he 'owned'.

'I suppose you've never banged her head into the wall or tied her up, either.'

He blinked at her, seemingly untroubled. 'Why are you out to get me? I've never done anything to you.'

'That may be true. But you don't have to do anything to me. I stand up for all victims, especially those who can't stand up for themselves.'

His chains rattled as he shifted to cross his legs. 'I suggest you mind your own business.'

'That would make life easier for you, wouldn't it?'

'It might make life easier for you, too,' he mumbled, but he was shifting again and spoke so low Evelyn could barely make out the words.

'Excuse me? Was that some sort of threat?'

'A few words to the wise.'

She folded her arms as she studied him. 'I'm having a doctor look at your sister. I hope, for your sake, she has no scars or other injuries.'

'Even if she does, you won't be able to prove she got them from me.' He came to his feet. 'And, like I told you before, you can't rely on her testimony. So why waste your time? It'll only drive you crazy, thinking she's some unfortunate I'm using for my own pleasure when you can't do anything about it.'

Evelyn straightened her spine. 'Seems you've thought of everything. But if you've been abusing her, I'll prove it. And I'll make sure you never get the chance to hurt her again.'

He approached the glass. *'Stay out of my life, Evelyn.'*

'Or . . .'

His eyes seemed to bore into hers. 'I think you already know . . .'

'Why don't you spell it out for me?' She needed him to reveal himself on tape, to show his true nature as much and as many times as she could get him to do it.

A half smile curved his thin lips. 'You wouldn't want to provoke the wrong person.'

She got up and crossed over to the plexiglass, stopping when they had only that between them. 'After what I've been through, *you* don't scare me.'

He didn't come back at her, didn't lose control or outright threaten her, as she hoped he would. He glared at her, remaining mute no matter the challenge she tossed out, no matter how many times she asked him what he'd done to his sister – and his mother. His eyes gave away everything *he* wouldn't, but how could she ever sell that to the police, or a jury?

Those flat, cold eyes. She recognized them, had seen similar 'dead' eyes when she was being tortured in that shack by Jasper . . .

Finally, she stopped talking. They remained locked in a silent power struggle for several long minutes – until she chuckled as if he were some kind of joke and pressed the button that would call the COs.

After they took him away, she stopped the recording and sank into her seat, glad that she had a few moments to herself. She couldn't have dealt with any inconsequential conversation right now, couldn't have continued to hide how upset she was.

She'd riled Bishop up, all right. But she was afraid nothing good would come from it.

Charlotte Zimmerman Pine didn't like being out after dark. Ever since Mandy had died and Evelyn Talbot had contacted her to warn her that she could be in danger, she felt as if she had a target painted on her forehead. She'd read the true crime book a man named Daniel Piedmont had written about Evelyn's experience, would never forget some of the chilling details he'd related about the torture she had endured – and how much Jasper had enjoyed inflicting that pain. Charlotte found it difficult to believe the boy she'd flirted with in biology class could be the person Piedmont had described, but there was too much proof to deny it. Jasper had committed three murders besides what he'd done to Evelyn, and he'd disappeared right after.

Was he the one who'd killed Mandy? Would he come after *her* next? She thought of Evelyn in that shack, watching her best friends decompose in the heat while knowing Jasper would be back to rape and torture her again as soon as he got out of school . . .

Gripping the steering wheel with both hands, she turned out of the neighborhood. She couldn't imagine going through what Evelyn had been through, knew she wouldn't have held up nearly so well. Dealing with the regular ups and downs of life proved difficult for her. She'd been on antidepressants and anti-anxiety drugs ever since she'd landed her first high-pressure job, with a law firm, right out of college. She wouldn't risk going anywhere tonight, except her friend – another paralegal in the firm where she worked, who was also a single mother and new to the area, with no friends or family – had a sick kid she needed to take to the emergency room and she'd asked Charlotte to stay with the baby. How Charlotte was going to get through the night if that hospital visit took very long she didn't know. She was terrified to be alone, especially in a strange house.

But she couldn't let her husband join her, as he'd offered. She preferred he stay with their own kids. Although they were old enough to stay alone, she didn't want to risk anything happening to *them.* And she kept telling herself that she'd be safe, too. If she was at someone else's house, how would Jasper ever find her?

That was how she'd felt *before* leaving the house. But only a block away, her eyes flicked, time and again, to the rearview mirror. That terrible feeling was back – the creepy sensation that she was being followed.

Was it merely apprehension, getting the best of her?

When she came to a stop at the first light, she glanced down at her cell phone, which she'd pulled from her purse and placed on the console between the seats for easy access. She had no good reason to call and alarm her husband. She hadn't seen anyone who looked like Jasper – no one who looked remotely dangerous or was acting suspicious.

Still, she picked up her phone and cradled it in her lap to keep it even closer.

There was a blue minivan behind her. Had she seen it before? Driving down her street?

It seemed she had, but she couldn't be sure. There were so many blue minivans in Boston . . .

Quit freaking yourself out. If she wasn't careful, she'd fall into a full-blown panic attack, and she couldn't let that happen. Maxine needed her. Besides, Evelyn had admitted that there might not be any danger. *I'm just being a big baby – jumping at shadows . . .*

The light turned green. With a final glance at the driver of that minivan, Charlotte gave her Acura some gas and tried not to let her fear grow beyond her ability to rein it in. The minivan turned off before she reached the entrance to the freeway, which made her feel more comfortable. That meant, even if she had seen it before, it didn't matter, because that minivan wasn't following her.

Her husband called as she took the entrance ramp. 'You there yet?'

She adjusted her Bluetooth as she accelerated. 'Not quite. GPS says I have ten minutes. What's going on?'

'I thought you might want to talk while you drive. Thought it might calm your nerves.'

Hearing his voice helped. So much that she forgot about watching her rearview mirror. She began to feel more and more like herself as they discussed whether or not he'd get a raise from the accountant he worked for, what their daughter needed to purchase for her art project at school and if they should allow their son to go with a friend and his family to Disney World over spring break. Before she knew it she'd reached Maxine's house and was parking at the curb.

'I'm here,' she told him with a sigh of relief.

'Good. Should we keep talking?'

'Not now. Let me greet Maxine and help her get on her way to the hospital. Then I'll call you.'

'I'll be here.'

She hit the disconnect button, gathered her purse and climbed out. With her attention solely on reaching the front door as quickly as possible, so she wouldn't hold Maxine up, she almost didn't see the van. She was about to step onto the porch to knock when a flash of blue in her peripheral vision caused her to turn as it rolled slowly down the street.

Was that the same vehicle that'd been behind her when she left her house? The one she thought had turned off?

Couldn't be, she told herself. As she'd acknowledged before, there were a lot of blue vans in Boston. She watched it disappear around the corner, then paused before knocking to see if it might come by again, but she didn't get the chance to wait very long. Maxine, her twentysomething face too young to be as pinched and tired looking as it was, opened the door.

'Saw you pull up,' she explained. 'Thanks for coming.'

Charlotte yanked her gaze away from the end of the street, where she'd been watching to see if that van reappeared. 'No problem. Is there anything I should know? It's been a while since I had a baby in the house.'

'I made a bottle and put it in the fridge, in case Ariel wakes up.

But she's nearly a year old now, so that shouldn't happen. She typically sleeps through the night.'

Sympathy welled up as Maxine bent to pick up her three-year-old boy. He was in footie pajamas and his cheeks were flushed with fever. 'How's he doing?'

'Not so good. I'll feel better when he's seen a doctor.'

Charlotte took the heavy bag that kept falling off Maxine's shoulder and gathered the boy's blanket and a stuffed animal he was crying to take along and helped get everything into the beat-up Ford Escort that was Maxine's only vehicle. 'I hope he's going to be okay.'

'Me, too.' Maxine got behind the wheel and put the key in the ignition.

'Call me when you learn what's wrong,' Charlotte said.

'I will. I really appreciate you coming, especially on such short notice. I don't know what I would've done if—'

Her voice wavered, telling Charlotte she was close to tears. The strain of her recent divorce, the move, her son's sickness – it was all taking a toll. Because of that, Charlotte didn't dare mention that she had her own worries. 'It's nothing,' she broke in. 'I'll make sure everything's okay here. Don't worry for a second. Just take your time and do whatever you need to do.'

With a grateful smile and a quick nod, she started the engine and backed down the drive.

Charlotte watched her go. Then she checked one end of the street as well as the other. No van.

Thank goodness.

Hurrying into the house, she closed and locked the door before peeking in on the baby. Ariel seemed to be sleeping soundly, so Charlotte went back to the living room and called her husband.

'Maxine's off to the hospital.'

'That's good. How's her son?'

'He's definitely ill. I hope it's nothing serious.'

'So do I.' They chatted as she wandered around the house, trying to familiarize herself with the layout. But they didn't get to talk for long. After a few minutes he had to help their daughter with homework, so Charlotte told him to check in with her later and turned on the television.

Maxine didn't have cable or satellite. She probably couldn't afford the expense, so there wasn't much to choose from. Even if there'd been a better selection of programs to watch, Charlotte wasn't sure she would've been able to completely relax. She kept getting up to peer out the window, looking for that blue van.

She didn't see it, but about thirty minutes later a thump at the back of the house made her catch and hold her breath.

What was that?

She was just creeping down the hall, trying to figure out the source of that noise – to make sure the baby hadn't tried to climb out of her crib and fallen to the floor – when the sound of breaking glass nearly turned her knees to water. The fear that swept through her was so arresting, so debilitating, she had to grab on to the walls to keep from sinking to the carpet.

Her phone! She was digging it out of her pocket when the baby started to cry.

It was too late to call anyone. She needed to get out of the house. Right away. But she couldn't leave Ariel behind.

Somehow Charlotte found the strength to remain upright and moving. She burst into the child's room to find Ariel standing up, hanging on to the slats of the crib with one chubby hand while rubbing her eyes with the other. She cried even harder when she saw Charlotte, whom she didn't recognize, but Charlotte didn't hesitate. She scooped the child out of her bed and turned to run.

But he was on her before she could even get back into the hallway.

Nineteen

That night Evelyn stayed late to help Jim Ricardo make some progress on the brain scans. She felt like she had to mollify him before his frustration boiled over and she ran into staffing problems again. She'd already had to cancel her and Amarok's attendance at his wife's dinner party, since Amarok had been out of town, and Jim hadn't been pleased. He'd been counting on Evelyn's support to help make Annie happy.

Not too long after they got started, however, Annie called, demanding he come home to eat. At that point, he hurried out without so much as a backwards glance. Evelyn was just shutting down her laptop so she could take it with her when Stacy Wilheim, the only other female on the mental health team, poked her head into the room.

'I bumped into someone named Samantha Boyce when I was in town a few minutes ago. Have you met her?'

Refusing to grimace at the name, Evelyn kept her expression neutral. 'I haven't met her, no.' She'd seen her, though – in those pictures in Amarok's attic and in the flesh that one night at the Moosehead.

Stacy came inside and took the seat across the desk. 'You're aware of who she is, though.'

'I am.' Although she'd been trying not to think about Amarok's ex, especially since she'd allowed Amarok to make love to her without any birth control, which made their relationship more serious than it'd been before, she'd be lying if she said the woman hadn't crossed her mind about a thousand times in spite of everything that was going on with Bishop and Jasper and the recently deceased Moores.

'Can't say as I like her,' Stacy said.

Although it wasn't kind to feel any sort of satisfaction at hearing that comment, Evelyn figured, in this type of situation, it was natural. 'Why not?'

'She's *so* damn pushy and assertive! *Too* assertive, in my book.'

'I guess that doesn't come as too much of a surprise. From what I hear, she can hunt and fish as well as any man. That would take a certain level of . . . boldness. Why? Where'd you meet her? Don't tell me you were having a drink at the Moosehead . . .'

'Are you kidding?' she scoffed. 'I wouldn't be caught dead in there. Too many drunken clouts stumble around that place for my taste.'

Stacy had the luxury of having her husband and her dog to keep her company. She was also intrigued by and devoted to their work, and she fell into the demographic that preferred a good TV program before bed to a raging party. Not everyone was so easily satisfied. 'We *are* living in Alaska. There's not a lot for folks to do here during the cold months, except drink away their boredom and wait for spring.'

'The only thing more plentiful than weapons is booze. Far as I'm concerned, that's not a good combination.'

The people in this part of the world were typically far more conservative in their politics than most of her colleagues from the East Coast. 'That's why Amarok has to spend so much of his time there,' she said. 'It's a far different life than the one we knew back in the Lower 48. So where did you meet Samantha? At the Quick Stop?'

'The gas station. I stopped to fill up on my way home. Then I realized I'd left the files I'd been planning to take with me in my office.

So I had to drive back. You never know when another storm's going to roll in. I don't want to get stuck without my work.'

'Did Samantha introduce herself to you or what?'

'Sort of, except the exchange wasn't nearly that polite. Let's say she *engaged* me. Had all kinds of questions about what we're doing here and what we hope to accomplish. Made sure to let me know she doesn't believe our work will amount to a hill of beans, that Hanover House would never have been built if she'd been in the area. Blah, blah, blah.'

Evelyn felt her stomach muscles tighten. 'Did she explain how she would've stopped it?'

'Said she has some sway with the folks around here. That they would've listened to her, banded together and made sure the "damn" thing was built somewhere else.'

Taking a deep breath, Evelyn threaded her fingers together. 'I guess we can be glad she wasn't around then.'

'Samantha asked me about you, too,' Stacy said.

'What about me?'

'She wanted to know how old you are.'

Evelyn curled her fingernails into her palms. 'Did you tell her?'

'No. I said it was none of her business.'

'And she said . . .'

'That you'd have to be a lot older than Amarok to have accomplished all you've accomplished.'

'How nice of her to bring *that* up.'

Stacy's mouth took on a derisive slant. 'See what I mean?'

Amarok insisted the seven years between them didn't bother him, but they bothered *her.* She had enough insecurities, what with trying to overcome her past so she could trust again. She didn't need to add any more doubt into the mix.

Leave it to Samantha to go right for the Achilles' heel of their relationship. 'Did she act like she's expecting to get him back?'

'She acted like that's why she came home – to claim what's "hers".' Stacy gestured toward all the land that lay beyond the window. 'Not just Amarok. She acted like *everything* in Hilltop belonged to her and we're mere interlopers.'

'She may have a point. You plan on going back to Maryland eventually, don't you?'

'I do. When I accepted the job, I committed to five years. I won't stay longer than that. *I* could take it, but my husband couldn't. He's already anxious to go home.'

'Most everyone else will go when their commitment is up, too.'

'I think the question is whether *you're* planning to go back – at least for her.'

Could she abandon her family permanently when her mother was so afraid for her up here? Give up the future she'd always envisioned for herself once she had Hanover House up and running and on stable political ground and settle here permanently?

When she hesitated, Stacy gave her a sympathetic look. 'I can see you're not ready to tackle that question quite yet.'

'No.'

'Then I wish you luck figuring it out. I just wanted to warn you that Samantha might not make your experience here very pleasant – and to tell you not to let her bother you. She can't hold a candle to you, and I'm sure Amarok would know that better than anyone.'

Except Samantha fit in in Hilltop. And that was as important as anything else, wasn't it?

Evelyn offered her colleague a feeble smile. 'Thank you for that.'

With a confident nod, as if she didn't doubt it, Stacy left to get her files and head home.

After she finished packing up her briefcase, Evelyn called Charlotte to see if her old friend was feeling safe and secure this evening or if she'd seen or heard anything that would give them reason to believe there might be trouble.

'Hello?'

The low, raspy male voice that answered *definitely* didn't belong to Charlotte. It didn't sound like a normal human being – was more like something from a horror movie.

'Hello?' Evelyn said. '*Who's this?*'

'Evelyn, I can't tell you how wonderful it is to hear your voice,' came the response. 'When I saw Hanover House come up on caller ID, I couldn't resist answering.'

Her breath caught, and she began to sweat. She couldn't say she recognized whom she was speaking to. He was whispering as well as disguising what he normally sounded like. But something about the way he'd said her name, the familiarity behind it, made her nauseous. And then there was the obvious – why would someone like that be answering her friend's phone? 'Is Charlotte there?' she asked above the rapid *boom-boom-boom* of her own heart.

She heard a low snicker. Then he said, 'I'm afraid she's a bit . . . indisposed at the moment.'

'*Jasper?*' she cried, but he'd already hung up.

Amarok was at the Moosehead. Evelyn saw his truck as she drove home and wanted to stop. She knew he'd expect her to. But she had to get near a phone. She imagined Samantha being there at the bar, too, hoping to reconnect with him and catch up. Even if Evelyn weren't worried sick about Charlotte, she wouldn't want to witness the two of them together. She was already wrestling with jealousy – not because she distrusted Amarok or thought he wanted to get back with his ex, but because she believed he'd be better off with Samantha (or *someone* else, anyone who didn't bear her scars or the responsibility she'd taken on as a consequence of what she'd experienced). Although Amarok didn't give that much consideration when she spoke of it – said he'd catch Jasper eventually – for now, Jasper was still out there and Evelyn feared he'd just killed another one of her friends. After that guy who'd been speaking in such a fake, creepy voice hung up on her, she'd called Charlotte five or six times. No one had picked up. Evelyn had then contacted Boston PD and asked them to go to Charlotte's house.

Makita greeted her enthusiastically as soon as she walked through the door, and she bent to hug him. A mere pat or a scratch wasn't enough. She needed his unconditional love. Sigmund came the moment he heard her, too, and when she was finished rubbing her face in Makita's soft fur she picked up her cat and carried him into the kitchen, where she tried, once again, to reach Charlotte.

She heard her friend's voice telling her to leave a message and wished she had Charlotte's home number or her husband's number. But she didn't. She'd only ever talked to Charlotte on Charlotte's cell phone. For now, her only other option for information was the police, whom she was hesitant to call again. They had to have the chance to do their jobs.

She changed into a pair of leggings and a big sweatshirt of Amarok's, simply because wearing something of his made her feel better – like Makita's hug and her cat purring in her arms. But the minutes continued to tick away and she didn't hear anything from Charlotte or the police.

Finally, she gave in and called Boston PD. The gruff cop who answered told her someone would get back to her, and that was it. She was left waiting and wondering and pacing a hole in the carpet.

After an hour or so, Amarok came home. 'What are you doing here?' he asked as he walked through the door. He was obviously put out that she hadn't joined him at the Moosehead since she went past the bar on the drive from HH, but his glower disappeared the moment he saw the look on her face. 'What is it?'

'I think something's happened to Charlotte,' she replied.

'Your friend from high school.'

She nodded.

He bent to scratch his dog behind the ears. Makita, so excited by the homecoming of his master, was prancing around and whining for attention. 'What makes you say that?' Using a more measured tone, one devoid of the pique that had been there a moment before, Amarok gazed up at her.

'Someone else answered her phone.' She blinked rapidly, trying to stem the emotion, and the memories, that threatened to overwhelm her. 'And I think it was Jasper.'

Forgetting about poor, eager Makita, Amarok slowly stood. 'Did you recognize his voice?'

'Yes. No.' She shook her head. 'I don't know. He was doing this thing so that I couldn't tell what he sounds like. "Hello?"' she croaked in the same scary way.

'Maybe it was her husband – some kind of joke,' Amarok said. But he was merely probing for other possibilities, wasn't serious. What kind of husband would carry out a joke like that when a murderer was on the loose, one who might have reason to target his wife?

'Except she hasn't called me back. And I've tried her about a million times since. All I get is her voice mail.'

'Have you spoken to her husband?'

As she explained the situation, Amarok came over, caught her hand and tugged her to the couch. 'Let's take a second and think this through, okay?'

With a nod, she sat down and tried to focus on the warmth of his hand to help calm her.

'Jasper killed his parents last Wednesday – in San Diego,' he said. 'We know that.'

'We're assuming it was him, yes,' she said.

'Considering the situation, and the way it all played out, it almost has to be him.'

She couldn't argue. 'Probably.'

'Charlotte lives in Boston.'

'So?'

'That's clear across the country.'

'Doesn't mean anything,' she insisted. 'He killed the Moores on Wednesday. That's when the fire was started to hide the crime. Boston's only a five-hour flight from California. He could've gone to Boston on Thursday or Friday. Or maybe he doesn't live in Arizona like we thought. Maybe he lives in Boston and just went home.' Tears filled her eyes despite her attempt to hold them back. Was Charlotte being brutally tortured, as Evelyn had been tortured in high school? Or was this a quick kill, more like what he'd done to his parents? 'I wish I knew if she was okay.'

'How do we find out?' Amarok asked.

'That's the problem. I called the police to report what happened. But we have no way of knowing what's going on until we hear back from them or someone else.'

'The police will update you as soon as they can.'

She dashed a hand across her cheeks. 'Do you know how many friends I've lost, Amarok?'

'Too many.' He pulled her against him before she could communicate where her mind was drifting next: what would she do if she ever lost him because of Jasper?

Envious that she was getting all of Amarok's attention, Makita, who'd followed them to the couch, rested his muzzle in Amarok's lap and stared up at him with those cerulean blue eyes.

Evelyn could feel the muscles in Amarok's chest flex as he stroked his dog while comforting her at the same time. 'Remember when it was difficult for me to let you hold me?' she asked once she'd managed to stifle her tears.

'How could I ever forget? You said you couldn't stand to be "held down",' he said with a chuckle.

She smiled, too. 'I like it now. Now it makes me feel better instead of worse.'

He kissed her on the head. 'See? We've made a lot of progress. And we're not going to let Jasper screw that up.'

'Was Samantha at the Moosehead?' His ex-girlfriend wasn't a subject Evelyn looked forward to discussing, but Samantha was about the only thing that had the power to distract her from the horrible images that came to mind as she worried about Charlotte.

'Yeah.'

Of course. She's probably been dying *to see him.* 'Did she speak to you?'

'For a few minutes.'

'What'd she say?'

'Nothing much.'

'Is she glad to be back?'

'Seemed like it.'

'Did she ask to get together?'

'Said we should do lunch.'

And his ex's efforts to reel him back in had officially begun . . . 'Did you set a date?'

'Not yet. I told her I'd see when you're available.'

She lifted her head. 'No, you didn't . . .'

'Why wouldn't I? She claims she'd like to meet you.'

What Samantha had said to Stacy didn't sound nearly so friendly, but Evelyn didn't repeat that. 'Wouldn't having lunch with both of us be a bit awkward?'

'Not for me,' he said. 'But if you'd rather not, we don't have to go.' He touched the tip of her nose. 'Anyway, why are we even talking about Samantha?'

'Because as unappealing as that topic is to me, it's not murder.'

The phone rang. Feeling as if she might finally get some information, Evelyn leapt off the couch and ran to the counter. But when she saw caller ID, she hesitated.

'Who is it?' Amarok asked.

'My mother.'

'Aren't you going to answer?'

Had Lara just seen a piece on the news related to Charlotte? Or had she received a call from someone who'd heard something through the grapevine? Lara and Grant still lived in the neighborhood where Evelyn had grown up, still socialized with all the same people. It wasn't inconceivable that they'd learn Charlotte's fate before she did.

Amarok came toward her. 'Do you want me to get it?' he asked, but she shook her head and picked up the handset.

'Hello?'

'Evelyn?'

'Yes?'

'It's Mom.'

She'd known that. But she was so afraid of what her mother might say she hadn't shown the usual recognition. 'Sorry, Mom. I was . . . I was preoccupied with something else and . . . Anyway, how are you?'

'Not good.'

Evelyn gripped the phone that much tighter. 'Why not? Is Charlotte okay?'

'*Charlotte?* Charlotte who?'

So her mother *hadn't* been calling for the reason Evelyn had assumed. Still, *something* was wrong. Evelyn could hear it in her voice. 'Never mind. What's the matter?'

'That other psychiatrist – who helped you launch Hanover House?'

'Fitzpatrick?'

'Yeah. The one you didn't really like there at the end?'

Evelyn had good reason for not liking Fitzpatrick, but she hadn't shared that reason with her folks. She'd merely said he was difficult to work with and she was glad when he quit. Her folks worried enough about her being so far away, living in such a harsh climate and working with hundreds of dangerous men. She didn't need to share every other little problem she had. 'What about him?'

'He called tonight.'

Feeling for a bar stool, Evelyn slipped onto the first one her hand encountered. 'Why would he call *you*?'

'Said he was worried about us. Said Jasper was back in Boston and we should leave the area as soon as possible.'

'He stated it that unequivocally?'

'He was adamant.'

Fitzpatrick knew something had happened tonight. He *had* to know, given the timing of his call to her parents and the panic behind it. How had he learned so quickly? The police hadn't even called her back, and she felt she'd be higher on their list than he would.

'Could he be right?' Lara asked.

The last thing Evelyn wanted to do was upset her folks. They'd been through so much. Lara was already on antidepressants to help her cope with it all. Evelyn wasn't convinced her mother could tolerate any more violence. But hearing that scratchy voice on the phone tonight when she'd called Charlotte – the way that man had said her name, almost like a caress – worried Evelyn. 'I'm afraid so,' she replied.

'Then it *was* him that killed Mandy.'

'Probably. And I should tell you that someone murdered his parents a week ago, too.'

'*Someone?*'

'The police aren't certain it was him, which is why I haven't said anything to you.'

Evelyn expected more railing and recriminations, maybe even tears, but after a protracted silence some steel entered her mother's voice. 'It's about damn time.'

'What did you say?' Evelyn cried.

'I don't care if it sounds harsh. They deserved what they got. It's *their* fault we've continued to suffer as we have all these years. Finally, they received a taste of what their son has put us through.'

'I understand how you feel, Mom, but now they won't be around to help us, even if they could. And Amarok thought he was finally getting through to them, which is why we think Jasper killed them. He seems to be on a rampage. There was Mandy, then the Moores, and tonight I learned that he may have killed another of my high school friends.'

'Charlotte,' her mother said, cluing in immediately. 'That's why you asked about her.'

'Yes.'

'When did this happen?'

'Earlier this evening.'

'Oh God . . .'

'I'm sorry, Mom.'

'Will this never end?' she wailed.

Evelyn couldn't help feeling partly responsible for the fact that the battle between her and Jasper continued to wage. Sure, it was Stan and Maureen who'd shielded him from the consequences of his actions twenty-one years ago. But her parents had pleaded with her, many times, to go into a different field, to live a life that wasn't so public. She would almost certainly make more money in private practice than working for the federal government, she wouldn't be interviewed on television for her 'groundbreaking' work and she would be in far less danger. Only she couldn't do it. She'd felt it was her duty to fight back, was so compelled she couldn't do anything else. And, thanks to government funding, she finally had the tools. Knowing that support could ebb and flow made her feel as if she had to take advantage of this opportunity while she could. 'I hope it will.'

'Same old story.'

'I wish things were different.'

'Where will we go?' her mother asked. 'My friends and most of my family are here in Boston. I don't want to leave.'

'You've talked about touring Europe. Maybe it's time you did that.'

'Your father doesn't like to travel. That's why we've never been.'

They'd never been because they didn't want to spend the money. They were too conservative to drop a fortune on something they considered extravagant. But they had the funds. And what better way to spend those funds than keeping themselves safe? 'Surely he'll see the wisdom in this.'

'What about your sister? We can't leave her here.'

'No, of course not. She has to go with you.'

'She has work! I doubt she'll be able to pick up and go on a moment's notice. Not for any length of time. And a week or two won't make much difference. Jasper will just be waiting for us when we get back. We've been hoping for *years* that he'd be caught and it hasn't happened yet.'

Evelyn squeezed her eyes closed. 'I understand your frustration and anger, Mom. Still, we have to do what we have to do. See if Brianne can arrange to be gone for a month.'

'A *month*?'

'Yes. If necessary, you can always stay another few weeks.'

There was a long silence. Then she said, 'One month. Two months. Will it *ever* be safe to come home?'

Not as long as Jasper was out there . . . But Evelyn did what she could to reassure Lara, promising, at the end of their conversation, to call in the morning.

After she hung up, she explained what was going on to Amarok and then she called Fitzpatrick.

Her fellow psychiatrist answered on the first ring. 'Finally!'

Evelyn wished he'd quit inserting himself into her life, even if he was trying to help. 'What's going on? Why'd you call my parents?'

'They're not safe, Evelyn.'

'Because . . .'

'Do I really need to answer that? No one who's close to you is safe. I told you Jasper would strike again. And he has.'

Evelyn heard that scratchy voice in her mind, *Hello . . .* 'You're talking about Charlotte.'

'Yes.'

Bowing her head, she closed her eyes. 'What's happened? How do you know she's been hurt?'

'When I drove past her house tonight—'

'You drove past her house?' she interrupted.

'Yes. I've been doing that every night since . . . since I found a certain picture in your junior yearbook.'

'The picture where I'm making a Homecoming sign with my friends.'

'That's the one. It stood out to you, too?'

'It did.' She'd guessed he'd come across that. 'But why were *you* looking through my high school yearbook, Tim?'

'I was trying to prevent another murder!' he snapped. 'I kept thinking, wondering, if I could stave off another attack. Or, at the very least, get a license plate number or some other piece of information that might lead us to Jasper before he can strike again.'

Tim didn't get that he shouldn't even be thinking of her or of anyone associated with her. He'd always shown more interest than she welcomed. But maybe this time he really was trying to do a good thing, trying to make up for before. 'I'm sorry, I just—'

'This isn't about you and me anymore, Evelyn. We need to put our differences aside and work together to catch Jasper – or more people could be killed.'

'You mean other than Mandy and . . . and Charlotte.'

'Yes.' He made an attempt to sound sorrowful, but he came off more vindicated for having predicted Charlotte's demise. That bothered Evelyn, but she supposed she could see why he'd feel as he did.

Amarok pulled another bar stool over and sat next to her, turning the phone so that he could hear, too.

'How'd you find out?' she asked.

'There was a cop car parked out front of her house with flashers on. I guessed something terrible had happened, so I went to the door. And I was right. The whole house was in upheaval. They'd just been told that . . .'

'Charlotte's dead,' she finished.

'Yes.'

Evelyn felt Amarok's arm go around her. 'How'd it happen? Please tell me it wasn't her children who found her.'

'No. She was stabbed to death, but it didn't happen at home.'

'Then where? And who discovered her body?'

'I'm trying to tell you. Apparently, when a friend couldn't reach her, they called the cops. The cops got hold of her husband, who told them she was babysitting for a work associate. But by the time they could get to that work associate's house, she was dead.'

Evelyn was that 'friend', the one who'd called the cops, but she didn't enlighten him. 'How many kids was she babysitting?'

'Just one. A baby, less than a year old.'

Her breath caught as she came to her feet. She feared the answer to the question that rose to her lips so much, she almost couldn't ask it. 'Please don't tell me he killed the baby, too.'

'No, fortunately, the baby was found next to her body. But she was crying in a puddle of blood. It's not as if he took the time to make sure she'd be safe. He didn't care one way or the other, didn't bother to put her back in her crib or anything.'

'He was in a hurry.' He'd spoken to Evelyn, knew she'd sound the alarm. So he did what he'd gone there to do and got out without allowing himself to be distracted – and without a single thought for the family Charlotte would leave behind or the baby she was watching. As far as he was concerned, nothing mattered except what *he* wanted.

Twenty

I *can't tell you how wonderful it is to hear your voice—*

Evelyn woke in a cold sweat. She'd been dreaming – of that voice on the phone, of babies wallowing in blood, of her own baby being cut from her womb, of finding Amarok crumpled in a heap on the front drive when she got home, his body cold as ice.

Taking measured breaths, she slid her hand over the mattress, relieved when she encountered him and he was plenty warm. His chest lifted and fell in a regular rhythm, which also helped calm her.

Still, she couldn't go back to sleep. She stared, wide-eyed at the oppressive darkness, knowing it would linger long after the clock indicated it was daytime. Alaska had so few hours of sunlight this time of year. She'd been coping with that just fine until last night, but now, suddenly, she hated the pervasive darkness, felt as if she couldn't survive here – as if she had to go back to where the sun made a longer appearance each day.

What time was it, anyway?

Shifting carefully, so she wouldn't wake Amarok, she checked the alarm clock on the nightstand. Three. She'd only slept, in fits and starts, for four hours. But there wasn't any point in continuing to lie in bed. She couldn't go back to sleep, and if she kept tossing she'd disturb Amarok. Why let that happen? *One* of them might as well get some sleep.

Sigmund remained curled up at the foot of the bed, but Makita stirred from where he'd been dozing on the floor as soon as he heard her get up. The tags on his collar jingled as he walked over to investigate. She felt his wet nose on her bare leg before she could pull on a robe to protect against the cold.

'Hi, 'Kita,' she whispered, and let him out of the room with her.

She figured she'd only drive herself mad if she flipped through TV channels or rambled around the place, waiting until it was time to go to work. She preferred not to face Amarok when he got up, anyway, preferred not to have to acknowledge that she'd had a bad night, since it seemed like she always gave him reason to be concerned about her. She couldn't help thinking that Samantha probably wasn't having nightmares, wasn't stirring at this late hour . . .

Once she was showered and dressed, Evelyn took Makita out, shoveled the snow behind her SUV and scraped off her windshield. She hadn't even realized it'd stormed last night, but waking up to more snow than they'd gone to bed with wasn't unusual.

Once she started her SUV and backed out of the drive, she hoped she'd feel some sense of relief that she was at least off on her own and not cooped up at the bungalow, trying so hard to keep from waking Amarok, but she didn't. An isolated, lonely feeling swept over her as her headlights fell on the thick drifts that lined the roadway and the snow-draped buildings of Hilltop. There wasn't another vehicle on the road – just a few parked here and there along the sides as she passed by, all buried in snow. The residents here basically rolled up the streets once the Moosehead closed down, and some nights the tavern closed earlier than others, depending on the weather and how many people were eating or buying booze. There was no such thing as standard operating hours in this little outpost.

The sign for The Shady Lady Motel, where Jennifer Hall had stayed, glowed orange as Evelyn passed it. The sign for Quigley's Quick Stop, several blocks down, glowed white. They were the only businesses this far from Anchorage that even attempted to stay open all night. But it was mid-week *and* mid-winter, so they were deserted, too. Evelyn longed to grab a cup of coffee at the Quick Stop but figured coffee wasn't reason enough to drag Garrett Boyle, the tough old widower who owned the store and lived in the back of it, out of bed to let her in.

'All the conveniences of home.' She missed Boston – and that made her once again consider the possibility that she might be pregnant. Surely she wasn't. Why worry about that on top of everything else?

Once she arrived at Hanover House, the guards were surprised to see her, of course. 'What are you doing here at this time of morning, Doc? . . .' 'Getting an early start on it, huh? . . .' 'Didn't you just leave? . . . Jeez, I know you work hard, but this is ridiculous.'

She responded vaguely to the first few comments and laughed at the last as they checked her through. Then she hurried up to her office. But she didn't stay there. She dropped off her briefcase and made her way over to the prison side of the institution.

She wasn't sure what drew her to Lyman Bishop's cell. She supposed she was paying him a visit because he would soon be gone and she'd no longer have the chance. She still thought she could learn something of value, some way to more effectively combat Jasper. Who better to tell her what one killer might do next than another?

Several of the inmates snored loudly as she made her way down the long corridor. A few others coughed or even talked in their sleep. There was no sound coming from Lyman Bishop's cell, but she stopped there, at D-128, and gazed through the bars, taking in as much as she could in the dim light. It was never totally dark in prison. Darkness was too dangerous.

'Is there something I can do for you?'

Evelyn started when he addressed her. He sounded wide-awake even though she hadn't said anything. She hadn't expected that, was still trying to decide how to respond when he followed up with, 'Evelyn?'

'How'd you know it was me?' she asked. 'That it wasn't a CO doing a routine bed check?' After all, he was lying down and couldn't see her yet.

'Your footsteps have a higher pitch than the heavy boots worn by the guards.'

'I see.'

'I try to remain very aware of my surroundings,' he added. 'I think that's prudent in here. Don't you?'

'I would say so, yes.'

'Do you always haunt the prison at night? Or is there something about *this* night that's particularly troubling for you?'

'Every now and then, I have difficulty sleeping.'

'Ah. Of course you do. As you might've guessed by now, I'm a night owl myself,' he said, but he wasn't a night owl at all, not in the harmless sense that idiom was typically meant. He was a predator. 'What brings you to this side of the facility?'

'You,' she replied.

'*I'm* the one keeping you up at night? I'm flattered. But why? Don't tell me you're worried about Beth.'

'I'm definitely worried about Beth.'

'Have you come here to plead with me to put her in an institution?'

'I haven't. I know you won't give her up. I'm just hoping you'll be honest with me.'

'Why wouldn't I be? I can trust you, right?'

'At least as much as I can trust you,' she replied with an equal amount of sarcasm.

He laughed.

'You're not going to deny that you're my enemy – continue to pretend otherwise?' she asked.

'You said you came here for some honesty. I might be able to afford you a bit of that, since it's only the two of us, with no cameras, no recordings. Having someone to talk to during such a long night is better than sending you away. What's on your mind?'

'Jasper has murdered another one of my high school friends.'

'You thought he'd stop?'

'Killing? No. I'm not quite that naïve. But he's getting bolder. Targeting people who are connected to me personally, even though that removes part of the "random" element that's made it so hard for the police to catch him in the past.'

'He likes to imagine how what he's doing affects you. Knowing he's upsetting you, frightening you, brings him pleasure. That's what makes it fun. The risk doesn't matter in light of the reward.'

She rested her hand against the cold, gritty cinder-block wall. 'I guess not. But . . . what's next?'

'You're the end goal, of course. You don't need me to tell you that. He's just taking his time, enjoying the chase.'

'How will he do it when the time comes? And who else might he hurt in the meantime?'

'I wish I could tell you that,' he said. 'But this isn't the movies.'

From the wry humor in his voice, she guessed he was referring to Jodie Foster's relationship with Hannibal Lecter in *Silence of the Lambs*. 'I understand that. But you've studied Jasper. I know you have. When you were sentenced to Hanover House, you read everything you could find about me and my case.'

She heard movement. Fortunately, he was merely sitting up and didn't walk over to the cell door. He seemed content to give her some space, to have this quiet conversation in the semidark as if he wasn't excited by the thought of getting closer to her. 'How can you be so sure?'

Judging by his reaction, he was curious, maybe even a little impressed. 'You're the kind of man who would educate himself. Like you did with the polygraph.'

'We were just getting along. Let's not bring up that sore subject.'

'You were trying to manipulate me into believing you were innocent. You can't blame me for trying to fight fire with fire.'

'You're right, of course. I did prepare for that polygraph and hoped it would go much . . . smoother. *And* I studied everything about you, including Jasper, as you said.'

'So now you *are* being honest.'

'I am. You're very good at what you do, you know.'

She blinked several times, surprised by the compliment. 'Thank you.'

'The problem is . . . Jasper's even better at what he does. And what he does is kill.'

'That's what I'm afraid of,' she admitted. 'You have no suggestions for how the police might catch him?'

'None. I can only tell you to be on your guard. He'll come for you eventually.'

She shivered as she recalled the nightmare she'd had earlier, where she'd found Amarok dead on the driveway. 'Even *here*? Where he'd stand out?'

'He'll figure out a way to fit in.'

Of course. She'd known he'd follow her to hell if he had to – that there would be a reckoning someday. That was why she'd been so sure he was back last year. 'I'm sorry I disturbed you,' she said, and turned to go.

'Evelyn?'

She hesitated.

'Leave Beth to me,' he murmured.

'And if I don't?'

'You won't have to worry about Jasper.'

She stared into his cell, trying to make out the barely discernible shine of his eyes. 'You've made that threat before.'

'It's not a threat.'

It was a promise . . . 'Your sister has no other defender,' she said. 'That leaves me no choice.'

'Then you'll leave *me* no choice. I hope you realize that.'

A debilitating fear welled up, far more powerful than if he'd been screaming obscenities at her and threatening her life. She heard plenty of that from the men she worked with – an explosion of temper, the result of impotent fury. But the inmates who typically screamed those things weren't about to be let out, where they could act on their threats. Bishop's quiet words carried such conviction. She had no doubt he meant them. And she had so much more to lose these days, so much more than she'd ever had.

Still, she couldn't allow the fear he inspired to get the best of her, couldn't allow Jasper or Bishop or any other psychopath to rule over her, or what was the point of having survived when she was sixteen? Of gaining the education she had to help combat the problem? Of being here, in the middle of nowhere? 'May the best person win,' she said, and walked away.

When Amarok woke up, Evelyn was gone, but he found a note stuck to the coffeemaker: *Took Makita out to go potty so he'd let you sleep in. Hope you got to do that. Talk to you soon. XO*

He hadn't heard her leave, wondered how long ago that was. She'd had a rough couple of weeks. First her friend Mandy had been murdered. Then they'd received news of the double homicide of Maureen and Stanley Moore, which eliminated their best source of information and, along with it, their best hope of finding Jasper. As if that weren't bad enough, last night Charlotte had been stabbed to death. Evelyn had to be feeling she was losing the battle she waged against Jasper. He seemed able to strike at will and take anyone he wanted – in any state. Even her parents and sister could be in danger.

Amarok believed Evelyn would've been much better off moving to some quiet corner of the Lower 48 and going into private practice, like her parents wanted. Maybe then she could've escaped all of this. Until eighteen months ago, Jasper had seemed content to remain in hiding and do his own thing. It was possible he would've looked for her, come after her again, eventually. But the publicity surrounding Hanover House had made that far more likely. Not only did seeing her face on television remind him that she was still living and breathing, the news coverage gave away where she was and what she was doing. Someone like Jasper would view that almost as an invitation.

Amarok hated that Evelyn was so exposed. But if she hadn't made the choices she did – if she hadn't come to Hilltop to get Hanover House off the ground – he never would've met her.

The danger of her work wasn't the only thing bothering him today, anyway. He couldn't help feeling as though he'd let her down. He'd promised her so much, and none of it was coming through. Now that Maureen was gone, he wasn't sure how he'd stop Jasper. He'd never faced a rival or a challenge he couldn't beat – not if he put enough effort into it. But this . . . this had to shake Evelyn's confidence in him and in their future.

Hell, it was undermining his own confidence . . .

With a curse, he crumpled the note, tossed it into the garbage and put on some coffee. It was two hours later in Arizona, nearly nine, so he felt comfortable calling Detective Sims in Peoria. Amarok had just been there on Friday, so Sims hadn't had a lot of time to make progress on that multiple homicide Amarok believed to be Jasper's work, but now, with the possible exception of the attack on Vanessa Lopez in Casa Grande, those killings might be all he had left with which to fulfill the promises he'd made to Evelyn. After how Maureen had reacted when he mentioned where those women were murdered, Amarok was more convinced than ever that Jasper was responsible for those deaths. The fact that he'd gone on such a rampage seemed to confirm it. By contacting the Moores and asking about those women in Peoria, Amarok had rattled Jasper's cage. He'd been getting close, and Jasper hadn't been happy about it.

'Detective Sims here.'

He'd gotten out the milk and cold cereal, so Amarok went to the cupboard for a bowl. 'Sims, it's Sergeant Murphy. I realize it hasn't been—'

'Amarok!' he broke in. 'Glad you called. I have good news for you, was just looking for your card.'

Amarok had taken a spoon from the drawer and started across the kitchen. At this, he froze. He could use some good news. 'I can't tell you how glad I am to hear that. What's up?'

'The pathologist who did the autopsies on the victims here in Peoria sent their fingernail clippings to the lab, and one victim provided a small amount of genetic material that was not her own. They're working on developing a DNA profile.'

'Wow. That *is* hopeful.' Except Boston PD didn't have Jasper's DNA. There'd been a screwup at the lab that was processing Evelyn's rape kit and, somehow, the evidence had been lost. Evelyn believed Jasper's father paid someone to destroy it, but that had never been proven. The loss had been credited to an 'accident'. 'That'll be helpful – if we can ever catch him.'

'It might tell us if the same person who killed my five victims attacked Vanessa Lopez. She fought when he grabbed her, and managed to scratch his arm. Casa Grande PD is trying to get a DNA profile from what was under her nails, too.'

'A match would be great.' Then at least they'd know they were chasing the same guy. 'Did the lab give you any idea *when* they might have a profile?'

'Usually takes thirty to sixty days, but they're rushing this one,' Sims said. 'They understand that we need to stop this guy before he kills again. They told me they should be able to finish the test in a couple of weeks.'

'The sooner the better.'

'Do you know if your man smokes?' Sims asked.

'I have no clue.' According to Evelyn, Jasper hadn't in high school, but that was over twenty years ago. 'Why?'

'We also recovered some cigarette butts not far from the burned-out building. Most have been too damaged by weather to even bother trying to get DNA. But one was knocked under a plastic tarp that was out there along with some other junk, so it's in fairly good shape. We're thinking we might be able to glean some DNA from that, as well. If it matches what we find under those fingernails, we'll not only know that our perp smokes, we'll know the brand. I realize that's not a lot, but every little bit helps.'

'I agree.' Amarok finished crossing over to the table. 'Thanks. I needed to hear this.'

'There should be more,' he said. 'I'll keep you informed.'

Amarok hung up and tried calling Evelyn. No doubt she could use some good news this morning, too. But she didn't pick up. He figured she was in a session or busy with a study. 'Call me when you can,' he said, leaving her a message.

He'd finished eating and was getting up to rinse his dishes when Makita dashed over to the door and began to bark.

'Whoa, settle down,' he told his dog, but he knew someone – or maybe an animal – had to be approaching the house.

A knock confirmed it wasn't an animal.

Although he was surprised to have company so early, he was the only police officer in town, so he was the go-to guy if anything went wrong, from a serious car accident, to a caribou carcass on the road, to someone who couldn't get his or her car out of the snow. But when he swung the door open, he knew this wasn't police business. Samantha stood there.

'Hi.' Wearing a heavy coat, boots and a knit cap, she smiled brightly at him.

He dipped his head. 'What's up?'

She lifted a bag and a 'to-go' coffee with one gloved hand. 'Brought you some donuts and your favorite brew – from The Dinky Diner.'

Her breath misted in the cold air, but he was hesitant to invite her in. 'I've had breakfast,' he said. 'And coffee.'

'So?' She gave him a look of exasperation. 'It won't hurt you to take it.'

He accepted the bag and the cup. 'Thanks. Is there . . . anything else?'

'I missed Makita while I was gone. Was hoping to see him.'

That made sense. She'd always been an animal person, had asked him for Makita when they broke up – not that his dog was something he could give up. Stepping out of the way, he motioned toward the living room. 'Sure. Come on in.'

As soon as she was inside, she removed her gloves and hat, tossed them on the couch and got down on her knees to pet a tail-wagging Makita. 'You missed me, didn't you, boy? You're a lot more excited to see me than your human is.' She tossed Amarok another meaningful glance, but he didn't react to it. He went over and finished rinsing his dishes, giving her the chance to get all she wanted of playing with his dog.

'Looks like he's doing great,' she said as she got to her feet.

'Good thing. I don't know what I'd do if anything ever happened to him.'

'I know. You felt so bad when you broke up with me that you would've given him to me, if you could have.'

'I considered it,' he admitted.

She chuckled. 'I wish you could've loved me that much, Amarok,' she said, sobering. 'And sometimes I wonder if . . . if you'd ever be willing to try again.'

He closed the dishwasher, turned it on and swung around to face her. 'Samantha, you know I'm with someone else.'

'I know you're with someone who can't be a very good match for you.'

Resting his hands on his hips, he scowled at her. 'What's that supposed to mean?'

'Some uppity psychiatrist from the Lower 48? Come on! You're a rugged man who likes the outdoors, who thrives on wide-open spaces and the freedom to roam. And you like women who can embrace all of that with you, someone who can handle it.'

'She's handled more than most,' he said.

'Crime and violence, maybe. But that has to have left some scars. Those scars are apparent by the wary look in her eye whenever anyone so much as walks into the Moosehead. Besides, can she hunt? Shoot? Fish? Ride a snowmobile or a four-wheeler? Do *any* of the things you love?'

'Lay off it, Sam. We have plenty in common.'

'Are you sure?' She lowered her voice. 'After what she's been through, can she even make love the way you like? With any kind of abandon? Or do you have to worry about every little move you make for fear you'll scare the hell out of her?'

'Stop it,' he said. 'We aren't having this conversation.'

'*Someone* needs to talk some sense into you. I admit there's some self-interest at play here, too. I've missed you. I won't lie about that. I've already told you that I wish things would've worked out between us, that I'd like to try again. You're everything I've ever wanted. But even if you don't want *me*, you owe it to yourself to find someone other than Dr Talbot, someone who fits you and your lifestyle a lot better than she does.'

'She's adjusting to Alaska. She'll be fine here.'

'Really? Because from what I've heard, most of the doctors at Hanover House have signed only a five-year commitment. How long is *she* planning to stay?'

He refused to admit that she hadn't made that clear. 'Her plans are none of your business.'

'It's anyone's business who cares about you. Trust me, I'm not the only one in town who feels this way. I'm just the only one bold enough to say it. She's not for you, Amarok. She's a cheechako.'

'That's ridiculous!'

She threw up her hands. 'No, it's not. That type of thing makes a difference. You know what happened with your mother, how miserable she was here. Do you want the same thing to happen with your *wife*?'

'You're out of line. I can run my own life,' he said, but she wouldn't back off.

'How old is she, anyway?' she asked.

'Doesn't matter,' he growled, but as Samantha came closer he couldn't help remembering how much simpler everything had been with her. Was he making a mistake devoting his life to someone as complicated as Evelyn? Would she ever be as committed to him, and to Alaska, as he needed her to be?

'Why take on all of those problems?' Samantha asked. 'Why get involved with someone who will only break your heart?'

'She didn't ask for what happened to her.'

'No. And I feel bad for what she's been through. Don't get me wrong. That kind of violence is sick, not fair to anyone. But she's an attractive woman. I'm sure there are plenty of men who would love to be with her. Let her find someone else – in Boston.' She unzipped her coat and lifted his hand to her breast. 'Remember what *I* feel like? You liked me well enough at one time.'

For a moment his libido flared and he was tempted to curl his fingers around that soft mound. She was sexually familiar and acting as if he still had the right to touch her wherever he wanted. But he set her away from him. 'You need to go,' he told her. 'Now.'

Frowning in disappointment, she zipped her coat. 'Fine. I'm going. Just know that . . . I still love you.' Standing on tiptoe, she tried to brush her lips across his.

Gently but firmly, he set her aside again, this time before she could make contact. But she lifted her chin to show him she wasn't put off. 'You belong with me,' she said, and gathered her hat and gloves before walking out the door.

'Shit,' he muttered once she was gone. Without a doubt, he knew he wanted Evelyn. But could he ever really have her?

Twenty One

After her encounter with Lyman Bishop, Evelyn had tried to chase away her demons by throwing herself into work. She'd finished some reports that needed to be written for her boss at the Bureau of Prisons. She'd called to find out who was working the Zombie Maker killings now that Detective Gustavson was gone and told his replacement, a Detective Lewis, what Bishop had revealed after he'd pulled off the polygraph equipment. She'd checked in with the social worker about Beth, only to learn that Louise Belgrath hadn't had time to get back out to Beth's house quite yet. And, besides holding a staff meeting over lunch where she went over the various studies they were involved in and the progress being made, she'd met with her regular subjects.

But news of Charlotte's death, the fact that Charlotte had also been a friend of Evelyn's in high school, was beginning to spread in Boston. Amidst everything else that was going on, Evelyn was bombarded with calls – some she was able to accept and some she wasn't, depending on what she was doing at the time. She'd spoken to Boston PD. Since she'd told them she'd been on the phone, briefly, with the killer the night Charlotte was murdered, they were very interested in hearing what she had to say. She'd spoken to various friends she hadn't heard from in years, all of whom were horrified for Charlotte and her family, if not downright frightened for their own safety. And she'd spent a few minutes on the phone with her father, not that it had gone any smoother than when she'd spoken to her mother the night before. They both insisted they couldn't leave the area, which left them vulnerable and frightened Evelyn.

Although she'd managed to dodge most calls from the media, that didn't last. At three ten, right when her lack of sleep was beginning to catch up with her, her assistant buzzed her office to say that Brianne was on the phone. Since her call was one of the many she'd been unable to take earlier and she didn't want to put her sister off any longer, Evelyn tried to pick up, but accidentally answered the wrong line. She found herself on a call with Sebring Schultz from *The Star Tribune* – the same reporter who'd reached out to her about the planted panty evidence in Lyman Bishop's attic and not someone she particularly cared for since he sympathized with Lyman Bishop and not Detective Gustavson, putting them on opposite sides of that issue.

'Dr Talbot, are you aware that Charlotte Zimmerman Pine has been murdered?' he asked as soon as she said hello.

'I am,' she replied. 'It's a tragedy – like Mandy's death was a tragedy. But I'm very busy, Mr Schultz—'

'Do you think Jasper is on the hunt again? That he's behind these killings?' he interrupted instead of letting her beg off.

Torn as to whether or not she would allow this interview, Evelyn stared at the blinking light on the line she should've picked up. 'I absolutely do, especially now that there has been a second victim. Both were schoolmates of mine – as well as his. He would've known them, too.'

'So you believe he's now living in the Boston area? That he's come back – if he ever truly left?'

'Whether he's living in Boston or not, he's obviously visiting. He abducted me from there eighteen months ago. I'm sure you're aware of that, since it was in the news. Anyway, I'm not trying to start a panic among all of my old friends and acquaintances. I'd merely like to take this opportunity to warn everyone to take care. There's no telling who he'll go after next.'

'You're saying there *will* be another victim.'

'Two murders can hardly be called a pattern, Mr Schultz. But given the situation, we have to acknowledge that it's a possibility. There's no telling what he might do. He's a sadist. Everyone should remain on their guard.'

'Charlotte's husband said you were in contact with her before she was killed. Did you know she might be a potential victim?'

Evelyn brushed some lint off her slacks. 'I guessed she might be targeted, yes. That was why I reached out.'

'Why her?' he asked. 'How'd you "guess" – accurately, I might add – that she'd be next?'

'She seemed the logical choice,' Evelyn replied, and explained about the picture in her junior yearbook.

'Are there any other photographs in that yearbook that might indicate who the next victim will be?'

'None that stood out to me, not like that one.'

'Was Charlotte able to convey anything to you that could be helpful in solving this case?'

Irritated that he seemed to feel entitled to push regardless of what *she* wanted, she hesitated. She was tempted to hang up simply because she didn't care for him. But, given her situation, it was never wise to make enemies in the media. So she forced herself to answer. 'No. She was nervous because Mandy had been killed – that's all. I was trying to calm her, give her someone to talk to who understood the fear she was feeling.'

'Your interaction gleaned nothing that could be shared with police . . .'

'I've already been in touch with the police, told them everything I know. I want Jasper to be caught more than anyone.'

'Then you don't believe it could've been Tim Fitzpatrick.'

The blinking light Evelyn had been watching went dark. Her sister had hung up. But Evelyn paid that no mind. She could call Brianne back. Schultz had just said something shocking. 'What do you mean?'

'Certain neighbors have reported seeing an unfamiliar blue

minivan in the area. One woman, a Lulu Crouch, got the license plate number of the van while she was walking her dog. She thought it was suspicious that the driver kept going around the same block – Charlotte's block. According to a contact I have at the DMV, who will remain nameless, that plate is registered to your former colleague.'

The suspicion that'd plagued Evelyn once before where Fitzpatrick was concerned reared up again. A previous subject, who was now dead *because of his hatred and suspicion of Fitzpatrick,* had told her Fitzpatrick was as much a psychopath as anyone incarcerated at Hanover House. Some of Fitzpatrick's actions and personality traits suggested that might be true – the way he'd tried to manipulate her and everyone else on the team, his need to be in control regardless of what was best for the group, the careless way he'd used her image in front of dangerous men, the stalking behavior.

He'd been going through a rough year since all of that came to light. But surely he hadn't resorted to *murder* . . .

'Dr Talbot?'

Evelyn drew her attention back to the conversation. 'Yes?'

'Aren't you going to answer the question?'

Tim had been searching her yearbook. He'd admitted as much. He was almost as obsessed with her as Jasper was, but would he go to such lengths? Had he fallen *that* low, grown *that* desperate to feel important again?

'It would be a mistake to jump to any conclusions,' she said. 'Whether or not Tim Fitzpatrick is involved is something the police will have to puzzle out.'

'I understand that. But you are an expert on human behavior, so your opinion should be valid here. You worked quite closely with Dr Fitzpatrick for several years, getting the funding and support for Hanover House. Would you say he's capable of such a heinous crime? Could this be revenge for how your relationship ended last winter?'

'Tim and I disagreed on certain policies here at the institution, and he quit. That's hardly any reason to begin killing innocent people.'

'Except his career is now in ruins. He hasn't been able to recover, and he could easily blame you. I have a source who tells me he'd like to get his job back, but you've refused to speak to him since he left.'

'That's not entirely true. Maybe I'm not willing to have him come back to Hanover House, but I've spoken to him twice this week. Our relationship is amicable enough.'

'So you would or you wouldn't be surprised?'

Now that I'm not actively involved in . . . in anything productive, I'm lost, Evelyn . . . I have to be part of something that matters or my life has no meaning. 'I would believe it's Jasper long before I'd believe it was a fellow psychiatrist.'

'That doesn't really answer my question.' Schultz was after a better quote for whatever piece he was writing, but he wasn't going to get it from her.

'I'm afraid I have to go. I have other commitments. Have a good day,' she said, and disconnected.

'What is it?'

Startled from her thoughts, Evelyn glanced up. She hadn't heard Penny come into the room. 'Nothing. Is there . . . something you need?' She hoped nothing else was seriously wrong. She had enough to contend with.

'I've seen that worried look before . . .' Penny gave a remonstrative shake of her head, but she didn't push the issue. The phone was ringing out front, as it had been ringing for most of the day. 'You never picked up that call from your sister. She's on the line again, and she's growing frustrated.'

For good reason. They hadn't been able to connect all day. 'Right. I'll grab it now,' Evelyn said, and Penny hurried back to her own desk.

Being careful to push the right button this time, Evelyn got her sister on the phone. 'Brianne?'

'Jeez, what does it take to get hold of you these days?'

'I'm sorry. I was . . . interrupted before. What's going on?'

'What do you mean – what's going on? Mom and Dad are freaking out. Everyone's freaking out. There's been another murder here in Boston.'

'I know. It's terrible, upsetting. I've tried calming Mom and Dad down, but . . .'

'There's no way. I've tried, too. Do you really think we aren't safe here? That we should *move*? Because that's what they're telling me.'

'I don't have a crystal ball, Brianne. I have no idea what might be best. I just don't want anything to happen to any of you.' And, since their parents hadn't moved since Evelyn dated Jasper in high school, Jasper knew where they lived. For that matter, so did Fitzpatrick. Brianne had relocated recently enough that it was possible she wouldn't be quite so easy to find, but she hadn't done anything to conceal her whereabouts, so a simple forwarding address could provide that information.

'What started this up again?' Brianne asked. 'It's been eighteen months since Jasper tried to abduct you the last time – and twenty-one years since he did what he did before that. Why would he suddenly start murdering your high school friends?'

Evelyn didn't know – unless it was Fitzpatrick, growing desperate over his failed career and his inability to recover from what he'd done last year. Fitzpatrick had to know that 'resurrecting' Jasper was the one way he could get her attention and possibly tempt her into accepting his assistance.

Now that she'd had a few minutes to think about it, Evelyn realized that there were differences in the methodology of Mandy's and Charlotte's murders, too. Jasper toyed with his victims for as long as possible before he ended their lives. She knew that from experience, and from the body of Shelly Walsh found near the shack where he'd taken her eighteen months ago. Shelly had gone missing nearly three months before she was killed. Mandy had been tortured, but she'd been killed quickly. Charlotte had died a violent but quick death also. Neither had been taken to a second location. Not only that, but the houses where they'd been murdered hadn't been burned.

Evelyn wondered – were the Boston murders merely foreplay to Jasper, a way to scare her before he came after her again, as she'd assumed? Did that account for the change in his methodology? Or were those murders a carefully constructed ruse to make her – and everyone else – believe Jasper was hunting down her old friends so that Fitzpatrick could jump in and act like the expert with all of his insider knowledge?

Regardless, she chose to leave Fitzpatrick out of it – for now. 'There could be a lot of reasons,' she told Brianne. 'Maybe he and his wife split up, so he doesn't have the same limiting factors he's been dealing with. Maybe it's the first time he can move freely around Boston. Or he saw or heard something about me that brought the old desire back into sharp focus. Mom could've told someone that I'm finally in a relationship, and that information could've been relayed to him through his parents. It's even possible he stumbled into Mandy – that the encounter was purely coincidental, but seeing her made him realize how easy it would be to upset me by killing her.'

'Which gave him the idea to continue.'

'Yes.'

'What are the police saying?' Brianne asked. 'Can we expect any help from them?'

'They haven't said anything yet. They're at the start of this thing.'

'It seems they never have anything to say,' Brianne grumbled.

'Trust me. I'm as frustrated as you are.'

'I know. I'm sorry. Don't listen to me. And don't worry about Mom and Dad. I'll talk them into going out of town for a couple of weeks, if I can. Then we'll decide what to do from there.'

'Sounds great. But what will *you* do? You'll go with them, won't you?'

'No. I'm seeing someone. I'll move in with him for the next little bit.'

Evelyn came to her feet. 'Whoa! This is a new development. When were you going to tell me you had a boyfriend?'

'I didn't see any point in telling anyone. I wasn't sure it was going anywhere.'

'And now?'

'It's actually moving quite fast.'

Evelyn couldn't help smiling at the pleasure in her voice. 'Could he be "the one", Bri?'

'It's possible.'

'What's his name?'

'Jeff Creery.'

'Jeff. Wow! Does Mom know?'

'Yes. I just told her.'

'She's got to be thrilled by the prospect of a possible wedding.'

'The news brought a ray of sunshine into her day. But we're not making wedding plans yet. Please don't mention the *w* word to her. I'd rather not get her going.'

'I won't. But this is good, for all of us. It gives us something to think about besides the past, our fear, the murders.'

'When you put it that way, I'm not sure I can conscionably let Jeff join this family.'

She was mostly joking, but that was how Evelyn felt about Amarok. 'I'm so happy for you, Bri.'

'I knew you would be.'

Penny knocked on the wall, since the door was open. 'Dr Ricardo called. He says you were supposed to meet him in Lab #8 ten minutes ago.'

Evelyn checked her watch. *Damn.* He was right; she was late. 'Listen, I've got to go,' she told Brianne. 'It's a crazy day here.'

'You're always so busy.'

'I'm sorry.'

'I understand. I miss you. I wish Alaska wasn't so far away. You'd be closer if you lived in Europe!'

Evelyn experienced a wave of homesickness. 'Not by much, but

Europe sounds appealing. There's no way it could be as cold as it is here.'

'Can you come visit this spring?'

'Yes. Definitely.' She said good-bye and hurried to meet Dr Ricardo so she wouldn't draw any more fire from him for slowing down the empathy study, but she had a difficult time concentrating on something she normally found fascinating. Her sister was falling in love. Somehow that made everything Evelyn was dealing with so much easier to bear. She hoped it had the same effect on their mother. Because if their mother couldn't cope, if things got any worse, Evelyn would almost *have* to go back to Boston.

When Jasper got home, it was late. He peered through the swish of his windshield wipers, which were working hard to keep up with the thunderstorm, to see that Hillary's car wasn't in the garage. That surprised him. He couldn't imagine where she might go this time of night, not with him gone and the kids having school in the morning.

After parking in his usual spot, he grabbed his duffel bag from the backseat, tore off the baggage ticket that gave away the fact that he'd been on a plane – God, he was getting sloppy – and braced against the rain to throw the ticket in the trash can out back before proceeding into the house.

The lights were off, even the kitchen light Hillary usually left on in case one of the girls got up in the night. The heat was off, too. Arizona didn't get all that cold, not compared to most places, but they were in the middle of some bad weather, so it was chilly tonight. He'd expected a blast of warm air to hit him the moment he walked inside, but the change in temperature hadn't been all that noticeable.

What was going on? Hillary never kept the house this cold . . .

The wind rattled the windows as Jasper turned on a light and started down the hall. Both Miranda's and Chelsea's bedroom doors stood open. He poked his head into Miranda's room, since he came to that first, but he couldn't see his stepdaughter – or anything else. It seemed . . .

He snapped on the light. Sure enough, she was gone. So was all of her furniture. He found Chelsea's room the same way.

What the hell?

Jasper strode through the rest of the house. Everything that belonged to Hillary or the girls was gone. She'd even taken the new king-sized bed he'd been looking forward to sleeping on after the nights he'd just spent on cheap motel mattresses.

'What a bitch!' he growled, and hurried to the garage to make sure she hadn't taken the box where he'd stuffed his phone.

Fortunately, that box was still there. She'd left most of the garage items, as well as a few pieces of old furniture she probably didn't want, anyway – like the dining table they'd been meaning to replace, a twin bed they'd stuck in the office as an extra when her mother gave it away last year, the desk that was also in the office and his clothes.

Flinging his wet hair out of his eyes, he sat at the desk and called his wife's cell. Frustrated when he got her voice mail and couldn't vent his rage, he hung up and called back.

You've reached the voice mail for Hillary Smith. I'm afraid I'm unable to come to the phone right now. Please leave a message and I'll get back to you as soon as possible.

This time, he waited for the recording to start instead of disconnecting. 'Answer, damn it. You'll have to talk to me at some point. What the hell's wrong with you? You can't wait until I'm home to leave me? How can you walk out on a man who's going through what I'm going through? I witnessed an inmate being stabbed, for God's sake – for the third time. Where's your compassion? What kind of woman abandons her husband when he's down-and-out?'

He hit the end button, almost called her back to rail some more, but wound up throwing his phone across the room instead. How dare she do this to him! He was tempted to go after her, to show her what standing up to him meant. He knew where to find her – she'd be back home with her parents. Where else would she go? He'd known for some time that they weren't fans of his, but he hadn't cared. He didn't like them, either. As long as *he* had control of Hillary, he didn't think it mattered what they thought.

But it mattered now. He could only imagine what they were telling her. *He barely talks to us when he comes here* – if *he comes in the first place . . . How can he leave you with the kids, disappear for days and not even stay in touch? . . . He* must *be seeing another woman, or he'd keep his cell phone charged so you could reach him. What if something happened to one of the girls while he was gone? . . . Let's be honest, you're not losing much. Until the past year, you basically supported him, and he rarely does anything with the girls. So what has he brought to the table?*

Visions of entering his in-laws' house and killing every single occupant danced in his head. He even went to the kitchen to see if Hillary had left any knives in the drawer. She had – but deep down he knew he couldn't touch her or the kids. That would only attract attention to him – as the spurned lover – and he'd be a fool to make himself the subject of a police investigation right now. He was trying to get on at Hanover House – if they'd ever fucking call him. Why hadn't they responded? He had the perfect résumé, had spent over a year crafting it. True, he hadn't been in corrections for very long, but he couldn't imagine they had people standing in line to work in such a remote place.

Impotent rage welled up at the thought that he might not get on. He'd based all of his plans on that one piece . . .

So he'd quit his job and go to Alaska, anyway, he decided. Get work in Anchorage. Try to hire on at Hanover House from there. They had to accept him eventually. They had no reason not to.

There. Hillary had done him a favor. She'd left him, so he was out of the relationship cleanly. She and her parents wouldn't be looking for him, wouldn't be blaming him for anything beyond being a bad husband and father. Basically, they'd be glad he was gone.

He was feeling better, so much that he almost started to whistle as he viewed the many empty spots where there had once been furniture. 'Good riddance. I should *thank* you,' he said aloud, and chuckled as he opened his laptop. He needed to turn in his notice – something he'd been looking forward to ever since the day he'd started.

He took great pleasure in crafting his resignation – great care, too, since he could still need a recommendation letter if he was ever lucky enough to get an interview at Evelyn's institution. But once he sent it off and was sifting through all the spam he'd received since he last checked his in-box this morning, he found something that made his breath catch in his throat: it was a message from Hanover House.

'Here we go,' he mumbled, and licked his lips before opening that e-mail.

> Dear Mr Smith:
> Thank you for your recent job application. We are happy you have decided to apply at the first maximum-security study facility of its kind. We are currently looking to fill five full-time positions, hopefully in the next few weeks, and would like to schedule an interview with you via Skype at your earliest convenience. If you could reply with three dates/times that you will be available, we'll send you an appointment.
>
> We look forward to learning more about you, your background and your vocational goals.

It was signed by someone named Brian Kincannon from Human Resources.

With a loud whoop, Jasper jumped out of his chair and went racing around the house, banging on the walls. He was good at interviews; he could get this job. Even better, after making him wait nearly three weeks for a reply they sounded like they were now in a bit of a hurry. Thank God he'd been so cautious with the way he'd worded his resignation.

'Wow,' he murmured when he'd finally siphoned off some of his excess energy and was able to calm down. He didn't care if Hillary was gone. He'd soon be rubbing elbows with Evelyn on a daily basis – and she wouldn't even realize who he was. Neither would Amarok. No way would either of them ever expect him to be so bold. He'd used another name when he'd bumped into the sergeant at a diner once, but how many people could remember the name of a complete stranger they met so briefly eighteen months ago?

After twenty-one years of keeping to the shadows, he'd be hiding in plain sight.

Twenty Two

Amarok kept a close watch on the door. He wondered if Evelyn was going to stop by the Moosehead tonight. Samantha was standing not far away. He wasn't too excited about that, guessed Evelyn would be even less excited. That was the reason he'd left Makita home – so Samantha wouldn't have the dog as an excuse to approach him. But it probably wouldn't make much difference in the long run. Living in such a small town, he and Evelyn wouldn't be able to avoid her, so there was little point in trying. His ex would hang out at the bar a lot. Samantha was single, after all, and there weren't a lot of other things to do, especially during the winter.

Still, he almost downed the rest of his drink and walked out. If Evelyn didn't see his truck she'd go on home, and he was fine with meeting her there. He might as well spare her the discomfort of watching Samantha smile and preen for him at every opportunity.

He picked up his mug to do exactly that – but Evelyn arrived before he could follow through. He spotted her the second she walked in. From the corner of his eye, he saw Samantha take notice, too, so he left his beer on the bar and walked over to sling an arm around Evelyn's shoulders. He didn't want her to feel like an outsider. She already dealt with that a lot. Although most of the townsfolk had come to accept her, even like her, Samantha was one of their own. Born and bred here, she understood the people and the area in a way an intellectual from Boston, who was so driven and focused on her own goals, probably never could.

'How was your day?' he asked as he guided her through the crowd and back to where he'd been sitting.

If she noticed Samantha watching them, she made no comment. 'Busy,' she replied, putting her purse on the bar and sliding onto the stool next to his. 'I'm exhausted. And frustrated.'

He returned to his own seat and motioned for Shorty to bring her a glass of wine. 'About what?'

'I just talked to the social worker assigned to Beth's case.'

'And?'

'She wasn't able to get out to Beth's house again today.'

'She probably has a lot of cases.'

Evelyn's expression turned into one of exasperation. 'I'd be willing to bet that none of them involve a serial killer. You'd think she could make this a priority.'

'The evidence that convicted Lyman Bishop was planted. Most people sympathize with Bishop at this point: the scholarly cancer researcher who, as it turns out, might be innocent of the heinous crimes for which he was convicted. You know how that must be playing out in the media. Adult Protective Services are going to be very careful with this case. No one wants to risk making another mistake.'

Evelyn picked a cashew out of the bowl of mixed nuts at her elbow. 'I understand that. But Bishop's attorney is pushing to get him released as soon as possible – and that shouldn't be too hard. Given that Bishop has no prior arrests and was an educated man doing important work, not the typical dirtball who's been in prison half a dozen times, the state's embarrassed and eager to get him home so that the media circus surrounding this incident will die down.'

'In other words, both sides are well motivated to expedite his release.'

'Yes.'

'That means you won't be able to hold him much longer.'

'Exactly my point. And Beth can't be there when he gets out, Amarok.'

'Jumping through all the hoops necessary to remove him as her guardian could take time, Evelyn. Investigations don't happen overnight. You might as well accept that, or you're going to have a miserable few weeks.'

'I can't shrug my shoulders and say *oh well*. He's sexually abusing her. I want that social worker to get her ass out there.'

Amarok was glad she was so fired up about Bishop. She might not even notice Samantha. But Samantha wasn't going to miss the opportunity to introduce herself. Although she took her time, talking to this or that person along the way, she moved constantly closer – until she tapped Evelyn's shoulder.

Evelyn had just received her drink. She thanked Shorty before turning. Then, to her credit, she managed to keep her smile in place. Amarok could see the subtle tightening around her mouth and eyes, however. She knew who Samantha was, even though, to his knowledge, they'd never met in person.

'You must be Evelyn,' Samantha said.

'Yes. And you must be Samantha.' Evelyn offered her hand. 'Amarok told me you were moving back. Welcome home.'

'Thank you,' Samantha said as they shook. 'I hear you're doing some interesting work here in Hilltop.'

'Can I get you something to drink, Sam?' Shorty interrupted, but Samantha waved him off.

'If you find human behavior interesting,' Evelyn said. 'Either way, someone's got to do the research. As I've told Amarok many times, psychopathy is a growing problem.'

'But not one *we* had to deal with,' Samantha said. 'Now there's no telling what might happen, right? I mean, look at last year. I hear Hanover House had prostitution, guard corruption and problems with the medical health staff. Not to mention the first murder – which turned into two murders – that we've had in Hilltop in over a decade. You certainly bring a lot of excitement to town.'

Evelyn studied her before responding. 'I understand that you're not happy with what I'm doing,' she said. 'Is there anything else you'd like to say to me?'

Samantha glanced at Amarok as if she feared he'd pile on. He was tempted. But Evelyn was handling the situation very nicely. She didn't need his help. 'I do have concerns,' Samantha responded, now a little defensive. 'A lot of people here do. And I believe they're legitimate.'

'As legitimate as they may be, I can assure you your opinion would change if you were ever to come face-to-face with a man like Jasper Moore. As indifferent as you may be about *my* past, I'm fighting to make sure you never have the same experience. Ignoring a problem won't fix it.'

'You don't want to challenge the doc, Sam.' Apparently, Phil Robbins had overheard part of the conversation while he was walking up. 'She's the smartest person in town.'

Obviously a little tipsy, he laughed, giving Amarok the chance to try to ease the tension with a smile that suggested they leave it right there. But Samantha didn't smile back. She didn't like that someone from Hilltop had taken Evelyn's side – or that Evelyn had put her in her place even before Phil showed his support. 'I just had a few questions,' she mumbled, and moved away without looking at Amarok again.

'Your ex-girlfriend doesn't approve of me,' Evelyn said.

'Aw, don't mind Sam.' Phil's voice, amplified by the alcohol he'd consumed, boomed overloud. 'She's sore that you got her man. That's all.'

Amarok motioned to Evelyn's wine. 'As soon as you're done with that, we'll head home.'

'I guess it's situations like these that make small towns a bit too . . . confining.'

'Yeah.' He leaned forward and pecked her lips. 'That's why I'm glad you don't have an ex-boyfriend running around this place.'

She afforded him a reluctant grin since he held her chin until she did. Then he helped her drink her wine so that they could get out of there even sooner.

'Do you think it could be Fitzpatrick?'

Amarok had been watching television while Evelyn spoke on the phone to her mother and then Boston PD. When she asked this question, he realized she was off and glanced up at her. '*What* could be Fitzpatrick?'

'My mother told me she saw his picture on the news as a possible suspect for Mandy's and Charlotte's deaths. So I called Boston PD and spoke to Detective Dressler, the guy who's investigating my case, to see why.'

Grabbing the remote, Amarok paused the television. 'Whoa. Wait a second. Are we talking about *Dr* Fitzpatrick? The same dude who quit before he could be fired from HH last year?'

'The one and only.'

'They think it might be him and not Jasper?'

'Apparently.'

Amarok rubbed his chin as he thought it over. 'What evidence do they have?'

She'd heard about the minivan, but she'd been surprised there was more. 'Besides the fact that he was driving a blue minivan that was seen in Charlotte's neighborhood quite a few times over the past several days?'

'What was he doing in Charlotte's neighborhood? Does he live nearby?'

'No. That's the problem. He had no reason for being there.' She would've already shared that tidbit, except they'd driven separately on the way home from the Moosehead and her mother had called the second she walked through the door. 'And it gets worse. He was placing calls to Charlotte – then hanging up on her.'

'Why would he do *that*?'

'To make her think it was Jasper. To cause some panic.'

'So that she'd call *you*. Then you'd know he was right – that she *was* in danger – be impressed that he figured it out in advance and loop him in on the case. He'd finally have the chance to prove how valuable he could be, once again, in the realm of criminal profiling, and you'd break down and allow him to return to Hanover House, or recommend him for some other position.'

Evelyn frowned at his summation. 'That could be the case.'

'You heard the killer's voice. Could the man you spoke to be Fitzpatrick?'

'Detective Dressler just asked me the same thing. But . . .' She shook her head. 'How would I know? The way he camouflaged his voice – that could've been *you* and I wouldn't have known it.'

'The mere fact that he camouflaged his voice suggests you might've recognized it if he hadn't.'

'That could be true for Fitzpatrick *or* Jasper,' she pointed out. 'I can't believe Tim would murder two people under any circumstances.'

'It's possible. He's obsessed with you, won't move on.'

'It's not only me. He wants to feel valued again, wants his old job back—'

'Or at least to rebuild his credibility in the industry.'

'Desperate people sometimes do desperate things. That's a cliché for a reason. But . . . even then,' she said. 'I've felt so bad for ever suspecting him of killing Lorraine and Danielle. I'd hate to make the same mistake twice.'

'Does he have an alibi for the nights Mandy and Charlotte were murdered?'

'He told the police he was home alone.'

'On *both* nights?'

'He's single, in his mid-fifties, and he's no longer working. Both murders happened on weeknights – a Thursday and a Monday. It's not inconceivable that he would be home. He's not exactly a social butterfly – never has been.'

'Just because he turned out to be innocent of murder last year doesn't mean he's innocent now, Evelyn. He wasn't down-and-out back then. He was on top, felt as if he was about to take control of Hanover House. The embarrassment and humiliation he's experienced since could've pushed him over the edge. He hasn't forgotten about you and gone on his way.'

'No, he's capitalized on Mandy's murder by getting in touch with me as soon as possible. But maybe he was only taking advantage of the opportunity that presented itself.'

'Question is . . . was it an opportunity he purposely created?'

Fitzpatrick had access to her high school yearbook, could've chosen Mandy and Charlotte from that picture as easily as Jasper . . . 'The methodology of these kills is different,' she admitted.

'I was thinking that, too. They seem to be more of a means to an end.'

'Yes. But if Jasper was killing my friends to scare me or upset me, he could have made it that simple. Go in, kill, get out.'

Leaning back, Amarok crossed his ankles. 'Four murders in such a short time, though, two on the West Coast and two on the East Coast, is a bit much for anyone to manage inside of two weeks, even a psychopath of Jasper's caliber.'

He'd pointed that out once before . . . 'Perhaps, but it's possible. It's not as if Mandy or Charlotte were killed on the same night as the Moores.'

'Still, it's not likely. I'm pretty sure Jasper lives in Arizona.'

'So you're thinking it might be Fitzpatrick.'

'It could be.'

He was the one who'd raised the alarm with her parents, who then called her in a panic . . .

'Are they going to arrest him?' Amarok asked.

'Not until they find some forensic evidence that ties him to one or both crimes. The fact that he was in Charlotte's neighborhood, that he had access and motivation, isn't proof. The DA wouldn't prosecute a case like that.'

The phone rang.

'I'll get it,' she said.

He grinned because he hadn't even moved to get up. 'You might as well. These days you get more calls than I do.'

'Now that I've warned off all the women who were chasing you before,' she teased, and walked over to the kitchen counter. 'It's Fitzpatrick,' she said, startled to see his name on caller ID. How'd he get Amarok's home number? 'Should I answer it?'

'I hate to keep giving him the attention he wants—'

'But I'm dying to see what he has to say,' she said, and lifted the receiver.

'Evelyn,' Fitzpatrick said in a big exhale as soon as she'd said hello. 'I'm so glad you answered.'

'What's going on, Tim? How do you even know this number?'

'You called me from it the other night.'

Of course. He'd captured it on his caller ID. She rolled her eyes. 'What do you want?'

'What do you mean, what do I want? I *told* you that Charlotte was in trouble. Now she's dead. Surely you've heard the news.'

'Of course I've heard the news. I'm heartbroken that someone else has been killed.'

'I tried to make sure that didn't happen.'

He sounded sincerely distressed. But what about the fact that he'd been implicated in the crime? 'My mother says that the police think you may have had something to do with it, Tim.'

Leaving the television on pause, Amarok walked over to listen to their conversation.

'No. Not really,' Fitzpatrick said. 'I mean, there's no way that'll ever come to anything. Because I didn't harm her. The police just wanted to ask me why I was in her neighborhood.'

'Why were you in her neighborhood?'

'You know why! I was trying to protect her, to keep her safe. I told you I was worried.'

'Is that why you kept calling her house and hanging up?'

'Yes!'

When he didn't even hesitate before answering, Evelyn blinked in surprise. *'Yes?'*

'I was hoping to spook her, to put her on her guard so that she'd be cautious.'

'You couldn't have called her and explained who you were and why you were worried?'

At this question there was a slight hesitation. 'I should have, but I was afraid if I was wrong and she told anyone that I'd called, claiming Jasper was killing people who were old friends of yours, I'd look like I didn't know what I was talking about. And my reputation couldn't withstand that. You rarely hesitate to stick your neck out that way, but your career is flourishing. I'm barely hanging on to mine.'

He'd pretty much lost it, wasn't hanging on at all. That was what had possibly given him the motivation to make it appear as if Jasper were back in Boston, killing the girls she'd hung out with in high school. But Evelyn didn't point that out. 'You didn't consider how that might play out if she was killed?'

'Of course not! I wasn't planning on letting her be killed. I even followed her that night, drove over to that house where she went to babysit to make sure she got there safe.'

'At which point you . . . what?'

'I drove around the block a few times to make sure everything looked okay, and left. I figured she'd be good for the night, never dreamed what happened could happen. I still have no idea how Jasper found her, since I didn't see anyone else following her.'

No one had reported another car, either. That wasn't a point in Fitzpatrick's favor. 'So where did you go when you left the place where she was babysitting?'

'Home.'

Which was why he had no alibi . . .

'You believe me, don't you, Evelyn? What reason would I have for hurting anyone?'

Evelyn pinched the bridge of her nose. Was he telling the truth? How would she ever know? Either way, she felt it was best to convince him that she was finally back on his side. If he was a murderer, upsetting him would only put more people in danger. 'Of course I believe you.'

'I'm *so* glad. I was afraid . . . Well, with everything that happened last year, I thought maybe you'd think the worst.'

She straightened as a horrifying thought came into her mind. He'd accurately predicted Charlotte's death. Sure, maybe that yearbook picture was all there was to it. But it would be pretty easy to predict the next victim if he was the one perpetrating the crime. 'Who do you think Jasper might go after next, Tim?'

'It could be anyone who was ever close to you,' he replied,

obviously pleased that she would ask his opinion. 'That's why I called your family. That's why I'm calling you now. You need to get them out of Boston.'

'I will,' she said. 'I'll get them out right away.'

'Particularly your sister.'

'Because . . .'

'Of her age. Jasper likes young, attractive women. When the police came by, I offered to help them put together a profile of what Jasper would be like now, where he might be living, who he might attack. But they weren't interested. It's so frustrating. Here I am, *trying* to help, and no one will listen. Maybe you and I can go over it and *you* can give them the information.'

'Sure. That sounds fine to me,' she said. 'But I'm going on very little sleep. Let me call you in the morning, from the office.'

'No problem,' he responded, clearly excited. 'Get some sleep. And I'll put together my notes.'

'Thanks,' she said, and hung up.

Amarok leaned around to look into her face. 'So? What do you think?'

'I'm scared,' she replied.

'Of Jasper or Fitzpatrick?'

'Both. But at least I *know* Jasper's my enemy.'

Twenty Three

The next two weeks were the longest of Jasper's life. He'd never been so eager to get through fourteen days. It felt as if he'd been waiting his whole life for this big move to Alaska.

Hillary didn't get the nerve to call him for nearly a week, but he could understand why. She assumed he'd be angry – she'd seen him angry before, knew how unpleasant it was. So he could imagine her surprise and relief when she finally called. He was cordial, but 'cordial' was easy for him since he was happy to let her go.

Nice though he was, she still cried a lot. She also told him that she'd done her best to love him, to be a good wife. He was just too unreachable. Too closed off. Too secretive. He let her talk without trying to justify his behavior, even told her she was right, that splitting up was for the best. Why say anything else? His interview with Hanover House had gone so well that they'd extended him the job. Since he was getting *exactly* what he wanted, he had no hard feelings. In the days after she and the girls had moved out, he'd been too busy to even worry about the 'family' he'd once had.

Once Hillary realized that he wasn't going to put up a fight, they'd made arrangements for her to move, after he was gone, back into the house they'd been renting. Since her name was on the lease, it would be her credit that would get destroyed if they didn't fulfill the obligation. But she wasn't unhappy about living in the house.

Returning to the neighborhood meant she wouldn't have to drive so far to get the girls to school.

No doubt her parents were relieved, too. Everyone had been anticipating a big fight.

See? I'm not such a bad guy, he'd told her, and she'd gone to great pains to assure him she'd never thought of him as 'bad'. She just couldn't 'fulfill' him.

More than once she'd indicated she wouldn't be completely opposed to a reconciliation. She was so damn afraid to be on her own. He'd always known that about her. But he didn't take the opportunity to try to win her back. He encouraged her to stay the course, told her she'd eventually find someone else who was better suited to her. He was being so nice that even her parents seemed to be rethinking their opinion of him and came by to store some of her stuff in the garage until he left.

He found it all quite amusing. He was killing them with kindness . . .

Other than what few dealings he had with his soon-to-be ex, he'd worked almost every day at Florence Prison, trying to fulfill his final shifts. He'd also arranged and paid for his airfare to Anchorage and spent quite a bit of time on the Internet, looking for the perfect place to stay once he arrived – a place with a basement he could use until he came up with other accommodations for his victims. He still had the money he'd taken from his parents when he killed them. He'd have his final paycheck, too. Hillary hadn't asked him for money, and he hadn't offered her any. Her kids weren't his kids; he shouldn't have to take care of them. And her job paid a lot more than his. As far as he was concerned, she should be glad he wasn't requesting spousal maintenance. Under different circumstances, he would have, but he didn't see any reason they should stay in touch. He was finished with her, never wanted to see her again.

Funny thing was, she called what they were going through an amicable divorce, seemed to take great pride in the fact that they could split up without the typical ugliness that occurred when a marriage didn't work. She didn't have a clue that she was only getting out of the relationship so easily because she'd fulfilled her purpose and wasn't standing in the way of anything he wanted.

He just had one more thing to do.

Stepping back, he shaded his eyes to take a final look at the RV. He hadn't liked taking his victims here. The damn thing was too cramped, too limiting. And it stunk to high heaven. It was just the best thing he'd been able to find. The type of shack he'd used in Peoria wasn't all that easy to find.

As he took the gas can out of his trunk and began pouring it inside, on the carpet and upholstery, he realized he had built some good memories here, though. He'd brought two victims to this place, would've brought three if that bitch who worked at the tattoo parlor hadn't jumped out of his van while he was driving.

Anyway, he'd make better arrangements in Alaska. There he'd have far more freedom and range. Instead of worrying about his victims dying in the heat, he'd have to worry about them freezing in the cold, but he never let fear for their safety trouble him too much. He wouldn't have a wife to placate in Alaska. Not while he was working at Hanover House and making his own money. That was why he might be able to keep Evelyn in his own basement. And if that didn't work? He'd find another place – even if he had to build a small cabin out in the mountains. That Bishop dude he'd read about, the one who gave his victims a lobotomy, might've had the right idea. Once he sliced into Evelyn's brain, she'd never defy him again. He doubted she'd ever even try to escape.

But after he did something like that, would she be the same Evelyn he knew? Making her into a zombie could take all of the fun out of it. Resistance was an important part of the experience.

He figured he could make that decision later. First he had to get close to her. The idea of working beside her, of rubbing elbows with her when she had no idea who he was, had to be the most exhilarating thing he'd ever dreamed up.

Nearly gagging on the gasoline fumes he left in his wake, he climbed out of the RV and walked the perimeter to make sure the graves he'd dug weren't obvious. Then he returned and tossed the match.

The RV went up with a *whoosh*, creating a giant ball of flame that made a magnificent sight, especially against the backdrop of an Arizona sunset and the flat, unrelenting desert, which stretched for miles around.

Too bad there wasn't anyone nearby to appreciate the spectacle. But it was privacy that had made it all possible.

And he'd have plenty of privacy in Alaska.

Amarok parked in the visitor lot, grabbed the sack he'd brought and braced against a powerful wind as he got out of his truck and headed toward the sally port at Hanover House. January had been bitter cold, and February wasn't promising to be any warmer. He frowned at the sky, watching the dark clouds scuttle closer, while trudging through the snow that hadn't yet been cleared away from this morning's flurry. He'd left Makita at his trooper post and hadn't bothered to put on any gloves or even his hat.

'Hey, Sarge . . .' 'What's up, Amarok? . . .' 'Good to see you, Sergeant.'

Grateful for the warm air that embraced him the moment he walked through the main entrance, he nodded at the greetings he received from the COs who ushered him through Security.

The warden was standing on a landing one story above him. Since Ferris happened to look down, Amarok waved before getting into the elevator that would take him to Evelyn's office. He didn't come inside the prison very often. He had enough to keep him busy in town. But he knew Evelyn hated sloppy joes, which was what they were serving for lunch. She'd mentioned it on the phone this morning. So he'd brought her a BLT from the Moosehead.

Evelyn wasn't in her office. Thanks to the interior window, he could see that as he approached Penny's desk. Her door stood ajar besides.

'Sergeant Murphy.' Penny nearly spilled her coffee as she jumped to her feet. He smiled to try to calm her, but that didn't help. Almost every encounter he had with Evelyn's assistant proved awkward; she made it far too obvious that she had a thing for him.

'Hi, Penny. I was hoping to talk to Dr Talbot. Can you tell her I'm here?'

'I'm afraid not.' Her eyes dropped to the sack, which smelled like the sweet potato fries he'd gotten along with the sandwich. 'But you could wait in her office until she returns.'

'From . . .'

'She's meeting with Lyman Bishop – told me not to interrupt for any reason, since this is her last chance to get anywhere with him.'

Amarok set the food on the edge of her desk. 'You've received the order to release him?'

'Came this morning. He walks out of Hanover House tomorrow, first thing.'

So the moment Evelyn had been dreading had come . . . 'I'm surprised the paperwork took that long.'

'The red tape involved in the criminal justice world is astounding. At least that was what Dr Talbot had to say a few days ago. But she also said this was one time she was grateful for that.'

He hated bureaucracy. That was part of the reason he lived in this far-off corner of the world. There was much less red tape in Alaska than in the overly regulated and overly legislated Lower 48.

'How will he get to Anchorage to catch his flight?' he asked. Hanover House hadn't been around long enough for anyone to be released under normal circumstances, let alone a vacation order. He was interested in how it all worked, but he was also asking because he wanted to know how quickly Bishop would be gone from the area. No way would he feel comfortable with a man Evelyn believed to have murdered at least eight women – not to mention the lobotomies he'd performed before committing those murders – running around Hilltop.

'I heard Dr Talbot tell Dr Ricardo that one of the COs will drive him, providing the roads are open. With the storm that's coming in, he may have to hole up at The Shady Lady for a day or two.'

Evelyn had been fighting like crazy to get Beth a new guardian, but the doctor who'd checked Lyman's sister hadn't found any injuries, at least none that he could say, without a doubt, were caused by abuse. And, as Evelyn had predicted, they refused to do an MRI. They didn't want to add insult to injury when it came to Lyman Bishop. The woman Evelyn had been working with at Adult Protective Services, Louise Something, had said that going so far would make it look like law enforcement was out to get him.

Once Evelyn had learned she'd have no ally in the doctor or the system in Minnesota, she'd gone up the chain of command all the way to the governor. But he wouldn't return her calls. He didn't want to touch Bishop's case, didn't want to get involved in the political hot potato it had turned out to be.

Bottom line, because of what Detective Gustavson had done, everyone was being very careful to give Bishop the benefit of every doubt. He'd probably sue the state for what Gustavson had done; no one else wanted to be involved in that.

So now Bishop was going to be let loose to do whatever he pleased. And to make matters even worse, he'd be right here in Hilltop until they could transport him to the airport in Anchorage.

'Shit.'

'I know,' Penny said. 'It's scary, right? I mean . . . what if he's guilty?' For no apparent reason – not one that could be tied to the conversation, anyway – a crimson blush crept into her cheeks when she met his gaze, and she looked away.

'What room are they in?' Amarok asked.

Penny seemed taken aback. 'You – you'd like to join them?'

'I'd like to meet him, yes.' Amarok figured he might as well get a feel for the guy. Once Bishop was released, he'd be Amarok's problem – until he was at a safe distance.

'Okay.' She fumbled around, obviously nervous, as she made the arrangements. But a few minutes later a CO arrived to show him to the correct location within the facility.

Before Amarok left the reception area, he pointed to Evelyn's lunch. 'Can you put that on Dr Talbot's desk for me, please?'

Her smile widened as if she was only too happy to please. 'You bet.'

After escorting him over to the prison side, the CO came to a stop in front of a beige metal door with the number five stenciled on the outside. 'They're in there, sir,' he said.

Amarok thanked him and stepped inside to see Evelyn sitting behind a utility desk facing a rather nondescript man on the other side of a thick piece of plexiglass. Lyman Bishop reminded Amarok of a shy bean counter. He sure as hell didn't look dangerous.

But that didn't mean he wasn't.

'Amarok! What are you doing here?' Evelyn asked in surprise.

He decided not to mention the lunch. She'd see it when she returned to her office. 'Penny told me that Lyman Bishop will soon be leaving the facility. I came to offer him a ride to the airport.' Amarok kept his eyes trained on the man in question, who now moved without the hindrance of cuffs or chains. They'd kept him on the other side of the plexiglass from Evelyn, thank goodness, but they'd done away with many of the usual security measures since, for good or ill, he was about to be released and would have them off in a matter of hours, anyway.

'That won't be necessary,' Evelyn said. 'One of the COs who lives in Anchorage will give him a ride. The warden said he'd arrange it.'

'If it's all the same to you, I'd rather escort him myself.'

'It's not the same to me,' she said.

She didn't want him anywhere near Bishop. That's how much Bishop frightened her. But Amarok felt as if it was his job. He didn't want to *hear* about Bishop boarding that plane; he wanted to see it with his own eyes. Only then, once he knew the Zombie Maker was out of Alaska, could he rest easy. '*I'll* make that decision,' he said firmly.

'What do we have here?' Bishop asked. 'A lovers' quarrel? I'd hate to be the cause of that.'

He'd picked up on the fact that there was more at play here than a psychiatrist speaking to the local law enforcement.

'This is Sergeant Murphy, the state trooper who's stationed here in town,' Evelyn explained.

'Ah, yes. I've heard about him. You're living with him.'

Evelyn didn't confirm that, but she didn't deny it, either. Like Amarok, she probably felt as if their personal relationship was none of Bishop's business.

He came to the glass and looked Amarok up and down – mostly up, since he was a great deal shorter. 'Why do *you* want to give me a ride?'

'Just to make sure everything goes smoothly.'

Bishop folded his arms. 'You want to shuttle me out of town as soon as possible.'

'I'm sure you'd like to get home.'

He pursed his lips. 'Except it's not like that. This is no . . . *courtesy*. Evelyn's convinced you that I'm a killer, that I might hurt someone in your town if you don't send me packing right away. You'd rather get me out, make me Minnesota's problem again, right?'

Amarok manufactured a pleasant expression. 'I have a truck with a plow, so I can get through when others can't.'

Bishop gestured toward Evelyn. 'Wow. Just goes to prove that once your reputation has been compromised, there's no getting it back. You both look at me like I'm some kind of . . . of cockroach.'

'You could change the way we look at you easily enough,' Evelyn said. 'We'd be grateful if only you'd tell us where you put Jan's body.'

'Listen to her!' Bishop flung his hand out emphatically. 'She won't give up.'

'Jan's family has been through quite an ordeal,' Amarok said, trying to help.

'So has *mine*,' he responded. 'But neither of you gives a damn about that. And, as I've explained to Dr Talbot many times, I can't help her. Only Jan's killer could provide that information.'

The sparkle in his eyes when he made that statement didn't match his words. The incongruity of the two sent a chill down Amarok's spine. This man was toying with Evelyn, all right, rubbing her nose in the fact that she knew the truth – and was powerless to do anything about it.

'If *you* didn't kill her, who did?' Amarok asked.

'Wish I knew,' he replied with a shrug. 'I guess the police will have to figure that out. If they can. To be honest, I don't have a great deal of confidence in them. They seem pretty . . . useless to me.'

Amarok got the impression Bishop was purposely including him in that statement, but Evelyn spoke before he could respond. 'And Beth?' she said. 'What will happen to her?'

A smug expression claimed Bishop's face. 'What do you think? I'll continue to take care of her, of course.' His head jutted forward as he stared at her. 'I'm not generally the type of person to gloat, but I admit I'm pleased by the fact that you lose all the way around.'

Evelyn came to her feet. 'It's not over.'

He started to laugh. 'Yeah, I think it is,' he said, and turned his attention to Amarok. 'My official release is at eight. I'll see you then.'

That evening Amarok found Evelyn's SUV parked out front of their bungalow. He'd gone by the prison so that he could drive her home like he usually did when it was storming, but Penny told him she'd left not long after meeting with Bishop. Taking the afternoon off was unlike her. He hoped she'd done so to beat the storm – something a lot of people did in these parts when the forecast called for so much snow. But she usually didn't let the weather stop her from putting in a full day. *Nothing* stopped her, which was why he generally had to take the plow over there.

Surely she hadn't learned of another murder in Boston. Her parents had refused to leave their home, had said they wouldn't allow their fear to drive them out of where they preferred to be, wouldn't allow Jasper to have that kind of control over their lives. Amarok secretly admired their stance, but he knew that Evelyn had been worried about them and her other friends. For good reason. Whatever was going on in Boston was not good.

Fortunately, everything had been quiet there – no one had been murdered since Charlotte – but whether that was because the police were keeping a close eye on Fitzpatrick remained to be seen. They still believed it was him, were working on gathering more evidence, and Evelyn had been playing along, letting Tim give her his ideas on the killer's psyche, which she recorded and turned over to the police – at their request.

When Amarok walked in with Makita, he could hear Evelyn on the phone and breathed easier despite the alarm in her voice.

'Beth, listen. If you can't give me something solid – some kind of proof – for what Lyman has done to you, I won't be able to get you out of there. Do you understand? This is important. I'm trying to keep you safe, but I need a little help from you . . . Forget about donuts. There will be plenty of donuts when I get this resolved, okay? . . . I'll send you some myself. I promise.'

Amarok watched as she tried to allay her frustration by closing her eyes and massaging her temples.

'Do you understand what I'm saying – what's happening?' she continued. 'We're releasing your brother tomorrow. That means he'll come home, and he'll force you to . . . to do things you don't want to do . . . Because if it makes you cry, you don't like it, right? And he has no business making you do it. You could live somewhere else, somewhere you don't have to do those sorts of things . . .'

Amarok had to go back out and help Phil. The snow was falling so fast one plow couldn't get the job done. He'd just stopped by to grab a sandwich to take with him and to check on Evelyn, to make sure she was safe and in for the night.

As he got the bread and lunch meat out of the fridge, he listened to her plead and placate and try to explain, in ever simpler terms, what types of things might constitute 'proof'. But he could tell she wasn't getting anywhere. By the time she hung up, she was almost in tears.

'Damn it!' she said, smacking her fist onto the table.

'She won't help?'

'It's hard to make her understand *how* to help – and even harder to get her to trust me enough to try. Now that she knows her brother is coming home tomorrow, she's too terrified. And I don't blame her. He'll punish her for telling me what she did. I shouldn't have let him know. But I never dreamed I wouldn't be able to get her out of there, that APS would be so busy protecting itself it wouldn't protect her! That's what the agency is for!'

'So what are you going to do?'

'I don't know.' She sighed. 'If I can't get proof, I'm all out of options, and that's hard to face.'

Amarok recalled Bishop's taunting smile. 'What about that woman you were telling me about – the lab janitor who cared for Beth during Lyman's trial?'

'Teralynn Clark? What about her?'

'Beth knows her, right?'

'Yes, but . . .' – Evelyn made a face – '. . . she's not much kinder than Bishop.'

'Still, Beth *knows* her,' he repeated. 'That's what's important. It means she'll probably let her in.'

Evelyn nibbled at her bottom lip. 'You're saying I could use her in some way.'

'As your liaison. Tell her you need help, make her feel important. Offer to pay her, if that's what it'll take. But get her to go over there tonight and comfort Beth, figure out some way to befriend her so she'll talk. Maybe she'll divulge some detail that will help. Teralynn could record the conversation. She might even be able to look around. There's got to be proof of Bishop's perversions somewhere in that house.'

'The police searched the house, his computer and his car. If there was anything there, they would've found it.'

'Then he's hidden everything at a remote site.'

'Which could be anywhere.'

'Except . . . he'd also want access.'

Evelyn's eyes widened with a burst of hope. 'The lab!'

'That's a possibility. She could go there tonight.'

'She's probably already going there, and she has keys to everything.' She rushed over to throw her arms around him. 'That's it! That's got to be it. If Bishop is as guilty as I believe he is, there's pornography, photographs, trophies, *something* he's hidden *somewhere*.'

He held her against him. 'Do you think you can get Teralynn to do a little snooping?'

'I bet I can, and I bet she'd have a better idea of where to look than the police did. Even if they searched his desk, I doubt they were able to go through the whole office or lab. That would invade the privacy of everyone who works there. Chances are the warrant didn't extend that far.'

'It's a shot,' he said.

It was a long shot, but Evelyn didn't seem to care. She'd already let go of him and returned to the phone. As he left, he heard her say, 'Teralynn? It's Evelyn Talbot from Alaska.'

Twenty Four

It was late when Amarok and Makita returned. Evelyn was relieved to see them walk through the door. Finally, Amarok would be able to get some rest after a long day, but she knew *she* wouldn't get much sleep. Ever since she'd spoken to Teralynn, she'd been trying to distract herself from the wait and the worry that this, too, would not go the way she hoped. But nothing had the power to divert her. Not the television, the housecleaning she'd attempted or the reports she'd brought home to finish. She couldn't quit obsessing over the fact that Bishop was getting home tomorrow night – and fearing the reckoning he would likely demand of Beth.

Makita barked and Sigmund came running to welcome him home. Since she'd moved in with Amarok, the two pets had grown surprisingly close. 'How bad is the storm?' Evelyn asked.

Amarok bent, as he always did when he first got home, to give Sigmund some attention. 'Fierce. I'm not sure I'll be able to get Bishop out of Hilltop tomorrow, even with a plow.'

She'd been listening to the wind whip around the house while he was gone, had seen how thickly the snow was falling when she pressed her nose to the window. Some of that snow clung to Amarok's hat and coat. 'Maybe it'd be best if he stayed.'

'Where?' Amarok demanded.

'At The Shady Lady, I guess. It's the only motel nearby. I can't imagine he'll be willing to sleep at the prison another night if he gets snowed in.'

Amarok shook his head. 'No way. I don't want him in *this* town.'

'It would give me another day to get Beth out of the situation she's in . . .'

He scowled, obviously reluctant to be talked into letting Bishop remain anywhere nearby. 'I hate to sound callous, but I don't know Beth. I do know, and care about, almost everyone here – and plan to keep them safe.'

She smiled. 'I understand how protective you are of this place.'

'It's my job.'

'It's more than that.'

'Maybe.' He tossed her a boyish grin as he stood to peel off his coat, hat and gloves. 'What'd Teralynn say?'

'She agreed to look. Said she thought she knew of a few places the professors or lab technicians might feel safe stashing something like the items I described.'

'Why didn't she ever think of checking those places herself?'

'Why would she? The police were doing the investigating, and they seemed to have everything well in hand, thought they had what they needed. I doubt very many people would consider launching their own search of the science building, even the janitor – especially if they have nothing personal at stake either way.'

'If he's the killer we believe he is, she could have something personal at stake.'

'True, but I doubt she would've thought of it that way in the beginning. She was too shocked that someone so mild mannered could even be suspected of crimes that heinous.' She came up to kiss him. 'Thanks for the lunch you brought to the prison today, by the way. That was very thoughtful.'

'Glad you liked it.' He went to the fridge and grabbed himself a beer, lifting it to offer her one.

'No thanks.'

'So when do you expect to hear something?'

'I have no idea how long it might take. Teralynn said she'd call when she could.' Evelyn assumed that would be sooner rather than later, but they spent an hour together, watching the rest of a movie they'd started on the weekend, and didn't hear anything. After that, she continued to wait while Amarok dozed right there on the sofa. Around two, she managed to drift off herself, but when Amarok woke and mumbled that they should go to bed she told him she'd be in soon and let him go without her.

After that, she just sat there, staring at Makita, who was looking at her with his head cocked to one side as if to say, *Didn't you see that Amarok left? The man we both adore? Aren't you going to follow him? Should I?*

'You go,' she muttered, and covered her face as he trotted off. Teralynn wasn't someone she should've counted on to begin with, she told herself. Teralynn had been eager to be involved, to feel important, as Amarok had predicted. But it didn't seem as if she was trying. She hadn't even bothered to call back, to keep in touch. Besides, what could she find that the police had not?

The despair that had been edging closer all night suddenly overwhelmed Evelyn. She lost more battles than she won when it came to the psychopaths she studied. Was she making any difference at all?

Tears were welling up when the shrill ring of the phone made her jump.

Scrambling to stop the noise before it could wake Amarok, she held her breath as she glanced at caller ID and lifted the receiver. It was Teralynn, all right.

Please. Let me be wrong. Let Teralynn come through. This was, after all, a last-ditch effort. If it didn't work, Beth would have to stay with Bishop until Evelyn could figure out something else – and who knew how long that would take? She'd feel as if she'd let Beth down—

'Dr Talbot?'

'Yes?' She stiffened as she waited to hear the results of Teralynn's efforts.

'I think I found something.'

Grabbing the closest chair, Evelyn sank into it as a sleepy Amarok came into the room, squinting against the light. 'Is it her?' he asked.

She nodded but lifted a hand to let him know she'd focus on him in a minute. 'What is it, Teralynn? What did you find?'

'A hooded mask, zip ties, a rag, some clear liquid in an old bottle – and an ice pick.'

When Evelyn gasped, Amarok moved forward but didn't speak again. He was waiting, listening. 'How'd you find that stuff?'

'Wasn't easy. I spent hours, searched the whole damn lab and every other place I knew Lyman went – without any luck. I was about to give up when I remembered how much he likes to play the piano. There's this old piece-of-crap piano in the professor's lounge, pushed back into the corner. Most professors are too busy to be bothered with it, or they don't play to begin with. But Lyman used to go there. There were times I'd find him alone, playing, when I came in to clean. He said music was soothing. Anyway, I pulled that piano away from the wall, which wasn't too hard since it's on coasters, and, after poking around a bit, I found this bag. Almost couldn't believe it myself.'

Evelyn's mind was racing. That Lyman was the only one to play the piano created a tie between him and that bag. So did the ice pick, considering the crimes he'd been accused of committing. But those were loose associations, nothing that proved beyond a shadow of a doubt that *he* was the one to hide those things – or perform the lobotomies.

'Teralynn? Can you please take a picture of each item – and all of it together – with your phone and e-mail those photographs to me? Then take what you've found straight to the police on your way home?'

'Will the police be mad that my fingerprints are on it? When I found it, I had no idea what it was. I took everything out.'

'No. It's natural that you would; you're not a forensics expert. Tell them you were cleaning when you came across it and that only Lyman Bishop ever played that piano. Ask for Detective Lewis. He's the one now working the Zombie Maker murders. And make sure you give those things directly to him so they can't get misplaced or handed off to someone who might not recognize the impact of what such a find means. The last thing we need is for this stuff to get lost.'

'I will. This is good, right? I mean, Bishop was getting out. This might mean he'll go back to prison.'

'That's exactly what it might mean. It's fantastic. For starters, it gives me something solid to work with. Now maybe I can get Beth out of that house.'

'Do you think they'll put my picture in the paper?' Teralynn asked.

Obviously, she was excited about the attention she would receive, but that didn't matter. She'd found what could save Beth from the abuse she'd suffered – and maybe she'd saved others from something even worse. 'I do. I know a reporter at *The Star Tribune* that will probably be very interested in talking to you.'

'Will you give him my number?'

'If that's what you want.'

'I do. Thanks!'

'You're on your way to the police, right?' Evelyn said, hoping to keep her on track until she could get those items into the hands of the detective.

'Yes. Leaving now.'

'Perfect.' After she hung up, Amarok lifted her to her feet and stared into her face.

'What is it?' he asked. 'What'd she find?'

Evelyn's exhaustion and fatigue rose to the surface, along with a jumble of emotions, causing tears to spill over her eyelashes as she told him.

He used his thumbs to wipe away those tears. 'That's wonderful.'

'It's a win for the good guys,' she said with a smile.

'There's a lot of police work yet to do – fingerprints, DNA, trying to trace that liquid as well as the ice pick to prove it was really Bishop who handled those things,' he cautioned, but he was smiling while he said it.

'He's smart. He managed to keep his kit out of the hands of police despite their earlier searches. I'm sure he assumes he's home free. But the connection should be there.'

'Gustavson had to have thought those searches would yield more than they did, had to have been shocked to find he could get nothing solid on Lyman.'

'That's why he resorted to planting those panties. He told me as much. But Bishop couldn't have prepared for *every* eventuality.' She reached up to smooth down Amarok's thick hair, which stood up from when he'd been sleeping. 'There will be something in what Teralynn found to show those items belong to him. I know it.'

Amarok pulled her into his arms and held her close.

'I believe we've got him,' she whispered.

Evelyn didn't dare go to bed. Minnesota was three hours later than Alaska, which meant it was already after seven there. While Amarok slept a little more so that he could get up to drive Bishop to the airport in Anchorage, she waited to give Teralynn time to reach the police station. Then she called Detective Lewis, who'd taken over for Gustavson.

To her frustration, Lewis wasn't in yet. She fidgeted and worried, watching the clock tick toward the moment when Lyman Bishop would be released, and waited for Lewis to call her back. Fortunately, during that time she did manage to confirm with a sergeant at the police station – the one who answered the phone when she called – that Teralynn had dropped off Bishop's 'kit'. Teralynn had called to say she'd *had* to leave it at the front desk, despite Evelyn's instructions not to. But when Lewis got in, he assured her that he'd retrieved those items and was heading down to check them into evidence.

'I'm sorry I missed Teralynn,' he said. 'Because now I need to get her back in here to give me a statement.'

Evelyn knew Teralynn would be more than eager to do that. 'I'm sure she'll be happy to accommodate you. It's just that she was up all night. She's exhausted, went home to sleep.'

'I've got her number. I'll give her a few hours before I call.'

'Do you have any way of getting hold of Detective Gustavson?' Evelyn asked, covering a yawn. 'I haven't been able to reach him since he resigned, but I'd like to let him know that Bishop's release doesn't mean it's over.'

'I agree. He should know,' Lewis said. 'Might stop him from wanting to jump off a cliff, poor guy. He's been catching hell from all sides, let me tell you.'

'I have no doubt it's been rough.'

'Deservedly so – to a point,' he said. 'He broke the rules. Even if Bishop turns out to be the murderer you and I believe him to be, that won't mean Gustavson will get his job back. But it should give him some peace of mind – that the sacrifice he made was for a good reason.'

'Yes. I'd like him to have that.'

'I'll make sure he gets the word.'

'Thanks.' It'd been an hour since Teralynn had found Bishop's 'kit', but the discovery still seemed a bit surreal. Drawing a deep breath, Evelyn rocked back in her chair. 'This is the bombshell we needed.'

'*If* we can prove Lyman Bishop put those items behind that piano, it is. But I'm optimistic. There's a number of ways we could do that – fortunately, all of them legit,' he added wryly.

'Even if we can't tie him directly to those items via DNA or whatever, what Teralynn found should cast sufficient doubt about his mentally impaired sister's safety that I can get her removed from his home. Don't you agree?'

'I can't speak for Adult Protective Services, but I have a hard time believing they'll fight you now. Can you imagine the negative PR they'd receive, and the number of people who'd lose their jobs, if Beth were to get killed after something like this kit was brought to their attention?'

Yes, Evelyn could imagine it. That was what brought such relief. The risk of *not* removing Bishop as Beth's guardian had just become greater than the risk of leaving him. *Thank God.* That was all Evelyn had needed – something to swing the pendulum over to the other side when it came to the county's liability. 'I'll let you go. We both have a lot to do. Bishop will be released from HH after he has breakfast.'

'Meaning he'll be home tonight.'

'Yes. It's three hours later there, but he's booked on a direct flight. It'll take only five hours.'

'Good luck,' Lewis said. 'Have whoever you're working with at APS call me if they need confirmation. I'll tell them this discovery hints at some pretty scary shit and they'd better get his sister out of that house while they can.'

'I appreciate it.' She let him go so that she could call Louise Belgrath, but Louise didn't pick up.

'Damn it,' Evelyn muttered. She tried again, to no avail. And then she must've dozed off. The next thing she knew, Amarok was entering the kitchen, freshly showered and dressed for the day.

'You've been up *all* night?'

She could hear the disapproval in his voice. He was worried about her; she had trouble knowing when to ease off the throttle. 'I'll take a nap as soon as I can. First I have to reach Louise Belgrath.'

He dropped a kiss on her head. 'Don't push yourself so hard. You've got all day. With this weather, we might not even be able to make the plane.'

'I'm not sure that comforts me, especially after what Teralynn found last night. I don't want you alone with Lyman Bishop in a motel room. So . . . figure out a way to get him on that plane. I'll do the rest.'

'And then you'll probably work the remainder of the day.'

'No, I'll clear off my schedule and sleep. I promise.'

The phone rang and, once again, she scrambled to get it. 'It's Louise.'

He walked over to put on a fresh pot of coffee while Evelyn answered.

'Thank God you called me back,' she said into the phone.

'I'm sorry to take so long. It's been a hectic morning. I just wanted you to know that I got your message and I'm working on it.'

'Working on what, *exactly*?'

'On getting Beth out of Lyman Bishop's house, of course.'

'You're kidding.'

'Not at all.'

Of course she wasn't kidding. This wasn't a joking matter. Besides, Louise didn't know how to joke – or didn't see any value in it. She was the most sober individual Evelyn had ever dealt with. But Beth was going to be taken to a safe place. That was all that mattered. 'How soon can you make it happen?'

'He gets home tonight?'

She'd left that information in her message. 'Yes. He lands at six. My guess is he'll be home no later than seven.'

'I'll have her gone by then.'

Closing her eyes, Evelyn breathed deeply. 'Thank you.'

'I hope we're doing the right thing,' she said, as if she wasn't entirely convinced.

'Excuse me?'

'Beth and her brother have both been through *a lot* in their lives. For the most part, they've only had each other. I don't want to separate them, and make things worse, if this isn't legit.'

She was referring to what Detective Gustavson had done, was lumping Evelyn and, possibly, the new detective, if she'd spoken with him, in with Gustavson because they also believed Bishop to be guilty. 'There are no easy answers, Louise. I'm sure you've come to realize that in your line of work. We can only do what we deem necessary at the time. And I can assure you that no one planted the bag that was found. Considering what was in it, don't *you* think Beth should be removed as soon as possible?'

There was a long pause. But then she said, 'Yes. I'll call you when it's done.'

'It's happening?' Amarok asked once she'd hung up the phone.

'It's happening,' she confirmed.

'Great. We're ninety percent there. I'll go get Bishop and ship that bastard home.'

'Will you be able to drive through the storm?'

'I'll do whatever I can to make sure of it.'

Evelyn got out of her chair to catch him before he could leave. 'Amarok?'

'I'll be careful.'

He knew what she was about to say, that she was concerned. But that didn't make it any easier to let him go. 'Can't someone else take him? Maybe Phil? Bishop knows . . . he knows I care about you. He caught on to that when you were in the interview room with us. And I can't speak for Bishop. I don't know him as well. But that would be enough to make Jasper kill you.'

'I can't trust Phil with someone like Bishop,' he said. 'Phil's a good guy but not especially . . . savvy. And I'll be fine. Bishop's excited. He thinks he's won, that he's going home to live his life however he wants – even if that includes destroying other people. I doubt he'd be stupid enough to try anything on me. Just don't tell him that Beth won't be waiting for him when he gets home. That could be a game changer.'

'There's no way he'd ever hear that from me,' she said.

Twenty Five

Bishop liked to talk. And, as Amarok had predicted, he was in a good mood. He had Amarok stop at The Dinky Diner so that he could get some 'decent' food before they left – not that he had much praise for the omelet he received. Then he chatted about how eager he was to get back to his work and how his associates at the college were going to feel so terrible that they'd ever doubted him. According to him, not one of them had offered him any support, not after news of those panties broke. 'Now that they know I'm innocent, they should line up to offer me their sincerest apologies.'

He seemed to enjoy imagining others as his supplicants, seemed to look forward to their attention and contrition. He talked about one woman, in particular – a fellow scientist at his lab – whom he seemed to admire a great deal. The repeated mention of her name made Amarok uncomfortable. He got the impression, if Bishop felt he could get away with it, she'd be next on his lobotomy list. Bishop reminded Amarok of Jeffrey Dahmer. Amarok had heard Evelyn say that Dahmer had tried to keep his victims with him as long as possible. She believed the lobotomy served the same purpose for Bishop – then the women he pursued couldn't leave him like his mother had – and that made a lot of sense to Amarok.

Amarok thought about that as he drove, but he said very little. When they came to a steep pass, which had been closed off because of the storm, he turned on his red and blue flashers, lowered his plow and continued on. But he could barely see for the blizzard raging around them, so he was surprised when he passed two different troopers, in separate trucks, and no one tried to stop him.

After what seemed like an interminable period of pressing on in some of the worst weather they'd had so far this winter, during which he could go only ten or fifteen miles an hour, they finally reached somewhat of a lower elevation, but the roads were slick and it was still snowing heavily.

'That was scary,' Bishop said when they could see Anchorage ahead of them. 'Not that I ever doubted your ability. You really know how to drive.'

Amorak glanced over at him. 'I've seen plenty of bad weather in my day.'

'Your day? What are you, *twenty-five*?'

Bishop had to know he was older than that, but Amarok didn't correct him. He was being facetious.

'What brought you to Alaska?' Bishop asked, breaking the silence yet again.

'I was born here,' Amarok replied.

'That doesn't mean you have to *stay*. This place is so cold and . . . empty. Well, except for here in Anchorage. What's the population in Alaska?'

'Last I heard, about seven hundred thousand.'

'And in Anchorage?'

'Probably half that.'

'What about Juneau? That's the capital, right?'

'Juneau's about ten percent of the population of Anchorage.'

'Anchorage is the largest city in Alaska?'

Amarok nodded.

'Three hundred fifty thousand people. That's half the population in the whole state? Wow. Still not a lot. I don't know how you stand it.'

'It's not always this cold. Even when it is, I happen to like it.'

'Maybe if you were born here and didn't know anything

different,' Bishop mused, frowning as he stared out at the whirling snow. 'But I can't imagine someone who's lived in warmer climes ever being able to adjust.'

'People come from the Lower 48 all the time,' Amarok said.

'To hunt or fish. Or take a cruise. They don't move here, do they?'

'Sometimes they do.'

Bishop adjusted his seat belt. 'I'd go crazy.'

Considering he was already crazy, at least in Amarok's estimation, Amarok didn't comment.

'I don't see Evelyn liking Alaska,' he went on, keeping his jaw flapping.

'Because . . .' Despite his earlier reserve, Amarok couldn't refrain from responding to this. What the hell did Lyman Bishop know about Evelyn and what she might or might not like?

'She's not the type. She's not . . . outdoorsy. I mean, after speaking with her as often as I have, I'd have to say she's more of an intellectual, like me.'

'You're no authority on Evelyn,' Amarok ground out.

A small smile curved his lips. 'I'm not pretending *that.* After all, you're the one who's sleeping with her at night.' He waited as if he hoped Amarok would confirm it, but when Amarok said nothing he went on, 'You know her much better than I do. I'm just saying I'd go stir-crazy out here.'

Amarok leveled a glare at him. 'Fortunately, you're leaving.'

'Yes. Thank goodness for both of us. I'm betting Evelyn will leave someday, too. That's my point.'

'She's got her work at the prison to keep her busy – and plenty of psychos there to study each day.'

'You think *I'm* a psycho,' Bishop said.

Amarok turned up the heater and didn't comment.

'You do. I can tell. Fine. Maybe that's a good thing. Maybe you'll believe I'm speaking as someone who should know when I say that Evelyn has no business dealing with the men she's dealing with at Hanover House. You should hear how they talk about her.'

This bastard was purposely trying to upset him, to elicit a

reaction. 'If you want to reach the airport, I'd shut up if I were you,' Amarok said.

Bishop blinked several times. 'What are you threatening me with? That you'll dump me out here in the middle of nowhere and make me walk the rest of the way? Or worse?'

Clenching his jaw, Amarok kept his attention riveted on the road.

'You'd really do something like that?' Bishop pressed. 'You'd risk losing your job?'

Slamming on the brakes, Amarok purposely caused the truck to go into a long skid, making sure they came dangerously close to the guardrail, which was the only thing separating the thin ribbon of road they were traveling from the steep slope beyond.

With a yelp, Bishop grabbed for the dash. 'What are you doing?' he cried, nearly hyperventilating before they came to a stop. 'Trying to *kill* us?'

'Of course not. It's just that you're making it awfully difficult for me to concentrate on my driving. And you can see how slick it is out here. With weather like this, I'd keep my mouth shut if I were you.'

His jaw sagged open as Amarok got back on the road. 'I can't believe you did that. We could've gone over the edge. I said you were a good driver, but that doesn't mean you can control something as heavy as a truck,' he complained, but when Amarok sent him a look that indicated he'd do it again he shut up at last.

Evelyn didn't go in to work that day. She called to tell Penny to cancel her appointments and let the other doctors know she'd be at home if they needed her. Then she crashed on the couch for several hours. She probably should've gone to bed. She could've rested better. But she couldn't stand the thought of being unaware of what was going on for a long stretch. She wanted to be sure the phone would wake her if Amarok or anyone else called.

Amarok did call but later than she'd expected, after she'd already awakened, checked her e-mail, returned her messages and started making beef stew for dinner. But at least, when she did hear from him, he was able to confirm that he'd gotten through to Anchorage and Bishop was off.

'I watched him go through Security myself,' he said.

'The planes aren't grounded?'

'The storm was letting up by the time we got to the airport. There were some delayed flights, but his was somehow on schedule.'

'Good. Except he should be behind bars – not flying home,' she grumbled.

'Boston PD has his kidnap kit. That should lead to the truth. Have you heard anything about Beth?'

'Just hung up with Louise. They've found a facility that can take her, which is great news. Louise is at her house now, helping her pack.'

'Have you talked to her?'

'Not yet. I asked, but she was too flustered to come to the phone. Everything is happening so fast. I'll call her once she's settled in her new place, try to help her remain calm. Are you on your way home?'

'Not yet. The road isn't open, and now that I don't have something as compelling as a serial killer in my truck I should respect that. I don't mind hanging at my dad's until the bulk of the storm has passed.'

'You won't be there overnight—'

'Hopefully not. I'll check the roads again in a few hours. Any more news out of Boston?'

'You mean from my parents?'

'And your sister.'

'They're holding tight. Fortunately, there haven't been any more killings. But I did find a panicked message from Fitzpatrick when I listened to my voice mail a few minutes ago. He claims the police are trying to pin Mandy's and Charlotte's murders on him instead of going after Jasper.'

'We knew he was a suspect. Does this mean they've found more evidence? Something solid?'

'He didn't say. I called Detective Dressler, but he wasn't in, so I decided to make you some beef stew while I waited.'

'My favorite.'

She smiled at the softness in his voice, knew that softness was reserved only for her. 'I know what you like.'

'You know exactly what I like,' he agreed. 'But does that mean you have something special to tell me?'

She set the spoon she'd been using to sample the beef stew on the counter. 'Like . . .'

'We've been making love without birth control ever since the motel, and you haven't had a period.'

'My periods are never regular. I can go months without one.'

'I know that. But this time, I'm wondering if a baby's the reason.'

'*That's* why you've been so worried when I don't get enough sleep?'

'After how Jasper abused your body, it might be hard for you to carry a baby. You need to be kinder to yourself.'

Since she wasn't sure she could get pregnant in the first place, she'd pushed the possibility to the back of her mind. She only knew that being open to having a baby with Amarok added a whole new dimension to their sex lives. She'd begun to initiate intimacy more often – and to enjoy it without any reservation. She supposed it was faith and trust that made the difference, and that was generated by the fact that he was so committed. 'How would I find out? I'm not about to walk into Quigley's and ask for a pregnancy test.' She chuckled as she thought of how quickly word of that would circulate around town . . .

'I could pick one up while I'm here.'

She touched her stomach, wondering if something significant had changed.

'Evelyn? Should I do that?'

'Sure.' She let her breath seep out slowly. 'That's a good idea. But will you be disappointed if the answer's no?'

'Not disappointed, exactly. It's nothing to stress about. We'll just . . . take our time. If it happens, it happens.'

'I never dreamed I'd have a baby,' she admitted. 'Not after Jasper. I'm almost afraid . . . I don't know, that it's too much to hope for.'

'Your doctors told you it might be possible.'

'"Might" being the operative word.'

'If you can't get pregnant, we'll figure out something else.'

'Are you talking adoption?'

'Nothing's off the table at this point.'

A sense of excitement she'd never experienced before swept through her. He made it all sound so easy, so possible – and that they'd deal with it if it wasn't. That created the exact sense of safety and security she needed. If she went back to Boston, would she ever be able to find someone she loved as much? 'I'm glad I met you,' she said. 'You've changed everything.'

There was a slight pause. Then he said, 'Good. Then maybe you'll never want to leave.'

Damn, it was cold in Anchorage! That was Jasper's first thought as he walked out of the Anchorage airport, but he was sort of grateful for the extremely low temperatures. The fact that Alaska wasn't the best place to visit during the winter had to have helped him land the job at Hanover House. No doubt they'd lost several COs – men and possibly women, who'd come to Alaska eager to work at the new facility only to give up and go home once they realized how miserable living in such an extreme climate could be. And he couldn't imagine there were a lot of people vying to fill those spots, not at this time of year. Even if there were, they probably didn't have previous corrections experience, like he did. That had created the perfect opportunity for him, made getting a job at Hanover House almost too easy, which was why he'd gone that direction in the first place.

He was supposed to pick up his uniforms and attend a four-hour orientation at the prison tomorrow afternoon and could hardly wait. He kept daydreaming of passing Evelyn in the halls. He'd have to be *very* careful, wouldn't even be able to look at her, not at first. He had to become a familiar face at the prison, gain some trust as one of the 'good guys', before he could risk so much as saying hello.

But just knowing she was close would provide a measure of excitement. Time would take care of the rest. He needed a couple of months to build out his basement, anyway. Creating the ideal place to keep her, somewhere she could never get away, would take weeks. Meanwhile, he'd kill Amarok, as he'd been longing to do . . .

Jasper cranked the heat a little higher. No, he couldn't kill Amarok. Not right away. That would put everyone in Hilltop on guard, start a big investigation and cause everyone to look at everyone else with suspicion and fear. He needed to be sure that Evelyn wasn't alarmed. He needed for her to continue to live with the false sense of security she no doubt felt as she went home to her cop lover every night.

So he'd wait, for now, and nab her once he had a place to put her where he could punish her indefinitely, toy with her for months – knowing all the while that Amarok was going crazy looking for her. Living in Anchorage instead of Hilltop would suit him well, would give him the space and privacy he'd need. And it wouldn't seem odd, since so many of the other COs commuted to Hilltop.

He smiled to himself. There wouldn't be a soul with any reason to keep tabs on him. As long as he continued to work at the prison and didn't suddenly go missing when Evelyn did, no one would have any reason to suspect him, even Amarok.

The wait would require patience; the kidnapping would require precise planning. But then?

He'd be able to do *anything* to her.

Amarok waited nervously outside the bathroom door. 'How long does it take?'

'Not long,' Evelyn replied.

'Seems like forever already.'

He heard her chuckle. 'Three to five minutes.'

'Can you let me in? So I can see the results when you do?'

'I had to pee on a stick, Amarok. Do you really want to be part of that?'

'Why not? I know you're not in there drawing blood for the test,' he said in exasperation. After the indignities she'd suffered at the hands of Jasper, she was more private than any woman he'd ever been with. Sometimes she shut him out even when she was only changing.

'Evelyn?'

'Okay.' She opened the door, and he walked in to see her sitting on the edge of the bathtub/shower combo, staring at a plastic indicator on the ledge of the sink.

He put down the toilet lid so that he could sit there. 'How will we know if it's positive?'

'We'll see a little ring in that window,' she said, pointing.

'How much longer do we have?'

She checked her watch. 'Two minutes.'

He reached out and took her hand, which was cold even though it was plenty warm in the house.

'Sorry. I washed my hands,' she explained.

'Good thing,' he joked, since she'd been so worried about including him in something that required urine. 'Just so you know, bodily fluids don't freak me out, not if they're yours.'

She gave him an abashed smile as she nudged him, but then her eyes returned to the indicator.

He cleared his throat. 'Do you want it to be positive?'

'In a way,' she admitted.

'*I* want it to be positive.'

'You're more of a risk-taker.'

'You're what I want. That's not a risk – it's a commitment.'

He thought she might reiterate all the things that could tear them apart and was relieved when she didn't. They both leaned closer as the minutes ticked down – but no ring appeared.

They waited another minute.

Still, no ring.

'Guess I'm not pregnant,' she said.

'Not this time.' He lifted her hand to his lips as he threw the indicator away. 'But that could easily change.'

She started blinking fast, and yet she was still trying to smile, so he looked a little closer. 'What's wrong?'

'I don't know.'

She'd wanted it to be positive as much as he had. She was just cautious not to set herself up for the disappointment that wanting a baby and not being able to have one could cause, so she wouldn't admit it. At least, he thought there was an element of that in what she was feeling.

'I must be tired from all the short nights I've had the past few weeks,' she explained, quickly gaining control.

'Tired,' he repeated.

'Exhausted.'

He tugged her toward the door. 'Then let's go to bed.'

Lately, she'd wanted to make love almost every night, so it didn't surprise him when she went for his jeans as soon as they reached the bedroom. He got the feeling she found the intimacy comforting and enjoyable in the way most people did – only, with her, there was an added element. She was reassuring herself that she could not only have sex, but she could also *want* it, even crave it, which had been beyond her ability at one time. As she learned what she liked and what she didn't like and how certain motions and positions helped her to climax, her confidence grew. Essentially, she was making up for lost time, and he didn't mind being the unwitting beneficiary.

'You're so good in bed,' she told him as he slid his hand down her pants and inside her panties.

He could have told her the same thing. She had a hold of him, was caressing him exactly as he liked. 'What can I say? You turn me on.' He was gaining confidence, too – confidence in the fact that he could touch her without frightening her.

'Good thing,' she told him. 'Because I probably couldn't make love with anyone else.'

'I think you're underestimating yourself, but you don't need anyone else. I know all your little pleasure spots.'

She moaned as he hit a favorite. 'Yes . . .'

'All the more reason to stick with me, babe,' he teased.

'I'm not going anywhere.' Her response grew breathy as the pleasure intensified. 'You're all I want.'

Feeling her fingers tighten around his hard shaft, he lowered his voice, his mouth at her ear. 'Tell me how bad.'

Nudging his hand away, she pushed him back on the bed. 'Let me show you instead,' she said, and peeled off her clothes before straddling him.

Twenty Six

Evelyn woke from a deep sleep. As she blinked against the darkness, she realized that Sigmund was on her pillow not far from her face and Amarok seemed to be everywhere else. She smiled as she remembered how crazy they'd gotten while making love – sex was getting to be so much fun for her, and he didn't seem to mind that she was gaining interest.

The ringing of the phone cut through her muddled thoughts. The noise had to be what'd disturbed her.

'Who's calling?' Amarok muttered, but he wasn't quite coherent. Taking most of the blankets with him, he rolled over to face the other direction.

'Don't worry, I'll get it,' she joked.

He didn't respond. He was dead to the world again.

Because she didn't want to take it in the bedroom – no way would he be able to continue sleeping if she did – Evelyn got up and grabbed her robe, belting it as she slipped out of the room.

Caller ID suggested it was Teralynn. At least, that was what Evelyn's blurry eyes registered when she saw the area code. 'Hello?'

'Dr Talbot?'

It *was* Teralynn, but the fear in her voice dispelled the grogginess that was making it so difficult for Evelyn to function. 'Yes?'

'He keeps calling me.'

'*Who* keeps calling you? Detective Lewis?' Makita came out of the room to join her as she yawned. 'He needs a statement.'

'Not Detective Lewis! I went in and gave him my statement before work this evening. I'm talking about Lyman Bishop!'

Evelyn straightened. 'What does *he* have to say?'

'He's furious that Beth is gone.'

'Does he know she's safe?'

'Yes. Adult Protective Services left an official letter on the table telling him he'd been removed as guardian.'

'So why doesn't he call them in the morning?'

'Because he's freaking pissed off, like I said. Maybe he's drunk, too. He's not sounding like the man I remember. He keeps asking me if I know where she is, why they took her. And he knows you had something to do with it. He curses every time he mentions you, wants me to give him *your* number.'

Evelyn had made no secret of her efforts to get Beth out of the house. 'He can call Hanover House tomorrow. The main number is on the Internet.'

'He doesn't want the main number. He asked if I have your home phone.'

'What'd you tell him?'

'That I don't.'

'Thanks. Please don't give it to him, no matter how insistent he gets. Have you called the police?'

'I left a message for Detective Lewis, but it's four o'clock in the morning. He's not at the station. And whoever I talked to said they'd have someone look into it, but I'm not sure they took me seriously enough.'

'Where are you?'

'At the lab.'

Bishop could easily go there, was familiar with the property. Perhaps he wanted to get that bag he'd hidden behind the piano. From his perspective, that would be smart – to get it back under his control. He wasn't aware it'd been found. 'How does he know *you* had anything to do with Beth?'

'I was the last one to help out with her, so he's assuming someone would've talked to me.'

'How many times have you spoken to him?'

'Only once. He's called back three times since then, but I haven't answered.'

'The safest thing you can do is play dumb.'

'But he hates me! He said if I would have taken care of Beth like he asked me to, none of this would've happened. It's because she was on her own that *you* got involved.'

Evelyn could easily imagine Teralynn's fear. 'Tell me a locksmith rekeyed the lab after Lyman went to jail.'

'They did. Of course they did. Until that business about the panties came out, everyone around here thought he was a serial killer. But . . . new locks or no, I'm afraid to finish up and leave. He could be waiting for me!'

Evelyn rubbed her right temple. 'He doesn't know where you live, does he?'

'No. He's never been to my house.'

'Good. Listen, you've got to reach out to the police again. Tell them you've been receiving harassing phone calls from Lyman Bishop and you need an escort home. I'm sure they'll send a patrol car to ensure you arrive safely.'

'Okay,' she said. 'I'm done here. I'm calling them now.'

Evelyn hung up feeling confident that the police would protect Teralynn tonight – but she knew the janitor would have to return to work tomorrow.

Lyman Bishop had been digging at his cuticles so incessantly they were beginning to bleed, but he barely felt the pain. He hadn't won. Those few exhilarating hours in Hilltop, when he'd thought he'd left Evelyn disappointed and empty-handed, had been an illusion. Even with everything that had suddenly shifted into his favor, the revelation of what the detective had done suddenly breaking in the news and everyone scrambling to apologize and get him released, Evelyn had not only stuck to her agenda; she'd managed to best him. A mere woman had done that, and a woman who believed in psychiatry – quack science, as far as he was concerned. Thanks to Dr Talbot, he'd never be able to touch or speak to his sister again. And Beth had been his greatest victory! None of his other lobotomies had turned out quite so well. He wasn't sure he'd ever be able to match his first success. He'd been trying to duplicate what he'd done to Beth ever since – with disappointing results.

He'd keep trying, however, wouldn't accept defeat. And he'd get even with Evelyn along the way. He'd told her to leave Beth alone, and he'd meant it. He'd start his revenge by driving two ice picks so deep into Teralynn's brain that she'd never recover. That would show Evelyn that she'd made a mistake getting someone else involved!

Wearing a heavy coat, hat and gloves to protect him from the cold, he sat in Teralynn's neighbor's hunk-of-junk car, which had been unlocked since it was up on blocks and couldn't be stolen anyway, waiting for her to come home. He'd left his Prius several blocks away and walked into the neighborhood – had had no trouble finding her place. She'd put her home address on her application for the cleaning position two years ago, and he'd been the one to interview and hire her. So he'd been here before, many times, trying to weigh the risks against the reward of taking Teralynn as his next victim.

Ultimately, he'd decided to choose someone else. He worked with Teralynn, would be questioned by police if she went missing. But he'd considered her as a possibility for quite some time. She'd be *such* an easy victim.

Something he was about to prove . . .

As soon as a pair of headlights rounded the corner, he slid down beneath the level of the window so that he couldn't be seen. This had to be her. She would've gotten off twenty minutes ago – the perfect amount of time to make the drive – and not many other people were up and cruising through residential neighborhoods at three in the morning.

Once he heard the car pass, he removed his hat and lifted his head enough to see her pull into her driveway. She sat there for several moments, looking around as if she was afraid to get out, and only opened the door when another car came down the street – a cop car.

Lyman ducked again and waited.

The cop got out and went inside the house for several minutes. Then the beam of a flashlight bobbed as he checked the side yard of Teralynn's house and went into the back. When he returned, Lyman could hear the drone of voices as the cop spoke to Teralynn at the front door. No doubt the police officer was assuring her that he hadn't seen anything to be alarmed about.

Lyman chuckled as the cop got back into his squad car and left. Teralynn would be feeling reassured at this point, would never see him coming. A year ago, he'd made a copy of the key she used to keep beneath the planter on the front porch, so even if she'd removed the spare since, it didn't matter. All he had to do was wait for her to go to sleep and let himself in . . .

He watched her house for thirty minutes – until all the lights went off. Then he waited *another* half hour. The cop hadn't returned, but Lyman thought he might do an occasional drive-by, so he'd been watching the road, as well.

At four-thirty, he slipped out of the wreck he'd been sitting in and walked quickly and quietly to the front door.

Teralynn's bedroom was in the back, on the right of a short hallway. He knew because he'd used his key before. He'd gone through her clothes and pictures, smelled her panties, even worn them. He'd also masturbated in her bathroom.

The floor creaked as he walked, but the heater camouflaged the noise. He got all the way to her bedroom, was about to turn the knob on her door, when he heard her say, 'Hello? Is someone there?'

The fear in her voice was gratifying, but the fact that she wasn't asleep posed a problem. If she were to call the police before he could subdue her, they could return before he was out of the house—

'Dr Bishop, is it you? . . . Hello? Is someone there?'

Lyman fingered the ice picks he carried in his coat pocket. He longed to speak up, to let her know he *was* there and had a surprise for her. But then headlights flashed through the front window of the house, and he had to flatten himself to the wall to be sure that he wasn't seen.

His heart raced as he waited. Had he walked into too precarious a situation? Although the car out front seemed to have driven away, he couldn't be sure . . .

He'd never attempted anything like this, had always worked from the advantage of being unexpected. Was he making a mistake? Being overly confident? Too bold? He'd waited years and years to get revenge on his mother. He'd be foolish to act too impulsively here. It was the waiting, the planning, the control he'd exhibited in the past that'd served him so well. If Detective Gustavson hadn't cheated he never would've been caught.

But since he *had* been caught, he was working at a distinct disadvantage, and he needed to take that into consideration. If he killed Teralynn, the police would come after him right away – everyone would be looking for him. Why not take advantage of being able to move freely about?

He stood silent and still for what seemed like forever – until he felt certain that Teralynn had to have relaxed and gone to sleep. Then he let himself out of her house and walked straight back to his car. He was frustrated that he hadn't achieved his goal. Since he had the key to Teralynn's house, killing her had seemed almost too perfect to resist. But he was glad he *had* resisted. It was Evelyn he wanted. He'd be a fool to do anything that would make reaching her any harder.

The moment he got home, he booked his flight to Alaska.

The next morning, Evelyn checked with Detective Lewis as soon as she got to the office. He told her that a squad car had followed Teralynn home and that he'd have a couple of uniforms keep an eye on her during the investigation. Her testimony about how and where she found that 'kidnap' bag could be important, and once Bishop learned that he was under scrutiny again – that because of Teralynn the police might have something legitimate on him as far as forensic evidence – there was no telling what he might do.

Lewis suggested, and Evelyn agreed, that to be safe Teralynn shouldn't talk to any reporters, including Sebring Schultz from *The Star Tribune,* until Bishop had been arrested. And they couldn't arrest him until they came up with a solid link between him and that bag with the ice pick.

Detective Lewis acted as though he had the situation under control. Evelyn had every confidence that he was working as fast as possible to have the items Teralynn found tested, but police work took *so* long. And having Bishop out on the street was dangerous. He'd killed Jan Hall as well as the others whose murders he'd been charged with; he could easily kill again.

After she hung up with Detective Lewis, Evelyn called the facility where Beth was staying.

'Hello?' Bishop's sister sounded as though she had her mouth full.

'Beth?'

'What?'

'This is Dr Talbot.'

'Who?'

'Dr Talbot. Remember me?'

The chewing grew louder. 'No.'

'I'm the one who sent Louise Belgrath to help you move. You remember Louise, right?'

'You're the one who gave me this room? And these donuts?'

Evelyn tried not to laugh at the level of enthusiasm that came into Beth's voice. 'Sort of. In a roundabout way, I guess.' Regardless, it wasn't worth trying to explain. 'How are you doing?'

'My bed is here – and my blanket. I have my clothes, too. All of them, even my underwear.'

'Well, I wouldn't want you going anywhere without those,' Evelyn said wryly, but Beth wasn't listening. She was still talking.

'And I have a mirror. And I have my toothbrush. And I have a TV. And I have a channel changer.'

Evelyn smiled and checked her e-mail while they talked. 'So you like your new place.'

'I do! They have cookies here!'

'I can tell you're excited about that, but I hope they're not letting you eat too many sweets. Donuts, cookies – and it's still early in the day.'

'Because it's a special occasion, I can have one donut and four cookies,' she said.

'What's the occasion?'

'Lyman can't hurt me anymore.'

'No, he can't.'

'Did I tell you they have cookies? One, two, three, four. That's how many I can have. And I don't have to take off my clothes – 'cept to wash.'

The fact that Beth had been rescued from Bishop made Evelyn glad she did what she did for a living. She often wondered if she was making a difference. There were times, many of them, when the small successes didn't seem to be enough. But she told herself that if she could improve just one person's life she should be satisfied. Today it was Beth who made all the risk and sacrifice worth it. 'I'm happy to hear that—'

'Louise!' Beth cried. Then she said into the phone, 'Guess what? Louise is here!'

'Can I talk to her?' Evelyn asked.

There was a long pause, during which Evelyn could hear Louise greet Beth. She could also hear Beth telling Louise about how many cookies she could have each day – counting again. Finally, Louise got on the phone.

'Sounds as though she's adjusting well,' Evelyn said.

'Like a fish to water,' Louise responded. 'I'm very proud of her.'

'I was worried. Who knows if it's true, but Bishop told me things didn't go so well the last time she was institutionalized.'

'You mean ten years ago?'

'Yes. According to him, it wasn't a great experience for the poor thing.'

'Her experience was a lot better than anything she's ever known at home.'

'You've looked into it?'

'Of course. Files are kept on that sort of thing. Lyman had a girlfriend then – one of the few love interests he's had in his life. So he wanted to get rid of Beth. She was suddenly in the way.'

'That's scary, considering how he gets rid of people,' Evelyn said.

'I doubt she was in danger of . . . you know. He wouldn't want to answer the questions that would arise if she turned up missing. And he likes the way having a sister like Beth makes him look – so magnanimous. His work associates have given him a lot of praise over the years for taking care of her. They always have him bring her to holiday parties and such. I'm guessing she was still valuable to him, but he was hoping to get serious with his girlfriend. Anyway, he put her in Sunset Homes Adult Care, and she was doing really well until Lyman's girlfriend broke off their relationship. Then he wanted her back.'

Evelyn felt as if she could guess the reason. Who else would he have to suck his tummy banana? 'So he went to get her.'

'Yes, and threw a big fit, acting as if she hadn't been treated kindly. That provoked an investigation, but there was never any evidence to suggest she'd been mistreated in any way. And we now know what was going on under *his* roof.'

Evelyn shook her head. 'I'm glad she won't be subjected to *that* anymore. I heard you left a letter telling Lyman that you were removing him as guardian.'

'Yes.'

'But he doesn't know where you've taken Beth . . .'

'I didn't reveal that, no. Of course, if he goes to trial and is found innocent I won't be able to keep her whereabouts from him. But until then, he won't know. And we're going to send her for an MRI. The results of that might help the prosecution's case.'

Forgetting about what she was finding in her e-mail, Evelyn pushed back her chair and came to her feet. 'You are? When?'

'I don't have the date and time yet. I'm still trying to make the arrangements.'

'How'd you get the approval?'

'I reported the ice pick that was found in the bag where Lyman worked.'

Penny had knocked a few minutes earlier. Now she was back and motioning that she had to talk to Evelyn. Since it seemed important, Evelyn thanked Louise, asked her to call as soon as she had the results of the MRI and disconnected.

'What is it?' Evelyn asked her assistant.

'Dr Fitzpatrick called.'

Evelyn barely refrained from rolling her eyes. 'He left me yet another message yesterday. What'd he have to say this time?'

'He was in tears,' she said, her eyes round with shock. 'Sobbing like a baby.'

'Because . . .' Evelyn was afraid she could guess . . .

'The police arrived with a search warrant this morning. They went through his whole house. Took clothes, tools, gloves, shoes, his kitchen knives . . .'

'Wow. They're serious about investigating him as a suspect.'

'He claims he's innocent. He's begging for your help.'

'There's nothing they can do without sufficient evidence. Unless they find that evidence, he'll be fine.'

'You won't call him back?'

Evelyn stood and stretched. Sometimes she spent far too much time in a chair. 'I have appointments this morning. I already had you reschedule my first one. But I'll call Boston PD, see what's going on. Maybe they'll share something that will enable me to reassure him.'

'Thanks, Dr Talbot. I know you don't like him. I didn't, either, when he worked here. But . . .'

'You feel sorry for him.' She'd indicated that before.

'Yeah.'

'I've got it.' She checked her schedule. 'Put off my session with Harvey Garber for fifteen minutes,' she said, and called Miles Dressler, who answered right away.

'Dr Talbot. How are you?'

She thought of Beth living in a safe place and of that bag of items

Teralynn found that could put Bishop back in prison, where he belonged. 'I'm having a good day. You?'

'Things are starting to heat up here.'

'What does that mean?'

'I'm talking about the investigation of your friends' murders, Mandy Walker and Charlotte Zimmerman Pine. We haven't been able to bring you justice, which pains me, but I'm feeling more and more confident that we're going to be successful in solving their murders.'

'You've found evidence that will lead you to Jasper?'

'I don't think it was Jasper.'

'Which is why you searched Tim Fitzpatrick's house this morning.'

'Word travels fast.'

'Tim spoke to my assistant a few minutes ago. She said he was crying like a baby. I have to tell you, Detective, that he has a plausible excuse for being seen in her neighborhood, even for following her. It might not sound reasonable to most people, but I sort of get what he was doing. He was trying to stay involved in what he used to do – and stop a murder at the same time.'

'Are you sure?'

'I can't imagine he was doing anything else.'

'I thought he was an unlikely culprit myself – an educated man like that with no criminal history. Until I came across one very important piece of evidence – and realized there was something he failed to mention.'

The somber tone of Dressler's voice caused a frisson of concern to snake through her. 'What's that?'

'He went inside the house where Charlotte was murdered.'

Evelyn didn't like Tim – and yet she felt her heart sink. Fitzpatrick hadn't mentioned that to her, either. 'How can you be so sure?'

'We found a footprint – in her blood.'

Penny had said they'd taken certain items from Tim's house . . . 'And it matches a pair of his shoes,' Evelyn said.

'Yes,' he responded. 'How'd you know?'

*

Jasper could hardly contain his excitement as he walked through the large front entrance of the imposing stone prison. Hanover House, with its tall columns and Gothic arches, reminded him of some of the big cathedrals from medieval times. When he'd come before, the prison hadn't been complete, so he couldn't help stopping to appreciate the architecture. This 'revolutionary new medical health facility', as it'd been billed by the press, didn't create a blight on the landscape, like most other prisons. It had some style, some class.

Good job, Evelyn. He would've expected nothing less of her . . .

A burly guard indicated the conveyor belt leading to the X-ray machine. 'Please empty your pockets into this dish before proceeding through the metal detector.'

'Right. No problem. I'm familiar with the drill,' he teased, hoping to make friends right from the beginning.

The guy seemed slightly taken aback that he was so amiable but managed a grudging smile. 'You sure you want to come work *here*?' he said under his breath.

Jasper lowered his voice. 'That bad, huh?'

'No different from any other prison – if you don't mind the cold.'

He breathed deeply as he looked around, hoping to catch a glimpse of Evelyn. If she was at the prison, she wasn't within eyesight. But no matter. He'd bump into her at some point. After twenty-one long years, he was right where he needed to be. 'I think I'm going to like it.'

Twenty Seven

Evelyn called her sister over lunch. She didn't want her family sitting on pins and needles thinking that Jasper was on a killing spree in Boston if Fitzpatrick was responsible for Mandy's and Charlotte's murders.

'It's me,' she said as soon as Brianne picked up.

'What's going on in Alaska?'

Evelyn thought of all the things she could say – about Bishop and Amarok and her current studies – but decided not to go into any of it. Bishop alone would take an hour to explain, what with Beth and Teralynn and what he'd said in the lie detector test, and she didn't have long before she had to return to evaluating those brain scans with Jim Ricardo. Focusing on that study seemed to be what was keeping him sane. He'd mentioned when he stopped by her office earlier that his wife wasn't pregnant, as they'd both hoped. Evelyn couldn't help feeling sorry for him, since she got the impression the bad news had only made things worse for him at home. She could even identify, to a smaller degree, with his wife's disappointment.

'Everything's pretty calm at the moment,' she said. In a way, that was true. Nothing big had happened in Hilltop or Hanover House *that day.* 'Have you seen the news?'

'The news? No. Why? Has someone else been killed?'

Evelyn hated that Brianne would immediately assume the worst, but she had good reason. 'They caught the man who killed Mandy and Charlotte.'

'Was it Jasper?'

'No, it was Tim Fitzpatrick.'

'The psychiatrist who gave you such a bad time last year?'

'Yes.'

Silence.

'Brianne?'

'I'm here.'

'Aren't you relieved?' She didn't seem to be . . .

'Of course. Mom and Dad will be, too. It'll be great to get back to our regular lives and stop looking over our shoulders all the time – if that's even possible after what we've been through. It's just . . . how long before the next thing pops up? It seems like we go through a big scare every few years.'

A rush of guilt made Evelyn uncomfortable. Her family had begged her to change her profession to something safer. Her work not only endangered her; it endangered everyone she loved. What Fitzpatrick had done was proof. But so did being a cop or a district attorney. Fighting crime contained inherent risk. 'I'm sorry for that.'

Her sister sighed. 'It'd be easier if we shared your passion.'

But they didn't. They wanted to forget the trauma of the past, to live their lives as if she'd never been kidnapped or tortured. Evelyn understood. Sometimes she felt she was being selfish to deny them that. But who would fight people like Jasper if she didn't? That was what it all came down to – what kept her going, despite their disapproval. 'Someone has to do what I'm doing.'

More silence. Then Brianne said, 'Don't mind me. I'm just a little disillusioned. Fitzpatrick was supposed to be one of the good guys, you know? How many killers will we have to worry about?'

Providing they were free and able, any of the psychopaths Evelyn had studied over the years – and that number was probably at a thousand by now – could come after her or her family. 'Hopefully we won't anymore.'

'Do you believe it was Fitzpatrick?' her sister asked. 'That they have the right guy?'

Evelyn couldn't say yes, not with any real commitment. Something about the situation felt off. But he *had* lied about being at the crime scene. They had his footprint in Charlotte's blood, so the police were convinced he was the culprit, and Evelyn had nothing concrete with which to disagree with them. Maybe she was doggedly hanging on to the suspicion that it was Jasper because she *wanted* to blame him for everything, had built his capabilities up so much in her mind that she'd come to believe he was all-powerful, all-seeing, everywhere at once. 'They have proof.'

'Okay. I'll tell Mom and Dad.'

'Thanks.' That would save her an even more difficult conversation – for now – since she knew her parents would once again plead with her to return to Boston and take up private practice.

Brianne was about to hang up when Evelyn caught her. 'How're things with Jeff?'

'Good.' Her sister's tone had finally warmed.

'You're still in love?'

'Most definitely.'

'That gives me something to smile about.'

'What about you?' Brianne asked. 'You've been with Amarok for a while now . . .'

'Yeah.'

'So what are you going to do? Marry him and stay there for the rest of your life?'

Evelyn pinched the bridge of her nose. She knew how well her family would take *that* news. 'I don't know,' she said.

As usual, Lyman Bishop was careful to blend in with the crowd as he followed the other passengers off the plane. He wore baggy, nondescript clothes under a heavy coat and had a hat pulled low, over his eyes. He didn't want to allow a clear image of himself to be caught on surveillance video.

Although he felt a great deal of pressure to act fast, before anyone could realize he'd left Minneapolis, he tried not to show that he was in a hurry. The fact that he'd gained three hours on the flight back to Alaska eased some of the pressure he felt. He'd slept most of the way, which also helped, since he'd been up the entire night once he got home and found that Beth had been removed from his care. Thanks to that four-hour nap, he was alert and ready for what lay ahead.

But he was facing a long night. By the time he rented an SUV and drove to Hilltop, it'd be eight, at least. That didn't give him a lot of time to put his plan into motion.

While Lyman waited at Baggage Claim, he stared at his feet and went over the next few hours in his mind. Not until several minutes after the luggage began to bump its way down the conveyor belt and the crowd around him began to thin did he lift his head to grab his own black, standard suitcase. He hoped Security hadn't searched it. The ice pick he'd purchased before getting on the plane wasn't a large tool – he'd slipped it right into his shaving kit – but the fact that he was carrying something that could be used to stab someone could raise questions. He was afraid, if TSA had found it, that they'd removed it and left one of those gold notes on top of his clothes in its place.

Because the pick was an integral part of his revenge, he was tempted to open his bag right there to look. They might've found the chloroform he'd paid a student to steal from the chemistry department, too. But he held off until he had his rental vehicle, was about to pull out of the lot and knew no one was watching.

'There you are,' he muttered when he found the pick and the chloroform right where he'd put them and zipped his bag back up. 'Those idiots couldn't find their own assholes,' he added, feeling strangely powerful to have escaped the notice of TSA. But then, that was what he did – he escaped notice.

Once he climbed behind the wheel, he turned on the cabin light and smoothed out the map he'd picked up at the car rental counter. He'd stop off and purchase the groceries and the rest of what he needed before leaving Anchorage. The woman who'd rented him the Ford Escape had circled a couple of spots on a nearby street where he could find the stores he needed. Then, providing the weather would cooperate – he felt nervous just thinking about that narrow mountain pass where Sergeant Murphy had swerved toward the guardrail – he'd drive to Hilltop.

Fortunately, it wasn't snowing. Bitter cold though it was, the storm seemed to have passed.

He started the engine to get the heat going and checked the paperwork he'd printed out at an office supply store before taking Uber to the airport in Minneapolis. The cabin he'd rented online looked remote. There'd be a bit of a drive to reach it, and it'd be pitch-black out away from the city lights. That caused him some concern. Getting stranded in Alaska at this time of year could prove fatal. But, providing he could find the cabin, he felt he'd be safe until he could figure out his next move.

Either way, there wasn't any point in ever trying to go back home. The police had something significant on him, or they wouldn't have taken Beth away. Teralynn had acted so strange when he'd spoken to her – and, after they hung up, she wouldn't accept any more of his calls. She hadn't been indifferent to him, like before; she'd been terrified, especially once he'd mentioned Evelyn Talbot. The psychiatrist who ran Hanover House was behind whatever was going on. He felt sure of it. She'd been determined to keep him behind bars, if possible.

May the best person win . . . She'd said that, but he wouldn't allow things to end as she hoped. If she was going to take Beth away, she'd have to replace her.

Amarok kept an eye on the door, but Evelyn didn't show up. She knew he had to spend some time at the Moosehead on Friday nights, especially when they had a boxing match. But she'd been going on such little sleep, what with the big push to get Beth away from Bishop and the murders in Boston. He couldn't blame her if she'd decided to go home and relax.

Because the fight – between a guy named Stu Stamper from Anchorage and Hilltop's own Tommy Gilchrist – promised to be a good one, people had come from all around. Almost everyone Amarok knew was there, including Samantha. She came over to pet Makita and struck up a conversation about her store. She said she planned to open in spring, talked about how excited she was to get started and then asked Amarok to dance.

He agreed – felt it'd be too rude to say no – but all he could think about was Evelyn. He wished he could go home and planned to do so as soon as the fight was over.

Too bad the fight didn't start until ten.

After the song ended, he extricated himself from Samantha's arms and returned to his seat, where Makita waited patiently. Then he nursed a beer and kept an eye out for any signs of trouble while scratching his dog's head.

Before long, Samantha was studying him as if she was tempted to approach again, so he slipped out of the main room, into the hallway where the bathrooms were, so that he could use the pay phone.

'Hello?' Evelyn said.

There she was. So she *had* left work – not always a given with her, even this late. He'd called the prison first, just in case. 'What's going on?' he asked.

'Not a whole lot. I'm sorry I'm not there at the Moosehead with you tonight. I pulled into the lot, but it was so full I couldn't find a parking space, and I was reluctant to leave my SUV down the street and walk. It's too cold out, and I wasn't wearing my boots.'

'That's fine. Just tell me you're not working. You need to get some rest.'

'I admit I'm trying to catch up on a few things for the BOP. But I'll get in bed early.'

He leaned one shoulder against the wood paneling that covered the wall. 'You're okay, though? You're not upset or worried about anything?'

'I'm not sure I'd go *that* far,' she said with a little laugh. 'I'm worried about Bishop and what he might do to Teralynn. She's at the lab, cleaning again. I keep imagining him breaking in while she's there or waiting for her when she gets out. But I've contacted Minneapolis PD. They say they'll look out for her.'

'You have to trust them. There's nothing you can do from here.'

'Truer words have never been spoken.'

He plugged his right ear, trying to block out the loud music. 'What'd you say?'

'I said, *Truer words have never been spoken.*'

'Right. Listen, I've got something to tell you that might improve your night!' he shouted into the phone.

'What's that?'

'They have a match on the DNA. In Peoria.'

There was a brief silence while she absorbed the news. 'The same person who killed those women in Peoria tried to abduct Vanessa Lopez from Casa Grande?'

'That's right. Granted, this would be more exciting if we had a sample of Jasper's DNA and could prove it was him. But we know from his mother that he lives in Arizona. And these murders aren't that old, not when you compare them to what happened to you and your friends back in Boston. They may yet yield some lead that will break the case. Detective Sims is determined to come up with something. He's afraid Jasper might kill again.'

'He *will* kill again. But having two police departments searching for him instead of one should improve our odds.'

'And we have a surviving witness, of sorts.'

'When did you hear this news?' she asked.

He stepped aside so that someone else could squeeze past him to get to the bathroom. 'This afternoon.'

'And you didn't call me?'

'I was saving it for tonight, thought we'd celebrate. But since you'll probably go to bed before I even get home . . .'

'Will you be late?'

'It'll be midnight, at least. With the way folks are drinking here tonight, it might be even later.'

'How's Vanessa doing? Have you heard?'

'I asked, yeah. She's recovered. Is back at work.'

'But no one has seen the guy she mentioned visiting that 7-Eleven.'

'No.'

'Something's got to give, Amarok.'

He ducked his head; the music seemed to be growing even louder. 'It will, babe. I promise. I'm having a tough time hearing you, so I'll let you go for now.'

'Okay. I hope Tommy wins the fight.'

'So do I,' he said, and hung up. He wasn't looking forward to the wait, not with Samantha hovering around, eager to use Makita as an excuse to talk to him again. But he quickly forgot about his ex. Almost as soon as he returned to his seat, Westin Pinnegar came rushing into the Moosehead, pushing everyone else out of his way.

'Where's the sergeant?' he yelled, and made a beeline for Amarok the second he learned the answer to that question.

'What is it?' Amarok asked. Clearly, the man was upset. His face, normally weathered and chapped red from all the time he spent outdoors, was chalk white, and he was breathing rapidly, as though he'd been running.

'Oh my God, Amarok. Oh my God!' he kept saying.

A crowd began to form around them as Amarok came off his stool. 'Calm down and tell me what happened.'

'I don't know what happened!' He spread out his hands and shook his head as if the vision in his mind was inconceivable, unexplainable. 'I-I can't figure it,' he stuttered. 'I just saw Sandy Ledstetter maybe an hour ago at The Dinky Diner. They stayed open late tonight, like they sometimes do, to take advantage of all the folks coming in for the fight, you know?'

Amarok *did* know. Shorty had complained that they were 'stealing his business'. He was the one sponsoring the fight, so he felt everyone should buy food at the Moosehead.

'She served me my chicken-fried steak,' Westin said, his voice cracking.

Dread welled up inside Amarok. The men in Hilltop didn't cry easily. 'And *now*?'

The tears that'd been in his voice filled his eyes as he choked out, 'She's swinging from a tree!'

Although he'd been standing along the periphery of the room, keeping a low profile, Jasper couldn't help craning his neck to see what was going on over by the bar with Amarok. Jasper had watched Evelyn's boyfriend ever since the trooper had walked in with his Alaskan malamute – had seen him pet his dog, talk to his friends and dance with a tall blonde. Evelyn didn't seem to be with him, but as far as Jasper was concerned, that was good. He longed to see her again, but as impatient as he was feeling, it would be better to slowly weave himself into the fabric of this small community without drawing her attention. Or the sergeant's, for that matter. By the time that happened, he hoped he wouldn't be considered a complete stranger in these parts.

The murmur that went through the throng indicated something terrible had happened. So did the way Amarok rushed out of the bar.

Several people followed despite how many times he gestured for them to stay back. That made it easy to get swept up in the crowd, which was buzzing with alarm.

Eventually, the entire Moosehead emptied out. All the patrons poured down the street to where a twentysomething-year-old woman dangled, obviously dead, from the branch of a big tree right at the edge of the parking lot of The Dinky Diner, where Jasper had once had breakfast.

'What the hell! . . .' 'It's Sandy . . .' 'No way! How terrible! . . .' 'What happened to her? . . .' 'Who could've done this?'

Several people grew instantly distraught. Jasper, however, gazed on to the scene with nothing more than detached curiosity. What an interesting and surprising turn of events, especially on his first night in town. Thank goodness he hadn't gone back to Anchorage after orientation at the prison, like he'd been planning to do. If he hadn't decided to stop in for a drink and be seen in his new uniform, he would've missed out.

Despite all the friends and family scrambling to get the woman down as soon as possible, Amarok wouldn't let anyone touch the body. He insisted it was too late, that she was 'gone', and pushed them all back – an action his dog helped with by barking and herding the crowd almost like sheep. Once everyone understood he wasn't going to relent on that, he called for someone by the name of Phil to run down to the trooper post and get a camera and some lights. Apparently, he was going to approach this as the crime scene it had to be.

How many murders could such a young trooper have investigated? Jasper wondered. *Especially way the hell out here?* More than the two Jasper had followed in the paper last year?

Regardless, Amarok wasn't stupid. He'd managed to tie Jasper to the five women near that old barn in Peoria, hadn't he? It wouldn't be wise to underestimate him . . .

The guy to Jasper's left, who'd been talking with Jasper at the Moosehead, nudged him. 'Not a good day to move to Alaska, buddy. I bet you're ready to turn around and head back to the Lower 48 after seeing this.'

'Naw,' Jasper said. 'I worked at Florence Prison before I got on at Hanover House. Believe me, I've seen it all.' He'd relished the violence – thrived on it – but he knew his new 'friend' wouldn't be able to relate.

'Makes sense this wouldn't hit you as hard as the rest of us,' he responded. 'You didn't know her. We did. And she was a real nice girl.'

Jasper had never seen a public spectacle like this one, but then he'd never spent any significant time in a place like Hilltop. Between all the weeping, the fear, the shock, and Amarok and Phil trying to calm everyone and retain control of the situation, the entire town was preoccupied. Anyone who happened to be outside this little epicenter could get away with *anything.* No one would notice.

Now *would be the time to commit a crime,* Jasper thought, eyeing the surrounding stores. And then, a mere second later, two things occurred to him. One, Evelyn wasn't at the murder scene – and

Amarok wouldn't be going home to her anytime soon. And two, there couldn't be a more engrossing or long-lasting diversion, no better chance to act on what he'd come here to accomplish despite all of his carefully laid plans.

This was called a golden opportunity, he decided. If he were to grab Evelyn in the midst of this uproar, there'd be plenty of time to get her out of Hilltop before she was missed, and whoever killed the fat chick swinging from the tree would get the blame.

That was *more* than a golden opportunity. That was a damn invitation.

Twenty Eight

Evelyn had the television on even though she wasn't paying much attention to it. She was too engrossed in updating the files on the inmates she met with on a regular basis, so engrossed that she didn't get up to investigate when she heard a noise outside. The many storms that rolled through Alaska could be loud – from booming thunder, to pounding rain, to the wail of the wind tossing tree branches or other items against the house. But a second thud pulled her mind out of her work, and she realized that it wasn't storming.

Was it Amarok? Usually Makita let her know well in advance when they were home. He'd race to the door, barking to announce their return.

Her cat jumped off her lap as she got up. One glance at her watch told her it was too early for Amarok and Makita to be back. Had Amarok decided to swing by before the big fight? Maybe he'd forgotten something . . .

She checked to make sure the porch light was on. It was, so she peered through the peephole, thinking she might see some sign of who or what was out there. Amarok could be moving around the house, putting the garbage cans away or whatever before coming in.

But she couldn't see anyone – and she wasn't about to unlock the door to go out in the dark to look—

A rustling sound coming from the back of the house caused her breath to catch in her throat. Something wasn't right. It wasn't just the noise; she felt an ominous sort of dread in the pit of her stomach.

Was someone trying to break in?

Her eyes darted to the phone. Should she call Amarok – or grab the rifle he kept near the fireplace and try to get her and Sigmund out of the house?

Afraid she wouldn't make it to her SUV or that it wouldn't start right away because of the cold, she grabbed the rifle, scooped up her cat and rushed over to the phone.

There was no dial tone. Either someone had hit a telephone pole and knocked out their service, or . . .

The 'or' convinced her that she was in trouble again. Fear rose up, stealing her strength. Considering the number of violent men she'd studied over the years, many of whom would like to kill her, she had to assume the worst.

Stay calm, she warned herself. *And get a coat.* She'd freeze to death if she had to be outside for any length of time. But just as she put down the gun and her cat so that she could suit up, she heard glass shatter in the spare bedroom.

Someone was coming in through the window.

Now. Forget the cold. She had to make a dash for it, even if it meant freezing to death later. But she had no idea where Sigmund had gone. Put out that she wasn't acting normal, he'd run off, was probably hiding under the couch or a chair so she'd leave him alone.

She prayed he'd be safe until she could get help as she retrieved the gun, grabbed her keys and bolted for the door.

She was so intent on reaching her SUV that she didn't see the trip wire strung from one support pole to the other. It caught her at the ankles. The gun went flying as she fell, hard on the icy pavement – and the next thing she knew, she was lying on her back, staring up at a dark shape leaning over her.

She thought it was Jasper. It *had* to be Jasper. He'd tried to abduct her again eighteen months ago. And she'd known he'd come back, that he wouldn't let her escape him in the end. The more successful she became, or he perceived her to be, the more he'd want to destroy her. She understood the fixation, not only because she'd researched so many psychopaths and the way they thought but also, instinctively, from those days when she'd been his captive and he'd been so incredibly cruel.

Frightened though she was, now that the moment had come part of her *wanted* to see him, to know how he'd changed. It'd been so long since she'd laid eyes on him. Because he'd been wearing a mask the summer before last in Boston, she hadn't been able to catch a glimpse of his face, and she'd so desperately wanted to provide the police with fresh details, an accurate composite sketch, something new to go on.

He wasn't wearing a mask now, but she still couldn't see him clearly, not with the way his body blocked the porch light.

'Jasper?' she croaked, her breath misting on the frigid air. Her body ached from the fall, and her ears rang. She'd hit her chin, nearly knocked herself out – yet, dimly, she realized he'd set a trap for her. He'd purposely flushed her out of the house, sent her running by making those noises and breaking that window.

He knew she'd charge out the only entrance; he also knew she wouldn't get far.

'Wrong,' she heard him say. 'The good news is that you'll never have to worry about Jasper again. The bad news is . . . I've gotten to you first.'

Lyman Bishop. He wasn't in Minnesota, stalking Teralynn. He'd gotten home, seen that Beth was gone, turned around and come back – for *her.*

'Help!' she yelled, but there was no one else around.

'Don't worry,' he told her calmly, full of a new kind of confidence. 'I'll be sure to knock you out before I operate. And you'll be glad to know that I've gotten good at going in through the eye socket. It only takes me ten minutes. When we're done, we'll put a pair of sunglasses on you and no one will know you've had any type of procedure.'

'Operate? Procedure?' Suddenly everything she'd learned about

Bishop – what he did to his victims – came tumbling back despite her dazed state. He was talking about a lobotomy! He was going to cut into her brain, make her compliant, destroy her ability to resist him – or do much of anything else.

With a surge of strength born of desperation, she tried to shove him away. But he was standing above her, had every advantage. She didn't have a chance, but she called for Amarok, anyway – until Bishop shut her up by holding a damp rag over her nose and mouth.

Although she continued to struggle, knew she *had* to fight if she wanted to be the same person when she woke up, a sweet acetone scent registered in her brain. Then even the dim halo of the porch light turned to black.

Bishop dragged Evelyn into the house and closed and locked the door. He was breathing hard from the exertion and yet, so far, he'd only gotten her into the entryway. Although Evelyn didn't weigh as much as some of his other victims, moving an unconscious woman was never easy. He wasn't as fit as he'd like to be, either. But at least he had a sharp mind. He should get more credit for being clever, should be more appealing to women than he'd always been. Look at what he'd been able to accomplish in his career!

Forget that, he told himself. What did it matter? He compensated for whatever he was missing, figured out a way to get what he wanted. Take tonight, for example. The woman he'd found turning off the lights and locking up at that diner was more than happy to tell him where Evelyn lived. Once he'd shown her the ice pick, she was willing to do *anything.* The information she provided had proven helpful, but it hadn't saved her life, as she'd been hoping in that moment. He'd needed a way to make sure Sergeant Amarok would be away from home – and occupied for hours.

Bishop had hung out in the shadows long enough to make sure that someone spotted the body after he hung it up. He'd even watched as that man nearly swerved off the road, returned to get another look, then rushed down to the bar. A few minutes later a horde of people had come pouring into the street, with the trooper leading the charge. So Bishop knew where Evelyn's boyfriend was and where he was likely to remain. And there weren't any neighbors nearby, no one else to get in the way. He'd checked the area before stringing that trip wire across the front door. They were out in the middle of nowhere – with the whole night ahead of them.

The table wasn't long enough, so he put Evelyn on the couch. That wasn't an ideal place to operate, but . . . what could he do? Once again, he had to improvise. The important thing was that he'd soon have a completely cowed and compliant Evelyn in the SUV with him as he drove out of town, never to be seen again.

It would take some real ingenuity to assume a new identity and start over somewhere else, but he'd have his disabled 'sister' to lend him instant legitimacy. They'd hide out in the cabin he'd rented for the first few weeks, to give him time to see how effective the procedure was. Everyone was different, after all; sometimes he had to do a second lobotomy. Once he was satisfied with Evelyn's behavior, they'd move on, figure out a new place to live and something he could do for work. People were always so supportive when he mentioned he was caring for his poor, unfortunate sibling. Evelyn would win him instant trust and the admiration he'd always deserved but been denied, just as Beth had.

One thing was for certain. Evelyn would never look down on him again. He'd see to that.

He lifted her left eyelid, looking for the best spot through which to jam the ice pick into her brain. *Eggbeater fashion,* he reminded himself. That was the best technique. Dr Freeman, who'd been famous for his lobotomies in the fifties and sixties, described the procedure that way in a video clip on the Internet, and, from his own experience, Bishop had to agree. That was how he'd done Beth's, and she was the best example of what he was looking to accomplish. She wasn't a drooling imbecile, like a handful or more women he'd done. She was still capable of sucking his tummy banana, which he enjoyed almost on a daily basis, yet she wasn't capable of surviving without assistance, which made it very unlikely she'd go anywhere or anyone would take much interest in her.

If Evelyn hadn't interfered, he'd still have Beth, would still be living in his comfortable house and working at his comfortable job and coming home to enjoy a woman's body in whatever way he chose.

Covering Evelyn's breast with one hand, he gave it an experimental squeeze. She made him hard, all right. She was beautiful, a step up from poor, pudgy Beth. Sadly, the lobotomy would change that, to a point. Evelyn's body would go soft, too, after a few years . . .

He wondered if he'd have time to have some fun with her after the procedure. He hadn't had sex in so long – ever since he was arrested. And he liked the idea of taking Evelyn right there on the trooper's couch. He'd never been able to get the type of women someone like the sergeant could, but this changed everything.

He reached into his pants, felt himself and decided he'd make time to consummate their new relationship.

'Everything I'm about to do is your own fault,' he told her, even though she was unconscious and couldn't hear a word.

Too bad he didn't have another ice pick. Then he could go in through both eyes at the same time. Freeman used to do that.

Jasper had no trouble finding Amarok's house. Not only had he spoken to a handful of COs after orientation; he'd chatted with that guy at the bar for quite some time, enough to have learned the layout of the whole town. He'd merely joked that if he ever got tired of commuting and decided to move to Hilltop he'd live right next to the trooper, since Amarok was the only cop in town. And he'd been told that there weren't any houses – or land, for that matter – for sale out on South Piper Street, where the 'trooper and the doc' lived. Most suggested he look a little closer to town.

That was what he loved about this place. Everyone was so helpful.

Because he didn't plan to stay at Evelyn's for long, Jasper pulled into the drive. He figured it'd be easier to get her into his vehicle that way. He'd learned a few things about finding and subduing victims in his day. Skulking about drew undue attention and wasn't necessary, but acting as if he belonged worked like magic. He would've gone right up to the door and knocked. He was wearing a heavy Hanover House coat over a Hanover House uniform, figured Evelyn would take him for a guard and open the door. He only needed her to trust him for a brief second, just long enough to give him a chance. But he saw a Ford Escape parked in front of the house that puzzled him. Did the trooper have two vehicles? Did Evelyn? Because there was also a Toyota Landcruiser under the carport.

He wasn't sure what their vehicle situation was like and didn't care to run into any unpleasant surprises, so he decided to take a look around before making an approach. That was when he found the broken window. The sight of it puzzled him. Cold as it was, Amarok would not have left that window broken and uncovered for any length of time. He wouldn't be able to. He and Evelyn would freeze to death in the sub-zero temperatures.

That meant the breaking had to be recent. *Really* recent.

The image of the dead woman, swinging from that tree in town popped into his mind. *What the hell!* Had someone created a diversion in order to get to Evelyn?

What else could be happening? It wasn't as if there were murders in Hilltop all the time. That woman had been hung in a place that suggested the killer wanted her to be found. And given the psychopaths Evelyn worked with, it wasn't inconceivable that there'd be another man hoping to lay hands on her.

Something was going down. The good news was that whoever broke that window wasn't gone yet, or one of the vehicles would be gone, too.

Fortunately, Jasper's outerwear was thick enough that he could crawl through the window without getting cut. And since the noisy part – the breaking of the glass – had already occurred, he barely made a sound as he went in. Whoever else was in the house didn't seem to be worried about visitors, anyway. Jasper could hear someone humming in the living room.

Creeping carefully down the hall toward that sound, he saw the back of a middle-aged balding man sterilizing an instrument with rubbing alcohol. 'I'm sure glad you had some of this,' that man said.

'I had to be careful what I purchased in Anchorage, didn't want to give myself away. I figured it was bad enough that I was buying rope. But it would sure be a tragedy if, after all this effort, you were to die of an infection. We're going to have a wonderful life together, you and I.'

Who was he speaking to? Jasper couldn't see anyone else in the room. But when the man turned and lifted the sharp instrument he'd just cleaned, Jasper recognized him from his picture on the Internet.

It was Lyman Bishop. And he was cleaning an ice pick!

Lyman didn't know what hit him. One minute he was walking around the couch carrying his clean ice pick, thoughts of stripping Evelyn's clothes off, of watching her rouse as he drove inside her, flowing through his head. The next he was sailing across the room. As he hit the wall, he assumed Amarok had come home. Whoever had shoved him was strong. But the person who rolled him over and lifted him by the shirtfront, his lip curled in hate and disgust, was not the Alaska State Trooper.

'Who – who are you?' Bishop cried, using his arms to shield his head from whatever was coming next.

The man didn't stop to introduce himself. He punched Bishop in the face and kept punching him – again and again and again.

At first, Bishop was so shocked he felt nothing. But pain burst upon his consciousness as the battering continued. A blow to the mouth knocked out two teeth; another broke his nose. He heard the bones crunch, could feel blood running from . . . everywhere, it seemed. The man was kicking him, too, right in the stomach, making him spit even more blood.

Although he covered up as best he could, he was no match for the ferocious onslaught. He whimpered; he cried; he begged. Nothing seemed to stem the rage inside the other man. He didn't deserve this. He hadn't been able to plan for it because it was completely unexpected.

Where had this person come from?

'Please,' Bishop moaned, barely able to speak for the damage done to his face. 'Stop. I'll do anything. I swear. You're going to *kill* me!'

'You're right,' the other man said, but the beating stopped. That made Bishop wonder if he'd gotten through to him. If there might still be a chance . . .

He tried to scramble for the door, but his attacker caught him before he could go three feet, and this time he had the ice pick Bishop had dropped when he'd been blindsided with that first powerful shove.

'What's that for?' Cowering, Bishop used his legs to propel his body toward the corner, but he couldn't escape. The rabid stranger advanced, wearing a gleeful, self-satisfied expression on his handsome face.

'You *know* what it's for,' he replied, and held Bishop's head back against the wall as he shoved the ice pick through Bishop's right eye.

Twenty Nine

As Amarok cut Sandy Ledstetter down, he had Phil use Makita to keep everyone back. He felt terrible having to be so firm. He knew these people meant well. They were her friends and family. Hell, he'd been her friend, too. She'd served him often at the diner, and he'd always liked her. But he couldn't think like a civilian right now. He owed it to her to think like a cop, couldn't allow anything to interfere with that, or he'd regret it later. He was all Hilltop had by way of police support. He couldn't let them down, especially now.

'This is a crime scene, Betty,' he said to her mother, but Betty was having none of it. She called him every name in the book as she fought to get to her 'little girl'.

'God, Amarok. This is terrible!' Phil yelled as he struggled to keep Betty away. 'You tried to tell us not to let Hanover House be built anywhere close by. And you were right. First last year, and now this. I'm sure we *all* regret it now.'

Phil assumed that someone attached to Hanover House had to be responsible for this. That had been the assumption last year, too, and it'd turned out to be true. Was this more corruption of some sort? Had someone escaped the prison? Or was this—

Amarok froze as he was about to snap another picture of Sandy's swollen face. He'd been so caught up in this tragedy that he hadn't considered all the ramifications. He'd been too busy securing and photographing the crime scene and trying to keep the crowd under control so it wouldn't get contaminated. He was doing his job. This was what he was expected to do. But that was just it. What if this was Jasper's handiwork? What if *he'd* gotten to Sandy? It didn't appear that she'd been raped or tortured. She'd been killed and strung up at the edge of a parking lot that bordered Main Street. Whoever did this knew it would cause an uproar. Was he also hoping it would divert Amarok's attention away from whatever he'd usually be doing, which was going home to Evelyn?

Shit! Whatever this crime was about, it wasn't about poor Sandy. She was merely a means to an end. And he feared Evelyn was that 'end'.

'Anyone who comes within three feet of this body will be arrested!' he yelled. Then he grabbed Shorty and Shorty's sister and told them to help Phil make sure everyone stayed well away.

'Where are you going?' Shorty yelled when Amarok took off running for his truck.

'I have to check on Evelyn,' he said.

'Now?' Phil cried.

'It could be a matter of life and death.' As Amarok jumped into his truck, he told himself that wasn't really true. Evelyn was fine. The terror that nearly had his heart bursting out of his chest was completely unwarranted.

Or was it?

'What a pathetic loser you are,' Jasper said as he gazed down on his handiwork. 'And you got blood all over me, you stupid prick.' He considered going to the sink so that he could wash off. He wouldn't want anyone to see him like this. But that would take more time and make a bigger mess. He was better off getting the hell out of there. Evelyn was beginning to moan, would come to very soon. It would be a lot easier to transport her while she was still out or at least confused and groggy. He figured he had about thirty minutes until she was fully recovered . . .

'Don't worry. I've got you,' he said as he lifted her from the couch. But the fact that the house was already getting cold reminded him that he couldn't take her outside without some kind of covering. It was twenty below tonight.

He put her down while he went to grab a blanket, which would be easier and quicker than a coat. Then he picked her up again and headed for the door.

He was safe to leave the house like this, wasn't he? he asked himself.

Yes, he'd be fine. When Amarok got home, he'd find a broken window and Bishop's vehicle out front, with Bishop dead on the floor and Evelyn gone. What would the scene tell him?

Did it make any difference?

Not if there wasn't anything to connect the crime to Andy Smith. And there wasn't. He hadn't even taken off his gloves. There should be no fingerprints, no DNA, nothing to lead anyone to the prison guard who'd just hired on at Hanover House.

He paused to look at the floor. No footprints, either. At least, none that he could see. Bishop had made it easy. Rarely did anything turn out like this. Jasper had been lucky, but he figured he deserved a bit of luck after waiting twenty-one years to get hold of Evelyn again. All the luck had gone her way eighteen months ago.

She groaned.

'Sh-h . . . ,' he said as he fumbled to unlock the front door without dropping her. It was no small feat and took a moment, but soon the cold slap of the wind hit his face. He was rushing toward the driveway when a truck came flying down the street and skidded to a stop behind his Chevy Tahoe.

Sergeant Amarok. In the split second it took for that to register, Jasper almost dropped Evelyn and ran. There was no other way out – unless he killed Amarok as he'd killed Bishop.

Amarok approached with a rifle. 'Freeze, or I'll blow your head off.'

'Wait! You don't understand!' Jasper cried.

Amarok's eyes darted to Bishop's vehicle. The fact that there were *two* SUVs that didn't belong seemed to cause a bit of doubt – and that gave Jasper the split second he needed to think.

'She – she needs a doctor!' he cried. 'We have to get her to a hospital. I was just . . . on my way there. Help me, please. I don't know what's wrong with her. When I got here, she was crying for help. I knocked, but there was no answer, so I had to find my own way in – through a-a broken window there on the side.' He jerked his head toward the window Bishop had broken. 'When I got in, I found some dude with your wife,' he said, purposely getting their relationship wrong in an attempt to make Amarok believe he wasn't that familiar with Evelyn or her situation. 'He had a sharp instrument he was about to shove in her head.'

Amarok's expression changed. There was still plenty of concern, but now Jasper saw more caution than fury and determination. 'Where is this man?'

'Inside, on the floor. We – we got into it. He might be dead. That's how bad it got. He was using that sharp thing, was trying to stab me, but he was older and not too strong. I gained control, and then I . . . I freaked out I was so panicked and terrified. Might've hit him too many times. But he wouldn't quit.'

Amarok's gaze flicked to Evelyn. He was tempted to take her. It was easy to see that he was worried about her, wanted to get her the help she needed. But he was smart, wasn't going to drop his gun too quickly. 'Who are you?'

'Andy Smith. I'm a-a new guard at the prison.' He stuttered to appear rattled. 'This was my first day. I had orientation a few hours ago. Can you believe it? Now look at me. I've got blood all over my uniform.'

'I know you from somewhere. We've met, haven't we? At the Moosehead?'

'I think so. Must've been. I came here a couple of years ago, before Hanover House opened. I was thinking of applying for work then, but I was still married and my wife refused to come to such a cold place.'

'This is *your* truck?' Amarok motioned to the SUV Jasper had rented until he could purchase a vehicle.

'Yes.'

Keeping a careful eye on Evelyn, Amarok stepped closer. 'What were you doing coming by here in the first place?'

'Looking for you. I saw a strange sight in town not too long ago. It appeared as if some guy was forcing a woman to do . . . something in the parking lot of The Dinky Diner. Because I thought it was suspect, I couldn't just drive home to Anchorage as if I hadn't seen anything. So I asked someone where I could find you, and they sent me here.'

That did it – that and another moan from Evelyn. Amarok finally lowered his gun. 'Put her in my truck,' he said. 'What's wrong with her?'

'I have no idea.' He opened the trooper's passenger door and deposited Evelyn on the seat. 'I don't think he had the chance to do any real damage. When I arrived, he was telling her she deserved whatever he was about to do. I'm guessing he drugged her.'

Amarok didn't ask any other questions. He was too eager to get help for the woman he loved, to take care of her, in case she was worse off than Jasper led him to believe. Besides, he felt he *could* relax, to a degree. Jasper's uniform lent him credibility and his story made sense. There was no way the sergeant could guess the truth, not with Lyman Bishop in the mix. That muddied the water too much. 'Thanks, Andy . . . Smith, did you say?'

'Yeah.'

'I'm really grateful for your help. I'll probably have more questions, but later. After I know Evelyn's safe, I'll see what needs to be done with Bishop – and everything else.'

'I can take her to the hospital for you, if you'd like,' Jasper said, stopping Amarok before he could get back behind the wheel. 'I don't mind.'

Amarok seemed torn between his heart and his duty, was obviously hesitant to let Evelyn out of his sight.

'You have a dead guy in your house,' Jasper reminded him.

'Right.' He seemed about to relent. No doubt he could see the sense in taking Jasper up on his offer. But, in the end, he couldn't do it. 'I'll take care of that when I get back. If he's dead, he's not going anywhere. The same goes for poor Sandy.'

'Who?'

He didn't answer. Setting his rifle in its rack, he jumped in his truck and took off with Evelyn.

Jasper stood in the cold and watched them go. 'Damn it,' he said when he could no longer see their taillights. He'd missed out on the perfect opportunity. The fact that he'd been so close made his disappointment all the worse.

But maybe this would turn out to be a good thing. What would make Evelyn – and Amarok – trust him more than the fact that he'd just 'saved her life'?

'There will be other opportunities,' he murmured, and chuckled as he imagined Evelyn and Amarok inviting him over for dinner to thank him.

When Evelyn opened her eyes, she was riding in a vehicle with Phil.

'Where . . . where's Amarok?' She reached for her head, which pounded so hard she thought it might explode.

'He's taking care of . . . of what's going on in Hilltop,' Phil responded. 'He didn't want to let me take you, but it made no sense for him to drive all the way to Anchorage tonight, not when he's needed at home.'

There was a terrible taste in her mouth. 'What happened?'

'Lyman Bishop tried to give you a lobotomy.'

A jolt of fear made her more lucid. 'Did he manage it?' Could that be why her head hurt so badly?

'No. Thank God. Amarok checked you over carefully. Bishop used chloroform or something else to knock you out. That's why you feel so terrible. He was interrupted before he could get much further.'

A snippet of memory floated before her mind's eye – Bishop standing over her, pressing a rag over her nose and mouth. 'He . . . he used a trip wire.'

'He what?'

She couldn't repeat what she'd said or explain it. Now that her fear had subsided, she was fairly certain she was about to be sick. She asked him to pull over so she could lean out of the truck and vomit on the snow. Afterwards, she began to feel a little better. 'Where *is* Bishop?' she asked. 'Does Amarok have him in custody?'

Phil reached over to pat her hand. 'Relax, Evelyn. Amarok's on it. Don't worry about anything.'

'I need to know. I feel so . . . out of touch, so . . . disoriented.'

'Amarok was in a hurry. He didn't tell me much. All I know is that Bishop killed Sandy Ledstetter to create a diversion while he came for you.'

'He *what*?' She swallowed, hoping to ease her burning throat. 'Sandy's *dead*?'

'I'm afraid so.'

'No . . .'

A sheepish expression claimed his face, which she could only see in the dim glow of the instrument panel. 'I shouldn't have told you,' he muttered. 'Amarok told me not to.'

'I need to know. Who found her?'

'Bishop strung her up in town, where she'd be spotted. Hung her from that big Shore Pine right there beside The Dinky Diner. After someone sounded the alarm, and the whole town came running, he broke into your house.'

How had she survived with her brain intact? 'Then Amarok came home?'

'Not Amarok. He was dealing with Sandy's murder. A new CO at the prison, guy by the name of Andy Smith, saw something strange at The Dinky Diner and was trying to report it. Didn't know it had already turned into a murder and been discovered. He stopped by, looking for Amarok.'

'He came to the house – when Bishop was there with me?'

'Yes. It's a fucking miracle – that's what it is, excuse my language,' he added.

'I'm not worried about your language.' She had much bigger things on her mind.

'Can you imagine stumbling into something like that?' he marveled.

She tried to laugh but couldn't quite manage it. 'We're very lucky Andy Smith was able to handle himself.'

'It could've ended much differently.'

She'd been saved by a guard at HH, a new hire. What were the chances of that? 'Please tell me *he* didn't get hurt . . .'

'Apparently not. Bishop got the worst of it.'

She leaned her head back as she tried to absorb this news, to use what Phil had told her to fill the time gaps in her mind. 'How bad off is Bishop? Because Amarok can't let him get away. After what he just tried – he'll go back to prison. We've got him; we've got the son of a bitch.' She managed a grin. 'Excuse my language.'

Phil smiled, too, and seemed to relax. 'I doubt he'll be going anywhere. I'm pretty sure he's dead, or I'd be driving him to Anchorage along with you.'

'Dead?' she echoed in surprise.

'Can't say for sure. Haven't seen him. I radioed Amarok as he was about to leave town with you and offered to take you instead.'

'That was nice of you.'

'Don't make it into anything selfless.' His smile turned grim. 'I couldn't bear to be in charge any longer, couldn't bear to see Sandy lying there with her family wailing all around . . .' His words fell off.

'I'm sorry it happened. *So* sorry.' She thought he might say something about Hanover House, something accusatory, but he didn't. 'Anyway, you were right to offer to take me,' she added. 'Amarok needs to be there. But I'm awake, so . . . can you turn around?'

Phil looked at her as if she'd lost her mind. *'Now?'*

'Yes.'

'Hell no! Amarok was very clear. He'll never forgive me if I don't get you to a hospital right away.'

'I'm fine, Phil. What I feel, it's the drugs. I'm having some sort of reaction to whatever Bishop used, that's all. It's not as if that kind of thing is good for a person.' And this was the second time it'd happened to her. Jasper had used a similar substance to subdue her when he'd abducted her eighteen months ago – before she got away.

'Makes no difference.' Phil wasn't remotely swayed. 'He made me promise to do exactly as he said, and that's what I'm going to do.'

Evelyn didn't want to be gone, not when she was convinced that Amarok could use her help and support. *Poor Sandy.* Amarok would mourn her as much as anyone. But when Evelyn continued to argue, Phil called Amarok on the radio and his response was as resolute as Phil's. 'You're going to the hospital to get checked out,' he said. 'I've got my hands full, but I'll be able to handle it much better knowing you're seeing a doctor.'

'I'd rather be there with you.'

'I've got it. There's nothing left on this end except cleanup. Both Sandy and Bishop are dead. You coming back won't change that. Now we know who killed Sandy, there won't even be an investigation.'

'Phil said someone by the name of Andy Smith saved my life.'

'It's true,' Amarok said. 'We owe him a lot – everything.'

Amarok had allowed Sandy's family to take her body home, so they could prepare it for burial in the small cemetery some of the older families used outside of Hilltop. He'd also sealed off the broken window at his place and driven over to his trooper post to get a tarp he could use to wrap Bishop's body in. He figured he might as well load Bishop into the back of his truck and take him to the State Medical Examiner tonight. The roads were slick and it was getting late. He would've waited until morning to make the drive to Anchorage, but he planned to go to the hospital to see Evelyn as soon as he'd finished cleaning up in Hilltop, anyway.

When he bent to roll Bishop onto that tarp, however, he realized that the man was still breathing and jumped back. 'What the hell!' *How could he be alive?* Amarok had checked. As soon as Phil had offered to take Evelyn to the hospital, Amarok had transferred her to Phil's truck and gone home to find Bishop slumped in the corner with an ice pick protruding from his right eye. Amarok hadn't been able to find a pulse. Neither had he been able to detect the slightest breath escaping Bishop's mouth. But he couldn't imagine anyone surviving having an ice pick jammed so far into one eye. So maybe he'd felt only what he'd expected to feel.

Bishop moaned, dispelling any further doubt. He was alive, all right. Regardless of how Amarok had arrived at the conclusion that he was dead, he'd been wrong.

'Help me,' Bishop rasped. 'Please.'

As the man's good eye focused on Amarok, Amarok's heart leapt into his throat. This was a whole different situation. The psychopath who'd killed Sandy and all those other women was alive, even though he didn't deserve to be. Bishop had also attacked Evelyn. If not for Andy Smith, Evelyn would be no different from Beth right now, *if* she survived the procedure Bishop had intended to perform in the first place.

Amarok was tempted to do nothing, to let him die. Surely it wouldn't be long. He deserved to be taken out of this world. Everything would be so much simpler. There'd be no money wasted on his medical bills, his trial, his incarceration.

But Amarok had no interest in playing God. That was what made him different from men like Bishop. At the end of the day, he had to live with himself. He was a cop, and he was determined to be a good one. That meant he had to uphold the law and allow the justice system to do the rest.

'Do you know where you are?' he asked Bishop.

'Yes . . . Please . . .'

'And you know who *I* am?'

He managed to nod.

'It's fortunate that you still have your faculties.'

'Why? Don't tell me . . .' – Bishop gasped for breath – '. . . you won't help me . . .'

'I might be persuaded – if you make it worth my while.'

Bishop struggled to gather the strength to speak. 'How?'

'Tell me where you disposed of Jan Hall's body. Evelyn would be encouraged to have that information, and, as far as I'm concerned, you owe her that much.'

His good eye slid closed.

'Are you checking out?' Amarok asked. 'Because I have to admit, that would make my job a whole hell of a lot easier.'

'How do I know . . . how do I know I can trust you?' Bishop asked without looking at him.

'You don't,' Amarok admitted. 'But this is your only chance. So I suggest you take it.'

Bishop didn't answer right away. After a moment, however, that eye opened again and, with great effort, he said, 'Okay, I . . . I'll tell you.'

Epilogue

'How are you, babe?'

Evelyn opened her eyes to see a beam of pale yellow sunlight drifting into her room from the window on her right and Amarok standing over her bed to the left. 'I'm okay, I think.' She touched her forehead. 'My head still hurts. But I got some sleep last night. What about you?'

He motioned to the chair in the corner. 'I grabbed several hours myself.'

'Where's Phil?'

'I sent him home, said I'd look after you from here on out.'

'When did you get here?'

'Last night.'

'You've been here that long and you didn't let me know?'

'I didn't see any reason to wake you. The doctor had given you a sedative, because he felt you needed to sleep and not be awakened by all the noise and commotion around here. I decided to respect that.'

'So . . . what time is it?'

'Mid-afternoon.'

'I've slept *all day*?'

'Most of it. But that's okay. That's what you were supposed to do.'

'What happened last night? Did you get Bishop's body to the medical examiner?'

'No. He may not wind up at the medical examiner's.'

'What do you mean?' She shifted to be able to sit up, but he pressed her back.

'Relax. Bishop is alive, Evelyn. He's in the hospital here with you – under guard, of course.'

'Wait. Phil made it sound as though—'

'I thought he was dead. I couldn't see how anyone could survive what happened to him in that fight with Andy Smith. But he's a stubborn bastard, won't give up.'

She grimaced. 'I can't say I'm excited to hear he's still breathing.'

'I didn't think you would be. But' – he lifted her hand and kissed her fingers – 'don't despair. I've got something that might make his still being in the world a little easier to take.'

She felt her eyebrows go up in expectation. 'This sounds interesting.'

'It is. Bishop gave up where he put Jan Hall's body.'

This time when Evelyn insisted on sitting, he raised her bed. 'Where'd he put her?'

'Behind a warehouse on the edge of town, back in a copse of trees. That's the gist of it, but he provided the exact location, as well.'

'Are you sure she's there? That he wasn't lying?'

'He wasn't lying. I called Minneapolis PD as soon as I got to Anchorage last night. Detective Lewis went out first thing this morning, and, sure enough, he found a body buried right where Bishop said it'd be. There was no identification or clothes on the body, but there was a necklace that belonged to Jan. They're pretty sure it's her. Testing will confirm it.'

'That's why you finally woke me.'

He grinned. 'I just got the call, couldn't wait to tell you.'

'That's wonderful!'

'I thought you'd be happy.'

'Have you told Jennifer?'

'I was hoping you'd get to do that, but the detective blew it.'

'*He* called her?'

'As soon as he recovered Jan's remains.'

'I can't blame him. He had to be anxious. After what happened with Gustavson, the whole police department has to be eager to save face.'

'No doubt. I wish he would've waited, but I got something else out of Bishop while we were driving to Anchorage last night, so maybe that'll make up for it.'

'I'm just happy Jennifer can put her sister to rest while her mother is alive. That's such a relief.'

'So you don't want to hear the rest?' he teased.

'Stop. Of course I want to hear. What else did he tell you?'

'He *did* give his sister a lobotomy.'

'I *knew* it!' she exclaimed. 'And the MRI, when they finally get around to it, will prove it.'

A knock sounded at the door. A man with thick sandy-colored hair and blue eyes, wearing the uniform of a Hanover House CO, entered the room carrying a bouquet of flowers. 'Hope I'm not interrupting anything.'

'No, now's a good time,' Amarok said. 'Evelyn, this is Andy Smith, the man who saved your life.'

Evelyn accepted the flowers Andy handed to her and took a moment to admire them before setting them aside. 'How nice. I'll have the nurse bring me a vase first thing. Thank you – especially for what you did last night.'

'It was no trouble,' he said. 'I'm glad you're okay.'

'We're *both* grateful to you,' Amarok added.

Andy waved him off. 'Like I said, it was no trouble. Thank God I showed up in time.'

Evelyn studied Andy Smith a little closer. 'Have we ever met before?'

'Not that I know of. Why?' he responded. 'Do I remind you of someone?'

'No one I can name off the top of my head.' She looked to Amarok, but he shook his head as if he had no idea what she was talking about. 'There's just . . . I don't know . . . a certain familiarity.'

He grinned and scratched his neck. 'I must have a common face. I get that a lot.'

Evelyn supposed it was nothing. She'd met a lot of people over the course of her career. Andy Smith probably reminded her of a former classmate, a colleague, a reporter, or a CO.

'I'd better go,' he said. 'I don't want to be a nuisance. I just got off my first shift at HH and was on my way home, thought I'd stop by to make sure you're recovering nicely.'

'I'm good as new – thanks to you,' Evelyn said.

His lips curved into a gratified smile. 'I'm happy to hear it. I feel bad for what happened to that other woman, though. Wish I could've stopped him sooner.'

'I'm sorry about Sandy, too.' She squeezed Amarok's hand. He'd known Sandy better than they did, had to feel even worse. 'It's not fair.'

Andy folded his arms across his broad chest. 'I hope the people of Hilltop won't blame HH.'

Some were bound to. Some would even blame *her.* Evelyn wasn't looking forward to trying to overcome the animosity Sandy's murder would inspire. Getting the locals to trust her, to like her, had been difficult enough. 'He wouldn't have returned to Hilltop, if not for me.'

'If not for you, he would've returned to Beth and continued to torture her,' Amarok said. 'He would've continued to murder other women, too. And maybe he would never have been caught.'

'But this is a woman you *know,*' she said softly.

'All those other women would've had friends and family, too,' he responded.

'What makes men like Lyman Bishop do what they do?' Andy asked. 'I can't wrap my mind around it.'

Evelyn shoved her hair back, out of her face. 'That's what I'm hoping to find out.'

'I'm excited to be a part of it.' He took out his keys. 'To help in whatever small way I can.'

'We need good men like you,' she said. 'Welcome to Hanover House.'

Find out why her nightmares began . . .

Psychiatrist Evelyn Talbot has dedicated her life to analysing psychopaths. Why they act as they do. How they come to be. Why they don't feel remorse. Her only goal is to use her knowledge to find and stop them.

Having been tortured and left for dead when she was just a teenager by her high school boyfriend, Evelyn is determined to understand how someone she trusted so much could turn on her. Establishing a revolutionary new medical health centre in the remote town of Hilltop, Alaska, where she observes these killers is the final step in years of studying which will give her the answers she needs.

Keeping these killers inside and the residents of Hilltop safe is Evelyn's responsibility, but it will only take one little thing to go wrong for the danger they pose to become all too real . . .

Available exclusively in ebook now.

978 1 4722 4187 0

And if you missed the first full-length novel in the Dr Evelyn Talbot series, look out for

Dr Evelyn Talbot has learnt to live with fear.

As a teenager she was targeted by her killer boyfriend, Jasper Moore, and survived days of torture. She escaped with her life, but Jasper disappeared before he could be caught.

Now she lives in a world of psychopaths.

As the pioneering head of Hanover House, Alaska's first mental health facility for psychopaths, Evelyn engages daily with killers who have no conscience, no remorse and an ever-increasing desire to murder her, in an effort to try and work out how to stop those that remain free.

But then a mutilated body is found in her sleepy Alaskan town and Evelyn is forced to question everything. Her work, her life and whether her darkest nightmare has come back to haunt her . . .

Available in paperback and ebook now.

978 1 4722 4097 2